THE CANDLE MAN

Also by Alex Scarrow

Afterlight
October Skies
Last Light
A Thousand Suns

THE CANDLE MAN

ALEX SCARROW

First published in Great Britain in 2012 by Orion Books,
an imprint of The Orion Publishing Group Ltd
Orion House, 5 Upper Saint Martin's Lane,
London WC2H 9EA

An Hachette UK Company

1 3 5 7 9 10 8 6 4 2

A CIP catalogue record for this book is
available from the British Library.

ISBN (Hardback) 978 1 4091 0818 4
ISBN (Trade Paperback) 978 1 4091 0819 1

Typeset at The Spartan Press Ltd,
Lymington, Hants

Printed and bound by CPI Group (UK) Ltd,
Croydon, CR0 4YY

The Orion Publishing Group's policy is to use papers that are natural,
renewable and recyclable products and made from wood grown in sustainable
forests. The logging and manufacturing processes are expected to
conform to the environmental regulations of the country of origin.

www.orionbooks.co.uk

To my wife, Frances – my partner in crime.

PROLOGUE

1912, RMS Titanic

She was tilting already, he could just detect the subtle hint of it; enough of a tilt that the service trolleys, all on well-oiled castors, seemed to have quietly drifted to the far end of the reading room.

He looked up from his brandy glass and watched as men in evening suits outside on the promenade deck rushed past the saloon windows, gawping at, laughing excitedly at, the slowly receding peak of the iceberg. No more than an interesting diversion for them, like an unscheduled port visit.

But the fools haven't noticed the engines have stopped.

'Mr Larkin, isn't it?'

He turned in his armchair. 'Yes?'

It was one of the stewards he rather liked: a short, cheerful, ruddy-faced man called Reginald. He was pushing a wheelchair occupied by a pale-looking young woman.

'Would you mind Miss Hammond sitting with you awhile, sir? There's a lot of commotion going on about the deck . . .' He smiled disarmingly. 'A lot of unnecessary runnin' around, if you ask me. The lady will be better off in here for now, I fancy.'

He nodded. 'Yes . . . of course, Reginald.'

The steward parked the chair opposite him and turned to leave.

'Reginald, you'll not forget her, I hope?'

'Sir?'

'When you start loading up the lifeboats? You'll not forget her, I trust?'

'*Lifeboats*, sir?' The steward's eyebrows knitted together above a vaguely patronising smile. 'Oh, I certainly don't think we'll be getting those out tonight, Mr Larkin.'

Larkin glanced at the young woman sitting opposite him, little more than a girl, really. The mention of lifeboats had turned her skin a shade paler. He spread his hands apologetically.

'Of course . . . of course. Perhaps I'm over reacting.'

Reginald's eyes met his and in that fleeting moment confirmed what he already suspected. That the ship was going down, albeit very slowly. Gracefully, even. But she was going down nonetheless.

'Aye, Mr Larkin, sir . . . no need for any undue alarm. You'll be all right here, won't you, Miss Hammond?'

She looked at Larkin uncertainly.

'Don't worry,' he said. 'I'll take very good care of her.'

'Right you are, sir.' The steward turned to leave them with a touch more haste than perhaps he'd intended.

Alone now. Just the two of them in the reading room, the crystal chandeliers jangling softly like wind chimes, the growing mélange of voices from the promenade deck and the deck below muted to a background hubbub through the closed windows.

He glanced up from his brandy glass at her. She wasn't just pale. She was clearly very ill. Perhaps even dying. Something, then, the pair of them had in common. His eyes wandered down from the pale and delicate oval of her face to the painfully thin frame of her body. She looked as fragile as a freshly hatched chick.

'Is there not someone else travelling with you?'

Her eyes darted from the windows to him and then back outside to the excited gentlemen in their dinner jackets.

'My guardian. She went outside to find out what is going on,' she replied in a small voice. She caught his eyes studying her. 'If you are wondering . . . I have a muscle-wasting disease. The family physician believes I will not last until the summer.' She sighed. 'One more summer would have been nice.'

The old man leant forward. 'Then I'm afraid we both will miss this summer,' he said.

'You are unwell too?'

He nodded. 'I have a cancer. I shall be lucky to enjoy more than a few more months.'

She smiled sadly. 'Then you're right. No more summers for either of us.'

'I fancy we won't be missing much. Another summer of grey skies and wet days.'

She laughed softly.

They listened to the animated chattering of the men outside, rubbing their hands and fidgeting from one foot to the other to stay warm. Plumes of breath and cigar smoke clouded the promenade.

'Why did you ask about the lifeboats?' the young woman asked. 'You don't think we're in trouble, do you?'

The old man swilled the half full glass of brandy in his hand.

'Mr Larkin? It is Larkin, isn't it?'

He nodded absently.

'Do you think we will sink, Mr Larkin?'

He was tempted to offer her a platitude. A verbal placebo. But then he suspected, despite her sparrow-like fragility, that she was made of sterner stuff. It appeared she'd already accepted her mortality; that, for her, there was a very clearly bookmarked ending to her life. He could patronise her, but perhaps that didn't do her justice.

'Yes,' he replied. He nodded towards the service trolleys gathered in a conspiratorial huddle against one wall. 'Do you see? We are already listing to the stern.'

'They say she's *unsinkable*.'

He laughed at that. 'Now doesn't that sound like hubris to you?'

She shrugged.

'I would imagine a big enough hole will sink *any* ship.'

She gave that some thought. 'The steward *was* frightened. I'm certain of it. I could hear it in his voice.'

He nodded. 'It'll be his job now – Reginald and the other stewards – to pretend all is well for as long as they possibly can whilst preparations are made.'

'The lifeboats?'

'Only for the lucky few.'

She frowned. Dark caterpillar eyebrows above piercing, intelligent eyes. 'I take it you have counted them too?'

He smiled, wondering for a moment what things this clever young woman might have gone on to do, to achieve, if her bookmark had been advanced to allow another dozen chapters in her life.

'Indeed. I should say there are enough boats for only a third of the people aboard.'

She nodded. 'I did wonder about that.'

He looked out of the saloon windows at the men outside. 'There will be boats for the first-class passengers, of course. And the crew. But those unfortunate people on deck "C" and below will be without.'

'They will have life-preservers, though?'

He shrugged. 'I presume so, but this sea is freezing. I'd imagine they'll not last an hour in it.' He pursed his lips. 'Which is why I rather fancy staying put here. Since I don't have a great deal of time left . . . someone else might as well have my place.' He laughed softly. 'And I shall imagine my sacrifice is made for some young soul with great plans, who will change the world for the better.' He drained his glass. 'And this brandy will make that sacrifice a great deal easier.'

He got up from his armchair, wandered over to the bar and retrieved another bottle of Rémy Martin from the glass cabinet. He closed the door. Slowly, it swung open again.

He rejoined Miss Hammond and set another glass on the table.

She looked at it meaningfully. 'You think I've been *left* here, don't you?'

He said nothing as he refilled his glass.

'You think the steward was under orders to just leave me here, don't you? A cripple in a wheelchair?'

'I think poor Reginald has a lot of things on his mind, principally hoping he has a place reserved aboard one of those lifeboats.' He sniffed the brandy in his glass. 'Sat down in here with me, you're one less thing he has to worry about.'

She glanced at the empty glass. 'Go on then . . . I shall join you.'

He poured her a half glass, more than one would normally pour into a brandy bowl, and passed it to her. 'The more we drink, my dear, the less we're going to care.'

She nodded and took a hefty swig. She made a face as she swallowed it. 'Urgh! I've never drunk brandy before.'

He laughed. 'And now you have.'

She recovered her composure and smacked her lips appreciatively. 'I think I like it better than the sweet sherry my aunt insists on serving.'

They sipped from their glasses in silence for a while, listening to the whoop of excitement from the promenade deck as an emergency flare was launched and exploded high in the night sky with a soft pop.

'Are you travelling with anyone?' she asked after a while.

He shook his head. 'I am alone.' He studied her face, a second question written in the arc of one raised eyebrow. 'I wanted to visit America,' he added.

'To see the sights? Myself too.'

'To find someone, actually.'

She looked intrigued. 'Find someone? Family?'

He nodded.

'To say goodbye?'

'Indeed.' He was reluctant to give her any more than that.

Her skin had a touch of colour now: faint florets of pink on the side of her pale neck.

'Someone once told me that on every deathbed there's a story to be told.' She shrugged. 'If you're indeed right, I suppose we shan't get to lie on our deathbeds now.'

'Perhaps tonight's a better way to go for the pair of us, then?'

Her face flickered with a moment of fear that slowly transformed and relaxed into a sanguine expression of acceptance. Perhaps the brandy was working on her; perhaps it was the realisation that going down with the ship tonight was going to save her the weeks, maybe months, of bed-ridden pain ahead.

'Truth be told, I wouldn't have much of a deathbed story. I'm nineteen. I've done little with my life but attend one school after another.' She tossed her head back and emptied her glass. 'What about you? I suspect you've lived long enough to acquire a deathbed tale or two.'

He smiled. 'Perhaps.'

She held out her glass for a refill. 'Tell me your story, then,' she said with a teasing smile and the slightest slur. 'I won't tell a soul.' She giggled.

He filled her glass and topped up his, the bottle of brandy already a third empty. He settled back in his armchair.

'My story?' His rheumy eyes found a place inside him: old memories, dusting them off one last time. 'My deathbed story?'

She nodded.

He gave it a few moments' thought, then finally nodded. 'Why not?' He sipped his brandy. 'I should say it happened . . . let me see . . . just about five years before you were born.'

Miss Hammond frowned. '1888?'

'Yes.' Larkin stroked his cheek absently. 'And it all happened over the summer and the autumn.' His grey eyes twinkled with moisture as they met hers. 'London. Whitechapel, to be precise.'

'Whitechapel?' For a moment she hesitated, placing the name in some vaguely recalled context. 'Is that . . . is that not where those horrible, ghastly murders took place?'

He nodded slowly. 'That very year.'

She stared at him with eyes wide, her small mouth slightly open.

'Is it *about* those murders? Is that it? Your story? About . . . *Jack the Ripper*? They never found him, did they? He just vanished!'

He sipped from his glass and savoured for a moment the burn of alcohol on his lips. A passing consideration as to whether it was prudent after all these years to tell a perfect stranger about those few weeks, months, those things . . . regrets . . .

'Forgive me,' she said. 'I . . . I think I just spoke out of turn. I'm sorry.'

He found himself smiling. Perhaps that too was the brandy at work. 'It's quite all right,' he continued. 'Quite all right, my dear.'

Her cheeks coloured. 'It was a foolish notion . . . to tell stories like this.' She leant forward in her wheelchair and placed a hand lightly on his. A gesture emboldened by the drink. 'I'm so very sorry. You must have lost someone?'

'Not really.' The smile remained on his lips, but slowly changed form. An expression that shared both regret and satisfaction, rival thespians sharing too small a stage.

'As for the Ripper? Let's just say . . . I *knew* the Ripper . . .'

PART I

CHAPTER 1

11th September 1888, London

Mary hastened along the alleyway: a dirty rat-run, little more than two shoulders in width of uneven cobblestones between dark, damp brick walls. She could hear the man calling after her, an angry foreign-accented voice promising to gut her like a fish when he caught up with her.

She lifted her long skirts as she stepped across a backed-up drain thick with faeces and the prone hump of a drunkard, or just as easily a corpse.

The man's shrill voice bounced off the brick walls, lost amidst the warren of gas-lit backstreets.

'Bitch! I cut you nose off . . . you bitch!'

She glanced back down the alley she'd darted into to see a dark shadow cast by a lamp slowly rise up the wall opposite. It loomed and wobbled, and then finally she saw the man's lurching outline as he passed by, not giving the dark alley a second glance. She listened to his slurred voice slowly recede as he staggered on, each new promised threat of mutilation growing fainter, each scraping foot-step more distant.

Finally sure she wasn't going to have to run again, she slumped against a wall, almost immediately feeling its clammy dampness through the thin material of her shawl.

Mary hunkered down to a tired squat, all of a sudden robbed of the adrenaline that had helped her escape . . . *this time*. And in the dark space she was sharing with a stream of shit, and with the light tapping of feet nearby of countless rats, she allowed tears to tumble down her cheeks.

Thruppence. This . . . for just a thrupenny bit?

She couldn't imagine for one moment what her parents would make of the pitiful wretch she was now. A girl with convent schooling, a girl who once upon a time wrote home weekly, a clever, bonny girl who enjoyed Austen, Dickens, even Mrs Beeton, and loved playing a few of Gilbert and Sullivan's easier parlour ballads on the school's upright piano. A young woman who had managed to talk herself into that job with such a wealthy, prestigious family . . . and now? In five short years she had fallen from being the bright, young girl from the Welsh valleys with dreams and goals, to being this twilight creature squatting in shit. This *thing* that offered to lift her skirts to any man for a quick fuck for no more than thruppence.

Often she couldn't bring herself to do it. On some occasions, with a man too drunk to manage it, she could get away with her modest fee by doing little more than tolerating several poorly aimed prods. Sometimes, clamping her thighs tightly around a probing member, she could fool a drunk man into thinking he'd made penetration and wipe the semen from her stockings later on. But occasionally, as on this occasion, her John was less drunk than she'd thought and quite well aware of some of the tricks tarts at the cheaper end of the market were prepared to pull to dodge their part of the contract.

This one had quickly realised in the darkness that she was presenting him with nothing more than the tops of her bare thighs and had angrily pulled a knife on her. Mary ran, taking the coin he'd paid, for services yet to be properly rendered, with her.

Mary, Mary, quite contrary, how does your little song go?

She replied with nothing more than a mewling whimper.

She knew that one of these nights she wasn't going to be able to escape. One of these nights she was going to end up like the prone form further back down the alleyway: another bundle of threadbare clothes lying in a drainage ditch. Ignored. Not missed by anyone. Forgotten.

All this for thruppence.

The price of a spoon of laudanum. A little alchemy. A little dose of cheer.

She wiped a string of snot from the end of her nose and the tears from her blotchy cheeks. She needed another couple of customers before the last business of the night was gone. Two more and she'd be able to buy some scran as well.

Mary pulled herself to her feet and began to pick her way carefully towards the far end of the alley where faint amber blooms of flickering gas light promised a little more business.

She was about to step out into the wider street, still a narrow back road, but at least wide enough to have its own grime-encrusted sign post – *Argyll Street* – when she heard a low moan.

Light pooled beneath two gas lamps and faded away across drizzle-wet cobblestones into darkness. On the periphery of faint light, she thought she could make out the huddled form of someone. A man, by the timbre of his keening voice, sitting on his haunches, rocking backwards and forwards with his head in his hands.

The clocks had chimed midnight nearly an hour ago and the public houses were all but emptied now. Dock workers and market traders had stumbled back home to their anxious wives, Dutch and Norwegian sailors back to their moored ships. The only potential customers she was likely to find left were *connoisseurs*; men who knew exactly what they wanted from a tart and were sober enough to make sure they got their money's worth. The type of customer she detested.

She watched the dark shape, gently rocking to and fro, moaning softly, and whimpering almost like a child. She decided he was drunk. She stepped into Argyll Street towards him. She had to walk past him anyway, but a closer look couldn't hurt. Her shoes clacked lightly on the greasy cobbles as she approached him.

Closer now, she could see he was no dock worker or market trader. He wore smart boots that glinted with polish, a dark, well-cut suit, a waistcoat and a cape draped over his shoulders. The dim light picked out the white rim of his shirt cuffs, dotted with dark, almost black, spots.

Mary had seen blood by gas light before. It was as black as ink.

She stopped opposite him. 'You all right?'

The rocking stopped.

'Sir? You all right there?'

Slowly his head came up from his hands and she couldn't help but gasp as she saw the drying blood on his hands, down the right side of his face and matting his hair in a thick, gelatinous tangle.

His eyes seemed to focus on her for a moment, then to roll with a will of their own. 'I don't . . . I . . .' The rest of his words became a confused mumble.

Mary took a step across the narrow street towards him, confident that he looked to be in too bad a way to pose a threat.

'What happened?' she uttered softly. 'Were you jumped?'

She hunkered down in front of him, like a schoolmistress consoling a lost child. 'You been robbed? That it?'

The man's eyes swivelled back onto her. Not really focusing. Judging him from the side of his face that wasn't caked in drying blood, she guessed he was a man in his late thirties. Fashionably cut sideburns and a well-trimmed and cared-for moustache. A gentleman.

His eyelids flickered, his eyes rolled upwards until she could see only the whites and slowly, like a mature oak being felled, he slumped over onto his left side.

'Hoy . . . hoy, mister?' she prodded him. 'Mister?'

She leant over his head and could hear his breathing bubbling through mucous. Still breathing. Still alive. He'd passed out was all. She leant closer and in the flickering gas twilight thought she could see a deep gash in his matted hair.

A cosh, or a club, even a dull-edged hatchet, could have done that. She suspected she was right: some young hoodlums must have cornered and mugged him. Without realising it, she found her hands were thinking for themselves. Already probing his pockets. She hated herself for doing that. Hated that this was now her first instinct: to see what the muggers might have left behind that could be lifted off this unfortunate bugger, what could be taken and pawned.

'I'm sorry, sir,' she whispered as she probed the folds of his cape and jacket. 'See, I need the money. I need it.'

The man's voice groaned a thick syrup of lost words.

Her hand found dampness on the side of his torso. She pulled it out and saw it was sticky with dark, cloying blood.

He's been stabbed too.

She fancied the poor gentleman was going to bleed out on Argyll Street before the morning came and some early trader on his way to work found him. She resumed her hasty search of his clothing and, just as she was about to give up, her fingers chanced upon the edge of a leather strap. She followed it down to his hip where the strap met the soft worn leather of a satchel flap.

Her hand probed cautiously inside and immediately felt a variety of things: the cool metal of keys on a ring and the smooth leather of what felt like a bulbous, well-fed wallet.

'Bleedin' Jesus!' she muttered.

Mary was about to probe deeper, to pull out her find one item at a time and examine them, when she heard the distant clacking of hooves on stone. She decided she'd chanced her luck enough for one night and eased the leather strap off the man's shoulder and quickly tugged it over his head.

She got to her feet and, with one last glance back at his slumped form, she hurried on down Argyll Street, the small satchel already over her own shoulder as if that's how she *always* wore this masculine-looking bag of hers.

Her quick steps took her onto Great Marlborough Street, far better lit and overlooked on both sides by tall townhouses with lace-curtained windows that still, here and there, glowed the soft amber of midnight oil.

Several carriages clattered past, taking gentlemen home from their drinking clubs. A hundred yards up the street, where wispy skeins of early morning mist covered the stone cobbles and small islands of horse manure, a dozen noisy young lads ambled drunkenly in the middle of the carriageway, hurling abuse at each other and laughing like chattering monkeys.

Mary hesitated. A pang of guilt stopping her where she stood. Once more she glanced back down Argyll Street at the faint hump of the man's body and knew leaving him like that, she was surely leaving him to die.

'Oh bugger,' she whispered.

CHAPTER 2

12th September 1888, London

He was awake for quite a while before he realised it. Looking up at a high plaster ceiling, discoloured a faint vanilla and riddled with the porcelain-fine cracks of drying and peeling paintwork.

Turning his head slightly on a pillow that rustled noisily beneath him, he could see a row of tall windows draped with net curtains that shifted in a gentle breeze and glowed the soft grey light of approaching dawn. His head throbbed at the movement and he lifted a hand to soothe the pain, finding a thick swathe of bandaging around his forehead.

His eyes flitted around the other things he could see without shifting his head again: he saw a row of beds opposite him, most of them occupied, he presumed, from the chorus of wheezing and snoring that echoed off the high ceiling.

A hospital ward.

That's what this was. That's exactly what this looked like. He wondered which hospital he was in and prepared to recite the list of hospitals in the proximity of where he lived when . . . he realised he couldn't actually recall where that was. He frowned. He couldn't recall his actual address nor, for that matter, could he even recall the city he lived in.

A small stab of panic made him shift in his bed.

Not even which *country* was his home.

Ignoring the waves of throbbing pain, he lifted his head off the pillow and looked around the ward. He saw a sign painted on a board screwed to the ward door: *Remember! Clean hands means clean beds!*

So, he was somewhere English-speaking.

But where . . . where exactly am I?

He began to feel lightheaded and dizzy. His head collapsed back against the pillow and a single tear rolled out from beneath a clenched eyelid, down his cheek, into the bristles of his sideburns . . . as his foggy mind processed another deeply unsettling thought.

I don't even remember what my name is.

'You don't recognise me, do you?'

He stirred at the sound of the voice and opened his eyes to see a doctor standing beside his bed. A young man with a sandy-coloured beard and spectacles.

He shook his head. 'No . . . I'm afraid not. Have we met?'

'We spoke for a short while earlier this morning. I saw you at the start of my rounds.' The doctor pulled up a wooden chair beside the bed and sat down. 'My name is Doctor Hart.'

'I'm sorry . . . but I can't actually tell you my name . . .'

Dr Hart smiled. 'I know. This is what we ascertained when we spoke. Apparently you have no memory of your name, or where you come from. But by the sound of your accent, I have a suspicion you might have spent some time in America? Does that sound right to you?'

'I . . . I really don't know. I don't even know where my home is.'

'Well, we shan't worry too much about that right now. These things will, I'm sure, come back to you in due course. They often do in these kinds of cases.' Dr Hart pulled out a metal cigarette case. 'Care for a smoke?'

He laughed feebly. 'I . . . uh . . . I'm not sure if I am a smoker or not.'

'Well, there's only one way to find out, isn't there?' He passed him a cigarette and then flipped a lighter. They sat in silence for a while, Dr Hart watching his patient draw on his cigarette.

'Well? Does that bring to mind any memories?'

He made a face at the taste of tobacco on his tongue. 'I don't think I particularly care for it.'

Dr Hart smiled. 'So there we are. Now we know you *aren't* a smoker. There's a little progress for you, eh?'

'Doctor, could you tell me . . . how did I end up in here?'

Dr Hart shrugged. 'You were brought in a couple of days ago by the driver of a hansom cab. I believe the gentleman in question found you down some backstreet. You suffered several quite nasty injuries. Several shallow cuts from a knife around your midriff, but the worst injury was the blow to your skull. The cranium was fractured and there was some haemorrhaging that needed to be bled off. I fully expected you to die, actually.' He smiled. 'But you seem to be made of sturdy stuff. I suspect you were probably robbed. That's most likely what happened. Robbed and left for dead by your assailant.'

'What hospital is this?' He looked around the quiet ward. 'I don't even know what city I'm in.'

Dr Hart studied him silently. 'Which city do you *think* you are in?'

He closed his eyes and willed his befuddled mind to produce a name. To produce *anything*. 'England?'

Dr Hart looked concerned. 'Now, you understand England is a country, not a city?'

Yes . . . goddammit, he knew that. 'I don't know why I said . . .' He shook his head, confused and frustrated with himself.

'Don't be so hard on yourself. Right now your mind is damaged and trying to mend itself. Things will be very confusing for a while. To answer my question, you're in London and this is Saint Bartholomew's hospital.'

He settled back against the pillow, feeling dizzy and nauseous from the cigarette smoke he'd just sucked in. 'Do I . . . did I have any possessions on me? Anything that might help me remember . . . ?'

'Nothing but the clothes you were wearing, I'm afraid. Whoever robbed you took everything you must have had on you.'

He felt sick. 'Do you have any idea how long this will last?'

'Before your memory returns?' Dr Hart shrugged. 'It is not a cut and dried thing. Sometimes it can all come back within hours. Sometimes the memories never fully return. Your brain has suffered some damage. It is quite a remarkable thing, the brain, you understand? It can heal itself without the clumsy intrusion of someone like me. There is little that we can do for the moment. You are now in a stable condition, the knife wounds are clean and healing nicely without any internal injury done as far as I can see. As for the fracture to your skull, the bone will knit together in time. We just need to protect it a little with dressing.'

'Will I remain here? In this ward?'

'Until I am happy your injuries are satisfactorily recovered.'

'And where will I go, then?'

Dr Hart patted his arm gently. 'Well, there's the thing, chap. Whilst you're in here, mending, I'm certain we shall have someone quite beside themselves with worry calling round various hospitals asking after you. Somebody will turn up for you, I'm sure.'

Someone?

He hadn't even begun to consider the notion yet that there might just be a wife, a mother, a brother, a father, out there looking for him. For a moment the thought of that lifted his spirits. That someone might at any moment come into this ward with a face twisted into a teary smile of relief at the sight of him. Someone who'd greet him with a hug, or smother him with wet and tender kisses. Someone who was going to use his name. He realised how disconcerting it was, how utterly disconnected he felt having no name, being nothing more than a disembodied 'I'.

Someone who could at least tell him what his name was, someone to answer the million and one questions he had about who the hell he was.

'You really should rest,' said Dr Hart. 'You have been through quite a tangle.' He got up from his chair and pinched out the stub of his cigarette. 'And I must say, you really are jolly lucky to be alive, old chap. Maybe the Almighty isn't quite ready for you yet,' he said, patting him gently on the arm once more. 'I shall see you later at the end of my shift. Hopefully you'll remember me and this conversation.'

'Yes . . . yes, I shall try, doctor. Try very hard.'

'That's the spirit.'

CHAPTER 3

Two months ago
13th July 1888, Whitechapel, London

'So, who's the tart, Bill?'

Bill Tolly pulled the lollipop stick out of his mouth. 'Shush yer questions now. Yer know how it is: less yer know, less yer can squawk 'bout later, right?'

He led the pair of women along the street. Mid-morning, the market was busy, full and bustling with noisy vendors calling out their prices over cart tables laden with soil-clad vegetables and fish that still flicked and jiggled, calling to workers' wives carrying wicker baskets and angling to make a shilling stretch as far as it could go.

'I thought we was doing this *tonight?*' hissed Annie. 'Not the middle of the day!'

Bill shook his head. 'Just don't bother thinking, love. You'll do yerself a mischief.'

Annie chuckled at the insult. Nerves. She and her friend Polly were both giddy with nerves.

Bill checked the scrap of paper in his hands. 'It's down here, ladies,' he said impatiently, leading them away from the market, down a less busy street – Cathcart Street – which was no less quiet. One side was lined with a row of archways beneath a railway bridge, each archway occupied by a variety of different one-man businesses. All of them, it seemed, in competition with the others to make the most noise: a cabinet-maker breaking down and recycling old furniture, a saddler beating tacks through coarse leather, a butcher sawing through the carcasses of pigs.

On the other side of the road was a row of tidy-looking terraced houses that each sported a tiny fenced front garden. The two women hesitated a moment, looked at each other anxiously.

'Bill, this is all posh,' said Annie. She turned to him accusingly. 'You said she was just some street girl.'

He looked around at them both standing still, unwilling to proceed another step further. He winced. One of the traders on the other side of the street was looking up casually from his work.

We don't want to be seen . . . don't want to be remembered. Not by anyone.

'I ain't pissin' around out here,' he snarled. 'Let's just get the job done.'

He reached for Annie's arm and dragged her along, making a show of a friendly smile and a mock laugh for the benefit of the mildly curious worker looking across the narrow road at them. Expecting their momentary sharp exchange to develop into an amusing shouting match, the workman quickly lost interest and returned to his task.

'She *is* just a street girl,' hissed Bill into Annie's ear. 'And a foreign one at that.'

'Well 'ow comes she's livin' in a bloomin' nice bloody manor house like one of these?'

Annie's voice was lost beneath a percussive symphony of hammers, mallets and saws. It didn't matter anyway; they were here now. Right outside number twenty-six.

He looked at the dark blue painted door, the paint peeling in places. It was one of the grubbier properties down this cul-de-sac. A rented property, neglected by some absentee landlord for some time by the look of it. But still, compared to the doss houses these two scabrous old tarts were used to, he mused, it probably did look like a proper manor.

He turned to them at the rickety gate, leading on to six feet of weed-strewn garden. 'Both of you clear on what's to be done?'

They both nodded sombrely.

'You can get rid of it proper?'

Annie nodded. 'Done this before.'

He took a deep breath and realised even he was a-flutter with nerves. Yeah, for sure, ol' Bill Tolly had killed before in cold blood. Three times before, if truth be told. Although he was happy for associates to believe it was a great deal more than that, reputation being what it was in this particular line of business. And for sure, there were no doubt others he may have killed or maimed during his thirty-six years. Bill had been in too many drunken scraps to remember, and he'd be surprised if he wasn't responsible for one or two more grieving wives or mothers out there whose stupid sons or husbands had annoyed him over a pint and received the jagged end of his glass in return. But there were only three people he'd ever murdered in cold blood specifically for a fee.

Three jobs. Three hits. And all three 'jobs' had been men.

This time it was a woman and the scrawny little bastard of hers. A woman. Even if she was just some shitty foreign tart, that was still going to be awkward for him. Quite honestly, he wasn't sure how he was going to feel until after he'd done the deed.

Annie and Polly both claimed they'd done their part of this job many times before. 'Just like tapping a rabbit,' Annie had said last night. 'Swing it by the legs and smack its head on a table. All done in two shakes of a lamb's tail, love.'

Last night, the pair of them had been very matter-of-fact about the whole business. Just a bit *too* casual, a bit too cocky. Perhaps that had been the bottle of malty-flavoured genever they'd been sharing between them doing the talking. All the same, he knew they'd done the deed for several of the more notorious baby farmers out there.

'Wouldn't believe 'ow many *unwanteds* end up being flushed down the sewers, Bill. Me and Poll know what we doin', love. You can rely on us.'

That was then. Last night, when presumably they'd imagined he'd be taking them to some grimy, stinking, shite-hole lodging house down their neck of the woods. Some cheap little tart, barely more than a child herself, and her freshly-sprung bastard, still purple-skinned and coated in dried fluids, nestling in a laundry basket full of dirty clothes.

This nice house, with its own front yard, seemed to have thoroughly spooked them.

'Come on . . . job ain't gonna do itself,' he grunted.

He pushed the gate aside, walked up the front garden and pulled the chain on the front door. The noise from across the narrow street was too loud to hear if a bell had actually rung inside and he was about to try again with a firm knock on the door when it cracked open.

'Oui?'

He could see a slender face framed by wisps of dark hair that had spilled from a tidy bun. Large, bleary brown eyes blinked sleep away whilst a pair of dark eyebrows arched in a wordless enquiry about his business. She tucked a tress of hair behind one ear. 'Yes?'

Bill smiled at her, careful to keep it polite and congenial: the weary but courteous greeting of a tradesman going about his rounds. She looked like she'd just woken up from a snatched sleep; her cheeks were blotched with fading pink, her eyelids heavy, one dusted with a little dry crust of mucous.

Still, a real beauty, though. A real beauty. Some rich bastard's tumble.

'Lan'lord sent us, miss. To come take a look at the pipings on yer out-'ouse.'

She frowned for a moment, struggling with his cockney accent. Her gaze quickly fell on the two women behind him. A man knocking on his own perhaps might have made her suspicious enough to query the unscheduled call.

'This *is* number twenny-six, ain't it, love?'

She nodded. 'Oui . . . yes, twenty-six.'

'Right, I gotta take a look atcha plumbings,' he said, waving a piece of paper around. 'Lan'lord, see?'

She hesitated a moment longer, glanced once again at Annie and Polly standing in the front yard. They both offered a courteous smile. 'D'accord. All right. You come in, please?'

She stepped back to let them pass into her narrow, dimly lit hallway, polite nods exchanged between them all as they wiped their feet on her doormat. And as she gently closed her front door, she was not to know that the rest of her life and her baby's life were, at best, going to be measured in mere seconds.

Bill saw Annie and Polly looking at him. He could almost read the accusation in their eyes.

You said she was just a tart! Just a cheap tart!

'You say you are come to . . . ?' Her slender face creased as she struggled with her English. 'What is this you come for?'

Bill's smile was stuck rigidly on his face.

She ain't no cheap slapper. The woman didn't have the wrecked look of a prostitute: the pallid skin riddled with sores and dry flaky patches, powdered and rouged to look tolerable; the florid blossom of burst blood vessels; the red eyes of too much drink and worry. That's what he'd assumed. That, or she'd been some flirtatious housemaid who'd tempted her employer once too often.

But this foreign woman, she almost looked like a *proper* lady. One of them ones you could see taking the air in Hyde Park on a Sunday morning, all bonnets and bustles.

'W-wha' you waitin' for, B-Bill?' snapped Annie quickly. 'Do it!'

'All right, all right!' he grunted.

The woman's bemused frown deepened to concern as she looked from him to the other two. 'Que est-ce que . . . ?'

His hand tightened around the long wooden handle in his jacket pocket.

'Bloody well DO IT, Bill!'

'All right! ALL RIGHT!' he snapped angrily. His hand was out of his pocket and the tip of the twelve-inch blade embedded into her petite waist before he realised he'd done it. The woman looked down at the army bayonet, her sleepy eyes wide awake now. She started to scream. His other hand clamped over her mouth.

'SHUT UP! SHUT UP! SHUT UP!'

He tugged the long serrated blade out of her guts, pushed her up against the hallway wall so hard the back of her head smacked against the plaster. He turned the bayonet blade sideways, then rammed it into her bare throat. He punched the blade so heavily into her neck that the tip crunched its way through vertebrae and ground into the plaster behind her.

Her muffled scream suddenly became a wet gurgle, blood pulsing between his fingers as the heels of her feet thrashed and drummed against the skirting board below.

'Shhhh,' he whispered. 'There's a good girl. Nice an' easy now.'

Polly stifled her own muted cry and Annie swore under her breath.

'What you two fuckin' starin' at?!' snapped Bill. 'Go an' do yer business!'

The two women, frozen to gawping statues by shock, finally stirred. They hurried past him, Polly crossing herself, while he continued to hold his hand over the French woman's mouth as she squirmed, struggled and kicked against the wall, blood pouring down the front of her blouse and pooling on the wooden floor.

Bill watched her eyes – such pretty eyes too – slowly lose their focus and begin to roll uncontrollably as she went into shock. All whites now as her dilated pupils seemed to fixate on something up on the ceiling.

Last night, after he'd finished discussing the job with the girls, he'd tried to imagine what it would be like *shanking* a woman. Of course, he'd slapped around a few in his time, tarts trying to short-change him, tarts who really should know better. But he'd never *stabbed* a woman.

It wasn't as difficult as he thought it might be. Not now he'd started. Just a little more squirming from her and it was all going to be over.

It was unusual though, to say the least: some gentleman actually putting a price on a *tart's* head. Mind you, this one . . . she was clearly no ordinary tart. She had some class, some poise. He wondered if she was something more than a maid. Perhaps a governess? He knew some of the posh buggers in London – the really posh types – paid for educated ladies from places like France to come and teach their children a bit of culture.

She finally sagged, her body's dead weight suspended by the blade of his bayonet still wedged into the soft plaster wall. Bill looked at the small triangle of pale skin at the hollow of her throat: the only skin below her beautiful oval jaw not covered by a dark tributary of blood. He wondered what it would be like to fuck a woman of class, albeit a dead one. He grinned. An added little perk to the generous money that gent was paying him to do this. He could feel the bulge in his trousers pressing against her narrow-framed body. He was fumbling at his buttons before he knew it, wanting to enter her before the warmth of her body had begun to wane.

Annie and Polly found the baby's cot up a flight of stairs in a small front room. It was a sparse room with bare floorboards, but the woman downstairs seemed to have gone some way towards making it more homely. Several threadbare teddy bears and stuffed farm-yard animals sat side by side beneath the small window.

'Oh, lord, 'elp us,' gasped Polly. 'Look at it!'

Annie was. It wasn't freshly born as Bill had promised them. It looked to her eyes like a baby several months old. She steadied her resolve with a mantra, one she silently repeated over and over whenever she had to do a job like this.

Not even properly human yet. That's how Annie rationalised it. Not like her little daughter who died of meningitis a few years back. Two years old, a cheeky smile that melted her heart and a mouth always full of jibber-jabber half-words. A real little person. Not like this fleshy, slug-like creature.

They ain't human 'til they can walk an' talk.

'Oh god, Annie! It's not freshly born!'

'Just an *unwanted*, Polly, s'all it is, love.'

·23·

'We . . . we . . . can't—'

'Ain't even a *proper* baby 'til someone says they want it, right?'

'It's a little boy.' Polly stared in silence down at him, legs and arms kicking fitfully as he lay on his back fast asleep. This wasn't what she was used to. The brats her and Annie had disposed of looked no different to piglets: squirming folds of discoloured flesh that promised to suck a young woman dry like a parasite, promised to turn a young working girl's life to shame and ruin.

Every one of those bastards they'd gotten rid of had been un-wanted; every one of them like a monster in the corner of a room, the mother cowering away from it in another. But this one – she looked at the row of soft toys – this baby was *loved*.

'It ain't right,' uttered Polly.

Annie turned on her. 'The mother's dead now, stupid! What you gonna do? Look after it yourself?'

Polly shook her head silently.

'Bill's payin' us good for this one.' She glanced down at the baby in the cot, stirring in his sleep. 'It's just a fuckin' *crib-rat*,' said Annie. She reached down into the cot. 'An' what do we do with bloody rats, girl?'

Polly shook her head as Annie tossed the blanket aside and grabbed the baby's bare feet. She turned to look away as her friend lifted him out of the cot by his feet, the baby now wide awake and squirming in her tight grasp. 'We bash their little 'eads in, is what we do!'

A mewling wail spun through the air and ended with a soft thud against the wooden floor. Polly clasped her hands over her face and whimpered at the sound of impact. She heard a second, softer smack against the floorboards.

Outside, the muted clatter and bang of the businesses opposite filtered through the grimy window, filling the silence of the room. Polly heard the rustle of Annie's clothing, her letting out a breath of long-held air. More than just a sigh.

'It's done.'

Polly opened her eyes and immediately shot them away from the pale little body on the floor.

'You can bag it,' said Annie dryly, 'since it was me 'ad to do the thing.'

Polly could only nod as she opened the canvas grocery bag she'd brought along for the job and knelt down beside the small corpse.

She touched a bare foot, still warm, pebble-stone toes still flexing and curling post-mortem.

How many times had she and Annie done this before? Too many times to count. *Baby farming,* that's what the papers called their business, wasn't it? All your troubles and worries gone, for a one-off payment. An assurance to the tearful and frightened young lady that their baby would be found a home, loving parents eager to adopt an' all that. That's what they were told. What they heard her and Annie say. Lip service. Polly suspected half the young women they'd saved from shame or a life of drudgery knew their assurances were an empty promise.

The papers liked to portray women like her and Annie as wicked witches, monsters who no doubt cooked and ate the freshly born babies they spirited away into the backstreets of the East End. But as Annie quite rightly said, although what they did was for money, it was a service to the community. A good thing. The streets were choked enough with abandoned or orphaned children. Many starving to death. A slow and horrible way for a life to end. What they offered, to her mind, was a service not so far removed from the many backstreet abortionists she knew operated from grubby front rooms they deigned to call 'surgeries'. All that differed was the matter of timing: a week, a day, an hour even, was all that separated her and Annie from those sorts.

In or just out of the womb, that's the only difference. They're still unwanted.

She lifted its foot, no longer than her index finger, and cradled its small lifeless body in her other hand. Its head, misshapen now, lolled on a shattered neck as she lifted it into the grocery bag.

But this one, this little life, had been around for some time, maybe even several months. Long enough to have a name, perhaps. She glanced at the tin rattle in the cot. Long enough to have a few possessions of his own, even.

Not 'he'. 'It.' She chided herself. *It. It.*

'Come on,' snapped Annie. 'We're done here.' She grabbed Polly's arm and pulled her to her feet. They made their way out of the small bare room, the grocery bag swinging by its handles as they clumped noisily down the stairs to the hallway.

'Bill? You there?'

'I'm in 'ere,' came his voice, muffled from behind a door off the hallway. Annie stepped towards the door and began to push it open.

'Hoy! Don't come in! I'm busy in 'ere!'

'What you doin'?'

'Finishin' up. You done *your* business?'

'Yeah.'

'Then off yer go with it. I'll see yer tonight with yer share.'

'Right. And dontcha be late with it. I mean it, Bill!' Annie said.

There was no answer through the closed door, just the shuffling, bump and slide of movement. 'Bill? I said don't—'

'I 'eard! Now fuck off! I'll see you two later!'

Annie turned to Polly and nodded toward the front door. 'Let's go.'

Bill heard the front door close and watched them through the net curtains, stepping out through the garden gate and walking back down Cathcart Street with their grocery bag swinging casually between them as if contained nothing more than several pounds of potatoes. He turned back to the work at hand.

The head was completely off now and covered like a badly wrapped gift in a length of tarpaulin. The body was stripped naked, the clothes ripped and bloodstained and in a pile on the floor. He was going to have to bag them up and burn them later. The headless body he was going to roll up in the bloody rug on the floor and tonight, after dark, drop it into the Thames. The head? Well, he was friendly with a brickmaker who let him use his kiln from time to time for a few coins, no questions asked.

Bill nodded. A very easy two hundred pounds earned, that was.

Very easy indeed.

He was rather pleased with himself, with the fore-planning, deciding to do the job in the middle of the day when all that noise from across the street was likely to cover a solitary scream. As opposed to the still of night, when a voice could carry.

Well done, Bill.

Two hundred pounds. A skilled craftsman might take half a year to earn that kind of money. And he'd earned it in the space of a few minutes. The girls were asking for ten pounds each, but he knew they'd done baby farming for far less. Tonight he was going to give them half that, and if they got all leery about it, maybe fifteen between them with the certain warning that if they asked for more, they'd be asking for a slapping.

He hunkered down beside the naked form of the headless body and studied her pale, unmarked skin.

She was such a beauty, though.

Certainly no common tart. Slender but none of the sharp edges of the malnourished, none of the bruises, scratches and scrapes that came as normal with the whoring profession. Perhaps a maid, then – a household maid who'd managed to catch her employer's eye? A scullery maid from one of them big tall houses in Holland Park?

Bill knew not to ask questions. A professional didn't ask questions. The gentleman who'd met with him had given him everything he needed to know: an address, a description of her and, in carefully nuanced language, what he wanted done with her and the child. But no one needed to be a genius to work out some west end toff had found his way into a very awkward situation. This unlucky girl presumably had been put up here for a while. She no doubt had assumed her fate had been sorted, the matter resolved; that her gentleman lover was going to provide for her like this indefinitely. A regular monthly allowance and a roof over her head. Never again having to work. But, the gentleman in question had opted for a far cheaper solution for this nameless foreign girl, presumably with no family in the country. To simply make her disappear. Another *no one* lost in the sprawling dim and dark beehive of humanity. London lost 'no ones' all the time. They pulled them out of the Thames nearly every day.

The gentleman hadn't even bothered to ask what Bill would charge for his services. If he had, Bill would have, poker-faced, insisted on fifty pounds and not a penny less. Although, truth be told, he would have let it come down to thirty and still have been reluctant to walk away from such easy money.

But two hundred pounds the gent had offered! Even a nib with education and decent clerk's position would struggle to earn that over six months toil.

He stuffed the last of her blood-soaked clothes into the bag. Not expensive clothes by the look of them, but certainly not the stained and second-hand frills and lace most working women wore to threads every day.

He could imagine the girl in her new home with a crisp folded finny in her purse to spend on a brand new wardrobe, then taking herself on a hasty shopping trip along Oxford Street. Perhaps thrilled with the experience of possessing so large a denomination. Five pounds. A fiver! Being called 'ma'am' by some store girl her own age, who yesterday wouldn't even have deigned to acknowledge her if she'd entered in her maid's uniform.

As he lifted the last of her things into the bag, something heavy slipped from the folds of material and thunked onto the soft rug between his knees. He reached down and picked it up, turning it over and over with his bloody fingers. He thumbed a clasp on one side that opened the item and saw within an image that took him several moments to register.

An image that was going to allow him to ask for ten times the gentleman's fee!

A photograph. This woman, a baby and a man. A very important man with a face he vaguely recognised. Bill felt the first prickle of concern on his scalp. The gentleman who'd approached him for this job was doing it on behalf of *this* man – an important man? – in the photograph.

There's more to this than just one randy gent cleaning up his own mess.

To his mind it meant one of two things: opportunity – or danger.

Or perhaps a bit of both.

CHAPTER 4

12th September 1888, Whitechapel, London

Mary's fingers explored the dark folds of the man's leather bag. It was like a cross between a sailor's duffle bag and a school satchel; an odd bag for a gentleman to be carrying around with him. It looked old, the leather well-worn.

Outside in the passageway beyond the door to her rented room, she heard the clumping of heavy feet and the muted giggle of a woman. The tenants from upstairs returning from a night's drinking. She glanced at the net curtains that hung down in front of her small grimy window. The first pallid grey stripes of dawn were leaking into her room. She reached over and turned out the wick of her lamp to save on the oil. In the grey gloom of dawn, she picked the satchel up and took it over to the stool by the window.

Outside in the street, through the broken panel of her window, she heard the clack of boots: men off to work.

The backstreet reminded her of home. Llangyndeyrn. The rows of terraced houses and cobbled roads. The threads of smoke from breakfast hearths from a thousand chimney pots rising to a horizon of craggy peaks. Mary smiled wistfully at how far she'd risen and fallen in five short years.

Eighteen when she left Saint Mary's convent with ideas in her head far too big for a modest Welsh valley town. No, it was *London* she wanted. Her parents, long used to dealing with their stubborn, wilful daughter, could only plead tearfully that she be awful careful and write often as they emptied every last jar of coins they had into her travel bag.

Eighteen she'd been, travelling alone to London. She remembered that day so well: grinning with excitement with her bag clutched in her hands, staring out of the window as the train pulled through the suburbs west of London. She saw the tall spires of factory chimney stacks, cranes on the horizon and workmen-like ants crawling along the rafters and scaffold of tall new buildings. She felt the magnetic pull of the beating heart of the capital. The pull of the most powerful city of the British Empire. The very centre of the civilised world.

What a place to be. What a place for someone like her: young, energetic, with big ideas. Oh, she had plans, didn't she? Naïve plans, looking back now. But back then, to that grinning eighteen-year-old, they'd been plans that were perfectly plausible. She was going to offer her services as a piano teacher. She was going to knock on the doors of the richest houses in London and present herself confidently and proudly. And soon after establishing herself as a tutor, she was going to find herself teaching some adorable young bachelor, with a bobbing Adam's apple and a dry tongue who was going to fall head over heels in love with her coy smile and her gentle, playful teasing.

Marriage would follow soon after that, of course, and her young husband was going to support her setting up a music school, which, naturally, she was going to run. Their home would become a place to entertain musicians, composers, poets, writers, painters, even actors. The more sophisticated dailies would be filled with stories about their fantastic parties, and the glamorous hostess in the middle of it all, Mary Kelly – or whatever surname she'd be using then.

She sighed.

Five years on and those grand ideas of her silly younger self were so ridiculous that she laughed every time she recalled them. A bitter laugh, and usually accompanied by a tear or two. She'd got some of the way there, though, hadn't she? Some of the way. Then she was stupid, careless, and threw it all away.

And now she was here, in this one room. In a room that reeked of damp wood and mothballs, and the vinegar-burn tang of stale urine from the tenant before who was either too sloppy with his night-water bowl, or just too lazy to use it and so pissed in the corner.

She looked back down at the satchel in her lap. Her hand stole in again under the flap. A thief. Occasional pickpocket. That was her now. And a tart; not even an honest tart. She tried to convince herself that the only thing which put her one modest step above all the other 'girls' she kept company with now was that a part of her old self was still alive somewhere inside. Still believing there was a way out of this dead-eyed existence.

But then stealing this bag from a *dying* man? Was it possible to sink any lower? She wondered whether he'd died or whether that approaching cab driver had found him, perhaps even done the *decent* thing and taken him to a hospital? Saint Bartholomew's was just a stone's throw away, wasn't it?

Her cheeks burned with shame. She could have called out for help to the cabbie, or gone and looked for a patrolling policeman. But no. She'd taken this bag off him and run.

What've you become, Mary?

It was then that her fingertips found the feathery-fan texture of the end of a tight bundle of paper. She fumbled by touch, heard the rustle of paper inside the bag. Gently she pulled it out of the satchel and held the bundle up in front of her face. She frowned, not quite sure of what she was looking at at first. She pulled the net curtain back a bit to allow a little more of the meagre grey light into her room.

'Oh my . . .' she whispered hoarsely. 'Oh my . . .'

CHAPTER 5

13th September 1888, Saint Bartholomew's Hospital, London

Mary Kelly turned in through the entrance gates of Saint Bart's. The one-way arc-shaped driveway was already busy with traffic: hansom cabs and private coaches bringing in hospital visitors or taking away patients well enough to return home; food vendors wheeling in hand-pulled traps to sell in the hospital's foyer.

This morning had been an agonising tug of war for Mary. Money. *So much money* in that bag, she hadn't even brought herself to consider counting it yet. But enough in there, surely, that she'd never need to do a stitch of work again in her life. Ever.

She was troubled though. Not so much on the ethics of the situation. Bugger that, the money was hers. But, she was troubled by more practical matters. A lingering concern pricked her bubbling euphoria. There was a lot of money being carried by that gentleman. She wondered whether it was being transported from one place to another. It was *somebody's* money. Somebody who had a lot more of it? Somebody powerful and rich? Somebody who was going to be looking for it? And god help the poor wretch holding onto it when that somebody found out who they were and came knocking at their door.

Mary was almost certain that she was safe. As long as she was discreet and clever about it, she was going to be fine. *Almost* certain. She'd be a lot happier if she knew for certain that the gentleman in Argyll Street had been brought in dead, though. He'd seen her. He'd looked at her. It would put her mind to rest to know for sure that he'd bled out.

If he'd been found by that cab driver or someone else later on yesterday morning, then the body would still have been brought here to this hospital, the nearest one. It was a matter of careful enquiry. And if she found out that he'd not survived his wounds, then the matter was settled. The money was hers!

I mustn't be silly with it.

She would need to be so very discreet. Pay her rent and leave. Perhaps come up with some sort of a cover story to tell the other girls. She'd tell them her parents had sent enough money for a ticket to take her back home to Wales. She'd have to leave Whitechapel promptly and find herself somewhere else to live on the other side of London. Why London though? Perhaps even another country. Some far corner of the empire? America? Africa? India?

Mary stifled an excited smile. She could become someone else. She'd have to come up with a new life story, a new name. Mary could do that. She could play at being someone else. Do all the proper talk with a little practice.

She looked up at a starling swooping across the roof of the hospital. Flying free.

That's me. Flying free.

But one last thing. This last thing. To be sure. To be safe.

She pushed her way through the large oak and glass doors into the hospital's foyer, the high ceiling echoing and ringing with voices and the bustle of activity all around her. Weaving her way through the hospital porters and food vendors, she passed by wooden benches crammed with seated, waiting patients clutching bloodied rags to foreheads, hips, arms, thighs. The usual casualties of spill-out time from the public houses. She looked for her gentleman amongst them but saw no one who looked remotely like the man.

'Help you, love?' asked the sister manning the front desk. She look flustered and impatient.

'I . . . I wonder if you can. I, well, I'm enquiring about a gentleman who might have been brought in late last night. Poorly thing. I think someone had stabbed him and beat his head.'

The sister looked tired; end of a long night shift. 'The one from near Soho? Argyll Street? Well-to-do sort?'

'Yes!' said Mary. 'Yes, that's right. It was very late, early hours even . . .'

'That's right.' The woman checked an entry book. 'Came in just after two.'

Mary steadied her nerves. She could feel her voice fluttering anxiously. 'I wondered, how is he?'

The woman looked up at her and saw the anxiety written on her pale face. 'Are you related?' Mary sensed the woman evaluating. A few fleeting moments as the nurse took in the crisp new bonnet that Mary had bought this morning, and the shawl that covered the threadbare seams of her jacket. 'Are you family?' There was a hint of cynicism in her voice.

Mary hesitated a moment too long to get away with trying to say 'yes'. She realised she was trembling.

'A friend then?' asked the woman more softly. 'A *close* friend?'

Mary nodded, even managing a tear that tumbled down onto one pale cheek.

The sister sighed sympathetically. 'Shouldn't really do this, love . . . not if you're not proper next of kin, but—'

'Oh my lord, is he—?'

'Dead?' The sister smiled, reached a hand over the desk and gently squeezed one of Mary's. 'No. But the poor chap's feeling very sorry for himself this morning. He's very much alive, my dear.'

Mary's cheeks dampened with several more tears. She smiled. But inside she felt panic beginning to bubble up and give her away. She wondered where the devil she was going to take this exchange next.

'Come with me, love,' said the nurse sympathetically. 'You can look at him briefly, but not too long. He needs his rest.' She turned to ask a colleague to take over on the front desk and, with a firm arm around Mary's shoulders, guided her away from the hustle and bustle of the foyer, through a pair of heavy swing doors.

'I . . . I don't want to be any trouble. I—'

'I'm finished for today anyway,' the sister said. 'Staff cloakroom's along this way anyhow. It's no trouble.' She looked at Mary, glassy-eyed and pale. 'He is going to be just fine, the doctor said.'

They walked down the hushed passageway, finally taking a door on the left leading to the men's ward. Heavy, dark wood doors again with frosted glass. The sister pushed one of them open a few inches and nodded towards the row of hospital beds on the inside.

'Third one along on the right. That's your gentleman.'

Mary could see a man with bandages around his head like a comically large Indian turban. He was fast asleep.

'See?' said the nurse. She smiled. 'You can relax. He's on the mend, so he is.'

'Could I . . . ?'

'Go in? No. No visitors until the doctor says otherwise,' said the nurse. 'He's still very poorly and not up to seeing anyone, I'm afraid.'

'Oh, right.' Mary nodded. She struggled to wrestle back a puff of relief.

'Speaking of which . . .' The nurse nodded politely at the doctor as he approached the double doors.

'Sister,' he said, looking at Mary. 'I'm sure you know there's no visiting on the ward yet? Not until I've done my rounds.'

'Sorry, sir. The lady here was awfully worried about the gent who came in early this morning. I was just showing her that he's perfectly fine, doctor.'

He made a face. 'Ahh . . . I see.' He scratched his cheek. 'I wouldn't say he's "perfectly fine". The head trauma was quite severe.' He noted the flicker of reaction in Mary's face. 'I mean to say he'll live, but he's experiencing some disorientation. Some confusion.'

'Confusion?'

'A forgetfulness.' The doctor shrugged. 'This can happen with a heavy blow to the head. "Amnesia", we call it. A forgetfulness of everyday normal things. Most often it's a temporary condition that fixes itself in due course.' The doctor deployed a well-practised reassuring smile for her benefit. 'Even the most severe cases of complete forgetfulness, when a patient doesn't even remember their own name, these things, these memories, can fully return eventually.'

Mary looked up at him. 'Is he . . . is he *that* bad?'

The doctor shrugged. 'It's very early yet. He has some swelling, a lesion inside his skull, which we're tapping to ensure the swelling does not cause any more harm to his brain. May I suggest you give him a day or two's rest? Then I shall have a clearer understanding of his condition?'

'Yes.' Mary nodded. 'Yes, of course. Whatever you think is best.'

The doctor nodded politely. 'Now, if you'll excuse me, I need to get started.' He hesitated in the doorway, the door half pushed open. 'Oh, what is the gentleman's name, by the way?'

Mary stared at him, frozen with panic. She hadn't anticipated that: conjuring up a name.

'His name? It's for our records, you see.'

Mary's mouth opened. 'It's . . . it's John.'

'John . . . ?' The doctor raised an eyebrow, awaiting the rest.

Her mind was blank. Panic-blank. She licked dry lips as she raced to engage it, make it produce a credible name out of thin air. She saw the man huddled over on the street, bathed in the flickering amber glow of the street lamp, and beyond him, on the side of a brick wall, a street sign.

'Argyll,' she said finally. 'John Argyll.'

CHAPTER 6

15th July 1888, Whitechapel, London

'It wasn't nothin' like you said, Bill.' Annie challenged him with a stare over the table. 'You said it was some cheap slapper. But she was class, you could see that. She ain't some Miss Nobody from Who-Pissin'-Well-Cares. Somebody's gonna miss her, an—'

'And her nipper?' Polly interrupted. 'We told you, we only do *fresh-born* ones.'

Bill waved them silent. 'Doesn't fuckin' matter, girls. S'all done now, right?'

'The baby was old enough to be . . . I dunno, *christened*,' snapped Polly, her voice rising above the rasping whisper they'd been sharing until now. 'The baby could be written in somewhere!'

Bill grabbed one of her hands and squeezed the knuckles until they bulged and ground painfully together. 'Keep yer fuckin' voice down, Polly,' he hissed.

'You're hurtin' me!' she whimpered.

'Course I'm fuckin' hurtin' you, love, 'cause you keep blabbin' so loud we're all gonna end up swinging on rope at the tuck-up fair. So you can either speak softly, or shut yer trap.'

She nodded mutely.

'Now . . . tell me what you two did with it.'

Annie spoke, tapping her clay pipe on the table and dusting the ash off with her hand onto the floor. 'Like we does every other time. It's just pieces now. Different places.'

'Good.'

'An' what about the woman, Bill?'

He shrugged. 'That's my business. She's gone.'

They sat in silence for a while, watching the inn's patrons from the corner booth. Watching the usual evening's pattern unfold: working men delaying the moment they have to return home with one final mug of the wet stuff; a row of tarts propping up the bar, puffing on clay pipes like royal trumpeters blowing a fanfare of smoke.

'Like I told yer, we been paid a pretty penny for this,' said Bill. 'A gentleman put his pecker in the wrong place an' we tidied up his consequences. That's all there is to it.'

'We was talking,' said Annie. 'Before you turned up.' She glanced at Polly, who offered her the slightest nod of moral support. 'Reckon, 'cause you wasn't straight up with us, 'cause of that posh street where she was livin', and on account of the baby not being a newborn . . . we ought to 'ave twice as much as we said we'd do it for. S'only fair, Bill.'

He eyed her silently.

'If you'd been straight with us from the first, we would've asked for more. That wasn't just a normal crib-rat.'

He could hear the wobble of fear in her voice.

Silly bitch is scared of me.

Of course she was. She'd watched him nearly behead the woman in the hallway. Watched him do it calmly and professionally, like it was no trouble at all. Like he was cutting himself a slice of bread from a loaf.

He casually drew a circle in the spilled beer on the wooden table, taking his time to answer. The thing was, given how much the gentleman was already paying, he could easily afford to double what those two had asked for. Better still, that locket he'd found – that precious little locket that had fallen from the woman's clothes, tucked away, something so precious, so valuable – that locket made this job a whole different thing.

A different business contract altogether.

His other hand absently stole into the pocket of his coat, played with the warm, smooth surface of the locket, flicked open and closed the clasp.

A very different situation altogether.

He smiled. Why not let these two share a little of the good news? Not that he was going to tell them what he was holding in his pocket, or what it meant, but it wouldn't hurt for them to know there was chance of a little more gravy coming out of this pudding if they played along like good girls.

He was seeing the gentleman tomorrow. An agreed rendezvous in a dark place where matters could be discussed and payment made. Bill had never actually done business with a man who spoke like this one did, like some duke or lord. Not just posh, but *old posh* . . . the kind that went back generations, had a coat of arms, went back to olden times.

He realised if he was going to play games with the gentleman, then he was going to have to play oh-so-cleverly. If he was going to tell him what he'd found on the woman, and that this little discovery was going to significantly alter the original agreement, he'd better be bloody careful about it.

Gentleman like that don't walk around the docks all on his lonesome, does he?

A gentleman like that most probably had a couple of lackeys tucked away beyond earshot and out of sight, but close enough to jump and chiv him at a sign: the lighting of a match, the deliberate stroking of a nose.

And it would be a proper foolish thing pulling that item out of his pocket as proof he'd found what he'd found. Far better to turn up at their meeting without it. To describe it in detail as best he could and assure the man it was being looked after elsewhere before moving the conversation on to how much the gentleman in question was going to have to pay to get the thing back.

Bill smiled. He could be so very, very shrewd when he tried. As cunning as a fox.

'Well?' said Annie. 'You ain't sayin' so much about what I just said.'

He sat forward. 'Polly? Why don't you go an' get yourselves a coupla cups of mecks, an' a pint o' gatter for me? I need to talk a moment with Annie in private.'

Polly's eyes flashed irritation, but she got up. 'S'pose.'

She slid out from the wooden booth and weaved through the pall of pipe smoke towards the bar.

'Annie . . . 'ow long we known each other?'

Annie took a match, struck a light and touched it against the nest of tobacco in her clay pipe. 'Years, Bill. Years.'

'And you can vouch for Polly?'

'She's not tapped as many cot-rats as me. But she can do it. She's—'

'I'm asking if you can *trust* her?'

Annie cocked a head. 'She's a mate. I'd trust her more than I fuckin' would you,' she replied with a dry, wheezy laugh. She meant it, though.

'All right, then.' His fingers played with the locket, turning it over and over. 'I'm seeing our pay man tomorrow night.'

'I know that.'

'I'm gonna be asking for a *lot* more swag than we settled on before.'

Her eyebrows arched. 'Oh, and 'e's goin' to pay up, is 'e, Bill? Just 'cause you've decided to ask for more?'

Bill smiled. 'Our pay man will cough up, love, because I found summin' special on the girl.'

'Special?' She pulled the stem of her pipe from her lips. 'What?'

'Summin' that I don't think 'e even knows she 'ad on 'er.'

'What?'

'Summin' nice an' shiny . . . a keepsake.' He was tempted to ease it out of his pocket, flash her a glimpse of it. But the public house was chock full of pocket dippers, cly fackers, petty crooks whose magpie eyes would more than likely pick out the faint glint of polished gold in the gas-lit gloom of their nook.

'It's a whatcha call it . . . a locket. There's a portrait in there. Portrait of a chap with the dead woman. A penny to a farthing tells me that's the gentleman who can't keep his pecker behind his buttons.'

Her eyes widened. 'Serious?'

'Oh, yes. And I'm quite certain it wouldn't take a person too much 'ard graft to find out the name what goes with the face.' He was going to add that he actually recognised the face; just couldn't work out where he'd seen it before. Yet.

She looked at him with hooded, sceptical eyes. 'Now, see, I would've thought you'd keep summin' like that all to yerself. It's not like you to share out unless somebody's got their fingers wrapped round yer curlies.'

'You're gonna look after it, Annie. Keep it safe for me while I go and have me chat with our man tomorrow night.'

'Oh.' She smiled. 'So you *do* trust me, Bill?'

'I trust you not to be a silly bitch and cross me. How about that?'

Annie looked over her shoulder at the bar. 'And Polly?'

'She follows yer lead, don't she? If yer trust her, then that's good for me. But,' he said, sitting back on the bench, 'either of yer mess me around, and you'll both find yerselves bobbing in the Thames.'

'So? Where's this locket, then?'

Not here . . . not now.

'I'll give it you tomorrow before I go see the man. And you be sure to find a safe place for it. *Very* safe.'

CHAPTER 7

15th September 1888, Saint Bartholomew's Hospital, London

His dreams seemed to know more about him than he did. They filled his restless sleep with stories that made no sense but promised him glimpses of things he might have seen. He saw a city of tall buildings, a wide street humming with life and activity. Instinctively he knew it wasn't London. It was a city far off, across an ocean.

Is that a place I have been? He asked himself. *Is that it? Is that where I come from?*

Perhaps he'd only visited there and his dreams were teasing him with a fleeting memory of that. But he was also wary of ideas creeping in to fill his empty memory. The ward room was busy all day long with visitors coming and going, the high-ceilinged room echoing with broken pieces of conversation, sometimes whispered considerately, other times loud and thoughtless. The young man in the bed next to his had lost several fingers in an accident. A bone saw in an abattoir and a moment's distraction was all it took. His colourful, boasting description of the incident to one of the ward sisters had become material for his empty mind to make mischief with. This afternoon's sleep had been full of splashes of blood and rib cages and metal pails full of offal, and the high-pitched screams of the young man next door, parted from his fingers. A memory or a dream? He shook his head. He had no way of knowing.

'Ahh! You're awake at last.'

He turned to see the ward matron: a tiny woman, no bigger than a child, but with the commanding air of a general. Her lean face was pulled taut by her brown hair tied back into a conker-sized bun; a hard face with a permanent scowl that seemed to intimidate even the duty surgeons.

'How are you feeling this afternoon, Mr Argyll?'

Yes. Argyll. Mr Argyll. John Argyll. He tried the name silently again. It still seemed so odd to have that: a name. But pleasing. So much better than nothing at all.

'Mr Argyll?'

He nodded. 'A little better, thank you, ma'am.'

'Splendid,' she said perfunctorily. Then her scowl momentarily softened with the slightest hint of humanity. 'Because . . . I have some news for you.'

'Yes?'

'You have a visitor.'

'A visitor?' He felt something lurch inside him. A spasm of nervousness, of excitement. 'For me? Are you sure?'

'Of course I'm sure.' The scowl was back as if it had never been away. 'Now, do you feel well enough to see her?'

Her?

'Who . . . who is she?'

'She says she's *a friend*.' He sensed a note of reproach in the matron's voice. 'She's been waiting in the main hall since breakfast.'

A friend. He begged his mind to try and produce something . . . someone. A face. A name. He got nothing back but the foolish young man next door and his flying fingers. 'I . . . I don't know . . . I really . . .'

'I could send her away if you're not ready?'

'No . . . no, please don't do that! I think I'd like to see her. Perhaps she'll help me get my memory back?'

'If you're absolutely sure?'

'Yes. Please.'

The matron turned with a squeak of shoes on the polished linoleum and headed down towards the end of the ward and disappeared through double doors of frosted glass.

Her? Argyll realised he was trembling as he watched indistinct outlines move beyond the frosted glass of the doors, dark shapes passing to and fro, lingering, conjoining, receding. Anyone of them could be his visitor slowly approaching. Whoever she was, she *knew* him!

A friend. That's what the matron said, wasn't it? Not family; a friend.

He hefted himself up on his bed, plumped his pillows up. His head pounded from the exertion of doing it.

A friend? Or – good grief – a lover, perhaps?

He adjusted the collar of his pyjama shirt. Rubbed his eyes in case they were gummed with sleep. It occurred to him that in a few short moments, he was going to have something valuable. He was going to be talking with someone who knew who he was; knew the person that existed beyond the bubble of this hospital cot existence. The frosted glass clouded with two dark blobs growing quickly more distinct. One shorter than the other: Matron and his lady visitor.

Good god, get a grip, man, he told himself. He wasn't just trembling, he was actually shaking.

With a creak of hinges that echoed through the quiet ward, the double doors swung inwards and he caught his first glimpse of her. She was slight, trim, and her clothes looked fashionable to him, as best he could tell. Auburn hair piled up and topped with a bonnet, and a pale oval face dusted with hayseed freckles. Her green eyes were hopping from one bed to another until, finally, they settled on him.

She clasped gloved hands and let out a small yelp before she quickened her pace and hurried towards him.

'Oh my, I've been so worried!'

She was beside his bed and her arms snaked around his shoulders tightly, squeezing him. 'My darling!' she whispered in his ear. 'John, I thought you were dead! I . . . I thought I'd lost you!'

The ward matron caught up with them and the young woman released him, straightened up and dabbed away the tears from her cheeks.

'So . . . Mr Argyll, this young lady has been very, very anxious to talk to you,' said Matron gruffly.

His female visitor gasped. 'Good lord, yes! When you didn't come home, John, I got so worried about you! I . . . I must have called into half the hospitals in London!'

The doctor – Dr Hart – had told him his name was John Argyll last night. *John.* It hadn't triggered a flood of memories as the doctor had hoped it might. And it had sounded so odd, so alien at first. But *John* . . . yes, he could sort of imagine himself as *John*. A dependable name. A reliable name. A neutral name. Now, hearing it on the lips of this beautiful young woman, he was absolutely certain it was his name.

He stared at her. 'My name *is* John.'

'Yes . . . of course it is, my love.' The young woman looked concerned. She turned to the matron. 'Is it really that bad? His memory?'

Matron nodded. 'He remembers absolutely nothing. Not a single thing.'

She bit her lip. 'Not even . . . *me?*'

'Might I enquire as to your . . . relationship with Mr Argyll?' There was a tone of suspicion in the matron's voice.

The young woman looked at the matron, then back at John. She lowered her voice to little more than a muted whisper. 'We are . . . we're . . . this is a bit awkward . . .' She bit her lip. 'You really don't remember me?'

Argyll frowned, pushing his mind to reach in and pull something out of the fog. He studied her face intently: the pointed chin, the look of concern and anguish. Something in all of that *did* feel vaguely familiar. But then again, he'd woken from sleep not half an hour before believing he might once have worked in an abattoir. He wasn't sure he could trust any instinctive feelings. It might just be that he *wanted* to remember such a beautiful face. And that intoxicating voice of hers . . . a hint of some accent in there, some sing-song lilt that he found utterly charming.

He would love to genuinely lay claim to her; love to say he remembered whatever relationship it is they had.

'Anything, Mr Argyll? Any recollection at all of this young lady?' The matron spoke his name with the same cynical tone.

'The face . . . the face is, yes, I think it is familiar to me.'

'It's me, my dear. It's me, Mary!'

He struggled to unite the name and her face. The name. Mary. Mary. He imagined saying 'I love you, Mary'. 'Mary, my darling.' Hoping they might stir some dormant images. Nothing came to him. But her face . . . Mary's face. It was most certainly familiar.

Then again, maybe he just wanted it to be. Perhaps he just wanted to know he wasn't entirely alone in this awful, listless limbo.

'Do I assume you are *Mrs Argyll?*' asked the matron.

Mary's cheeks coloured pink and she shook her head. 'No . . . we . . . we are . . .'

The matron waved her hand, preferring not to hear what the young woman was struggling to say. 'Fair enough. Say no more.' The suspicious edge in her voice seemed to have wavered and been replaced with her usual stern authority. 'Perhaps then, *Miss*, you can assist me with some paperwork now that we have someone who can vouch for his identity.'

The matron turned to him and that passing expression of

professional warmth returned to her face. 'There you are, my dear –
didn't I say someone would come calling for you soon enough?'

Argyll nodded, looking pitifully relieved to have someone. 'You'll
come back, Mary?'

'Yes . . . yes, my love, of course.'

'I won't keep her from you for long, Mr Argyll.'

CHAPTER 8

16th July 1888, Victoria Docks, London

Bill heard the hour chimes coming from Saint George's. The last stain of the day coloured the tumbling clouds overhead, painting them a soft and vulnerable fleshy colour – the belly of a salmon, the powdered blush on a whore's cheek.

He was watching the dock workers unloading a coal barge across the Thames; little mole men, coated black with the dust. The horizon across the placid, wide river was black, paper cut-out silhouettes of chimney pots and the vaulted roofs of warehouses lined up side by side along the busy quay. He could hear the distant bark of voices, the clatter of unloading, the irritable bray of a mule. The docks were always busy.

This side of the river, however, the south side, was quiet. Quiet enough to hear the soft sound of grit beneath approaching boot heels.

'Good evening, Mr Tolly.'

Bill turned around to see his gentleman client a dozen feet away. Just like last time, their face to face meeting was at twilight: dark enough that beneath the felt brim of his topper there was only shadowed detail, but not so dark that business was going to be conducted blindly.

The gentleman had given him a name, quite obviously a pseudonym. 'Good evenin', Mr Jones.' Instinctively he deferentially knuckled his forehead and then kicked himself inside for doing so.

For the moment, a pause. The soft lapping sound of the Thames at low tide, riding the silt and pebbles, and the clanking of halyards and block and tackles against the masts of barges moored nearby filled the silence.

'So, is the . . . uh . . . matter . . . dealt with?'

'The tart and the baby are in pieces,' Tolly replied matter-of-factly.

The gentleman looked away for a moment. A gesture of discomfort. A man used to talking in delicately veiled euphemisms, not so bluntly as that.

'Fine,' he replied eventually. 'I have the balance of your fee here, Mr Tolly. The second one hundred pounds as agreed, which we believe satisfactorily settles the matter.'

We?

Bill cocked his head slightly at that. We? The only other time he had met Mr Jones – here at the same time three weeks ago – he had talked as if 'the matter' was his and his alone. Up until five seconds ago, Bill had been entertaining the possibility that the man in the locket's portrait might actually be Mr Jones himself, hence his vague familiarity – the gentleman with a penchant for young, French domestic staff.

Bill had a little speech organised. Something he'd been rehearsing all day, knowing full well he didn't have the clever talk and the long, smart-sounding words that Mr Jones did. And what he was about to say needed to sound very clever. It needed to sound very business-like.

But the word 'we' changed matters somewhat.

Bugger that. Just say your piece, he urged himself.

'Mr Jones,' he began. 'I reckon the *transac-shun* ain't quite done yet.'

He could see the gentleman's head turn from looking out across the Thames. A glint of twilight in one of his eyes told Bill that he was looking directly at him. 'Pardon me?'

'Your tart wasn't exactly that, was she? She 'ad a bit of class about 'er. Foreign, too. French, right?'

Mr Jones remained silent and perfectly still.

'Was she your bit of stuff?'

Bill decided to bring the word 'we' into the discussion.

'Or wozzit the tart of a friend of yours? Huh?'

The gentleman looked back out across the Thames again, at the dim shapes of mole men hefting sacks of coal onto the quayside.

'You'd be best advised not to continue with questions like these, Mr Tolly. The matter is settled and I have a sizeable amount of money to give you right now. Shall we just conclude our business and bid goodnight?'

'I want more, Mr Jones. I want two thousand.'

Bill could see the man's outline recoil ever so slightly.

'See, I found a few things on the girl. Things she 'ad on 'er that I think she weren't meant to 'ave.'

'Mr Tolly, I really have no interest in whether you've decided to rummage through her things and pawn them for—'

'*Jewlerry*, Mr Jones. Special *jewlerry*, which I don't s'pose she bought for 'erself.'

'I beg your pardon? Jewellery?'

Bill grinned in the dark. He had this man's full attention. He felt a buzz of nervous excitement and satisfaction at seeing this smug stuck-up bastard lose his cool inbred demeanour, if only for a fleeting moment.

'A gift. A keepsake – gold by the look of it – with an interestin' pattern on it and a proper maker's mark on the bottom of it. Best bit, though, Mr Jones, the best bit is a real nice portrait photograph on the inside of it. *Luverly* picture of a gentleman, a woman an' a nipper. Very much in love, by the looks of it. How's it go? Very much the 'appy family.'

Bill hushed now, satisfied that his speech had come out pretty close to the way he'd practised it.

'I see.'

He wanted desperately to look around, behind himself, to check and see if Mr Jones had brought with him some hired knuckleheads. But he knew he needed to remain calm, remain in control, remain *businesslike*.

'If you were to show this particular piece of jewellery to me, Mr Tolly, I might actually believe you.'

This is it, Bill, mate . . . this is where you go very careful.

'See, I'd be a right fuckin' fool if I brought it along 'ere tonight, dontcha think, Mr Jones? A right fool.' He glanced around now. 'I'd say you mighta brought a chiv man or two along tonight.'

The gentleman stared at him silently. In the failing twilight, the faint dark patches that hinted at eyes, nose and mouth had merged into one shape now beneath the brim of his hat. 'You are playing an exceedingly dangerous game, Mr Tolly. I would strongly advise against that.'

'I ain't playing a game. This is a business deal, Mr Jones. I'm a business man.'

The gentleman wheezed a soft, sputtering laugh. 'No, you are not.

You're a common crook who believes he's stumbled across something of value.'

'But, see, I have, ain't I?'

'You have a trinket that might – at worst – cause embarrassment to an associate of mine. That is all. You go and fetch it, bring it back here and, if you are quick about it, I shall be prepared to give you another hundred pounds for the errand and not a penny more.'

Bill shook his head. 'Nah, that's all right. It's safe with me bizness partner. Think it can stay where it is for now.'

'Partner?' The word filled the space between them. 'Now, you *assured* me you work alone, Tolly.'

Bill realised the mention of someone else involved in this deal was deeply unsettling for Mr Jones. Just as unsettling, in fact, as hearing Mr Jones refer to 'we'.

'So? I 'ad a little 'elp to do the job. A coupla 'elpers to be sure.'

'And they . . .' A long pause. A very long pause. 'And they *know* about this trinket?'

'Oh, yes they do, Mr Jones. But don't worry, they won't flap their mouths. Not when there's some decent money to be 'ad out of you.'

Bill realised he was trembling; not out of fear, but sheer damned excitement. He could hear an unsteady warble in this gentleman's voice and knew this was going perfectly. Far better than he could ever have imagined.

He's fucking scared shitless.

'Please understand, Mr Tolly, that we . . . uh . . . we could find you very easily. And if we decided to do that, you and your colleagues would end up in a very unfortunate way.' The gentleman took a step closer, but Bill stood his ground.

Brass it out, Bill. Show 'im who's boss here.

If Mr Jones had brought along with him a pair of knuckle-heads, then now would be the time he'd beckon them forward, he figured.

'Mr Jones, you ain't gonna find this nice little piece and the picture in it, not if you do anything to me. It's safe with a friend of mine. Anythin' funny 'appens to me and it'll get took to one of 'em penny papers.'

Mr Jones stopped where he was. 'It would be desirable to have this item back without any more blood being shed.' He waved a hand. 'The money is inconsequential. But discretion, you understand; discretion – that's something we value far more.'

'I can un'erstan' that, Mr Jones. Summin' like this in the paper would be very embarrassin'.'

'Hmmm,' replied the gentleman. He turned to watch the last of the crimson stain disappear from the twilight sky. Silent consideration of the way ahead that lasted long enough for Bill to prompt him.

'So . . . Mr Jones?'

'So, it seems, then, our little matter is not going to be concluded tonight. You and I will require a second meeting. I don't have that sum of money on me right now.'

Bill shrugged. 'Of course not. Didn't expect yer to. But I'll 'ave me hundred pounds now, Mr Jones, if that's all the same to yer. And the rest when yer got it.'

'I shall need to make some . . . uh . . . arrangements first.'

'Do what you 'ave to, but you don't want to keep me waitin' too long, Mr Jones. I tend to get impatient.'

CHAPTER 9

21st September 1888, Saint Bartholomew's Hospital, London

'Is he awake yet this morning?'

The ward matron turned at the sound of her soft voice. 'Ahh, here she is again! Good morning, Mary,' she said with a polite nod. 'Yes, he's up and about. Had a cup of tea and making quite a nuisance of himself so far this morning.'

'Oh, good,' Mary replied cheerfully, striding along the polished floor of the hallway towards the nurses' station, a bunch of fresh daffodils under one arm and a basket of fruit from the market in the other.

'Good lord! Are those grapes! Goodness, lucky Mr Argyll!'

Mary smiled as she passed by. 'Yes, I heard tell they were good for a weak constitution,' she replied, self-conscious that she was over-egging her 'h's.

Over the last week, she'd been working so hard on that, and other things. Listening closely to the way more refined ladies than her spoke to each other. This morning, stopping at Covent Garden on the way in to Saint Bart's, she'd discreetly followed two well-to-do young ladies all the way around the market, listening to the sounds of the words coming out of their mouths and the sorts of things they talked about. Mary had all new clothes now. Nice clothes, better than she'd ever worn before. And walking around the market, if she kept her mouth shut and just practised the measured little steps of a properly *finished* lady, if she didn't swing her arms like she was used to doing but kept them occupied holding a small purse, she could almost pass as one of them.

Almost?

No, not almost – she did. Men – the nice gentlemen – tipped their hats, offered polite smiles and stepped aside for her. And the tradesmen and stall owners! Good lord, there were even faces amongst them she recognised, men who would have crudely wolf-whistled at her only a few days ago, or slapped her behind playfully or even grabbed at her cleavage. Now they doffed their caps politely and with exaggerated and misplaced 'h's enquired *hhhhall hhhabout 'er 'ealth.*

Mary bustled into the ward and instantly spotted John Argyll sitting in striped hospital issue pyjamas, a dressing gown and slip-pers on his bed, frowning at the morning paper. The dressing on his head had been replaced a couple of times, on each occasion with somewhat less wadding, so that it looked not quite so comical now.

'Good morning, John!'

Argyll looked up at her, his tanned face splitting instantly into a broad smile. 'Am I happy to see you. This damnable word right here is driving me crazy. What is it?' he said, pointing to the column of text for an article about domestic sanitation. She leant over his shoulder and narrowed her eyes at the word his finger was hovering over.

'Basin.'

He squinted and leant closer. 'Good grief, I think you're right!' He shook his head, confounded and annoyed with himself. 'I kept looking at it, spelling all the letters out correctly, and yet just couldn't make sense of the damned thing!'

'You shouldn't fret about it, John. You know what Doctor Hart said: that there might be things that don't make sense to you at first. But they'll come back to you.'

He nodded. 'I know, I know, but it's the fact I can read all the other words. It's just so damned irritating. Doesn't make any sense.'

'Your damaged mind will get better.' She squeezed his shoulder affectionately. 'It will, love.'

But, please, not too quick.

She sat down in the visitor's chair by his side. 'You're remember-ing things better now, aren't you? What about the things we talked about yesterday evening? Can you remember?'

They'd been playing cards – cribbage – and speaking in hushed tones so as not to disturb the others in the ward. Argyll had been asking about them, what they had meant to each other before the incident, how they met, where they lived, what he did for work. A million and one questions that Mary had managed to answer cautiously. The surgeon, Dr Hart, had suggested it best that, at first, she should not tell him the answers to too many things; that she should let him ask the questions, then try and reach for the answers himself. It might be better for his healing brain to be worked rather than spoon-fed. And at the very least, if he started to learn things about himself that he hadn't been told, then it would be a sign that some degree of his amnesia was clearing up.

He nodded proudly. 'I remember everything from yesterday.' He laughed. 'I remember you cheated at crib.'

Her jaw dropped in mock horror. 'John! How could you say such an awful bad thing? Me? A cheat!' Her horror dissolved into a polite giggle as she squeezed his hand.

'I remember how little I know about us,' he said after a while. Sadly. 'I wish I could remember how we first met, how we felt . . .' He shook his head.

'The doctor said I have to let you see if you can find those things yourself. I'm sorry.'

He stroked his chin, thick with bristles, much in need of a wet shave. 'But you, Mary, you have it all in your memory. You remember us.' He looked at her. 'And . . . and did you . . . ?'

Her cheeks flushed slightly. 'Did I love you?'

He looked desperately hopeful. Puppy-dog pitiful in his pyjamas. 'Yes . . . yes, I do, John.'

Relief spilled across him. An odd expression on such a mature face. Mary supposed the man must be in his mid- to late-thirties; crow's feet arcing down across sun-browned skin that she imagined had seen a lifetime of wonderful and exciting things in America. And yet there was the smile of an innocent child on his craggy cheeks.

'I'd be so lost without you.' He looked around at some of the other men, old and young, in the row of beds opposite. Some of them had yet to receive a single visitor, as if they were entirely alone in this world. Unmissed. Unnoticed. But he was lucky. He had this wonderful young lady. A breath of fresh air, a spoon of sugar in a bowl of oats. Her chirruping voice lightened the oppressive gloom of the ward, which was otherwise a sea of sighing breaths, moans and sleep-talking threats and curses.

'Doctor Hart said I may not need to remain in the hospital much longer. A few more days at most to make sure the swelling has gone down and to remove the stitches in my side.'

'That's . . .' Mary smiled. 'That's wonderful news.' Her stomach flipped. So distracted with her daily visits here, dodging the other girls in her lodging house and their inevitable probing questions as to what the devil she's been up to these last few days, and pretending to be someone she wasn't, she'd given little thought as to what happened next. She wasn't even sure why she'd been coming to visit John this last week. Surely the prudent thing to do would be to run. Get out of London now, before this sham fell apart. But she found herself coming here, dutifully, every morning. What was that? Guilt? Concern for this lost soul? Something else?

'I can't wait to come home,' he said quietly. He tossed a conspiratorial nod at the old man in the next bed. 'The chap over there keeps breaking wind during the night.' His face wrinkled. 'Most awful bloody smell.'

Mary smiled. But her mind was racing. Home. The moment he checked out of the hospital and they asked for a contact address, this little sham was all going to be over.

John squeezed her hand. 'Can't wait to come home.'

'Yes.' She leant close to him, kissed him tenderly on the cheek. 'I'm going to take good care of you, my love.'

CHAPTER 10

22nd September 1888, Saint Bartholomew's Hospital, London

'Provided there are no problems, no complications, I would say he could be discharged by the end of this week. But you must understand: Mr Argyll suffered a severe blow to his head. Beneath the skull, a degree of haemorrhaging occurred which—'

'Hemmer . . . ?'

'Internal bleeding, Miss Kelly. The blood wasn't able to find a way out and was thus causing a build up of pressure inside his cranium . . . his skull. It's this pressure that I believe has caused significant damage to his brain.'

Dr Hart could see the poor young woman was hoping to hear a more positive prognosis than he was giving; an assurance that the man's memories would all come flooding back fully-formed in one moment of blinding epiphany. But the truth was there were absolutely no assurances he could make. He'd seen enough cracked and caved in skulls to know that the damaged brain behaved in no predictable way. A man might receive a tap on the head and be reduced to a vegetative state for the rest of his life; another might be bludgeoned until his head looked like a misshapen potato and yet still walk away proudly sporting stitches that would one day make a scar worth boasting about.

'I'm sorry, my dear, there really is no knowing for sure how much of a recovery he will make. Or how soon. If, indeed, ever.'

'But will he be able to walk properly again?'

John could manage a stilted shuffle. His right leg seemed to operate perfectly normally, but his left appeared to exhibit signs of partial paralysis.

Dr Hart pressed his lips together. 'My hope is that it will get better as his mind knits the damage that has been done. From my experience, the harder he works to recover, the better the chances are for him that he will make a full recovery, in time.'

She sucked in a breath. 'Then I'll have to be a hard taskmaster,' she said with a firm nod.

Dr Hart smiled encouragement. 'That's the idea.'

He looked out of the window of his consultation room at the ward across the passageway. He could see Mr Argyll playing chess with another patient. 'So he's an American? Is that right? Is he visiting London? A business trip perhaps?' The exotic twang of the former colonies was certainly somewhere there in the calm, deep drawl of his voice.

'Uh . . . yes, that's right. Yes, he is American.'

'How did you both meet?'

Mary Kelly's cheeks prickled with crimson. She looked flustered. 'I . . . well . . . it's . . .'

Dr Hart waved his hand. 'I'm sorry. Very nosy of me.'

'No, honestly, that's all right. We met in . . . Covent Garden.'

He smiled. 'I see.'

He suspected Matron was right about one thing: Kelly was a working girl. No doubt about it. It was in her diction. So careful and deliberate in the way she talked. But every now and then she let slip and missed a consonant, or dropped an 'h'. A girl quite obviously working very hard to disguise it.

Matron's instinct at the beginning of the week was to suspect this girl was on *the make* somehow. Some scoundrel looking to hoodwink the unfortunate chap. She'd told him about a story she'd once read in one of the penny papers about a scurrilous housemaid who'd hoodwinked her way into the will of a senile old millionaire, convinced him he had no living relations or heirs, that he was entirely alone. With a cautionary cocking of an eyebrow, she'd alluded that perhaps 'that girl who keeps visiting our Mr Argyll' might be up to similar tricks. But then there was no one quite so cold-hearted and cynical as Matron. And even she was now prepared to admit that perhaps she'd probably misjudged the poor girl.

Dr Hart liked to think he had a fairly good measure of people; after all, he met and fixed up all manner of people here who drifted into St Bartholomew's at every hour of night and day. And Mary Kelly, to his eye, looked very much like a young woman hopelessly in love.

And why not? It irked him so that his parents' stuffy generation still invested so much stock in a person's class. That a person should be condemned to never better their station because of an accident of birth, an accident of accent and diction. What with Mr Argyll being an American, he was certain something as old-fashioned and uniquely English as *class* meant absolutely nothing to the man. Dr Hart sometimes rather fancied he'd be more at home in a country like America, where a person was a measure of what they actually achieved rather than merely being the sum of their manners and bearing.

An American gentleman and a working-class English girl in love? Good grief, the world was full of far more unlikely things.

'I suspect you will make a first-rate nurse for our patient when you get him home, Miss Kelly. First-rate.'

'Yes.' She smiled. 'I'll have him back to his old self, so I will.'

'I'm certain you will. He seems a very resilient gentleman, does Mr Argyll. And, I suspect he's a jolly lucky man to have someone like you to care for him.'

Mary sipped tea from the cup. Fine china and a slender handle that allowed only a couple of fingers through its eye. She spread her little finger out, like the other ladies in the tea shop were doing.

What now?

Dr Hart thought John was almost ready to be discharged from the ward. He'd even asked her if Mr Argyll's home had suitable access for a wheelchair, as initially he would need one.

She'd nodded, but in actual fact her mind had been racing. The lodging house? Her room? No. She couldn't take John back to that squalor. Even his befuddled mind would instantly work out that they couldn't possibly have been living together there.

A hotel? She had the money.

No, that wouldn't do. She'd let slip to John they had a *home* together. A foolish bloody slip. But there it was; she'd said 'home'. She had only two or three days left now and then they were going to discover there was no home, that she was an imposter, a charlatan.

I should run. Right now.

She toyed with that idea as she carefully forked at the cake on the plate before her. She could take that money of John's and disappear. It was back home, under her bed. She could go back, grab it and run away. Another city, another country, another life. But she dismissed the notion without even being sure why.

Yes . . . why?

She fished for an answer to that question. And the answer came back surprisingly easily.

'He needs me,' she uttered softly, then immediately scoffed at her own fuzzy-headed sentimentality.

He's not your child, your lover, or your husband. He's NOT your responsibility!

Mary chided herself for being soft and foolish. She should have been long gone by now. Like that starling, swooping off to some far-off hot country. He was a grown man and whoever had jumped him, beaten him, knifed him, *they* were the ones who should carry any burden of guilt. Not her. Anyway, she had to look out for herself, since no one else was going to. She was in the position she was in – whoring, thieving in order to pay the rent on that piss-stinking room – because she'd been stupid and naïve enough to let her heart rule her head.

That wonderful plan of hers. That plan that seemed like a lifetime ago. As it happened, she'd found work not as a piano tutor, as she'd hoped, but as an au pair. A nanny for a wealthy family – Mr and Mrs Frampton-Parker and their two boys – living in a beautiful, crescent-shaped drive in Holland Park. Such a lovely place. They had another home in Italy they went to in the winter months. Six months abroad, then returned for spring and summer. They were *that* kind of rich.

Mr Frampton-Parker, a man fifteen years older than her, married to a woman ten years older than himself. Quite clearly a marriage for money. His eyes wandered; of course they did. And they'd very quickly rested on her. Eighteen then, just turning nineteen. Still a child, she realised now. So she had wholly believed him – stupidly believed him – when he said he was going to announce to his wife that he had fallen out of love with her and was going to instigate a divorce. That they would be free to be together and could live just fine on his half of the divorce settlement.

But then, of course, one day not too long after they'd 'started', his wife caught them out. A careless tryst in a dark corner of the large house and the man, in a blind panic, had turned savagely on Mary. Blamed her for everything, for flirting with him, throwing herself at him. That he'd succumbed to a moment of weakness in the face of Mary's relentless campaign to steal him away from his wife.

She wasn't going to get any work like that again. She wasn't ever going to get a job like that again. It was the need for a reference that finished her chances. Even chasing jobs as a shop girl, they wanted to know her life story. She did actually manage to get work on a stall in the Covent Garden market for a while, but the money wasn't enough. Nowhere near enough. The other girls who worked on the stalls there lived with their families still; their money contributed to a family pot. Mary's money was all she had.

And that was where her slippery slope began.

She placed a forkful of a gloriously light sponge topped with thick cream and jam into her mouth and savoured it with eyes firmly closed. Luxury she hadn't enjoyed in over four years. Not since she'd packed her bag and been escorted out of that house by the Frampton-Parkers' cook and valet.

I could make a home for us.

Mary opened her eyes. The idea had popped into her head from nowhere. But she could; she actually, really could. The Frampton-Parkers left their home for Italy at the beginning of September, didn't they? Like bloody clockwork. Every year. It would be closed for the winter, the furniture dressed in dust sheets, the window drapes drawn. And it remained like that until late February, a week before they returned, when their staff came back and dusted, cleaned and aired the property, and fired-up the coke-burning boiler in the basement ready for their return.

She knew Mr and Mrs Frampton-Parker left the keys to their home with a property letting agent in the hope that a convenient and 'acceptable' short-term tenant could be found. But they bemoaned the fact that the agent had been unsuccessful thus far in generating some income from their empty house.

Mary smiled. *I really could.*

She knew the house well. She knew where she could break in without alerting anyone. Or better, if she had the brass nerves to do it, she could walk right into the letting agent's office and place six months' rent right there in his hand. He wouldn't know who she was – the scurrilous au pair who'd 'tempted' Mr Frampton-Parker. That was three years ago, anyway. So long as all the money was up front and she appeared to be suitably well-mannered.

I can do that.

There was something in that idea that provided a unified solution to variously conflicting dilemmas. Yes, she could run with this money – but she realised she didn't want to. Her wiser, older self rationalised that quite reasonably: 'John' might just be a business-man, as Dr Hart had suggested. A businessman with significantly *more* money back in America. Who knows? A business empire of some sort? Factories? Warehouses? Ships? Her wiser, older self calmly explained that she didn't want to run because there was, quite possibly, much more money to be made from this poor lost soul than the five thousand she'd found in his satchel.

But another part of her also couldn't help suspecting she didn't want to run because, well, truth be told, she was rather fond of John Argyll. There was something about him. A gentleness. A kindness. An innocence.

Oh, Mary. Get a grip!

She looked at the sponge cake, her appetite suddenly gone. Her stomach lurched and churned with butterflies. Nerves. If she was going to do this, she was going to need to be smart and calm, and not play around with childish fantasies and dreams of romance.

John's my investment. Nothing more.

CHAPTER 11

17th July 1888, Great Queen Street, Central London

'This has become very dangerous. Very dangerous indeed.'
    The others present nodded in agreement as they watched the crackling fire in the grate send phantoms dancing across the oak panelled walls of the Barclay Room.

'George, how the hell did this happen?'

Warrington stirred in the winged-back armchair, worn leather creaking beneath him. 'I used a local thug to deal with the matter. Local and not particularly well-connected. Awful scoundrel wouldn't have been missed by anyone.'

'But now this scoundrel appears to be *blackmailing* us?'

Warrington shifted uncomfortably under the gaze of the others. 'He claimed to have something in his possession. A memento, a keepsake. Some sort of damned locket. I would have given our chaps the nod to . . . deal with him then and there. But, I just thought we need to be sure if he's telling the truth or not. He could be trying to play us for silly buggers. Or he really could have found something.'

'Perhaps, George, whether he has something or not is irrelevant. The fact is he suspects there's *reason* to blackmail. That alone means I'd rather this low-life was at the bottom of the Thames and crab-food as soon as possible,' said Henry Rawlinson. His eyes twinkled beneath thick white brows and above drawn, liver-spotted cheeks. He stroked a bare chin thoughtfully as the others nodded in silent agreement.

'If the fellow even suspects there's some rich pickings to be had, then he already knows far too much,' said Rawlinson.

'My concern, Henry, is that he does really have something.'

Warrington wondered if there was ever going to be a better time to tell them the worst of it. 'He mentioned a portrait . . . a small photographic portrait. A miniature.'

A spoon clattered noisily against fine china.

'Good god!' one of them gasped.

'Warrington, are you serious?'

'That's what he claimed.'

'Please tell us you mean a portrait of the woman alone.'

If only.

'All of them, I'm afraid. "Very much the happy family." Those were his words.'

The men sat in silence, contemplating that information. The old man, Rawlinson, stirred his tea gently. The three others in their little group – The Steering Committee, which was Rawlinson's euphemism – waited to see what Rawlinson had to say.

'A photograph?' He shook his head and tutted.

'The stupid fool,' muttered one of the others.

'He's still so young,' said Rawlinson, 'and so reckless.'

'That's no excuse. The young man has to be much smarter than this. After all, this girl, she was French, wasn't she?'

'And Catholic. An artist's model, I believe.'

'The man is a damned liability!' growled one of them: Oscar Crosbourne. Warrington looked at the man as he agitatedly thumbed the stem of his pipe. Younger than Rawlinson, but still one of this unofficial committee of silver-haired elders. 'With these bloody problems we're having in Ireland, the troubles the press are stoking up in the East End, grumblings of revolution not only on foreign city streets, but right here in London! And the stupid young fool decides to get a foreign Catholic tart pregnant?! We'd be better off tossing *him* into the Thames!'

There was a long silence. Warrington watched the old men sharing glances that spoke of age-old allegiances and hidden agendas, accepted protocols and boundaries of behaviour.

'Let's not have any more talk like that in here, Crosbourne. We've all sworn oaths, you understand? No more talk like that.' Rawlinson turned his rheumy, old, grey eyes onto Warrington. 'Now, George, what are you suggesting?'

'I would suggest we need to treat Tolly's claim seriously.'

'Do we know where to find him? Surely he could be paid a visit, his rooms searched for the item?'

'He said he used some associates on this job. More than one.

There is a danger that if something unpleasant was to happen to Tolly, then his associates might panic, might flee, might go to ground . . . perhaps might even go to a newspaper with what they have, what they know.'

A log in the fire place spat a lump of glowing charcoal onto the tile hearth.

'God help us!' whispered Rawlinson, 'if that happened.'

'So, come on, George,' said Crosbourne. 'What are you suggesting?'

'Much as I'm appalled that this little . . .' He wanted to curse, but manners before his elders stayed him.

'You can call him a little bastard if you want,' said Rawlinson.

Warrington nodded. 'This little *bastard* thinks he has us in a fix, and I would be inclined to let him believe this is so. Let him think he will have the money he's asked for, in due course.'

'How much has he asked for?'

'Two thousand pounds.'

'Is that *all*?' gasped one of the others. 'Good lord, George, well *pay* the bloody man then and let's have that picture back!'

'But if we do, what's to stop them asking for more? What's to stop them taking our money, and then trying to get some more from a newspaper, for example?'

'Of course, of course, George is quite right,' said Rawlinson. 'We don't just need this item back – that is, if they really have it. We also need to be sure that there is no one, other than those of us in this room, who know about the woman.' He looked at them. 'More importantly, the baby.'

They were silent for a while, watching the flames licking around the glowing ends of the last log in the grate.

'Our mistake was assuming the woman had nothing left, nothing on her that was evidence of this . . . affair. And perhaps your error, George, was employing a local amateur.'

'I used Tolly because, well, he's expendable. That was the plan, gentlemen. This is what we agreed to. To make sure he did the job, then in turn was disposed of.'

Rawlinson reached out a hand and patted Warrington's arm. 'I understand why, George, but it has turned out to be a problem. An amateur has no reputation to preserve. An amateur is an opportunist, someone who might decide he would like a little more money later on. Perhaps after he has spent all his swag, acquired a gambling debt, spent it all on alcohol or opium or whatever that type spend their money on, perhaps an amateur like that would come knocking for more money.'

The old man settled back in his winged leather chair and tipped the last of the tepid cup of tea into his mouth. He smacked his lips thoughtfully.

'I have an old friend in New York. He's one of *us*.' He nodded assurance. 'They use a chap over there for problems such as this one. Bit of a bloodhound, I've been told. Good nose for finding people, finding things. Very, very reliable.'

'This man's in America? It will take weeks to get him here.' Oscar looked at the others. 'We need this Tolly chap dead now! Before he gets impatient and—'

'George, will he?'

Warrington stroked his jaw thoughtfully. 'I left Tolly with the assurance that he will get his money. But that it was going to take me some time to get hold of it. I think he believes that. To him, two thousand pounds is an unimaginable fortune. He'll be patient. He'll wait around for his money. For a little while yet, anyway.' He looked at the others pointedly. 'Just as long as he isn't spooked.'

Rawlinson nodded slowly. 'I shall send a telegram to my friend, then. See if he can contact this fellow they use.'

CHAPTER 12

25th September 1888, Marble Arch, London

Argyll looked on in admiration at the horse-drawn tram running on metal rails down the middle of the Strand. He shuffled in his wheelchair to watch it go past.

'You like the trams, John?' said Mary.

He nodded. 'They remind me of . . . something.'

'Do they have trams like these in America?' she asked, steering the chair around a fruit seller.

He rubbed his temple in a repeated circular motion, a habit she had noticed he'd developed over the last week, something he did when he was trying to coax something from his mind.

'Yes . . . I think so.'

She wondered if that was an answer he had drawn from his memory, or just an assumption he was making. She knew he had produced some fleeting images of his life before. Last evening, as they played cards again on his hospital bed, he was able to tell her he thought he lived in a big city once – tall buildings and busy streets. But it was not London he was seeing, he was almost certain of that.

America. That's where he was from, but no idea where in the country precisely. She knew nothing about the country. Nothing but the occasional things she'd seen in the penny papers: terrifying-looking Indian warriors and continent-spanning railroads.

Last night, John, beginning now to try and piece the fragments of his life together, had asked her how they'd first met. She replied with one of her rehearsed answers, one she'd practised several times over back in her lodgings, knowing the question was going to arise sooner or later.

'Covent Garden,' she'd said. She went on to describe how they'd bumped into each other quite by accident. He'd literally bowled her off her feet and had felt so ashamed and apologetic, he'd offered to make amends by buying her tea.

He craned his neck to look up at her. 'So do we live near here, Mary?'

'Not too far. Our home is in a place called Holland Park.'

'Is it a busy place, like this?'

'No. Quiet and peaceful. Just what you and I both need, I fancy.'

His bandaged head bobbed with approval.

'It's a beautiful place. A tree-lined avenue with a row of lovely, tall houses.'

Mary smiled. She'd done it. She had gone and done it. She'd walked bold as brass into the letting agents and enquired about Number 67. There'd been an awful moment when he'd looked up at her, and Mary had wondered whether a trace of the East End had been in her voice. Or that she might have swaggered in through the agency's double doors instead of gliding. But then he'd smiled warmly, and offered her a chair to sit in.

She had her ready-made story: her American cousin was convalescing in London after an unfortunate accident. They needed somewhere quiet for a few months, just the pair of them. The little park in front of the tree-lined row of houses seemed absolutely perfect. Oh, and was it suitably furnished?

Ten minutes later, the gentlemen had his bowler hat on and keys jangling in his eager hands as he showed her around bedrooms and stairwells she was already very familiar with. She nodded politely at his sales patter, laughed tolerantly at his gushing attempts to be humorous. And when he showed her the boiler in the basement and asked whether she would like to pay a little extra for the property's handyman to come in once a day to keep an eye on the coal burner, she declined.

'My father taught me how to run a steam tractor. I can manage a domestic boiler quite adequately.'

The deal was done, money exchanged, and her name – Mrs Argyll – tidily written on a rental contract by the end of the morning.

She slowly pushed his wheelchair along Oxford Street, past Marble Arch, on to Bayswater Road, and finally through to Hyde Park, where they stopped for tea and watched a brass band playing on the band stand and children chasing pigeons across freshly clipped lawns.

His eyes . . . John had eyes with well-defined crow's feet – a mature man's eyes. She could imagine them squinting back prairie sunlight from beneath the brim of a felt hat, counting heads of cattle. Or gazing out upon factory floors full of noisy machines and a thousand immigrant workers. Eyes of an intelligent man. Now, though, they lit up with childlike innocence and pleasure as the pigeons scattered, circled and swooped down behind their tormentors to resume pecking at seeds and breadcrumbs on the ground.

Mary realised, as she quietly studied his face, how far she had become immersed in this little fiction of hers. It had all started out as an impulsive gamble to see whether a dying man she'd callously robbed was alive or dead. Now . . . ? Now she was taking on the care of a total stranger. A boy-like man she knew absolutely nothing about. She smiled at John's little-boy delight at the fluttering of pigeons, at the toy sailing boats bobbing on the duck pond. She realised that although she had to be about half his age, in a funny way it was as if she'd become his mother.

Oh my . . . what am I doing?

Something one of the other street girls she knew often said: *In for a penny, in for a pound.*

As midday passed and the morning's sun ducked behind scudding grey clouds, she decided that it was time to take John home. To their new home.

Home. No longer that horrid room back in Whitechapel, that piss-stinking sparse room with damp patches on the low tobacco-browned ceiling, those walls with peeling paper and mottled black spots of mould, but a proud three-storey townhouse with a servants' floor at the very top.

Mary, do you really know what you're doing, girl?

As the afternoon greyed and became chilly, they passed along Bayswater and through Notting Hill, thick with market stalls and the pungent aroma of fishmongers, and finally off the busy thoroughfare of Holland Park Avenue and on to the quiet, leafy cul-de-sac that Mary had been returning to for the last couple of nights, preparing for John's homecoming: removing the various family portraits of the Frampton-Parkers, photographs, paintings and silhouettes.

'Is this our home?' asked Argyll.

'It is.'

He smiled up at her. 'It's very nice.'

'Come on then,' she said brightly. 'Let's get you inside and then I'll make us some supper.'

Argyll lifted himself out of the wheelchair and shuffled his left leg forward, taking the first of the half dozen steps up to the front door beneath the portico. Mary followed, reversing the chair up each step. At the top, she unlocked the front door.

'Home, my dear,' she said as it swung in, revealing old oak floorboards and a dark maroon hallway.

She helped him step over the threshold and onto a mat inside. 'I'll get a fire going in the front room,' she said. 'Then I'll go and get us something from the grocer's around the corner.'

He looked at her, almost reaching out to embrace her, but holding back. 'I'm so glad to have you, Mary. I . . . I'm not sure what I'd do without you.'

'We were very much in love, John. I wouldn't just abandon you.'

'I just feel so . . . so damned *wretched*, so guilty that I can't remember anything about us before, well, before you came and found me in the hospital.'

'You'll mend soon, my love. I'm sure of it.'

He turned to look at her. 'You know, I . . .' He shook his head.

'What is it?'

He suddenly leant forward and kissed her heavily on the lips. A clumsy, lurching gesture she hadn't been expecting. Instinctively, she recoiled a step.

'Oh, I'm sorry! Please forgive me,' he uttered immediately, awkwardly. 'That was improper. I . . .'

'Forgive you?' She lowered her gaze a little. 'We've more than kissed before, don't you know.'

His face flushed crimson. 'I feel like . . . to me, Mary, this is all so new.' He sighed. 'That was wrong of me just then. I . . . just . . .'

She touched his cheek. 'It's all right, John. I know this must all seem so new and strange to you. It'll all come back to you. I promise. You can't completely forget love, I'm sure of it.'

CHAPTER 13

29th July 1888, Great Queen Street, Central London

Dear Trusted Brother,

I received your telegram of 18th July. Firstly, business. I shall inform you that I have acted on your behalf as requested and established contact. I am assured through a middleman that he is on his way to England and will be able to meet with your representative on the date you specified.

Now, old friend, I think it advisable that I tell you all that we know about the man. His trade name is Candle Man. I have no notion of whether the name is of his choosing, or whether it is one that has grown out of the rich underworld rumour-mill that exists in and around the tenements and slums here in New York. I also have no notion of the significance, if any, of such an unusual name. Does he make candles? I have no idea.

I have asked amongst the Trusted Few in our club about the Candle Man, to contribute to the rest of the knowledge we have on him. It is clear that no one, anywhere, is aware of his true identity, his real name, or his origins. What we have on him are unreliable hearsays from the criminal fraternity and, of course, what little we learned about him on the several occasions that we have employed his services.

I shall start with our firsthand knowledge of him. He is utterly reliable. Should he agree the terms of whatever contract you propose, you may rest assured the task agreed will happen. He can be trusted with complete discretion. He has made it known to many a client that his professional reputation in this matter is of paramount importance, that he is a reliable keeper of secrets. I have no wish to pry into your affairs, Henry, but I am assuming *the matter you wish him to deal with has a sensitive angle. If so, then the Candle Man may be the perfect choice of man for the job. I say that as a person with direct experience of his craftsmanship. We used him to deal with a busybody poking his nose into our business affairs. The Candle Man was given instructions to make his demise look like the handiwork of a madman who tormented this city a few years ago with a series of brutal slayings. Suffice to say, that particular murderer was caught and hung for seven murders, only <u>six</u> of which were his!*

A note of caution, now. I am certain you have no intentions at all of reneging on whatever contract you propose to arrange with him. But be warned: although this is hearsay gleaned from unreliable quarters of the city, it is said that one of the more prominent Irish crime clan leaders attempted to betray the Candle Man. He disappeared shortly after. The story goes that his family received a parcel some weeks after, containing the putrefying remains of a human heart and a note that claimed it was the one part of the man's body he couldn't bring himself to 'consume' because it was 'rotten to the core'. I can't help but suspect it is a tale that has grown from a kernel of truth and been somewhat embellished upon, but I would say he is certainly not a man you would wish to double-cross.

Now, on to some background information I have on him. Treat the following with a healthy dose of scepticism. There are some who say he is originally from mainland Europe, suggesting he is possibly eastern European. However, there are also rumours that claim he is half Paiute Indian! Of those people who claim to have met him face to face, the estimate of age ranges from late-twenties to early-forties, of middle height and build, and nothing particularly remarkable about his appearance.

For myself, I have spoken with him on only two occasions. Once before on business of our own, and several days ago on your behalf. And this takes me directly onto the subject of how you should arrange to meet with him.

He will post an advertisement in the 'personals' in one of your London newspapers on the day you specified to meet him. The advertisement will have 'Candle Man' as its title, to ensure you find it. The message itself will employ a keyword alphabet displacement code. The keyword for his advert will be 'spirit'. Only he, you and I know this keyword. The advertisement will contain very specific instructions about how, where and when he will meet with you. I would strongly advise following this to the very letter, otherwise he will not make an approach and the liaison will fail.

His services are not cheap. I have no idea what fee he will ask of you for this task, but I assure you, for our last business arrangement, it was no trifling sum. Typically, he will accept half of the payment on acceptance of the contract and half on completion of the task.

On a final note, he may make some curious and unpalatable totemic requests. There is something about the man that is unsettlingly 'barbaric', for sake of a better word. He spoke to me once of cutting and curing the skin of one of his victims to use as leather. I suspect the man was humouring himself at my expense. I have a suspicion he attempts to cultivate this impression for whatever reasons he has.

If you follow his requests and instructions closely, and he agrees to the undertaking you assign him, I can assure you, whatever problem you have over there will be satisfactorily resolved. What is more, provided this contract works out to both parties' satisfaction, you may find he is agreeable to further work and will conclude his business with you by leaving behind a unique method by which you, and only you, may contact him again. Thus not needing myself to act further as a middleman.

Please ensure, having read this correspondence thoroughly and memorised all that you need to, particularly the code keyword stated above, that you burn this letter.

Sincere regards from your Fellow Trustee

CHAPTER 14

30th July 1888, Liverpool Street Station, London

George Warrington watched the platforms in front of him fill and then empty, fill and then empty, as steam trains came and went. A morass of people in their smartest wear, off for a fortnight out of the choking city to sip on the fresh, bracing air of the seaside, accompanied by porters wheeling trolleys stacked precariously high with travel trunks; businessmen and travelling salesmen in smart but well-worn suits and bowler hats on at jaunty angles, arms laden with canvas carpetbags full of product samples and testers.

The tea-house sat on the edge of the main concourse, a fenced enclosure of green-painted wrought iron swirls decorated along the bottom with potted plants. Inside the enclosure, several rows of cosy wooden booths and benches gave it the intentional feel of a railway carriage.

Warrington checked his timepiece again. The message from this chap had been quite explicit. It was this station, this tea-house, this booth – third one along – and this time. Warrington had wondered how this mysterious Candle Man could be so confident that this particular booth was going to be vacant for him to sit in, but it had been. The ones either side, he noted as he sat down, had both been occupied.

He watched the people milling outside the wrought iron enclosure, curious as to whether he would be able to pick this man out as he approached. A man conspicuously on his own, a man fresh from America, trying to make sense of the curious way the British lay out their railway stations. A man clearly off his familiar ground.

But he won't stand out, will he? Not if he is as good as they say he is.
The old man, Rawlinson, told him the Candle Man never made

face to face contact. That he guarded his identity as if it was his very soul.

A note, then. That's what Warrington expected now. Not a direct approach, but a hand-delivered note. He could imagine some errand boy, red-cheeked and puffing wind. 'I fink this is for you, mister!' Crushing a creased envelope into his hands. He looked around for just that: a mysterious stranger stooped over a small boy, waving a finger in his direction as he uttered instructions into a pink ear and pressed a shilling into a grubby hand. But he saw nothing like that.

'He's late,' Warrington muttered to himself, realising for the first time that he was actually a little bit nervous. The cautionary advice he'd been given, the parts of the letter from America he'd been allowed to look at, seemed to be mythologising him a little, turning him into something much more than what he was: simply a very well-paid shiv man.

A cannibal, for Christ's sake? He shook his head. Quite obviously that was the kind of fairground patter the Candle Man was happy to see propagated about him. Making him sound like some sort of monster, like some species of gargoyle arisen from the dark depths of the underworld to snatch another victim from the world above, to be taken down and cooked in a pot in some cavern below.

He smiled at the theatricality of it. Well, if their American colleagues were gullible enough to include that kind of nonsense in a communiqué – stories of crime bosses eaten for their sins – more fool them. Provided this chap was actually worth his fee, was discreet and not going to try and pull the same foolish trick as that thug, Tolly, then all would be well.

Two weeks since they'd last met. Tolly had sounded edgy and irritable then, demanding an advance payment of some of the money he was hoping to blackmail them out of. Warrington was there to placate him and actually did give a generous advance on the money and an assurance that if he could be patient, wait just a few more weeks, he'd be able to have all of the amount he was asking for.

But he had the sense that Tolly was getting anxious about the whole thing now. Perhaps worried that this situation was too big a bite for him to chew, bigger than he'd originally realised. Warrington had to wonder whether the man had been doing some homework. Whether Tolly had thought to investigate this trinket, to investigate who was on this portrait it supposedly contained.

Is it possible he's worked out who it is?

He'd decided probably not. If Tolly really knew, or even suspected he knew, then the asking price would undoubtedly have been increased. Substantially. He suspected Tolly didn't know yet, but maybe that was only going to be a matter of time. The newspapers printed regular photographs and illustrations of the man. Given that he was such a busy bee, at some point Tolly was surely going to catch a glimpse of his face on a front page and realise he recognised it. Realise exactly what he had in his possession.

But he doesn't know yet.

That much was for sure.

Tolly was clearly getting anxious; a journeyman trying to play a craftsman's game. Not for the first time, Warrington wondered whether he'd hired someone too low down the criminal fraternity. He'd wanted a cheap thug. After all, the target required little skill – just a tart and her baby. The hired man just needed to have a strong stomach, was all. But also, some thug who could be made to disappear afterwards without much fuss. A low-life without too many friends or contacts who might start wondering why their old colleague no longer seemed to turn up at his regular haunts.

Tolly, though, seemed to be getting a little too edgy now. Dangerously edgy.

'Excuse me.'

A whispered voice.

'What is the word?'

The voice seemed to be right beside his ear. Warrington lurched in his seat. Looked either side of him and saw no one.

'Tell me, what is the word?'

This time he detected the soft voice coming around the end of the booth divide. He twisted on his seat to look behind him. Above the shoulder-high wooden panelling was a frieze of decorative frosted glass, and through its foggy mist he could see the dark outline of the back of a head. Perfectly still.

'The keyword. The word that allowed you to read my message, if you please.'

He's right there. Warrington could feel his heart skipping a jig.

'Spirit,' said Warrington quietly.

'Very good. Now, best if you settle down. Turn back around. You don't need to be staring at this partition to hear me, do you?'

Warrington nodded. 'No, no, of course not.'

He heard the rustle of a newspaper. *'Do you have a paper to look at while we talk?'*

'Yes.' Warrington pulled the *Illustrated London News* from his coat pocket, shook out the folds and opened it up.

'*Splendid. Now, before we discuss the particulars, I'd like to know a little bit about who I'm dealing with.*' Warrington heard the man shuffle slightly on the other side of the thin wooden partition. '*I'd like to know a little about you.*'

'My name is—'

'*No, I don't need a name. It's best if we don't exchange real names.*' His voice was a little clearer. He must have shifted position so that his mouth was just around the edge of the booth. Just a few inches away from Warrington, just around the corner of a thin lip of wood. '*For the duration of our little discussion, I shall think of you as, let's see . . . you seem like a "George". So that's what I'm going to call you. And as for me? Well, you have my nom de plume.*'

Warrington shook his head with an uneasy incredulity at the man's lucky guess. 'What do you want to know?'

'*The sort of people I shall be dealing with, George.*'

'You have dealt with associates of ours before, I believe? In New York?'

'*Indeed. Reliable clients. Settled their fee promptly. I have no complaints. But what about you, George? Are you reliable? Will this particular contract end with both parties satisfied?*'

Warrington swallowed nervously. 'We've been informed you are wholly reliable. Full discretion assured.'

'*Of course, of course. I really wouldn't come so highly recommended if that were not so. But for my part, I need to know if I can trust you. No half-truths, George, no hidden arrangements, no contingency plans that I'm not aware of.*'

'Of course not.'

The Candle Man said nothing. Across the station's busy concourse, a platform attendant blew a shrill whistle to announce the imminent departure of a train.

'We have a man we paid to do a job for us. And now he's attempting to blackmail—'

'*The details can come later. Since I'm dealing directly with you, George, I want to know what kind of a person are you. Can you deal with me honestly?*'

'I shan't attempt to deceive you. We . . . uh . . . we've heard stories, rumours, of what happened last time a client tried to . . . uh . . . tried to con you. The cannibalism story. Whether that particular rumour is true or—'

He heard a soft chuckle come around the edge of the booth. *'Stories . . . The underworld does love its little fairytales, doesn't it? All part of the business of reputation.'*

Warrington noted that was not exactly a complete denial of the rumours. He felt something roll and flip lazily in his stomach. 'Indeed.'

'It does my professional reputation no harm at all, George, for little folk tales like that to proceed me. Keeps a client on his guard.' The newspaper rustled. *'Rest assured, I've been satisfied with the outcome of my business dealings thus far.'* That soft chuckle again. *'One way or another, my clients always settle up.'*

'Well, I'm certain there will be no difficulty agreeing on your fee.'

He seemed to ignore that. *'So tell me, George: what's this all about? I'm assuming there's somebody you wish me to locate, someone you wish me to deal with. But what is the motive? Tell me the "why".'*

'This is a sensitive area. It could lead to some sort of a scandal which we really can't afford to happen right—'

'Ahhh, a politician, is it? Someone's been naughty?'

Warrington was hesitant to give too much away. 'Perhaps one might say . . . careless.'

'A woman?'

He said nothing. Which was, perhaps, to the voice around the corner, everything. 'I think at this stage, it's best for us if I keep our briefing to the person we'd like you to deal with.'

A long pause. Long enough that he was beginning to wonder if he'd caused the Candle Man to be offended.

'Of course,' he said finally. *'Why don't we begin, then? Tell me who it is you're after, George.'*

CHAPTER 15

26th September 1888, Holland Park, London

A nightmare. He was watching them hack the young man to pieces. The first few strokes of the *tamahakan* buried deep through pale skin into gristle and bone, and caused the tied up young man to scream. A pitiful, shrill scream like a child's. The others joined in, a dozen of them, swinging and hacking, the wet *cracks* of impact quickly lost beneath somebody else's wailing voice.

He could see another pale body tied up on the ground next to him, naked like the young man. A woman, older, kicking, flailing, screaming with tormented anguish as if every blow was landing on her. The young man's mother. He knew that somehow, even before she started screaming her agony for him.

The young lad's own shrill cries had already stopped. The ferocious onslaught of rising, falling blades was beginning to wane now.

There were a dozen bronze-skinned men standing over the now motionless corpse, dabbed with chalk-white paint across their chests and faces; dark charcoal smears around their eyes made them look a little like sun-bleached skeletons that had come to life. They had worked on another couple of bound prisoners before the lad. He could see their tattered remains, barely recognisable as human cadavers now, just bloody lengths of butchered meat. From the end of one of them he could see a long blonde tail of matted hair; from the other, a pale and recognisably feminine shin, ankle and foot, unblemished, unspotted with blood. As if it belonged elsewhere.

He struggled against the twine binding that lashed him in a seated position up against a wooden stake. There were others, another three of them, tied up on the ground and desperately wriggling, squirming, knowing the same fate awaited them.

Why am I not on the ground with the others?
Why am I sitting up?
They want me to watch.

One of the chalk-white figures turned towards him then, holding something bloody in one hand. The savage stepped slowly towards him, holding it closer so that he could see it better. The thing in his hand lurched and twitched, reminding him of a mouse he'd once caught and tossed into a cloth bag; the cloth twitching, lifting, dropping, as the mouse scurried around in blind panic inside.

It was the boy's heart, still shuddering with post-mortem spasms. A part of him still alive, in a way.

The chalk-painted savage squatted down in front of him. Offering the heart and smiling; an almost friendly, inviting smile. Like that of a benign, favourite uncle, offering a drumstick from a steaming roast turkey.

He cocked his head and then began to eat it.

Argyll found himself sitting bolt upright, just as he'd been in the nightmare. But now sitting in total darkness instead of the light of day. 'Oh, god! Oh, dear god!' he cried, his voice every bit as shrill as that young lad's had been.

He heard a muted woman's voice. 'John?' The thud of bare feet on a wooden floor in another room. Then he detected the faint flicker and dance of a match lighting a wick. A moment later, through his bedroom door, open ajar, he saw the glow of a candle in the hallway.

'John, love? Are you all right?' His door creaked open wider and the candlelight entered his room.

There was a moment of puzzlement for him. The woman who entered was wrapped in a nightgown, a freckled face framed by a riot of untidy, pillow-messed hair.

'John!' she whispered. 'You having nightmares?'

The woman confused him. Familiar, but he was not sure for the moment who she was. She hurried across the floor, setting the guttering candle on his bedside table, and sat beside him on the bed.

'Settle back down, sweetheart,' she cooed softly, pressing his shoulder firmly. He did as he was told and reclined back against the cold, damp cotton of his pillow.

'Shhhh.' She stroked the hair from his still-bandaged forehead. 'It's just another horrible dream.' She whispered like a mother calming her own child.

She's not your mother. A voice from a far corner of his mind.

'Were you dreaming about what happened to you again?' she asked.

Her voice, that accent, managed to re-unite a collection of disparate and recent memories and the moment of puzzlement, sleep-addled confusion, was suddenly banished. Yes, it was Mary. Mary. How silly that he'd been confused as to who she was.

'Mary . . . I . . . I'm so sorry . . . I . . .'

She shook her head, discarding his needless apology. 'Nightmares, my love. That's all. Just them nasty nightmares again.'

She was right, of course. Mary.

He looked at her dishevelled strawberry blonde hair and freckled face still half asleep, and he realised again how beautiful she was. Not just the kind of beauty that makes a man's loins stir and twitch – he pushed that thought away. No, it was the glowing, warm beauty of someone he was certain cared for him with all her heart. Very much like the love of a mother for her baby. He wondered how alone, how helpless, he'd be without her. Still lost in a large echoing hospital ward without even a name for himself.

He knew he'd been crying in his sleep. 'I wish . . . I wish my damned mind would come back to me,' he uttered.

She nodded reassuringly, still stroking the sweat-damp tresses of his hair. 'I'm here, John. I'm going to look after you while we wait for it.'

'Thank you,' he whispered. He suddenly felt an overwhelming wave of gratitude towards her; gratitude and complete dependence. Yes, even utter devotion to her.

'Mary, I . . . I think I love—'

She gently placed a finger on his lips to hush him. He thought he saw the slightest wince of pain on her face. 'You save them three words for me, John. Save them 'til more of your mind comes back. 'Til you know me properly again.' She smiled a little sadly. ''Til you know for sure you mean it.'

She was right. There she was with her wise words again. Wisdom beyond her young years. He closed his eyes once more, soothed by the light touch of her fingers across his forehead, stroking and playing with the coarse hairs of his eyebrows, the whiskers beside his ears.

'It'll all come back to you, John,' she said softly. 'And if it doesn't . . . well, it'll be like us starting all over again.' He heard the rustle of her nightgown and felt the light touch of her lips on his right cheek. A polite kiss that suggested nothing more, right now, than concern and a genuine affection. 'And who but us is lucky enough to get to fall in love all over again, eh?'

He nodded sleepily, his mind beginning to slide back down into the muddle of sleep.

Please . . . I don't want that nightmare again.

Some of the details of it, at least, were already faded and gone. He still remembered woods, mountains and an untroubled blue sky, idyllic if not for the butchery going on down on the ground.

He could hear Mary singing a lullaby, a go-to-sleep song for a troubled child. It felt reassuring, the soothing timbre of her voice, the soft play of her fingers, the warm, embracing wrap of a mother's love. The womb-like comfort of feeling like a child. Snow-capped mountains and tall pine trees and crisp blue skies and dancing skeletons with bloodied hand axes, hacked carcasses of bloody human meat . . . spun away into a sleepy fog, like milk stirred into tea.

Just as he began to feel the gentle gravity-drop of sleep engulf him, he heard a quiet, mature voice, his own voice, but with just a little bit more of that accent the surgeon had guessed was American.

She's not your mother; just remember that.

He banished the voice. He didn't want to hear it again right now. He rather wanted to believe Mary was his mother and he was freshly born into this maddeningly confusing world. At least that would excuse him behaving like a foolish child.

He smiled, almost completely asleep again. How lovely if, in fact, it could be just the two of them, mother and child, in this room, this moment, this lullaby. A pleasant fiction to hold onto forever.

CHAPTER 16

27th September 1888, Hyde Park, London

'Please . . . no, Mary! I'll fall.'

'Come along,' she said firmly, holding his hand and tugging him gently.

Argyll looked around at the other people strolling along the tidy gravel paths of Hyde Park. 'I'll fall over!' He looked up at Mary, the shame and embarrassment of that possibility already on his face.

'I won't let you, John. I'll be right beside you.' She reached down to pull him out of the wheelchair as he awkwardly hefted himself up, cursing as an unlocked wheel rolled back slightly and his balance momentarily faltered.

He grabbed her shoulder to prevent himself from slumping back in the seat and teetered on his good leg as he probed the ground with the other.

'I can't feel a damned thing with this wretched leg!' he hissed.

'Come on, let's just walk for a few dozen yards. See how you get on, love,' she cajoled him.

Two young women passing by caught the slightest taint of the street in her vowels and the colonies in his. They glanced at each other and smiled patronisingly as they watched the unlikely couple struggle together.

She pulled out the crutches poking from the carry-bag at the back and handed them to him as he swayed unsteadily on his good leg.

The two young women glanced back once more over shawl-covered shoulders. Mary thought she heard the barely suppressed conspiratorial twittering sound of giggling from them. 'Ignore those silly cows,' she said quietly to him.

He manoeuvred the crutches under his arms and took the weight, steady once more. 'They're all watching me,' he muttered. There were some children standing beside the duck pond nearby, patiently waiting for him to topple over.

'No they're not,' she replied, louder than was necessary. *'They're minding their own bloody business!'*

Embarrassed faces flicked away from them.

Mary knew how it was here in the park. A quiet place far away from the vulgarity of the busy street. A place for sensitive social correspondence, for questions to be timidly danced around and finally hinted at, if not actually asked. For politely veiled inquiries to be made and tactfully ignored. For courtships to begin or be politely brought to an end. A place for quiet exchanges.

Nobody makes a scene here.

Argyll took his first tentative steps, lurching forward on his wooden crutches and doing the best he could to control his entirely numb and stubbornly useless leg.

'There,' she said, 'that's not so bad.'

He grimaced. 'This feels so ridiculous. My leg is just fine, after all. I just can't seem to tell the thing what to do.'

'You remember what the doctor said, though. The harder you work on it, the sooner you'll be able to walk normal again, John.' She pushed the wheelchair along beside him, keeping close enough that she'd have a chance to catch him in it if he started to lose his balance. 'It's like *teachin'* your leg to walk again. Just like you teach a baby to walk.'

He gave a dry, humourless laugh. 'I suppose that's what I am now: an oversized child for you to have to care for.' He sighed. 'Not a *man* anymore, eh?'

'I'm going to help you get better again.' She smiled at him. 'You're still the same *gentleman* I fell in love with, you know.'

'But . . .' He shook his head slowly, thoughtfully. 'I'm not, am I? I remember nothing of who I was. Nothing of where my home is, who my family are.' He turned to her. 'What was I like? What things did I enjoy? Tell me more about who I was. Please.'

Be careful, Mary.

'The doctor said I shouldn't tell you too much about your past.'

'Well.' He ground his teeth, exasperated. 'There's nothing coming back to me, Mary, not a thing. I hate being like this, so . . . like a blank page, like a damned blackboard scrubbed clean. I'm . . . I feel like *nothing*. Like an empty space! Please, Mary, please, for pity's sake, give me something about myself, more than just my name.'

Take care, Mary. She knew told lies had to be remembered like a well-told story. Not bandied about willy-nilly. A lie fired off without care had a way of coming back to bite you, always.

'Well,' she began, 'you already know you come from America.'

Her mind worked hard at all the things she'd heard him say, both awake and sometimes in his sleep. He'd said something about tall buildings once. She knew of only one place in America with tall buildings. 'New York, John; that's where you used to live.'

He nodded thoughtfully at that. 'It's like London, isn't it?'

Mary had no idea at all. 'Yes, exactly like London.'

'How long?'

'How long what?'

'How long since we . . . how long have you and I been together?'

Mary had originally planned to say they had been living as man and wife for the best part of a year. She'd even considered telling him that they had discreetly married, but that would require a licence as proof. He might ask which church. He might want to go there to see if it tugged a memory out of his mind. He might want to speak to the chaplain. And then her lie would be undone.

'Well, it's been thirteen months since you sent me flying. Ended up on my bottom in the middle of Covent Garden, my shopping all over the cobbles.'

He muttered an apology. Again. She'd told him about that moment before, but decided to tell it again. Reinforce the story in his mind.

'Ooh, don't be daft, my dear. It was very funny. You came bustling around the corner of a grocer's stall like a bleedin' steam train. Straight into me, you did. And lord, you were so embarrassed! So apologetic, so worried you'd hurt me. You picked me up, helped me gather my bits and pieces of shopping and then insisted on taking me to a tea shop.' She laughed gaily. 'You all but marched me to the nearest one and sat me down. Bought us some tea.' She reached out and squeezed his arm. 'The perfect gentleman.'

He sighed. 'Well, that's a relief.'

'And so we talked, you and me. Talked the long afternoon away until them market stalls started packing up and the lamp lighters finally came out.'

Her gaze was far off, indulging in the finer details of this particular little fantasy. Many a night she and some of the other street girls had played this same old game down the Firkin, cackling like fishwives over a beer-damp table and through skeins of pipe smoke.

The game? Not so much a game but the collectively authored fantasy of *Meeting the Perfect Gent*. Something they could all add their tuppence-worth to. A tall man? Yes, of course! Slender or muscular? Oh, he'd have to be a healthy man, all muscles an' that!

'And you don't remember a bit of that, do you?' she asked Argyll now.

He shook his head sadly. 'I would like to, though.' He then stopped, hesitated, with his weight balanced on the crutches. 'Please tell me that I—'

Her face split with a coy grin. 'That you *behaved* yourself?'

He nodded.

'Of course. Treated me like a lady, you did. All Mr Manners an' that. By the time we had to say good evening, you and me had arranged to take a walk together the next day.' She nodded towards the Serpentine, where a cluster of boys in shorts and navy tops played with model boats on the water. 'Right over there, as it happens. We've strolled in this park many times, John.' She smiled. The lie came easily. She'd rehearsed the Covent Garden story many times over; a part of the fantasy she'd made up with the girls: the mysterious and chivalrous gent, rich enough to whisk her away from the grime and the grinding poverty of the East End.

'We walked in Hyde Park the next day. Talked about this and that and everything. Your life over there in America and—'

'And your life?' He lurched another step forward, testing his weight on his numb left leg. 'What about you?'

She shrugged dismissively. 'Oh, my life weren't that much to speak of. Just a workin' girl.'

'Tell me again.'

Mary had this part of her fiction all worked out. She stuck to the truth as best she could. And when it wasn't truth, it was how her life could have gone if fate had been a little kinder.

'I used to live in Wales. As a small girl. Then I came to London when I was eighteen. I wanted to see the big city. To explore the very heart of our empire. I suppose I hoped I might find my fortune here, enough to eventually take me to some exotic far-flung corner of the empire.' She smiled wistfully. A huff of amusement at the naïveté of her younger self. 'As it happened, I ended up teachin' piano to rich and precocious children. Can't say I earned very much doing that, though.' She steered the empty wheelchair clear of a bench occupied by an elderly couple who were fast asleep with legs stretched out onto the gravel pathway. 'I suppose my job now is making sure you get better again, John.'

'Mary?' She sensed he had an awkward question. One he was having trouble finding the words to frame.

'Yes?'

'How old am I?'

'Oh, you're thirty-nine,' she replied, without missing a beat.

He shrugged. 'I thought I was much older than that. I was looking at myself in a mirror.'

'I should say you look much younger.'

'But you are, aren't you? Much younger?'

She allowed herself the briefest pause, wondering how much to stretch the truth. 'Twenty-six,' she replied. She added just three years onto her real age. Enough to narrow the gap between them to thirteen years. Not an implausible age difference.

'But, I could almost be your father!'

'You'd have to have been a very young one if so. More like an older brother.'

He nodded, then laughed.

'What's so funny?'

'Us,' he replied. 'I'm so much older, but it's as if *I'm* the little one, and *you're* my older, wiser sister.'

She turned to look at him, her hand gently resting on one of his broad shoulders. 'What a decidedly odd couple we make.'

CHAPTER 17

28th September 1888, Holland Park, London

'There,' she said. 'Breakfast: eggs, toast and butter, and a nice strong coffee.'

Argyll looked up from the chair in the bay window. 'Mary, thank you. Are you not having something with me this morning?'

'I have some errands to run. Just a few things.'

He reached out and grabbed her hand. 'You're doing so much for me. Caring for me, cooking for me . . . I don't know . . .' He smiled sadly. 'I can't help but wonder why such a beautiful young woman would want to spend time fussing around—'

'Because I love you. Because you've got manners and graces unlike the . . .' She was going to say *unlike all the young bumerees and mug-fisted tykes that worked down Spitalfields Market and fancied their chances with her out the back of the pub.* 'Unlike most of them young gentleman around town,' she said instead.

Impulsively, she leant over and kissed him on the cheek. 'Because you're a wonderful man, John. An' I aim to have you back with me. Now,' she straightened up and flourished a copy of the *Illustrated London News*, 'you enjoy your breakfast an' have a nice read. I'll be back later on with some groceries an' make us both a lovely broth for lunch.'

She kissed the top of his head, where his coarse brown hair was still unruly and sprouted like cactus plants from a night bedevilled by tossing and turning against a feather pillow. The bandage had gone now and the area of his scalp around the line of stitching, near his crown, was sprouting a fuzz of bristles as new hair had begun to grow in. She was going to have to take John back to Saint Bart's to have the stitches removed a couple of weeks from now. Dr

Hart would take that opportunity to see how John's memory was healing.

'See you later,' she said, stepping out of the front room and into the hall, closing the door behind her.

In the hall, another door beside the pantry stood closed. Gently, she eased it open to reveal a short, steep flight of stone steps down to the basement. She knew the basement well enough. On more than one occasion, Mr Frampton-Parker had found reason to follow her down there while she was collecting a bucket of coals for her bedroom on the top floor.

Their first awkward fumble had been down here in this grubby place. It was at the bottom of these steep stone steps that he'd offered to help her with her bucket, a hand reaching out for the brass handle and finding something else instead, by accident – on purpose. A muttered apology from him, followed very quickly by a declaration of his infatuation with her. She'd been aware he'd been looking sideways at her for a few days. Furtive glances at his wife first, to be sure she was engaged in whatever she was doing, then at her.

Mary had been a little mystified by that at first. Then more than a bit flattered by the idea. Then quietly and secretly guiltily, rather thrilled at the hold she had over Mr Frampton-Parker. Mary reached the bottom of the stairs where their 'affair' – if one really could have called it that – had first germinated.

John knew this basement was through that door and down these tricky steep steps, but had never been curious enough, or confident enough with his 'sleepy left leg', to try coming down. Which was just as well.

Because it was down here.

She stepped lightly across the floor of the basement, cluttered with several boxes of household tools, travel chests that contained smaller travel chests like Russian dolls. The chests were used infrequently when the Frampton-Parkers occasionally travelled further afield. In the corner was a small mountain of coal held in a wooden collecting frame, poured down a chute through the street-level hatch above. The chute had a padlock on it on the outside, which Mary knew could be jiggled open easily with bent wire. That was how she would have gotten in if she'd not had the brass nerves to walk into the agent's office and rent the place legitimately.

Pallid shafts of daylight shone through a small barred window, surrounded by thick cobwebs like candy floss. Checking that John wasn't watching her from the top of the steps, she knelt down beside one of the travel chests and lifted the lid to reveal the leather satchel inside. She opened its flap and her fingers found one of the bundles of notes. There had been twelve bundles when she'd first discovered the money. Now there were only nine. She'd paid six months of rent on this house: a tidy sum of four hundred pounds. And of course the clothes she was wearing and a small wardrobe of other clothes to wear, and some suits and casual clothes she'd bought for John, guessing at all his measurements.

There had also been the purchase of a few decorative knick-knacks around the house: some very neutral hunting prints in frames, a carved Red Indian savage for the drawing room – as she knew he was American – a set of faux Egyptian statuettes for chess pieces; sphinxes and pharaohs. Enough personal effects around to maintain the illusion that they'd been living together here for just over a year.

She took just a couple of the large five pound notes from the bundle, put the satchel back in the chest and hurried back up the steps to the hall. She closed the door and grabbed a bonnet and lace shawl from the stand in the hallway.

'I'm off out now, John!' she called.

'See you later!' he replied cheerily. She heard the rustle of the newspaper in his hands and knew he was going to be fine there this morning, sitting in the sun of the morning room bay window and watching the comings and goings of the busy avenue outside.

Argyll watched her through the window as she took the steps down to the pavement and waggled his fingers at her as she glanced up and waved at him, before briskly crossing Holland Park Avenue. The basket swung from one hand as she set off to do her shopping and run her errands. He settled back in the armchair, feeling that same warm glow he'd felt in the park.

To be blessed to have someone like Mary. Beautiful, cheerful, caring. The light fizz of her laughter was pure joy. And beneath that happy-go-lucky demeanour, she seemed to have a dedicated, earnest affection for him. But, despite what she'd said, he really couldn't understand what she saw in him. Looking at the wall opposite, in the walnut-framed mirror over the mantelpiece, he saw a complete stranger. A man with faintly tanned and leathered skin, with fine creases that perhaps told a story of a lifetime full of memories from far-flung places, but which were now all gone. Perhaps for good.

Now nothing more than a thirty-nine-year-old child.

He looked down at his hands holding the newspaper and for a moment it felt oddly like they were another person's hands. As if they could somehow tell him about the person he used to be. The curious faint scar running across his knuckles, the small swirl of ridged skin along the palm of his left hand, suggesting a burn from long ago? He wondered what job these hands used to do. Were they used to holding some craftsman's tool, a chisel? Or were these hands that used a pen? Perhaps even a typewriter?

Mary stubbornly refused to tell him these things. She seemed certain it would all come back to him in due course.

He let his gaze drift onto the paper. At least his mind had not forgotten how to read, or write, or a hundred other simple tasks. Perhaps he would only find out what other things he used to be able to do by trying them.

'Perhaps I can speak French?' he said aloud. He tried to think of how to say that same phrase, but nothing came. 'Perhaps not,' he muttered.

His eyes settled on the headlines in bold type:

Carriage Incident Maims Mother-to-Be
Holborn Viaduct Electrical Lights Fail – Again!
Chapman Murder Linked to Another

Chapman. The name sounded vaguely familiar. Perhaps he knew someone called Chapman. His foggy mind assured him of that. He read the column beneath:

> Rumours have been heard issuing from officers serving in Scotland Yard that the prostitute brutally murdered last month, Annie Chapman, 47, may have been the second victim of the same murderer. Another prostitute by the name of Polly Nichols was also murdered in a strikingly similar manner in Bucks Row, only a few streets away from where Chapman's body was found. Police have so far been unwilling to reveal the precise details of the Chapman murder, but what details are in public circulation bear a striking resemblance to the ghastly mutilations inflicted on Nichols. It is known that both women were initially killed by a deep and savage incision to the neck. Following this, it is common knowledge that both women were extensively

mutilated, with specific attention to their personals. A source from within the police service investigative force has hinted that the mutilations were of a 'ritualistic nature' . . .

Argyll put the paper down and sipped from his coffee cup.

I know that name as well . . . Nichols. Polly Nichols.

He wondered from where. A friend? Surely not the same person. A prostitute? Certainly not the same person. He closed his eyes and settled back in the armchair, willing, *bludgeoning*, his useless mind to conjure something up, anything. He sighed.

Nothing.

'I'm useless,' he sighed.

No.

That quiet voice again.

Your memories are all here, tucked away in boxes. Be patient.

Really? So little had been forthcoming thus far despite Mary's diligent coercion and encouragement, filling in a few of the smaller blank spaces in the hope that he might fill in the rest. All he seemed to have were the confused and fleeting images in his sleep. The tall buildings he could only presume were New York. That horrible vision of chalk-painted savages and their horrific butchery – was that even actually a memory? Or just some lucid nightmare? He could only hope it was the latter.

The morning sun streaming in through the bay window was warm on his face, warm through his closed eyelids. He breathed slowly and deeply, beginning to relax. Little by little, his grip loosened and the newspaper rustled, settling to rest, unread, in his lap.

. . . a knife buried into her neck up to the hilt. A woman. Polly, isn't it? Polly Nichols? With a quick jerk, he wrenches it forward, opening her throat in a jagged gash from beneath her left ear, almost all the way round to the other. She squirms and shudders, eyes wide and rolling like a startled pig in an abattoir.

'Shhhh,' he whispers to her softly, holding her head back to open the wound and ease the flow. 'Like this, just be very still . . . It's better, much, much quicker this way.'

She tries to gurgle something. Her boots scraping and slapping against greasy cobblestones.

'There's a good girl,' he whispers into her ear. He kisses her cheek tenderly. 'You can sleep soon enough, my dear. Sleep soon enough.'

Her struggling begins to slacken. She's still alive, barely. She can still hear him. 'This really isn't the real world. Don't you see? This world around us . . . it's just purgatory.'

Her legs flex beneath her and all of a sudden she is a dead weight in his arms. Gently, he lowers her to the ground. 'And now you're free to leave.'

CHAPTER 18

28th September 1888, Whitechapel, London

Mary's journey across London from west to east took much less time than she thought it would. The morning traffic was light and brisk. Just over a couple of hours and she was in her old haunting ground, her own manor: Whitechapel. Her heart sank as she walked along these familiar narrow roads. She crossed the small thoroughfare at the top of Dorset Street. Surrounded on all four sides by tall, grey painted brick buildings with small, squint-eyed windows almost opaque with grime; windows that had the milky boiled-fish look of a blind man's retinas. Even in the pallid daylight of mid-morning, the thoroughfare had a permanent twilight gloom to it; brickwork dark with soot, the grooves between cobbles in the street filled with a glutinous washed-aside collection of grime.

In the daytime, a forgotten rat-run like this was a place of only women and children. Wives already having to plan and prepare for their husband's evening meal in the few moments they weren't busy keeping a watchful eye over their scab-kneed young chavys playing toss and catch in the street. Prostitutes emerging bleary-eyed into the day, sitting on doorsteps and nursing heads sore from the cheap alcohol of the night before.

Mary's rented room was halfway down Millers Court, off Dorset Street; the ground floor of a forward leaning three-storey house of single-room tenants managed by a woman on the same floor. Marge Newing. She was a slight, rodent-like woman with a taut face and purse-string lips. She rented to single women only. Very deliberately. Single women of a certain kind – those who looked like they were teetering on the perilous edge of a downward slope that ultimately led to whoring as their profession. Women whose downing of any old cheaply-brewed *mecks* and an addiction to a pinch of laudanum was their only distraction.

For the poor girls who could only just about afford the money to take a room there, Marge inevitably ended up being their landlady, their madam – and their supplier. And in that inevitable order.

Mary had lived in her room for just over nine months now. So far she'd managed to avoid succumbing to the addiction of the opiates and the numbing allure of gin or absinthe. The bits and pieces she made from the late night hoodwinking of drunken, randy clients into parting with their money, the occasional petty theft, the infrequent morsels of legitimate work, were barely enough to keep the rent going and a little scran for her permanently rumbling tummy.

But Marge Newing was keen to see her go the way of her other girls; become a customer for the drugs she peddled as well as being one of her tenants. Like many a lodging house *mot*, she bullied and cajoled her tenants to become whores. Perhaps because that's what she used to be. It was her bitter medicine – to feel one step above her girls, one step out of the gutter. Which was why she had a particular dislike for Mary. Not until she was another lost soul, like the rest of the girls in her lodging house, would Marge be content; a lost soul on a slow, spiralling, drug-addled, pox-ridden descent to Hell.

Mary took the two steps up from the narrow cobbled street and pushed on the door, pondering a decision that had been slowly turning over and over in her mind like a hog on a spit. Whether she really wanted to – needed to – keep her room here. Rent was due, in fact overdue, and Marge was certainly not averse to tossing the possessions of someone in arrears out onto the street, keeping and pawning those personal effects that might yield a shilling or two. Mary stepped into the dark hallway. Luckily, it appeared that Marge had not got round to emptying her room out just yet. A key unlocked the door to her room, and quickly, hoping to avoid confronting her landlady, she stepped inside, then closed and locked the door behind her.

She looked around at the painfully dismal space. A bed, a small, scuffed writing table, a water faucet with a tin bowl beneath it, a small wood-burning stove and a row of hooks hammered along the picture rail from which her few changes of thread-bare clothing hung. Her version of a wardrobe.

Her old clothes. She looked at them: desperately sad attempts at feminine glamour. Second-hands and throw-aways. She'd managed to lay her hands on a fox-fur stole turning bald, a lace shawl shedding threads, and a soot-stained ruffle she had intended to stitch to the hem of her skirt when she could be bothered.

My old life.

To walk away from this, her old life, to let the room go; she'd thought of nothing else this morning as she'd taken several different trams across London. There was nothing about this old life she wanted, but if John's memory suddenly came flooding back and he realised he was being looked after by a tart attempting to trick him, then surely he'd turf her out, if he didn't call the police first. If she didn't end up in prison, she'd end up back here. And if her room and possessions were all gone, she'd be on the street.

Mary realised she was taking an almighty gamble. She was hoping, desperately hoping, that some lasting bond would have developed between John and her; that even as his mind came back into sharp focus, there would still be an affection there for her.

That's a terribly big gamble.

It was. But she knew, this wasn't a life she wanted to come back to. These four tight walls through which, almost every night, she heard a scream of pain or a slap, the snarl of a drunk's voice, pitiful moaning or, even more pitifully, the fake-cheer of drunken singing, and in the early hours, the soft sound of someone sobbing.

Not now. Not now she wore these clean, new clothes. Clean clothes without a rip or a tear or a stain. Not now she slept in a room that was restful at night, a room that didn't stink of stale piss and damp, a room that led onto a hallway and washroom that wasn't shared with a dozen others taking turns washing themselves down after a night of work.

And wasn't there more to this simple equation now? It was about the money at first. The smell of all that money in his satchel, and the intoxicating thought that this poor tourist gentleman must have a great deal more of it elsewhere.

But now . . . ?

Now there was something else. She daren't put a label on it. But it was a feeling that felt good, that was honest, even if she wasn't prepared to admit the word. A feeling that wasn't rotten to the core, that didn't smell like this whole house did, of desperation and selfishness. Of doing anything for enough coins to buy another bottle or spoon of cheer.

It felt wholesome and naïve. Hopeful and, quite probably, doomed.

'Love' was perhaps too strong a word at the moment.

Mary realised she felt affection for this stranger. This poor man who now swore blind his name was John Argyll; this man whom she'd named in a moment of panic. She felt something for him; actually wanted to care for him, to nurse him back to being a complete man.

And perhaps, just perhaps, when he finally discovered he'd been lied to by her, that she'd been exploiting his lost and broken mind, he might still forgive her. Even love her back and take her with him, home to America. She saw flashes of a fairytale ending. A brightly painted stone house with a grand portico and front lawns surrounded by white picket fences overlooking a fashionable and busy thoroughfare. And her on John's arm as he introduced her to New York's polite society as 'the English rose he fell for on his last business trip to London'. A spotless, clean household full of lovely things and chambermaids calling her 'ma'am'. And John: polite, charming, handsome in a distinguished, silvered way, and oh-so worldly. Her lover, her protector, her provider and her mentor.

No matter how things went, she knew she couldn't ever come back to this. If she did come back here, she knew the last of her resolve to do better for herself would evaporate. She'd end up like all the others: drunks, addicts and eventually, one day, end up as a carcass down a backstreet, a floater in the Thames, a small article in a parish newsletter, a nameless entry on a policeman's notebook.

Actually, this room could go fuck itself. The money in her bag she'd brought to pay up her rent was going to stay right where it was; let that bitch Marge Newing toss out her things into the street. There was nothing here of any value anyway, except a few personal things to remind her of better days, a childhood that promised to be so much more than this.

She began to gather them up. A hand basket, half a dozen penny-packets of tea and sugar, a hairbrush – once her mother's, a small, cracked porcelain-handled mirror – her grandmother's.

One last look at the grimy cell, the dark, peeling walls, the threadbare evening wear on wall-nail hooks, stained by the few drunks she'd stooped to selling sex to at her most desperate and hungry. She was burning a bridge she planned never to use again.

Outside, in the gloomy hallway, she heard the clop of shoes on bare floorboards.

'Mary?'

She turned to see one of the women who kept a room on the floor above. Cath Eddowes. One of the regular crowd of girls down the Firkin.

'Mary? That you, love?'

'Uh . . . hullo, Cath.'

'Look at yer! My god! All posh clothes an' all!' she exclaimed, reaching for the sleeve of Mary's blouse and rubbing the cotton between her fingers. 'New clothes! What, you done a bit a hoistin' up Chelsea way?'

Mary shrugged. 'Come good on a bit a swag. That's all.'

'A bit? You look like a right toffer in that get up!'

Cath's hands were all over her clothes, feeling her lace shawl. Her eyes wide and enquiring, a grin spread across her lips, revealing a piano keyboard of yellow ivories and black gaps. 'Gawd, look at yer, love. So how's all this brass come yer way all of a sudden?'

Mary felt a shade of shame steal onto her cheeks. Cath, a friend, along with Long Liz, Sally, Bad Bess, all the other girls who regularly gathered down the Firkin to seek solace in each other's company – they were friends she needed to walk away from. They were as much a part of the squalid prison she'd been living in as the walls of this room were. Drunks, most of them, and addicts at least half of them. Bit by bit, they were pulling her down, trying to make her one of them. Doing Marge's work for her.

'Come on! Don't be all coy! What's yer fiddle?'

'It's nothing,' she replied, shrugging off Cath's hands and pressing past her for the front door.

'Piss off! Yer got yer 'ands on a load a brass, didn't yer? Whatcha been up to?'

'Actually, I just got a bit lucky.'

Cath's eyes widened. She laughed. '*Ac-tu-ally!*' she mimicked grotesquely. 'Listen to yer! Yer even blimmin' talkin' all *la-di-dah!*'

Mary reached for the handle on the front door. 'I'm not coming back anymore. I'm all finished here. Tell Marge she can have her piss-'ole room back.' Mary realised she was subtly shifting back to her adopted version of an East End accent.

Cath put her hands on her hips. 'Oh, it's a man, innit? He got some brass?'

'I got lucky is all,' replied Mary. 'Found me some money.'

'Well, ain't yer gonna share it with the girls? One in, all in?' The motto they shared – that is, the motto they shared towards the end of an evening drinking. With the sound of closing time bells ringing and men shouting their orders over each other. One in, all in. The sisterhood of street girls. The code.

It was all just talk, though. They'd happily screw each other over if it meant getting their hands on a free bottle of liquid cheer.

Mary tugged the door open. 'Goodbye, Cath.' She said that in her new, very deliberate, accent.

But it angered Cath. 'Hoy! You! Mary! What's yer fuckin' game? Yer think yer better than us, dontcha? Think yer can jus' walk out on us like that!'

Mary looked around the grim walls of the hallway, the faded wallpaper and curls of peeling paint, the floorboards stained with spilled booze and, in one or two places, dark spots of what she suspected were probably blood. 'I can't live like this anymore, Cath. I never wanted this to be my life.'

'None of us does, lovey! But yer takes whatcha gets.'

Mary smiled; a small, wan, apologetic smile. She turned to go. 'I'm sorry. Goodbye.'

Cath's face darkened. 'Well, go fuck yerself then, yer stuck up bitch. Go on! Piss off an' leave us!'

Mary hovered, feeling a tendril of guilt. Her hand stole into her bag and pulled several coins out. She offered them to Cath. 'You and the others . . . this is for you. Have a few rounds on me.'

'Fuck me!' gasped Cath, wide-eyed once again. 'Fuck me! That's a . . . that's a *shilling?*'

Her grubby fingers snatched it suspiciously from Mary's hand, eyeing her warily like a pigeon feeding on breadcrumbs. Despite what she'd been saying about 'one in, all in', Mary very much doubted whether Cath was going to share that coin around. But it didn't matter; that was up to her. Mary took Cath's moment of bug-eyed amazement as she stared at the money in her hand to excuse herself and step outside into the heavy grey day, down the steps onto the cobbles, greasy now with the first spit of rain.

CHAPTER 19

8th August 1888, The Grantham Hotel, The Strand, London

'There you are, Mr Babbitt,' said the porter, bringing into the room a silver tray with a pot of tea, two smoked mackerel and a piece of toast.

'Thank you,' he said, and passed the young man a coin.

The porter grinned, thanked him and bowed out of the room, leaving him alone.

He settled down at the small breakfast table in his room. Positioned by the bay window, he had a pleasing view out onto Oxford Street below. A very nice hotel suite. As good as the best in New York.

His eyes, cold and grey – a demon's eyes, an Indian had once told him – watched the to-ing and fro-ing of carriages and milk carts, top hats and the fluttering plumes of ostrich feathers. The sounds coming up from the street below reminded him of Manhattan; the cry of street vendors, the clatter of metal cartwheel rims on stone, the hubbub of voices, the endless coconut-shell applause of horse hooves on stone.

I am Mr Babbitt.

Every job came with a different name. A name usually chosen quite randomly; perhaps one overheard in a conversation, a sign above a business, a name in a newspaper. On the steamship from New York to Liverpool, he'd come across the name on someone's travel trunk being hoisted into a cabin.

A G Babbitt. And just like that, he had a name to adopt.

The man he'd met a few days ago in the station, the nervous gentleman with a voice rich with privilege – 'George' – had explained in a low, faltering mumble the job they required him to do. A local shiv man from the East End by the name of Bill Tolly. A relatively easy man to locate, Babbitt imagined. The New York underworld was noisy with men like Tolly: blowhard thugs who boasted far too loudly about their handiwork after a few drinks. The trick was simply knowing which bars – he smiled, corrected himself – which *public houses* to frequent. To sit quietly in a corner and listen to the traffic of conversation. George had given him the name of one of the places this man regularly frequented. That was enough to get started.

Quietly taking a knife to Tolly was, frankly, a job any hired killer could do. But there was more to the task than just that. The man apparently had several accomplices, one of whom presumably had an item on him or her that his clients very much wanted returned. Tolly, therefore, was required to do some talking before he died and that's where some degree of professional experience was required. Again, any thug with a pair of pliers and a few basic instruments for inducing extreme discomfort and pain could extract a screamed confession of one sort or another. The trick of it was ensuring that the extracted information could be verified, cross-examined, con-firmed. Very necessary before the final business of finishing off the fellow was carried out.

And he was extremely good at that sort of thing.

The other matter was making sure that Tolly, and whoever else was involved, were disposed of in a way that could be attributed to whatever background violence appeared to be going on in the locale. Babbitt had been in London several days now. Enough time to pick up the local papers and read about all manner of grisly, gang-related violence, crimes of passion, crimes of a sexual nature. It appeared the East End of London was every bit as debased as New York: full of shallow-minded fools stabbing and hacking at each other for the price of a pint of ale, for looking at them or their girl in the wrong way. Like New York's dark underbelly, a place populated by animals with no grace, or ethics; insects with no communal purpose.

Recycled life, returned souls. That's what they were. That's why the world they all lived in seemed a far less moral place than it once was. Too many souls now were made of bad stuff. No place in God's afterlife for the rotten, and the only place to send them was back here.

No surprise then that this world was becoming a thickening soup of rotten minds and souls. Effluence. Nothing more.

The faster they killed each other for their petty, selfish gain, the faster they made new bastard babies that would inevitably grow up and one day throttle a whore, or open someone's belly with a knife just for the glistening silver timepiece in their waistcoat pocket.

Souls like that needed removing from this eternal cycle, like filtering muck and spoilage from drinking water. Souls like that needed snuffing out permanently. And Babbitt had been blessed with that skill, that *responsibility*; to not only snuff out a worthless life, but to look into the eyes of the dying, to look through their dilated pupils and see that coiling dark shapeless thing – the soul. And snuff that out too just as easily as one would quickly grasp between thumb and forefinger the glowing wick of a candle.

Babbitt smiled. George had wondered why he'd allowed himself to be dubbed 'Candle Man'. It most probably had something to do with the one lit candle he left behind after every job. Left behind to burn down until its wick drowned in a pool of its own liquid wax and went out.

CHAPTER 20

14th August 1888, Whitechapel, London

He watched the ebb and flow of patrons into the public house. He watched the flow of smudged faces and florid cheeks, crimson noses, gap-toothed grins, snarled greetings and exchanged curses, through pale blue wafts of pipe smoke, which hung above the churning mass of customers like a marsh mist. He watched and thought of the flow of patrons like a flow of shit into a cesspool; main channels of flowing shit, and side pools where things became stiller, quieter. That's what this place, this busy inn, resembled to Babbitt: a stagnant pool where the turds of humanity coalesced and bobbed together.

Babbitt had a stool at one end of the bar and nursed in his hands a tankard of warm and flat ale. He made it look like he was swilling thirstily from it, but was in fact barely deigning to wet his lips with the awful brew. He fitted right in with the noisy crowd; a few stolen clothes from the washing lines that dangled across the narrow streets of Whitechapel, several days' growth of bristles on his cheeks and he looked just as unpleasant, dishevelled and grubby as the rest of these mole-like creatures.

Why? Why would any soul want to exist like this?

He'd been watching an old prostitute for a while. An unappetising sight made worse by the clumsy, clown-like splotches of rouge on her cheeks and the complete lack of teeth in her mouth. But once upon a time, that caved-in witch's face might just have been attractive, or even beautiful. Her pay was ale, not money. A pint of ale. In the last hour, he had seen her propositioned by four different men even more unpleasant to behold than her. Men who took her by the arm to the gent's lavvy and returned on their own only minutes later. This poor wretch emerging shortly after, straightening her clothes and wiping her chin dry, eager to sip her flat and warm wages to wash away the foul taste in her gummy mouth.

Babbitt's keen ears caught the wafting shirt tails of conversations, his ears well-tuned now to make sense of the mongrel version of English these underworld creatures spoke.

'. . . an' the dirty bitch 'ad it cummin', didn't she? Fuckin' went an' spen' it all when I says I needed it . . .'

'. . . s'how it goes, right? You gonna take the piss, then yer gonna feel a fuckin' fist . . .'

'. . . don't care, mate. Ain't right. Just ain't right. 'E bleedin' well deserved wha' 'e got . . .'

'. . . all dirty bastards, love. You take 'em for what you can, 'specially them stupid drunk ones . . .'

Everyone of them preying on the other. Not a single cupful of kindness in this entire inn. Not even a thimbleful of it.

His ears had been hard at work all through the evening; the rest of him was slumped on his stool, looking almost asleep over his drink. Often his eyes closed so he could just listen to the rising, falling voices, the shrill slices of sneering laughter, the rough voices of hard men loudly stating their place in the inn's masculine hierarchy. Like monkeys in a cage: the ones squealing the loudest getting to sit on the highest perches in their little world.

Babbitt had left his timepiece back at his hotel room, quite deliberately. His mind was used to metering time. Just over three hours he had patiently sat like a man fit to topple onto the floor before his ears picked out one solitary word amidst the noise of strangled, slurred, mutilated language being spoken.

Tolly.

Intently, he focused his attention on the growling voice that had uttered the word, doing his best to pull it to the foreground and filtering out the rest of the hubbub, pushing it back into the shadows.

'. . . so 'ow much is it yer owe 'im?'

'Enough that fucker's gonna break summin' on me even before he finks to ask for it.'

A laugh. Not exactly a friendly or even a sympathetic one. 'Then yer a complete idiot, intcha, ol' son? I mean, losing yer tin to 'im, of all people. The bastard's a complete fuckin' nuttah!'

'Tha's why I'm lyin' low for a bit.'

'Well, yer bein' a fool comin' in 'ere. S'one of 'is regulars, this is.'

'I 'eard 'e's down the Cock tonight.'

'Bill don't always stick to 'is routine, mate. Yer a silly fucker chancin' it comin' in here.'

Babbitt's eyes cracked slowly open; the impression of a drunkard stirring to sip again from his tankard of old beer. His ears suggested an approximate direction for him to glance and he did, quickly identifying the two old men propping up the corner of the bar, ten feet along from him. The worried and regular glances over his shoulder by the one on the right clearly indicated which one of the two of them was the fool in debt to Tolly.

'. . . tell yer what, yer stickin' out like a sore thumb, keep lookin' over at the door like that.'

'Well, I ain't gonna let 'im sneak up on me!'

'Tell yer what, seein' as I'm facin' the door, I'll jus' nod to yer if he enters, right?'

A pause. 'Well, dontcha fuckin' miss 'im, or I'll make sure you get a smackin', too.'

Babbitt smiled. *Charming. Not even a thank you.*

He closed his eyes, once again the bar stool drunkard returning to his sleep, and let his ears continue to do their work. It was nearly another hour of exchanges between them, most utterly banal, before finally the one on the left said something quickly.

'Oi, fuck! Tolly's 'ere!'

Babbitt sat up and craned his neck to look over the milling crowd. In between jostling billycock hats and flat caps and plumes of drifting blue pipe smoke, he caught a glimpse of a tall, bull-necked man entering through the public house's stained glass double doors.

He saw one of the two old men quickly finish the last of his ale, slide off his stool and lose himself amidst the busy press of patrons. Babbitt's eyes returned to Tolly. He watched the man ease his way towards the bar, a respectful path clearing in front of him.

He's a 'name' in here.

Babbitt had suspected that. A neighbourhood thug. Every tenement block, every crowded street in the Five Points of New York, had at least one. A 'name'. Most people steered a wide path around them.

He knew Tolly's type: brutish, stupid. The type to act impulsively and think with his fists. If he ever threw his lot in with one of the organised gangs, he'd only ever be a foot soldier. A sergeant at best. The slightest smile stole out and spread across Babbitt's lips. This oaf was going to be all too easy to deal with.

CHAPTER 21

14th August 1888, Whitechapel, London

Tolly had had enough of those two silly bitches. He'd just spent the last hour down the Rose and Crown, their favourite haunt. It was quiet enough there to be able to talk without shouting, but noisy enough that a conversation across a table was unlikely to be overheard.

Both Annie and Polly were getting very itchy about it. They were in on the blackmail now. He'd decided to cut them both in, not out of a sense of fraternal charity but because he was being a right clever bastard. The gentleman client he'd done the job for was bound to hire some petty knapper to find out where Tolly's place was, break in and simply snatch the locket back. So, Annie and Polly could mind it between them. He trusted them not to fuck with him, not to pawn it, hock it, or lose it. Because if they did . . . well, they knew exactly what they'd get from him. Still, both of them, despite being keen to have a slice of the blackmail money, were getting decidedly hot-footed about the whole matter.

'He's *proper* rich, that man in the picture,' said Annie. 'You can tell it. An' proper rich 'as *means*, Bill, you know what I'm sayin'?'

Polly nodded.

''Course 'e 'as *means*, love; 'e's got money.'

'No, I'm talkin' about the secret stuff. Them proper rich buggers, most of them's in secret groups that 'elp each other out. So could 'e be.'

'Them secret groups?' Tolly laughed. 'Them secret groups is all story. Don't tell me you been tryin' to read the dailies again?'

'Fuck off, you can't read no better than me, Bill.'

Tolly grabbed her hair in one of his big fists. 'Tell me to fuck off again an' I'll cut yer nose in half.'

'Ow! Let go! That's 'urtin' me!'

''Course it is.' He let her go. 'Just mind yer fuckin' language in future. It ain't nice out of a woman, not even a slapper like you.'

Annie rubbed her head where he'd yanked at her hair. 'Just sayin', Bill. Just sayin' I ain't 'appy 'angin' onto that thing. It's been too long now. We should just get rid of it.'

'The gentleman's payin' up. It's just 'e needs to get the money in a way that's discreet. That's what 'e said. That's why the wait.' He smiled. 'You just sit easy. Goin' to be the easiest fuckin' money you two will *ever* make.'

'I ain't 'appy bein' the one 'oldin' it, though.'

Bill shrugged. 'So give it to Poll to 'ave for a while.'

Annie looked at her friend. 'Yeah?'

Polly looked unhappy at the suggestion but, with her two co-conspirators staring at her, she realised that unless she offered to do something useful, they were going to start questioning why the hell she was getting a share at all.

'All right.' She nodded. 'All right, I s'pose I got a good place to 'ide it.'

That was earlier. Bill excused himself from their company and decided to come down the Turpin for a couple of scoops. There was a stupid old soak who usually drank in here who owed him some money. If he found him, he could twist some of his dues out of the old fart. Just tap him for a few shillings and call it interest on the loan. Tolly knew that's how the banks on the big high streets made their lolly: not getting their money back, but getting the rent on that money. That was the clever bit. Money making money. He fancied, once they got their swag off the gentleman, he might set up his own little bank. Set it up right inside the busiest pub he could find in Whitechapel where his customers were going to be too drunk to realise how much 'rent' he was going to charge them for their loans.

As he entered the Turpin, he looked around the sea of faces for the gnarly old sod and, failing to spot him, decided the very next most important thing he needed to attend to was to have a big piss.

The gentlemen's lavvy was like any other public house's: a back room lined with cracked tiles and a stained porcelain gutter along the bottom of one wall in which all manner of unpleasant things sedately floated like tug boats down a piss-yellow canal.

Bill snorted and spat, adding his own glutinous vessel to the convoy as he unbuttoned his trousers and began to release a long, overdue torrent into the porcelain channel.

'Desperate for it, eh?'

He looked to his left to see a man as tall as him, all mutton chop whiskers and a cap.

'Yeah, straight in, straight out. Got a bladder smaller 'an a Jew's purse.'

The man chuckled at that as he released a torrent beside his. 'Makes you wonder why we pay for it. I'm sure I'm shootin' out nothing different to what I just been sippin'.'

Tolly sniggered. 'True.'

The man had the ghost of an accent in there. It sounded vaguely Irish, but he knew it wasn't. 'Where you from?'

'Me?' replied the man. 'New York, as it happens.'

'Yeah?' Bill was instantly interested in the man. 'New York, you say?'

'Aye.'

Bill had heard all sorts of things about the place. There were opportunities for a man with a businesslike mind, like himself. He decided he was going to buy this man a drink. 'You lived over there long?'

'Been there most of my life and I travelled the middle states some.' The man with mutton chops tilted a shoulder casually. 'Even seen some real Red Indians an' all.'

Bill's eyes lit up like Chinese lanterns 'Bleedin' 'ell! *Real* redskins?! Yer see 'em for yerself?'

'Oh, that's for sure. Right up close.' He chuckled. 'Maybe too close.'

Bill had finished and tucked himself away. He offered the stranger a hand. 'William H Tolly, but I'm known mostly as Bill.'

'Just gimme a second here,' the American said, pissing a little harder. 'It's a two-handed job for me.'

Bill sniggered at that. Presently the man finished and buttoned himself up before offering Bill a hand. 'The name's Charlie.'

'Well, Charlie, ol' son,' Bill grinned, showing a wall of tobacco-yellow teeth and a couple of gaps, 'can I buy you a pint?'

CHAPTER 22

14th August 1888, Whitechapel, London

He staggered through the front door of his lodgings. It rattled on old hinges as Tolly clumsily kicked it aside to reveal his dark hallway.

'Now, yer still got that jug of shandygaff with yer?' said Tolly, his voice slurring lazily. 'Welcome to me 'umble manor, Mr . . .' He straightened as a point of protocol suddenly occurred to him. 'Hoy! Here's yer comin' into me place for a piss up an' I don't even know yer proper name. It's Mr . . . ?'

His American guest smiled as he stood politely outside on the doorstep, waiting to be invited in. 'Oh? Is that a British custom?'

'Izza fuckin' East End custom, mate! Bad manners on my part. So? It's Mr . . . ?'

'Babbitt. Charlie Babbitt.'

Tolly swayed drunkenly in the doorway, his eyebrows arched. 'Babbitt, you say? Like . . . *rabbit*?'

Babbitt smiled again. 'Yes, just like rabbit.'

'Welcome in, Mr Rabbit, an' let's get that jug of yers uncorked.'

Babbitt stepped over the threshold into the hallway and closed the door gently behind him as Tolly shuffled up the hallway and stumbled through a door into his kitchen. 'In 'ere, Mr Rabbit-Babbitt. I got a nice bit of cheese 'ere somewhere.'

He entered the kitchen behind Tolly and watched as he scraped around in the semi-darkness, the only light coming from the faint amber glow of a gas light outside, stealing in through a small, soot-stained window.

'Ah! There we go,' he grunted, and the room flickered with the light of a struck match as Tolly drunkenly wafted it above the wick of a candle in the middle of a small kitchen table. He kept misjudging the distance. 'Fuck me! Must've drank more than I thought!' he said with a giggle.

'Allow me.' Babbitt took the match from him and deftly lit the wick. 'There,' he said, 'we can both see what we're doing now.'

'Siddown, Charlie! I'll get us a coupla mugs an' cut some of that cheese.'

Babbitt nodded politely and settled down, placing the corked jug of ale on the table. 'You live here alone, Bill?'

'All on me own.' He pulled two mugs from a shelf over his stove. 'With all me business dealin's goin' on, it's better I don't share me rooms with no one, if yer know what I mean?'

'Uh-huh.' Babbitt nodded. He could sympathise with that. 'I must say, I'm a bit of a loner myself.'

'Here.' Tolly thudded the mugs clumsily onto the table and then slumped into a chair opposite. 'Fuckin' cheese . . . Can't bloody find it.'

Babbitt uncorked the ale and poured some into each of their mugs. 'Oh, don't worry about that, Bill. I'm not so hungry anyway, if truth be told.'

Tolly raised his mug and clinked it against Babbitt's. 'Well, gotta say, been a real pleasure talkin' to yer, Charlie. Much more interestin' than all them other buggers down the Turpin. Fuckin' borin' shower, the lot of 'em. But you? Bet you seen some things, ain't cha?'

Babbitt nodded. 'Yes, I dare say I've seen quite a few things.'

Tolly made a face: half a grin, half a frown. 'You sounded funny just then.'

'My accent wanders a little sometimes.'

Tolly tipped his mug and slurped frothy ale. 'Y'think someone like me could do all right over there in America? In New York? You know, do good? Make some decent money?'

'Certainly. It's a place full of opportunities for the likes of you, Bill.'

'S'what I 'eard.'

'You'd fit right in.' Babbitt smiled.

Tolly smacked his lips. 'So you was sayin' earlier you come over 'ere for some work, right? You got any? 'Cause if you ain't, I s'pose I could help you out. I know people in this manor, people who could use a bloke like yourself to—'

'Oh, I'm just fine, Bill. I have a job already.'

'Yeah? What you got lined up?'

Babbitt smiled. Beneath the kitchen table, his left hand eased a nine-inch long blade out of a hip pocket. Nine inches long and barely a half inch wide. One side of the narrow blade was as keen as a surgeon's knife, the other side had small, serrated teeth that could saw through gristle and bone with ease. A knife he'd had purpose-made years ago by an expensive Swiss bladesmith.

'I have a job arranged. Some gentlemen have paid me quite a handsome fee to find something of theirs.'

'Well tha's all right then!' Tolly grinned encouragingly. 'Yer stayin' in the area? 'Cause if y'are, then I'll show yer round if yer like?'

'That's really rather kind of you, Bill.'

Tolly looked a little bemused. 'Yer speakin' totally different now. No offence, mate, but you sound a bit like a ponce.'

He recognised he was letting his accent wander. His natural American accent was becoming something else – dry, proper. Almost that of a British gent. The persona he'd begun to associate with the name he'd appropriated: Mr Babbitt.

He was letting his accent wander partly because it didn't matter any longer. They were all alone now and Tolly only had a few more moments of sweet ignorance left before Babbitt set to work on him. But partly because this bit was fun; the slow, dawning realisation was soon to come – the moment when Tolly's eyes would widen as he understood he'd invited death into his home.

'Actually, I like talking like this, Bill,' he continued. 'I prefer it to the mongrel English you speak.'

Tolly took that as a joke and laughed. 'Hoy! You musta learned off some posh bloke or summin'. Got a whole loada learnin' an' what 'ave you?'

Babbitt smiled. 'Yer . . . I got learnin' an' such.' A not too bad attempt at impersonating Tolly.

Tolly's good-natured smile was wavering uncertainly. 'Hang on . . . yer takin' the piss outta me or summin'?'

'I learned me that yer a bit of a stupid fool, ain't cha, Bill?'

Tolly's confused smile was entirely gone now.

'I've learned that you're a big, stupid oaf who's been very, very silly.' Babbitt's exaggerated New York dockside accent was gone entirely now as well; too much of an inconvenience for him to bother keeping up. 'I've learned that you're like a child. A stupid, lumbering child. And like a child, you take, take, take.'

Tolly's brow furrowed. 'You takin' the piss outta me, Charlie?'

Stupid drunken fool was still stuck on that.

'I've learned that you did a job recently, Bill.'

Tolly's jaw suddenly swung open.

'Did a job for some "posh" gentleman, didn't you?'

Tolly stood up clumsily, pushing his stool back so that it clattered noisily onto the stone floor. 'You get the fuck out now, 'fore I throw you out!'

Babbitt slowly produced his knife from beneath the table, caressing the long, thin blade. 'Best if you sit down. You and I have some talking to do.'

He could see Tolly's eyes were on the blade, that the man was considering making an embarrassingly obvious lunge for it. 'A note of caution, Bill. You are drunk . . . and I am not.'

That fact seemed to be registering on his florid face.

'Why don't you pick up that stool and sit down,' said Babbitt. 'And you and I will share this ale together as we originally planned, hmmm?'

Tolly finally stooped down for the stool, stood it up and slumped down heavily onto it. 'That . . . that gentleman,' he said after a while. 'S'pose he sent you, right?'

Babbitt nodded. 'Indeed.'

His eyes were on the knife still. 'All right, I ain't stupid. He don't wanna pay up. That's what this is about, right?'

'Oh, he was *never* going to pay you, Bill. You have to understand this, my friend. This particular client of yours has enough money to make *any* problem at all go away. And you? You're just a very small problem.'

He picked up the jug of ale and filled Tolly's mug. 'I suggest you have a little to drink. And look . . .' He poured some into his own mug, 'I shall join you. Two friends drinking together, hmmm?'

Tolly ignored the ale. A twitch of anxiety appeared on his face. 'I get it, I get it. All right.' He sighed. 'You go tell that fucker I'll leave him alone an' won't say nuffin' more 'bout the job.'

'It's ancient history now. The job is done. You got paid for it. The matter is closed, right?'

Tolly nodded eagerly. 'S'right. I got a decent enough pay out of him. Call it quits.'

'Excellent.' Babbitt smiled. 'There's a good chap. Shake on it?'

Tolly shrugged. ''Course,' and offered his hand.

The smack, like a claw hammer into an apple, echoed off the bare walls of the kitchen. Tolly took a couple of seconds to register the fact that his wrist was pinned to the table. The knife's slender blade was embedded an inch into the old, dry oak of the table, through the cluster of bones and tendons where his hand met his wrist.

Babbitt knew it was the shock of the sight of it that made Tolly whimper, not the pain; that was going to take a few seconds more to kick in.

'There,' said Babbitt. 'Now I know for certain you're going to sit still whilst we talk. The less you move around, by the way, the less damage you're going to do to your wrist.'

'My . . . my arm! My fuckin' arm! You've—' He reached for the handle of the knife to pull it out of the his wrist and the table beneath, but screamed with agony as he tried to waggle the blade loose.

Babbitt put a finger to his lips. 'Shhhh . . . Bill, I need you to hush and listen.' He watched Tolly squirming on his stool. 'And really, you should try and keep very still; the more you struggle, the more it's going to damage your arm.' He smiled. 'And I suspect it will be a two-handed job pulling that out.'

Tolly clamped his mouth shut and mewled quietly.

'Now then, this little job of yours . . . Getting rid of some tart, wasn't it? And her baby?'

Tolly nodded, grunting an affirmative.

'But you told your client – who, by the way, is now *my* client – that you found something on her, something that could *cause some difficulties*, shall we say?'

'Locket,' he blurted between gasps. 'Locket with a picture in it.'

'Yes. I believe it was a photograph, wasn't it?'

Tolly's head nodded vigorously. 'Please . . . pull the knife out!'

'So, that's the thing I'm after, then. If you just tell me where you've stashed it, you and I will be done here.' He smiled warmly. 'I'll un-peg you. I'll even leave you the ale, how about that?'

Tolly gritted his teeth; dots of perspiration were appearing all over his forehead. He huffed and puffed to keep from fainting. 'I ain't got it 'ere.'

Babbitt pursed his lips. 'Oh dear, that's a little bit disappointing. Someone else then; a friend of yours, perhaps?'

Tolly said nothing.

'Yes, my client said you mentioned to him you had a friend help you out on the job. I can safely presume it's with that friend of yours, then?'

'Yes! Yes! All right . . . I 'ad some 'elp. Please! Take this fuckin' thing outta me arm!'

'Not yet, Bill. I just need your friend's name and where he lives.'

'Don't . . . don't know where she lives!'

'A *she,* is it? Hmm.' Babbitt grinned. 'You're not very good at hanging onto secrets, are you, Bill?'

Tolly whimpered.

'So, let's start with her name, then.'

Tolly was not in the mood for loyalty. Honour among thieves? Fuck it. 'Polly! Name's Polly! Polly Nichols.'

Babbitt looked into his eyes as he said that. There were no tells, no giveaway moment of hesitation for a panicking mind to conjure up a fictional name. He could believe that sounded like the truth.

'And you say you don't know where she lives? A good friend like Polly?'

'Fuckin' tart! Moves round . . . place to place. Got no idea. Please? I . . . I . . .' Tolly was swaying. He looked like he was ready to faint.

Blood was pooling on the table beneath his wrist. By the look of things, his blade had managed to sever an artery. Babbitt silently cursed. He'd wanted to merely pin the man's hand, that's all; just pin him in place until he was all done with asking him questions. But Tolly's hand must have lurched too far forward as he'd struck down with the blade. The man was going to bleed out quickly and, as he started slipping into unconsciousness, he was going to become much less useful.

I have a name, though. A good enough place to start.

'Bill, does this Polly regularly frequent the same inn, like you do? Is there a place I'm likely to find her?'

Tolly's eyes were beginning to roll, showing their whites.

'Bill? Stay with me awhile longer, if you please. Just one more question, ol' chum, then I'll let you go and I'll bandage you up as good as new. I'd like you to tell me where I can find her.'

'There's bloody blood all over.' Tolly's voice slurred. 'Jus' like when I took 'er 'ead off.' He grinned like a naughty boy. 'Messy ol' business . . . so it . . . isss. The choppy chop chop . . . Loverly looker . . . she was an' all . . .'

'Bill? Come on now. Where can I find this Polly Nichols?'

'Rose an' Crown!' Tolly blurted, bleary-eyed. 'Them pair of stupid bitches . . .' His head nodded like a donkey, then finally drooped down to the table with a heavy thud, knocking his mug over. The blood and ale mixed together, forming a pink froth on the tabletop.

Babbitt stood up, leant over and lifted Tolly's head up by his hair. He wasn't dead just yet but he certainly wasn't going to get any more sense out of him tonight. He yanked the blade out of the table and the man's wrist. A curse of frustration. His aim should have been better.

It's the ale. Babbitt had had to drink a couple of tankards of that awful brew during the evening as he'd chatted and guffawed along with Tolly; all of a sudden, the pair of them best of friends. His judgement was impaired. His aim with the blade was slightly off. No matter; he had a name. And in a place like this, he wouldn't have to ask too far and wide before someone pointed her out to him.

Time to finish off. Needs to look random . . . violent. A drunken scuffle. Two men arguing over money or a woman. A fight that blew up out of nowhere and went too far.

Babbitt swiped his blade several times across Tolly's forearm. *Defensive wounds*. Then, with two quick jabs, Tolly's white cotton shirt started blossoming dark crimson roses around his waist.

He pushed the man off the table and he flopped unconsciously onto the stone floor. Babbitt kicked his own stool over, kicked the table hard enough that the jug of ale rolled off and shattered on the floor.

He studied his handiwork. A drunken brawl that got out of hand, a knife was pulled and William H Tolly, a low-life known round here for his short temper and violent outbursts, had become just another victim of the crime-ridden culture of this part of London.

The candle lay on its side, spilling a small puddle of wax onto the table, the flame guttering excitedly as the wick, freed from its straightjacket of wax, licked and melted a 'V' on one side. Babbitt stood it up and watched the flame calm itself once again as molten wax pooled around the base of the wick.

He licked his index finger and thumb and reached out to squeeze the flame's life away. The room was dark once more, lit only by the jaundice-yellow glow of light from the gas lamp outside leaking in through the small window. Enough that he could see a faint twist of smoke rising from the dying pinprick glow of the candle's wick.

He watched it curl, twist and then disappear.

One less putrid soul.

CHAPTER 23

29th September 1888, Holland Park, London

John's talking again. Just like he had last night in his sleep. A mixture of muttering and soft moaning like one half of a barely heard conversation. Mary had climbed from her bed in the back room, put on a dressing gown, crossed the hallway in order to listen outside his bedroom door for a while, but he'd quietened down before she'd got close enough to pick out his words.

Tonight, though, his voice sounded more agitated. She tiptoed out of her room, along the short hallway once again and listened at his door. She could hear him stirring restlessly, the creak of bed springs, a man's voice one moment, the whine of a child the next. Sometimes his words sounded pitiful, tearful; sometimes, cold, dry, admonishing and cruel.

'John?' she whispered. 'Are you all right in there?'

He was still making noises. She pushed the door ajar, stuck her head in. 'John, love?'

He didn't answer her. She crossed his bedroom floor and knelt down beside his bed. His head turned from one side to the other, rucking up the pillow, his legs peddling beneath the sheets.

'. . . s'all chop chop . . . ain't it? . . . an' so much bloody mess . . . hmmm?'

He sounded so peculiar. The soft, gentlemanly tones in his voice were gone, replaced by the sort of coarse street snarl she'd only so recently hoped to leave behind and never hear again. It was like listening to someone else, another person. He sounded like any one of the thousands of drunken bullies who staggered out onto the streets at night come closing time.

'*Fuckin' tart. Moves around from place to place . . .*'

Then a different voice. '. . . *there's a good chap, Bill* . . .' That one sounded more like John's voice. But she wondered who 'Bill' was; perhaps some of the memories of his old life were beginning to surface?

She hoped not. Not now. Not so soon. The thought of losing *her* John.

She caught herself. *My* John?

And why not? She reached out and curled a finger through a damp tress of his hair. Why not *my* John? She surprised herself with that. How possessive she suddenly felt.

Why can't I have a man like John?

She was no less a woman than the sort of pale-faced cows who regularly took the air in Hyde Park; always in pairs and threes, immaculately dressed; stuck-up cows who could detect in no more than a few words the accent she so nearly had managed to completely lose now. But it didn't take much for bitches like that to know she wasn't one of them, not properly; just one misplaced vowel for them to curl their lips at her pretence.

Mary knew she could please John in ways those precious young ladies could never dream of. She might not be quite as porcelain-pretty as them, nor be able to recite a soupçon of Tennyson or Wordsworth, but she could care for this man, love this man. She could travel the world with this man and not complain that the sun was too bright or that the air was 'too heavy for her constitution' or that her pretty little feet 'couldn't take another step in these awfully tight shoes'. She could be a companion to him in so many ways. And wherever he came from in America, a slipped vowel, a dropped consonant, wasn't going to mean a damned thing.

America.

She hoped so much that there was a way this game of hers could end with him whisking her away to such an exciting place. That come the return of his memories, she'd have managed to earn a permanent place in his heart.

'. . . *Polly?* . . . *Hmmm* . . .'

She looked down at him, still fast asleep. Blood instantly drained from her face, leaving her paralysed, trembling with fear.

Polly?

A terrifying thought occurred to her. *He has someone else.*

She had visions of another woman, probably American like John, frantically worrying about her . . . husband? Wandering frantically from hospital to hospital trying to locate her man.

'Oh, please . . . no,' she whispered.

And Polly was this woman's name.

All of a sudden, she realised this whole desperate scheme of hers was a foolish little bubble of hope, of make-believe, all paid for by money she'd stolen from him; a bubble long overdue to burst. Sooner or later, he was going to wake up in the morning and wonder who the hell she was and ask where in the world he was. That, or there'd be a knocking on the door and she'd open it to find that nice Dr Hart from the hospital flanked on either side by police constables, and one step behind a woman far prettier than her, far more sophisticated than her, with a face like thunder, and quite ready to press charges for the abduction of her husband.

Mary needed to find out more about him.

The only thing she had of his, the *only* trace of the man he'd been before someone had attacked him, was that leather satchel of his. And she was certain she'd searched it thoroughly.

But perhaps she hadn't. Maybe there might be something else in there: a letter, a note, a picture of a loved one. She was beginning to wonder whether finding all those folded pound notes had been all she wanted to find. That her probing fingers had chosen not to delve further or more thoroughly.

'. . . M'dear . . . dear Polly . . .' Argyll turned over on his side, still in a deep sleep, his broad shoulders rising and falling, his breath softly whistling from his nose pressed up against the pillow.

Go and look, she urged. She knew she wasn't going to get a wink of sleep tonight unless she went down to the cellar and had another quick look in that satchel. Just to be sure she hadn't missed anything in there.

Silently she left his bedroom and made her way down the old wooden stairs to the hall. A glimmer of shifting moonlight lanced through from the front room and by its faint light, she picked her way along the floorboards, past the flimsy hall table and the noisy brass clock Mrs Frampton-Parker insisted *only she* should dust because it was so fragile and expensive.

Mary stood beside the cellar door. There was a candle and a box of matches beside the clock. She picked them up, opened the cellar door and stepped inside onto the top step. Pulling the door closed behind her, she carefully set the candle down on the step, pulled out a match and struck it. In the momentary phosphorus flare she saw the bottom of the steps, the cracked and uneven stone floor below and the stack of travel chests.

The candle lit, she took the steps down to the bottom and crossed the floor to the travel chest where she'd stashed John's satchel. That old thing. So worn and well-used, something she suspected he must have owned for years. Perhaps the bag itself might have his real name, his initials, stitched or written or branded on it somewhere? She hadn't thought to look for that. She set the candle down, lifted the satchel out of the box and began to inspect it more closely. On the outside there was nothing but scratches and scrapes, a possession clearly very well used.

She lifted the buckled flap and her hands once again probed inside. By the flickering light of the candle, it was difficult to actually see inside, so instead she felt her way. There were the other bundles of notes tightly bound with string. She pulled them out one at a time and stacked them on the stone floor. She looked at the small pile of paper notes.

So much money!

The first night after she'd taken possession of this house, alone down here whilst John was still in St Bart's with a couple of days more before he was going to be allowed to go home with Mary, she'd taken the money out and dared to count it. Five *thousand* pounds! An unimaginable amount. She'd felt dizzy with excitement at how much there was spread out on the floor in front of her . . . and how much more there might be if her daring scheme played out right.

Alone in this house, down in this cellar, she'd *yipped* with excited glee.

Now her hands probed back inside the bag. She could feel nothing else in the bottom. Just the folds of the cloth lining of the bag. But then her fingers provoked a soft, metallic *clink*.

Coins?

She waggled her fingers and heard the sound again. Something caught in the folds of the lining. Her fingers tangled with threads and then found a hole worn through the lining. She felt the coarse edge of the leather and a stitched seam. And then . . .

Clink.

. . . Something metal. Not coins. It felt like a key. She got hold of it and pulled it out, tugging with it the bag's cloth lining, pulling it inside out. She untangled the threads of the lining from the key's teeth. It was on a brass ring, along with a small brass fob with a number stamped on it.

207.

She shook her head that she'd been careless enough to miss this. But then it had fallen through the threadbare lining. It had been missable.

She studied the brass fob. 207. Not the number of a house, surely? If it was an address, there'd also be the name of a street or a road. It was a hotel key. She turned it over and over in her hands. A hotel key, but nothing on the fob to suggest which hotel.

She heard the cellar door creak softly on its hinges.

'John?' she called out.

She heard a foot fall on the wooden floorboard of the hallway, then the rasp of mucous-thick breath. Her heart lurched. She held her breath.

'John! Is that you?'

No answer.

She picked the candle up and made her way to the bottom of the stairs. He was standing at the top, looking down at her with eyes that were blinking sleep away, unfocused. She took the steps up slowly as he stared at her silently. Closer now, Mary thought she could see something in the set of his face that looked like dawning realisation, more than a face waking up from sleep. It was a lost mind finding its way home.

Her mouth was suddenly very dry.

He knows. He knows! His memory's come back!

She was about to say something, to fumble for some kind of desperate explanation as to why she was down here, who she was and why she was looking after him, when John's mouth slowly flopped opened.

'I . . . I . . . think . . . I'm . . .' He cocked his head and frowned, looking quite confounded. Befuddled. 'Is it morning yet?'

Mary could have almost laughed with relief. He was sleepwalking.

'No, John.' She smiled. 'No, it's the middle of the night still.'

He nodded slowly. 'Oh . . . right.' His dark hair fluffed up on one side, his face puffy with sleep and standing barefoot in his pyjamas, he looked like a small boy roused from sleep.

'Come on, love, let's get you back to bed.'

CHAPTER 24

30th September 1888, Holland Park, London

Argyll watched her lay the breakfast out on the table in the front room. She worked with quiet efficiency: tablecloth, crockery, coffee pot and finally bread, butter and a boiled egg. Not one word said, not even a smile. So unlike Mary.

What's wrong with her?

'Mary?' he said, reaching out for her hand. She stopped her fussing and unnecessary fiddling with place mats and crockery. 'Mary?' he said again. 'What's the matter? Have I done something wrong?'

She looked so unhappy. So worried. Apparently anxious to talk about something but reluctant or unable to find a way to start.

'Something's the matter, isn't it?' he persisted.

She sat down at their breakfast table and looked out through the net curtains at the milk float *clip-clopping* past their house. 'John . . . you were talking in your sleep last night.'

He smiled apologetically. Apparently he'd been doing it every night, according to her. The dreams he woke up in the morning with were little more than fast-fading wisps of disjointed imagery. They often seemed to be jam-packed with bits and pieces he couldn't quite make sense of.

'I'm sorry. Did I wake you again, Mary?'

She poured coffee from the pot; something for her fidgeting hands to do. 'You said a woman's name.' She looked up at him. 'Do you remember?'

Argyll remembered absolutely nothing. That was the problem. 'No. I'm sorry, I don't.'

She wanted to say the name – it was on her lips – but she was waiting to see if he could come up with it. He shook his head. 'What was the name I said?' he asked finally.

'It was Polly.'

He stared down at the coffee he'd been stirring, the spiral of creamy milk twirling like a Catherine wheel.

Polly?

Like the rest of his lost life, the name meant absolutely nothing to him. But yet . . . the name triggered *something* in a shadowed corner of his mind. Just as the breaking crust of a stale loaf attracts a cloud of pigeons, or the smell of roasting chestnuts will pull an audience of hungry children, the name caused something in the darkest attic corner of his mind to uncurl from its roost and slide forward.

Polly? Hmmm?

'I . . .' He frowned, still watching his coffee spiral.

Polly, is it? That voice again. There was a harshness, an unkindness in its tone. Disapproval. Disappointment. Like an ambitious father let down by an unambitious son.

You know Polly . . . don't you? Oh, yes, you remember Polly. The voice offered him a fleeting image, just a momentary flash. Dark red, splattered in commas and dots across skin as white as unbaked pastry; an opened-up cranberry pie.

He felt sick. He shook his head, feeling a headache coming on. The voice returned once again to its dark corner, to its roost, satisfied with its morning's torment.

'I . . . I honestly don't recall a Polly,' he uttered. 'The name means absolutely nothing to me, Mary. Honestly.' That half-lie tasted like bile in his mouth.

Mary tried to hide a look of relief from him. She acted busy, buttering him some bread. 'Well, perhaps she's an auntie or cousin or something. You know, back home in America?'

'Yes, perhaps that's who it is.'

He tapped the egg with his spoon, breaking its crown and scooping it off to one side of his plate.

'How is it? The egg? Done how you like it?'

He kissed his fingers like an epicure. 'Done to perfection, my dear.'

She giggled with delight at his saying 'my dear'. The other day she'd told him the way he said those two words made him sound 'all dashing an' heroic, like one of them gentleman adventurers you read about in books'.

'I never get my eggs right normally.' She buttered some more bread and spooned jam generously on top if it. 'John?'

'Hmmm?'

'I shall have to go to the shops for our supper again today. Is there anything in particular you fancy?'

Argyll stared at the open crown of the egg, his mind a million miles away. 'Oh . . . uh . . . no, whatever you think is best, Mary.'

CHAPTER 25

15th August 1888, The Grantham Hotel, The Strand, London

Babbitt stared at the cracked and opened top of the egg. He'd once seen a head that had looked very much like that. Been responsible, in fact, for a head that looked very much like that. A troublesome juror who'd taken a very generous bribe but then made the foolish mistake of being greedy and asking for more.

That job had been one of the more satisfying ones. The man was rotten to the core.

'Everything all right, Mr Babbitt, sir?'

He looked up at the waiter. 'Yes, yes, quite fine. The egg is done to perfection, thank you.'

He'd decided to take breakfast this morning in The Grantham Hotel's morning room. It was agreeably quiet this late in the morning. A trim and po-faced woman with her two young daughters sat on the far side of the laid tables, clucking in a whisper at how they should sit at the table, how they should peck at their food; two miniature versions of her, destined to be pickle-faced shrews like her one day. A solitary, portly, ruddy gentleman sat by the crackling fireplace, making a copy of the *Times* last as long as possible.

Babbitt's attention returned to his own paper. His work of several nights ago had made a mere paragraph on the seventh page. One of a list of briefly reported murders and assaults. Just as he'd hoped they would, the police were assuming the killing to be a revenge attack perpetrated by some other villain with a grudge or a debt to settle. Tolly's landlady had found his body later on the next day and had commented that she wasn't entirely surprised that her tenant had come to such a violent end.

He found himself chuckling at the flowery prose used by the

paper. No different to the press back in New York, squeezing every adjective for all its worth:

> . . . violent criminal by the name of William Tolly was found brutally slain last night in his lodgings, on Upper Ellesmere Street. Said Mrs Amy Tanbridge, his landlady and the unfortunate soul to discover the body: 'he looked like he had been in a frightful scrap'. Mrs Tanbridge claimed 'there was blood all across the floor. I thought I had just walked into an abattoir'. Tolly is known to the local constabulary as a violent man with many local enemies . . .

Now, on to more important matters.

Tolly had helpfully given him the name of a couple of public houses and a woman. His best guess was that it was a pub in the same locale as he'd found Tolly: Whitechapel. Yesterday, he'd walked the area, noting them, their names, the names of the streets they were on, and annoyingly discovered that there were five 'Rose and Crown's within streets of each other and seven pubs with 'Firkin' as part of their name. Babbitt decided the one closest to the Turpin was where he was going to start. Just as he had with Tolly, he would dress the part, find a quiet corner and listen to the back-and-forth chatter. None of it was ever quiet. It always seemed to be bellowed out at full volume as if these people had only ever learned to communicate with a bawdy shout. And the trick of it was to arrive early in the evening and listen carefully to each new instrument as it arrived and added its tune to the orchestra of voices. And there was always a greeting from somewhere hurled out above the noise whenever someone entered, wasn't there?

He would listen specifically for that.

Polly Nichols, if she was a tart, would have her regulars; a dozen or more pockmarked and raspberry-nosed old men letching at her and wondering if she was 'up for it this evening'.

It was all about listening. Listening and watching and, most important of all, never ever being noticed. Just the slumbering drunk at one end of the bar.

If he had no luck tracking her down that way, he could ask amongst the men he spotted disappearing outside with other tarts. Those types had their favourites, didn't they? Babbitt could affect the behaviour of a maudlin old soak asking after the whereabouts of his favourite ol' girl.

'Luverly Polly. You seen her, mate? You seen my luverly Polly Nichols?' But asking around was an alternative he preferred not to resort to. Even drink-hazy memories could sometimes recall a distinctive face, a manner slightly out of the ordinary.

'Aye, sir, 'e was tall, so 'e was. Tall with a dark barnet, an' a pointy nose bit like ol' Boney. An' thinkin' 'bout it, 'e spoke different to normal. Foreign. Irish maybe. American p'raps? An' I 'member he was askin' for Polly that night. Wanted to know where to find 'er, 'e did.'

He dipped a soldier of buttered toast into the yolk. It really was done perfectly, just as he'd asked for it: firm white with a soft, liquid yolk. He made a mental note to tip his waiter and the kitchen staff generously when it finally came time for him to check out and return home. They were looking after him wonderfully.

Polly. Hmmm.

The trick wasn't going to be tracking her down. He anticipated that was going to be a relatively straightforward task. No, the trick was going to be convincing her to trust him enough to take him back to her place. The tarts here in the East End preferred doing their business in the open: backstreets, rat-runs, park benches. It kept business brisk and there was some notion of safety being outside where a scream or a shout would carry – and quite likely send an abusive client shuffling hastily away with his trousers and undergarment around his ankles.

The promise of the right money – no, showing her the right money, and exhibiting a manner that wasn't going to unsettle or worry her – that's how he was going to convince her to take him back to her lodgings.

CHAPTER 26

30th September 1888, Whitechapel, London

Mary had a good idea where to find her old acquaintances at this time of the day. Mid-morning, it's where they usually congregated: Ramsey's tea shop. Half a dozen of them usually sitting together around one table in the back, a thin veil of pipe smoke hovering above, and a table crowded with tea cups, a bottle of absinthe in the middle for those after a hair of the dog.

Henry Ramsey, the owner, was quite happy to have the tarts' business in the back room, away from the rest of the decent customers who sat in the front with the big shop window looking out onto Goulston Street and where the tables all had nice linen and lace tablecloths. The girls were usually quiet, not too bawdy, generally nursing sore heads from the night before and most of them starving hungry for his stodgy potato pies and pastries.

Mary nodded at Ramsey as she weaved delicately through the patrons taking tea in the front parlour, heading towards the back room. He knew her face, if not her name, and his eyes widened at the sight of her.

'Blimey!' he uttered. 'You gone an' nicked the crown *jools* or something?'

She ignored the question. 'The girls in back?'

'Aye.'

She continued towards the rear of the tea shop, down a hallway, past the water closet and then pushed her way through a heavy curtain into a room with its own small window and a door onto the tea shop's backyard, filled with sacks of tea leaves, flour and suet and stacked wooden pallets laden with freshly baked bread and an iron keg of milk.

She smiled. There they were. The girls.

'I'll be fucked!' gasped Cath Eddowes. 'It's Lady Muck 'erself!'

The others gawped at Mary's clothes, wide-eyed and slack-jawed. Then all of a sudden she was confronted by the noise of questions and exclamations; a mixture of squeals of delight and caustic put-downs, and jealous hands reaching out to appraise the texture and quality of her skirts.

She picked out the face she was after. Liz . . . Long Liz. A clay pipe bobbed from the corner of her mouth as she chewed on the stem and muttered something to Cath.

'Liz!' Mary's voice cut over the noise. She tipped her head at the backyard. 'Can I have a word in private?'

Liz shrugged, got up off her stool, pushed her way round the girls' table and stepped out through the open door into the yard.

'Excuse me!' Mary squeezed her way past the others. 'Could I just . . .'

'Ooh! Listen to 'er!' said one of them.

'Oh, 'scuse me awfully muchly, my lay-dee!' giggled another, with a mock curtsey thrown in for good measure.

Outside in the yard, four walls of soot-covered brick surrounding just enough space for them to perch amid Mr Ramsey's supplies. Above them the sky hung grey-white and featureless, as if London existed permanently beneath a drape of old sailcloth. Over the head-high yard walls, the clack and rattle of hooves and wheel rims echoed. Just another morning's business.

Liz was sat on a stack of empty pallets; Cath, uninvited but there all the same, sitting beside her. They came as a pair, those two. Partners in crime, always looking out for each other. They always solicited for business together. But Liz Stride was the prettier one of the pair. Tall, fair and fine-boned, whilst Cath was short and heavy.

Mary closed the back door, muting the giggles and mocking 'la-di-da's coming from inside.

'Cath told us yer come into some money,' said Liz. 'Howzat, then? You rob a bank?'

Mary laughed self-consciously. 'Maybe I did.'

Liz eyed her through a thin plume of smoke. 'You was always gonna get lucky. I knew summin' like this would 'appen for yer. What is it a gentleman client payin' yer good?'

Mary had decided to keep news of Argyll to herself. She side-stepped the question. 'I need your help.'

'You don't look like you need no one's 'elp,' said Cath. Mary ignored her as she fished around in the small bag on her arm and pulled out the key on the brass fob.

'This.' She held it out for Liz to see. 'It's a key . . .'

Liz made a face. 'Well done, love.'

'It's a key to a . . . room. A hotel room, I think.'

Liz plucked it out of her hand and quickly examined it. 'Looks that way. So?'

Mary shrugged. 'I don't know *which* hotel. It could be any.'

Liz, nearly forty years of age, was the know-things person amongst the girls, almost the mother-figure amongst them. Once upon a time, Liz had even a run a tea shop much like this one. Mary hoped she might recognise the hotel's mark on the fob, or at least know someone who would know.

Liz looked up at her. 'What's goin' on, Mary? You disappear for several weeks, an' me an' Cath an' the others was starting to get bloody worried about you, what with them nasty murders goin' on. And now, here you are, turnin' up dressed like Lady Muck. What's been goin' on?'

On her way across the city, she'd rehearsed this, answers to the questions the girls were inevitably going to bombard her with. But she'd resolved not to tell them a thing about her man. Because they would undoubtedly want in on her scam; a share of him, a piece of him. But this, all of this, her 'scam', wasn't about taking a vulnerable man for every penny he had. Silly and impractical though it sounded, a little feeling inside her was telling her this really wasn't about the money anymore.

'I ain't saying. It's my business.'

'Well maybe I ain't inclined to 'elp, then,' Liz replied curtly, her slender fingers closed deliberately around the fob.

She's not going to give me that back.

'I can pay you. I got some—'

Liz slowly shook her head. 'I ain't after yer money, Mary. I'm worried for yer, love. All us girls is. Yer don't get money like yer got without a bag full of troubles comin' wiv it. Tell me what's been goin' on with you.'

Mary felt the wall of her own firm resolve begin to wobble, crumble.

'Did you steal it, love? Is that it?' She reached out to her. Stroked her lace shawl. 'All this . . . the nice clothes and the proper talkin' – it ain't you, is it? What's goin' on? You in trouble now?'

Mary felt like crying for some reason.

Liz's voice softened. 'You in some trouble, dear?'

Lying, lying and more lying to John; she felt exhausted with the effort of it. Maintaining a fiction that with every new probing question of his was growing that much more elaborate and difficult to sustain. Trying to keep all that in her mind so that she didn't contradict herself. Coupled with that, this contrived make-believe version of herself. This act. She liked feeling 'posh', and she knew a man like John wouldn't ever consort with a common street tart, not even in the wildest fiction she could construct, but it was yet another layer of burden. To constantly keep in mind how to speak, how to step, how to hold herself. The daily trips out of the rented house in Holland Park to buy things for their supper weren't just shopping trips; they were an opportunity to draw a breath, to compose herself, to recuperate. To catalogue and order every little lie she'd told John, to be sure she wasn't going to trip herself up.

She realised she was exhausted. Worn down to a nub.

And the first tears began to roll down her cheeks.

'Oh, dear, oh, dear, come on,' said Liz. She grasped Mary by the arms. 'Sit down, poppet.' She pulled her down to sit beside her.

Mary didn't resist. She nodded.

'Now then,' said Liz, gently stroking her shoulder, 'why dontcha tell me what's been goin' on?'

Mary glanced up at Cath standing over them in the yard like Liz's guard dog. Liz seemed to pick up on Mary wanting to speak to her alone.

'Cath, 'ow about you join the others for a bit?'

Cath pouted like a child and then, with an irritable huff, she turned and headed for the back door. She pulled it open and, for a moment, the muted hubbub of conversation from the back room died away. Mary briefly spotted half a dozen curious faces from the gloomy back room craning across the cluttered table to get a look at what was going on outside. The door clattered closed and the muted murmur of voices inside continued once more.

'Now then,' continued Liz. 'What sort of a pickle 'ave yer gone an' got yerself into?'

CHAPTER 27

30th September 1888, Whitechapel, London

Mary told her everything, the whole lot: finding the nameless gentleman on Argyll Street and then tracking him down later in St Bartholomew's hospital, his mind wiped clean. She told Liz that none of it had been planned, it had just come as a sequence of opportunities, and she'd taken each one as it presented itself to her.

And now, perhaps the worst thing of all, she felt something for him. Instead of vanishing like she should have done with his bag of money, leaving him alone in the Frampton-Parkers' home to finally figure out he'd been abandoned by her, she was now hankering to get back to him, worried that he'd been on his own this morning far too long already.

'But I don't really know nothing about him, Liz,' she said. 'He . . . he might have a wife or . . . someone else lookin' for him. I just need to know because . . .' Because maybe the sensible thing *was* to take the rest of his money and run, to forget about him and her silly dreams of being Mrs Argyll. Not that she would ever be a Mrs 'Argyll'. He had another name that was sure to surface one day soon.

Silly dream. Nothing ever came of dreams, not really. Not outside of the fairytale books she'd read as a child in her convent school.

Liz looked down at the key still in her hand. 'And you want me to find out for you?'

Mary nodded.

'Do yer feel safe with 'im, love?'

'Oh, god, yes, Liz! He's as gentle as a lamb, so he is. Like a baby, in a way. I'm almost like his mam.'

Liz nodded sagely. As Mary had talked, she'd been intrigued by the notion of a person's mind wiped clean. 'Gentle he may be, but he's still a man, Mary. A man yer don't know nothin' about, really. Yer don't know nothin' about the man he is.' Liz shrugged and corrected herself. 'Or *was*. You got to be careful, Mary.'

Mary nodded quickly. 'But listen, Liz. Just you, all right? Don't tell the others, please. Just you.'

'I won't tell no one nothing. Promise.'

Mary fumbled in her handbag, into her purse, the coins jingling heavily. 'I'll pay you—'

Liz nodded. 'I'll take a florin. I think I know a bloke who'd take a look at this key and might know the 'otel. Dylan, 'e's a locksmith, 'e might recognise the fob, or the handiwork.'

'Let me give you something too.'

Liz shrugged. 'A sixpence for me troubles, I s'pose, wouldn't go amiss. But look, Mary, this man—'

'He's fine, really,' she said. 'Like I said, he's like a lamb.'

'You 'eard about 'em recent murders, though?'

She'd seen large type on the front of some of the papers and whispers of gossip from passersby. She vaguely knew of the killings. Not that her mind had been on London news recently. But it was hard to completely ignore the large headlines, the imaginative illustrations on the front of some of the pennies that made creative use of the few lascivious details bribed out of the mouths of Scotland Yard's detectives working the case.

'Oh, lord, not him!' Mary almost laughed at what Liz was suggesting. 'He wouldn't last no more'n two minutes here in Whitechapel before some shivering Jemmy ripped him off.' She laughed. 'Gawd, no. It's certainly not him.'

Liz shrugged. 'Yer know 'im best, I s'pose. Just yer be careful, though.' A thought occurred to her. 'Tell me, Mary – 'ave yer let 'im 'ave yer? Yer lifted yer skirts for—'

'No! It's not like that!' Mary frowned. 'He's been a perfect gent, so he has. He's treated me nicer than any other man ever has.'

Liz nodded thoughtfully. 'Good.' She smiled. 'So, I'll take this key with me? You all right with that?'

'Yes.'

'An' I'll see what I can find out. If I find out which 'otel 'e's in, yer want me to knock on the room? See who's there? Find out 'bout 'im?'

Mary wasn't sure she wanted that. The truth. It would almost certainly spell the end of her little fantasy world with John. There'd be a new name, wouldn't there? This time, his real name. And there'd be the reason he was in England and – for some reason she was certain of this now – there'd be an anxious wife called 'Polly'.

Mary nodded slowly. 'All right . . . yes. I s'pose I have to know.'

Liz cupped the warm bowl of her pipe in her hand and sucked on the stem. A faint curl of blue smoke twisted into the cool morning air in the yard. 'Cath tells me yer not stayin' in yer room in Millers Court no more?'

'I ain't paid my rent for a week. So maybe my room's gone by now.'

'So where yer livin' now?'

'Holland Park.'

'Holland Park?!' Liz's eyes widened. 'Posh 'ouse, is it?'

Mary shrugged.

'Want me to come to yours an' tell yer what I find out?'

She wasn't sure she wanted to give Liz the exact address.

'Yes, but . . .'

Liz smiled. 'I'll be discreet, love. Knock an' try an' sell yer summin', eh? And maybe there'll be a note amongst a posy of flowers for yer.' She winked. 'Somewhere you an' me can meet.'

Mary understood. Liz was smart. The only other girl amongst their informal sisterhood, apart from herself, who could actually read and write.

'All right, then.'

She told Liz the address in Holland Park and stood up to go. Poor John would be wondering where she'd got to and she had still yet to visit the market to buy something for their evening meal.

'You be careful,' said Liz. 'Remember, there's two girls like us out there been gutted like butcher's meat by the same mad man. Just you be careful, love.'

CHAPTER 28

31st August 1888, Whitechapel, London

'I'm scared, Annie. I'm so fuckin' scared!'

'Keep yer voice down, Polly!' hissed Annie. She looked around at the market traders either side of them, busy packing up their wares as the tumbling grey August sky above began to spit greasy drops of rain down on them. The summer, for what it was, had been warm and all too short. Now, autumn seemed impatient to get started, to soak London's streets and draw a cover over the possibility of seeing a slither of blue sky until the far side of spring.

Polly hastened along beside her, both of them keen to get off the street and inside before the sky opened up fully and drenched them.

'Someone's after us, Annie. I'm sure of it.' Polly tied her dark bonnet under her chin. 'Bill was—'

'Bill got in a stupid fight, is all!' snapped Annie. The big fool had a list of local enemies as long as one of his ape-like arms. She'd warned him of that. Warned him you didn't swagger around a manor like Whitechapel unless you're part of a firm, unless you got some back-up. But that's what Bill liked doing: swaggering, holding himself like some kind of 'Big I Am'. It was no surprise he ended up being stuck by someone. But the stupid sod might have bloody paid them the rest of their share of that job first. Now there was no chance they were going to see any of that. Neither she nor Polly had any idea who the gentleman client was.

'I 'ear someone sayin' he was cut up real bad. Just like the . . .' She looked at Annie. 'Just like the French tart he done in.'

Annie stopped in the middle of the thoroughfare, waiting for a young runner to pass by with a basket of foul-smelling fish scraps in his arms. 'We jus' need to forget all 'bout that bleedin' job now. All right? We ain't gonna see a single 'nother bleeding penny from it, so there's no point you and me wastin' no more breath on it either.'

'But they want *this* back,' said Polly, absently gesturing to the fine golden chain around her neck, hidden beneath her thick flannel collar. 'Bill said it was important, didn't he? That's why they was goin' to pay up so much!'

Annie resumed striding down the walkway between the stalls. 'Well none of that's 'appenin' now, is it? Bill was the job man an' now the stupid git is done in. So you and me, Poll', we're goin' to have to go back to business as usual and forget all about that now.'

'We could flog it?' Polly's eyes lit up at her own idea. 'Yeah, take it down the pawn shop an'—'

'No.' Annie frowned. Thinking. 'No. We should 'ang onto it. Maybe there's some money we can get out of this fuckin' muddle.'

Polly put a hand on her arm. 'Annie . . .'

'What?'

'The man in that picture.'

Annie looked up and down the walkway and either side at the traders packing their market stalls away into their carts. Probably far too busy to bother listening to two tarts hissing exchanges at each other. Still. Best they kept their voices down.

'The man in the picture, Poll,' she uttered quietly, 'is lucky we went and tidied his dirty little mess up for 'im an' now 'e can go back to whatever ugly wife 'e has and get on with 'is nice life. Only, first, maybe we can tap him for a bit of—'

'Listen, Annie . . .'

She looked at Polly's frightened eyes. 'What?'

'I think . . .' She swallowed anxiously. 'I think 'e ain't *just* a gentleman.'

Annie shrugged.

'I saw 'is face, Annie.'

That stilled her.

'I swear it. I saw 'is face. Same face as is in the picture.'

'Round 'ere?'

Polly shook her head. 'No. On the front of a newsie.'

Annie looked round at her. 'Which newspaper?'

'I dunno. Can't remember which one.' Polly's turn to look up and down the walkway of the market. The rain was coming down a little heavier now, spattering in puddles; a hiss of splashing, the rattle of raindrops tapping on tarpaulins and the clank and bang of tired tradesmen hefting crates of goods, eager to get home for the evening.

'I think 'e's in the guvver-ment or summin', Annie. 'E's important, I think.'

'Are you sure it was 'im?'

'Yeah.' She looked at Annie. 'I'm sure I seen 'is face before somewhere else as well. Like a paintin' or summin'.'

'A paintin'?' Annie felt the rain begin to soak through her shawl and chill her neck and shoulders.

They stood in a dampened silence for a moment, both of them considering what that might mean. *A painting? A painting famous enough known that even Polly would have seen it?*

'I don't want to look after this no more,' said Polly, beginning to fish for the chain under her flannel top.

'No, you said you'd take it for a while!'

'I ain't got lodgings no more! You know that! Me rooms is gone. Me money's gone. That's why I got to wear it round me neck, instead of stashed away!'

Annie knew Polly was in some straits. The half of money Bill had paid them up front was already gone for Polly, pissed away on too much mecks. Now she was back to doing business on the streets to pay for a bed night by night. She had been for a couple of weeks now.

Polly cautiously eased the locket out, turning her back on the few tradesmen nearby and inserting a grubby fingernail into the small frame to ease the miniature portrait out. 'Please, Annie, you 'old onto it for a bit—'

'It's your turn!'

'Then I'll just throw it away.' She pulled the small picture out and was about to toss it into a puddle.

'No!' Annie reached and snatched it out of her hand. 'No, stupid! It's bloody well worth summin', ain't it?' She cursed under her breath. 'Give it to me, then. I'll mind it for a bit.'

Annie had no idea what exactly she could do with it except some nebulous notion of selling it to one of the cheap daily papers. They seemed to like their scandals and sordid tales. But if she did do something like that, there was no way she was going to cut the proceeds with Polly. The woman – her so-called partner in crime – had been a complete waste of space on this job. Lost her nerve, so she had. Odd that, after all the other babies they'd 'farmed' over the last few years, this last job had rattled her nerves so.

'What if we tell the slops?'

Annie grabbed one of her arms. 'Police? You stupid cow! Are you really that stupid?'

'I'm scared, Annie!' From beneath the shadow of her bonnet, tears emerged down florid and pockmarked cheeks. 'Bill said they really wanted that picture back, so he did! You 'eard, too. And now look; 'e's stabbed-up an' dead! We should go to the police with it!'

'Streuth, Polly! We can't go to the coppers. What we gonna tell 'em? You an' me's both guilty of . . .' She fumbled for the fancy word Bill had once used. ' . . . infanticide! They'd bloody 'ang us soon as look at us! Do you understand?'

Polly dabbed at her blotchy cheeks.

'Do you want to be 'anged? Eh?'

Polly silently shook her head.

Annie sighed. 'Right. So we ain't talkin' to any police, or anyone, about this, all right? Because it's our blimmin' secret!' She softened her tone and leant a little closer, hunkering down slightly to look up into the dark shadows beneath the bonnet where Polly's frightened eyes glinted. 'Bill didn't tell no one else about our job. It was just you an' me. Bill may have been a stupid prat, but when it came to money, 'e was dead bloody careful. All right, love?'

She waited for Polly to nod.

'No one knows 'bout you an' me,' said Annie, tucking the small portrait into the inside pocket of her coat. 'An' no one knows we got this little picture 'ere.'

Polly nodded, dabbed her cheeks again. 'I . . . I better go,' she said unhappily. 'I 'ave to get some business tonight or I'm sleepin' in the rain again.'

Annie would have offered her a roof if she could, but the man she was currently sharing a room with was funny about his privacy and had a habit of making himself understood with his fists.

She reached out and squeezed Polly's shoulder. 'You go get some business. I'll see yer t'morra mornin'?'

Polly nodded, turned away and walked quickly into the rain, now hammering down loudly against the awnings either side. Annie watched her go, sidestepping the bigger puddles, and hunched over, trying to keep some of herself dry, little knowing it was the last time she was going to see Polly alive.

CHAPTER 29

31st August 1888, Whitechapel, London

The bells of Christ Church chimed the half hour. 'Won't get no more trade tonight, don't think, Polly,' said Emily Holland. She sniffed – a constant, irritating habit of hers that came, literally, after her every utterance. 'An' it's pissin' down. Any bloke with any sense is already gone 'ome, I reckon.'

Polly nodded. It didn't look good for business. She'd stupidly spent her earnings from earlier this evening on a bottle of cheap rancid wine. Her stupid fault. Now she needed one last trick to pay for a shared flop-room out of the rain. That's all. Just one more customer.

She'd been edgy earlier this evening, still worried every shadow might contain some knife-wielding man eager to get that locket and that little photograph back. Now she was beginning to realise Annie was probably right. Perhaps she was just jumping at shadows.

Two-thirty in the morning. Polly needed one more bit of business.

'I'm off,' Emily said with a sniff. 'I'm pissin' cold, wet an' fed up.' She glanced at Polly. 'Comin' or what?'

'Ain't got no money. I need to stay on a bit. There was still boozers in the Crown not so long ago. Might get trade off of one of 'em.'

Emily shrugged before she turned away to walk up Bucks Row. 'Be careful,' she called over her shoulder.

Polly watched her go up the road. On one side, a row of two-storey terraced houses, on the other, a warehouse and the edge of Essex Wharf. She watched until the last thing she could see was Emily's pale frock merging with the gloom. She listened until the clack and scrape of her heels were finally lost beneath the hiss of a steady drizzle, the sputtering water cascading from the roofs and guttering of the row of terraced houses, and faintly, the restless slap of the Thames against the hulls of a row of tethered-up barges.

Just one more. And if he was drunk enough, she might even try and make a grab for his wallet. It didn't concern her that she would most probably be stealing food from some family's mouth. Everyone here learned to do without from time to time. It wasn't uncommon not to have a proper meal for days. You just made do. Or you made enough for a drink or two to forget how empty your tummy was.

She snorted. The best thing about being hungry was that it took less booze to get you so you didn't have a care in the world. She realised it was the last couple of drinks she'd had that was still keeping her warm now, despite her rain-damp clothes.

'You look a sort.'

The words sounded dead, muffled in the drizzle. For a moment she thought it might have been her wine-addled mind playing a game with her.

'You look a sort, you do.'

Polly glanced around. There was some light from the gas lamp nearby, a sick orange halo around it that caught the intermittent flicker of raindrops, and a weak pool of light at the bottom of the lamp post that spilled across slick cobbles and gave in all too quickly to the darkness.

'Hoy! Who's 'at, then?' she said, with a forced playful tone. 'You after a little bit of the other before you go 'ome, then?' she asked the darkness. 'Five pence will do yer. Seven if you wanna go in the back way. Whadya say?' She had no intention of actually letting anyone take her like that, but in the dark, if he was drunk enough, he'd probably think he was getting what he'd paid for.

'Yes . . . you'll do.' The voice whispered out of the gloom.

'Come on then, where are yer?' she called out, still straining to make her voice sound playful and sporting for some fun. It bounced, a little too shrill, off the walls of the row of terraced houses across the narrow street.

She heard the clack of shoe heels and then saw the hazy shape of a figure emerging from the darkness. Moderate height and build, a face partially shadowed from the pallid glow of the gas lamp by the peak of a felt cap.

'Ah! There you are, love!'

The man drew closer. She could smell pub on him: the thick

odour of pipe smoke, the stew of stale beer, the meaty odour of a workman's sweat. Rain pattered on his cap as he stood perfectly still, his eyes hidden in shadow.

'So come on then, what's it to be, dear?'

'I like it in private,' said the man. 'Not out in the street.'

'Oh, there ain't no one around, love. We'll be just fine out 'ere.'

'Only dogs fuck in the street. It's undignified.'

His voice didn't sound like how he looked, how he smelled. He sounded like a bit of class. There was something comforting in that. The educated ones didn't think with the backs of their hands. They tended to be somewhat bashful, polite even. Paid better, too, if you gave good service.

'I don't 'ave any place to go, love. It's 'ere or nowhere.'

'Then how about over there,' he said, pointing towards a wooden gateway. It stood ajar and led into the stable yard of the small quayside warehouse. 'We might find somewhere sheltered. Dry, even.'

A coarse, leery voice and Polly would have been wary of his suggestion, would have stood her ground and insisted it was out here or not at all. She'd been *taken* roughly before by drunks who thought she was doing this for fun, not money. Somewhere private was the first thing they asked for. But this one seemed, at the very least, quite polite.

'I don't think so.'

'I'm sorry,' said the man. He took off his cap, and for the first time she had a glimpse of his face: lean and tanned, dark sideburns and dark hair, coarse and tufty. Under different circumstances, quite an attractive man. He held his cap awkwardly, twisting it between balled fists. She could tell he was feeling uncomfortable about this.

First-timer? Most probably a married man and this was his very first time actually paying for it. She took pity on him. He seemed harmless enough.

'Go on then,' she nodded towards the open gate. She reached out and grabbed one of his hands. He flinched nervously at her touch.

Polly cackled. 'I'll look after yer, love. Treat yer gentle!'

She led him across the road and through the open gate. Beyond, the small stable yard was big enough for only two or three carts side by side. Tonight it was empty, save for a pile of empty canvas sacks in one corner, sodden from the rain. On the far side, padlocked double gates to the stable were overhung by a lip of several feet of roof. It was dry over there.

Polly clacked unsteadily across uneven cobbles until she rested a hand against the dry wood. She turned around to look at the man. He hovered uncertainly a yard from her. She couldn't see his face now; the gas lamp out on Bucks Row was behind him. He was just a silhouette.

'Need to come a little closer, love, if you want—'

'I was watching you earlier,' said the man gently.

'Excuse me?'

'Hours earlier, back in that pub . . . The Rose and Crown.'

'Oh?' She laughed. It sounded forced. 'Like what you saw, then, eh?'

He shared the laugh, insincere and cool. He didn't sound quite so much like the nervous first-timer now. 'Oh, yes, you're a right beauty.'

Polly shrugged at the compliment. It was nice to hear it even if she knew it was a facile attempt at small talk. She was no beauty; that's why her best trade tended to be at the latter end of an evening.

'Your name's Polly,' he said.

'Aye, Polly's the name! Everyone knows me in that pub, one way or the other,' she said with a chuckle, a hand impatiently reaching out and tugging on his belt buckle. 'Now then—'

'Polly Nichols.'

She hesitated. Everyone knew her as Polly, her trade name. But they knew no more than that.

'Yes,' said the man, 'I know your name. And I know something was troubling you.'

She let go of his belt. 'I . . .'

'Yes, something playing heavily on your mind, Polly. Your hand – the one not busy holding a cup – was telling me all sorts of things.'

'Whatcha talkin' 'bout?'

'Your hand. It kept fumbling for something around your neck. A nice necklace, perhaps? A piece of jewellery? I saw your fingers stealing beneath your neck cloth, feeling under folds of flannel. Something right there,' he said, pressing a finger against the subtle bulge at the base of her throat beneath the collar of her jacket.

'I . . . I ain't got nothing in there that's any yer business, love.'

'Oh, but you do have something, Polly; something very important to us. You know that, don't you?'

Her jaw shuddered with that word. 'Us?'

Babbitt grinned. 'Yes.'

She took a step back from him, reversing into the stable's wooden-slat wall. 'Oh dear god . . .'

He rested a hand lightly on her shoulder. 'We need to have a little talk, my dear.'

Her jaw trembled, wobbled up and down, showing him a mouth full of missing teeth. 'Oh god! P . . . p . . . please don't 'urt me!'

He shushed her with a finger placed lightly against her lips. 'Now, I know you helped a certain William H Tolly with a job some weeks ago, didn't you?'

She stared at him, wide-eyed and frozen.

'I know, Polly. I know, because William, or shall I say "ol' Bill", told me all about you. So shall we take it that there's really no point your trying to pretend you don't know what I'm talking about?'

She managed a quick jerk of her head.

'Bill told me you found something on that French woman. A very nice gold locket; the sort of gift a foolish man besotted with a beautiful woman might give. And inside this locket there was something else.' He looked into her eyes. 'You know, don't you? Why don't you tell me?'

'P-picture. A . . . p-photograph.'

'That's right. Well done, Polly.'

'The . . . the woman . . . and the m . . . man. They . . . were lovers . . .'

He smiled. 'Good girl. You keep this up, keep being this helpful to me, and I promise I'm going to let you go.' He patted her shoulder affectionately. 'And I might even give you a couple of shillings for your troubles.'

She swallowed anxiously. 'The man in the picture. I . . . I . . . seen 'is face again.'

Babbitt cocked a brow. 'Really?'

Her head nodded vigorously. ''Is . . . face . . . in a newspaper. Handsome . . . young man.'

'And do you know *who* he is, Polly?'

She shook her head. 'No . . . no. But . . . but, I . . . I think . . . I . . . 'E could be in the guvver-ment or summin'?'

Government. Babbitt gave that a moment's consideration. It would certainly make sense with the amount of money these gentlemen were prepared to pay him to fix this mess of theirs.

'Can you tell me *which* newspaper you saw his face in?'

Her face flickered with effort, her eyes darting up to one side in a desperate attempt to haul something useful out of her head. "No . . . I . . . I . . . don't remember . . .'

'Not to worry. Now Polly, my dear; why don't you pull out that nice bit of jewellery and give it to me?'

With trembling fingers, she delved under her frock and lifted the chain and locket out over her collar. Fumbling, she tried to lift it over her head but the chain caught on her hair, on her bonnet.

'Here, allow me,' he offered solicitously. He reached around her head, almost like a tender embrace, and undid the chain's clasp behind her neck. 'There,' he said softly.

'Picture ain't in there n-no more,' said Polly quickly.

'Oh?'

He held the locket in his hand, warm from her body-heat, the size of a large flattened walnut. He fiddled with its clasp until it opened. As she said. Just an empty frame and a pink velvet inlay.

'Where is it?'

Polly's lips were quivering, reluctant to blurt out any more. Babbitt sighed. He reached into a pocket inside his jacket and pulled out his long, slender knife. Its blade glinted, a faint shard reflecting the pallid orange light from the lamp on the street outside. Her eyes instantly widened and she began to moan.

'Ah yes, it's not a pleasant sight, is it, hmmm?'

She swallowed and shook her head, tears rolling down her cheeks.

'Frightened?'

She nodded.

'Yes, you jolly well should be. See, it's this very blade I used to gut your friend Bill.'

'Oh . . . g-god . . . oh . . . n-no!' Her deep moan became a mewling whimper, thick with mucous and horror.

'Now then, that picture; where might I find it, my dear?'

She sniffled something through the snot and tears.

'Again please.'

'A-Annie.'

Babbitt cocked his brow. 'Would this be another helper Bill had on this job?'

'She . . . she . . . was the one did the baby. I gave it 'er . . . this . . . this evenin'. The picture . . . I g-gave it her earlier.'

He let the tip of his blade flick back and forth in the small space between their faces. 'Annie who? I'd really like her full name.'

'Chapman! Annie Chapman!'

'Chapman, is it?' He smiled, charming and wide. 'Thank you, Polly. And do you have an address for me?'

''Onest . . . I d-don't,' she replied, her eyes on the serrated side of the blade. 'Sh-she moved in wiv a man last week. I think . . . b-but I d-don't know . . . 'Onest I d-don't . . .'

He could well believe that. Her type were all no fixed abode. Flop houses, workhouses and lodgings, from one to the next, to the bed of any man who promised to look after them.

'Annie's like you and Bill though, isn't she? She has her favourite public houses?'

Polly nodded, lips pressed together as if that last morsel of information was going to need to be prised out of her.

'I promised you some shillings, didn't I? The same goes for Annie. I don't want to hurt either of you. I'm just getting back what shouldn't have been taken in the first place.'

'Was it r-r-really y-you . . . that k-killed Bill?'

He sighed. 'Yes, I did. But then, between you and I, I don't think he was a very nice man, was he?'

She shook her head. He could see a glimmer of hope in her eyes.

Good. There was no need to make her any more frightened than she was. And hope . . . Hope was a good thing to be grasping hold of in the last few moments of life.

'The . . . the Swan . . .'

The Swan. He'd done his research. He knew of the public house. Not so very far from here, as it happened. 'Thank you,' he said softly. 'You've been immensely helpful.' He reached down for one of her cold hands and cupped it in his. 'Don't look so worried. Here.' He pressed a couple of shillings into her hand. 'This is for your time.'

She looked down and caught the dull glint of coins in her palm. Her eyes lit up, a mixture of overwhelming relief and joy.

'Thank you!' She gazed wide-eyed at the money in her hand. 'Thank you! I—'

His knife was suddenly buried in her neck up to the hilt; with a quick jerk, he wrenched it forward, opening her throat in a jagged gash from beneath her left ear, almost all the way round to the other. She looked up from her coins, still trying to work out what had just happened. Then blood tumbled and spattered onto the stones between them. She shuddered in his grasp, eyes wide and rolling.

'Shhhh,' he whispered softly, holding her head back to open the wound and ease the flow. 'Like this. Be very still. It's better, much quicker this way.'

She tried to gurgle something. Her boots scraping and slapping against the bottom of the stable wall.

'There's a good girl,' he whispered into her ear. He kissed her cheek tenderly. 'You can sleep soon enough, my dear. Soon enough.'

Her struggling, shuffling, began to wane. 'This really isn't your mortal life, Polly. Don't you see? This world around us . . . it's purgatory.' Her legs flexed beneath her and all of a sudden she was a dead weight in his arms. Gently, he lowered her to the ground.

For a few moments he studied her still body, growing damp beneath the heavy patter of rain, the blood that had begun to pool beneath her neck washed away by a miniature stream of rainwater that snaked towards a gutter and sewage drain across the small courtyard.

He would have liked a candle to hand, to light, to watch the flickering flame for a few moments. Instead, he struck a match and gazed at the glow for a moment before extinguishing it with his fingers.

'And now, my dear, you're free to go . . . whichever way you must go.'

A clock chimed the quarter hour. It was 2.45 in the morning. He stirred from his reverie. There were tradesmen that would be getting up within the hour.

He crouched down over her body.

Make it look the work of madman . . . not a hired man.

He stabbed at her abdomen several times; hard, ruthless thrusts that were deliberately uncontrolled, artless and vicious.

CHAPTER 30

30th September 1888, Holland Park, London

Argyll was standing in the hallway, staring at the front door, working up the courage to open it and step outside.

'Come on, John,' he muttered to himself. 'It's just a little walk. You can do that at least, can't you?'

This morning, after finishing his breakfast and reading his paper, he decided to set himself a challenge. To do something for himself instead of relying quite so much on Mary to nurse him. He was beginning to wonder whether the poor young girl might be having second thoughts about the commitment she'd taken on. He certainly couldn't blame her if she was entertaining the notion of leaving him. Caring for a man so many years her senior, a shuffling invalid no less, with an empty vessel of a mind and nothing noteworthy to say for himself. He wouldn't wish that on anyone.

In truth, he was sure a beauty like her could be stepping out with any young man she chose. A wonderful girl like her, so vivacious, so charming, a wholesome quality that made her fresh freckled face look out of place amongst all the other sallow, sickly faces of London. But she appeared to be prepared to stay by his side, for whatever it was that she saw in him. The thought made him feel guilty. And frightened – terrified – of losing her.

'Come on, you pathetic fool,' he snapped at himself irritably, and reached for the door, pulling it open. A rare stream of autumn sun warmed his face and immediately the stifling quiet of the hallway, marked only by the ticking of a brass clock on the side table, was flooded with the noise and bustling activity of Holland Park Avenue.

He shuffled his still-numb left leg over the dust mat onto the top step outside. The bad leg was behaving itself this morning. He decided he no longer needed the walking stick that Mary had bought him a couple of days ago. It made him look, feel, older than he was. As for that wheelchair, it was already just an embarrassing memory tucked away in the back room, out of sight and mind.

He took the steps down carefully, one at a time, through the wrought iron gate and onto the pavement, tapping his forehead in a polite gesture at the police constable passing by on a bicycle.

The fleeting sunlight felt good; he savoured the warmth on his face, the noises of midday business going on around him. He looked up and down the street. To his right, he remembered, was Hyde Park, a mile or so along. And halfway between there and here was Notting Hill with, as he recalled from their last walk to the park together, a number of pleasant-looking teashops and cafes.

A walk. And perhaps a little something to eat?

He realised he was getting peckish. Mary had been gone awhile now and it was almost lunchtime. He had a pocket full of jingling coins and a rumbling stomach.

'Why not?' he uttered resolutely. Pleased with himself so far. He smiled. Mary was going to be impressed when he told her later that he'd actually managed to take himself out for a walk and order something to eat and drink. All by himself. She was going to be so pleased with him.

Half an hour later, a faltering and cautious stroll had brought him to Notting Hill, busy with a farmer's market; a cacophony of traders' barking voices and chattering women; carts parked on one side of the road, ponies and horses tethered together to railings on the other. The main road was thick with small mounds of drying manure that he didn't fancy stepping in. On the far side of the busy road he saw a nice-looking tea house with broad, sunny windows that were trapping the fleeting sunlight. He hesitated and took several abortive steps into the road. Hesitated long enough that an old woman eventually reached for his arm and helped him across. Argyll doffed his hat and thanked her on the far side, pink-cheeked at the thought that she'd been helping him instead of the other way round.

A bell jingled above the door as he entered the tea shop. He picked a small round table for two by the front window, sat down and watched the market through a window spattered on the outside with spots of pigeon droppings, until an old woman with raw red hands and a crisp white apron asked him what he fancied. He ordered a pot of tea, a round of toast and butter and a slice of bacon, quietly pleased with himself for his impressive show of independence. His life story might still be a complete mystery, but good grief, at least he was able to order a spot of lunch.

Ten minutes later, he was enjoying the activity of the market, sipping tea and savouring the warm toast thickly spread with melting butter. He watched a fishmonger in a leather apron behind a propped up pallet of filleted mackerel; fillets lined up like soldiers on parade, the shimmering blue of their scales interlaced with the puckered pink of exposed flesh. A fat greengrocer almost lost behind a veritable mountain of soil-covered potatoes, each the size of a boxer's fist. A butcher hacking at cuts of mutton, observed by the dead eyes of a row of pigs' heads arranged along the edge of his stall like jurors in a court. The space between the stalls was teeming with bonnets and feathers, bowlers and tops hats, flat caps and forage caps; a painter's palette of so many different-looking faces all intent on the same errand, the same mission: *something nice and tasty for our tea tonight.*

He looked at them.

Yes, why not? Go on . . . take a good look at them.

Argyll stirred uneasily. He recognised that voice and his good mood soured. The voice brought with it an unpleasant sensation; the notion of things left undone, obligations unfulfilled. A spiteful, mean-spirited little voice that he was certain didn't approve of him merely sitting here watching the world go by.

You're right. Because you are not looking closely enough. Look at them. Look at them, 'John'. Do you see that fishmonger putting spoiled fillets in behind the good? Do you see the butcher trimming rancid corners off his meat? Do you see that gentleman walking with his wife and yet his eyes lingering on the baker's boy? Do you see the beggar over there with crutches he pretends to need? Do you see that small boy flicking dirt into his baby sister's face behind his mother's back?

He saw those things, like the small background details of a giant painting; brush strokes that told stories hidden amidst swirls of oil paint.

They're all rotten, all spoiled stock. The good people, 'John', all the good people went on from this world long ago. In far better times than this.

He hated the tone of the voice, the unpleasant sharpness to it. It was the hectoring of a disapproving tutor. The nag of an unsatisfied creditor. The persistent chase of a debtor. The spiteful ridicule of an older sibling.

Do you remember anything?

His eyes narrowed. There'd been another dream last night, hadn't there? In it he was young, much younger, perhaps in his early-twenties. He remembered catching a glimpse of a reflection of himself in a store window: a wild-looking young man in deerskins and a threadbare and faded red polka dot shirt staring back at him. He looked like a frontiersman. A trapper? He vaguely recalled docks and sailboats, steamships, wagons. Someplace busy, just like the market out there.

Then a second strange, dislocated dream that made little sense to him again. He had a feeling that chronologically, it was some years earlier. He remembered an Indian, ghostly white with chalk powder, standing over him and shouting something he didn't understand, pushing him and pointing a finger. The Indian had the same shrill, nagging tone as the voice. He had the distinct impression the Indian was saying the same thing in his coarse, guttural tongue.

'*Do you see? Do you see? Do you see?*'

And then he saw a village of those tall, cone-shaped tents that Indians live in. Yes, tepees, that's what they're called . . .

. . . *They're burning. Flames licking from the top of one tepee to the next, smoke blowing across snow-covered prairie grass. A thick blanket of snow stained a startlingly bright crimson in places. Militia men in forage caps with thick winter beards, wearing navy blue army greatcoats and riding thundering horses that blast plumes of breath into the early morning air. And the men are cheering, laughing, 'yee-hawing' at the thrill of the chase.*

Between the flaming tepees, they're chasing down terrified squaws; and their children and old men, hardly ferocious savage warriors, all of them half-naked, clearly freshly roused from sleep. Chasing them down, running the slow ones through with their sabres rather than waste the cost of a bullet.

Do you see? Do you see the baby bayoneted against that small fir tree? Left there, lifeless, dangling like a decoration. Do you see those three men and the young squaw? Do you see what they're doing to her? Don't look away. Look! And look down now . . . look down at your own hands. Do you see what you're holding . . . ?

He'd awoken then, last night. Awoken in his dark bedroom, not quite sure if he'd screamed, if he'd roused poor Mary from her slumber yet again.

Oh, so you're remembering just a little more now, hmmm? Argyll did his best to ignore the spiteful voice. *Let me ask you . . . do you know what this place is?*

'Of course,' Argyll whispered, almost immediately angry with himself for acknowledging the voice with an answer. It was only going to encourage the voice in his head.

Hmmm, yes, you do hear me. I know you do. So, what is this place, 'John'? Where are we?

'This is London.'

The voice laughed at him. Most amused at his naïve answer.

No, you fool. This place, this world, is purgatory. You're as blind as everyone else, aren't—

'Be quiet!' Argyll slapped his hand against the table. A couple of coke-men on the table next to his, broad-shouldered with coal-black hands that left finger marks on their sandwiches, stopped mid-conversation and turned to look his way curiously. The waitress with the red raw skin and the crisp white apron bustled over.

'Everythin' awl-right, sir?'

Argyll looked up at her and looked around at the other eyes resting on him. 'Uhh . . . yes, ma'am. Yes, I'm fine.'

'Would you care for a top-up of your tea, sir?'

He looked down at the cup: old chipped porcelain, the blue and gold flower detail rubbed away on the handle. It was all but empty, the dregs of his tea long since gone cold. He realised he must have been sitting here for quite some time, gazing out through the window in some sort of a trance.

'No . . . err, no ma'am, thank you. I'm fine.' He fumbled in his pocket for some coins and pulled out a handful, frowning to make sense of them as he pushed them around the palm of his hand.

'How much do I owe?'

She smiled sympathetically at his awkwardness. 'Thruppence, farthing, sir.'

He picked at the coins, turning them over one after the other to read their value.

'Shall I help you, sir?' said the waitress. Argyll held his open hand out to her and she plucked out the coins. He thanked her before she turned to deal with the men sitting on the next table.

He pushed himself up from his seat, a piece of toast and a rasher of bacon left on his plate uneaten. All of a sudden, his appetite was gone. All of a sudden, he wanted to be back home. Back with Mary where things made sense. Their simple little world for two.

It was mid-afternoon by the time he clambered shakily up the steps to the front door. The noises of Holland Park Avenue, the faces, the confusion, and that hectoring voice had upset him. Confused and frightened him. He wanted to be back home. Somewhere safe and quiet and comprehensible. He saw the net curtain in the bay window of the front room twitch and a moment later the front door swung inwards.

'John!' cried Mary. 'Oh, god help me, I was so worried about you!'

He smiled, pathetically pleased to see her, even if she was going to scold him like a small boy. 'I went for a walk, and a spot of—'

'You've been gone hours! I thought you'd *left* . . .' Her voice caught. 'I thought you'd got lost, forgot where we live!'

Her eyes were red-rimmed. She'd been crying.

'I'm sorry, Mary.' He reached for her arm. 'I must have lost track of the time.'

She grasped his hand and all but dragged him into the hallway and slammed the front door shut behind him. Argyll swallowed nervously, expecting her wrath now. But instead he heard her breath catch and saw in the dim light that her shoulders heaving gently.

'I thought you went and left me,' she whispered.

He reached out to her. 'I . . . I think I'd be so very lost without you, my dear.' He said it and realised how much he meant it. He was at sea in churning waters, a turmoil of confusing, frightening memories and dreams that blew across his mind like a storm front. And Mary was the only thing standing still for him. A lighthouse, a beacon . . . a guttering candle.

Before either of them could utter another word, they were locked together hungrily, the hallway echoing their fluttering gasps, and the *tac-tac-tac* of the clock on the side table calmly measuring what remained of the little time they were going to have left together.

CHAPTER 31

8th September 1888, Whitechapel, London

Annie Chapman looked down Hanbury Street. She could still see another two of them beneath the gas light halfway down, chattering in noisy voices in the stillness of the early hours. She recognised their faces, even if she didn't know them by their names. They were the last girls on the street, apart from her. No doubt forlornly hoping for one more customer before the sky started to lighten with dawn and the early-risers came for Spitalfields market.

Half an hour ago, they'd both spotted an old man staggering and tripping his way home. They'd caterwauled at him to come over, both lifted their skirts to show stocking tops and bare thighs in an attempt to entice him, but he was too far gone to even acknowledge them.

She sat on a low wall in a pool of darkness, far away from the nearest lamp. Normally, like those other two, she would gravitate to the glow beneath a lamp for the sense of safety it provided, but also to be able to show herself off to any passing potential customers. Tonight, though, she wanted to be entirely invisible until the morning returned and the streets were full and she could feel safe again.

And she so wanted tonight to hurry up and be gone.

Foolish. Stupid. She could have been tucked up in the relative safety of the lodging house she's been using this last week. She'd bloody well paid for tonight with the last of her money, but then she'd had a fight with that bitch, Eliza, in the next room earlier this evening. A stupid fight that had flared up in mere seconds down in the washroom. A fight over a bloody bar of soap, would you believe.

Annie was inclined to agree the incident had been more her fault than Eliza's, not that she'd admitted as much. So Annie borrowed her bar of soap and lost it and then Eliza had started accusing her of trying to steal it. Well, she'd lost control of herself and fists flew. The others there were unanimous in saying that Annie had thrown the first punch.

Possibly they were right. Annie wasn't herself. Was very much out of sorts. In truth, she was a jangling skin of sharp-ended nerves. Ever since she'd heard the news that Polly Nichols had been knifed up. Quite horribly, if the Chinese whispers were to be trusted.

She was dead. That much was true. And then the morning after Annie had heard that news, one of the men in the lodgings, who bought the occasional paper, had spotted a small notice in the local reports. Just a couple of paragraphs.

Just another unlucky tart.

Polly was right, that's what Annie realised now. Certain of it. 'They', whoever the hell 'they' were, were going to come for her next. Absently, she fingered her bag. All that she owned was in there: a comb, a nice piece of muslin, some cheap brass rings that her last man had bought her (just a few days before he'd kicked her out for another, younger, tart) and, of course, kept safe in an envelope she'd found in the lodging house – that picture.

It's what they want, ain't it?

She felt like the small, oval-shaped photograph of the young gentleman and that pretty French woman holding the baby was like a fox's scent, drawing the hunting dogs. She was tempted to just tear it into little pieces and toss it away. In fact, several times she nearly had. But then that would do no good. Them hunting dogs would still come for her, photograph or not. She had to keep it with her for now. Keep it because, perhaps, somehow, she might be able to use it to bargain for her life.

Or . . . the other alternative. Take it to one of the newspapers, just like Polly had suggested she do the last time she saw her. Take it to one of them and, of course, ask for money. They were clever men who worked for the papers. They'd know exactly who the gentleman in the picture was. Oh, yes . . . there'd be some money for her. But the trick would be explaining how she had the picture. The trick would be in knowing how much to say. Certainly nothing about how she had played her part in making sure the pretty woman and the young baby were no more.

And if they did pay her some money – and not summon a constable to arrest her immediately for infanticide – it wasn't going to be anything like the king's ransom Bill had assured them they were going to get. But at least it would be something. But more to the point, if the story of this man's indiscretion, and the picture to prove it, were in the press, then surely there was no point in setting the hunting dogs on her anymore. Right?

The man.

Oh, good god, the man. She thought she had an idea who it was now. Not a hundred percent certain, but it looked so very much like him. Images of him, both photographs and 'artists impressions', had been in a paper only this morning; an official visit he'd made to some cavalry barracks in Yorkshire. There he was, shaking hands, greeting young cavalry officers. The look of a carefree man whose troubles have all been taken care of for him.

The two girls further down Hanbury Street stepped out of the pall of light from the gas lamp and crossed the road together. Annie's heart sank. Even though neither of them knew she was perched in the darkness up this end, they had felt like company. She watched them cross the narrow street from one pool of dim amber light to the one on the far side, their boot heels clacking and scraping as they passed beneath it and then finally disappeared from view down a rat-run between two rows of terraced houses.

All alone, Annie.

She wished she'd had just enough money to drink herself unconscious this evening, rather than tremble the night away. At least unconscious, if the shiv men found her, she'd take the blade in her sleep; not even know it had happened to her.

God help me.

Just tonight. Just the few hours left of tonight. That's all she had to get through. She nodded. The gesture heartened her, firmed her resolve. Yes, tomorrow, that's exactly what she was going to do: take it to the first newspaper building she came across on Fleet Street and then, money or no money, she was going to be done with this. Let them worry about what to do with that portrait of a man and woman in love; a small picture of Queen Victoria's son, Prince Albert, with his French tart.

It takes patience. An immense amount of patience to do this sort of thing properly. Even so, Babbitt was beginning to wonder whether those two wretched tarts were ever going to move along. Whether, in fact, they were just going to stay rooted beneath that gas lamp until it was finally put out by the lamplighter and the morning was about its business.

He watched them leave and then returned his gaze to the low wall opposite. He knew Annie Chapman was sitting right there, utterly convinced she was invisible in the night. But he could just about see the faint, ghostly outline of her white bonnet bobbing in the dark.

The woman appeared to have no idea she'd been watched all evening. He'd picked up on her at just gone eight when she'd wandered into the Swan, asking around for favours, offering herself more cheaply than she would have normally on account of the bruises and scratches on her face. But all poor Annie had received were shaking heads, and the all too predictable grunted, single-syllable abuse from those shaved and clothed monkeys.

Savages, animals, these people.

What was it his tutor had once told him? A long time ago now, back in better times, the innocent time of childhood. Back before his family undertook their doomed trek across God's wilderness. Before the Indians. Before that shaman had showed him his *calling*.

What was it his tutor said?

'It is the capacity for acts of genuine kindness that separates humans from the animals.'

He remembered that insight so well, even being so young. Remembered looking at the world slightly differently thereafter and categorising people he met as either animals or humans based on their capacity for altruism.

He remembered a hectic summer, full of packing and preparations. 1858. His father had decided fantastic business opportunities awaited him on the far side of America, even though his various businesses were doing a healthy trade in New York. It was a place called Oregon that he was certain would make him rich. So the whole family was going, with just their dearest heirlooms. Everything else was for sale.

That summer, only nine, he'd been a silent observer, judge and juror for the procession of people who entered his parents' parlour to wish them *bon voyage*, or enquire about a business detail. He'd silently judged them on the simplest, most casual gestures. A trades-man who might enter the house, see him standing in the foyer and offer him a friendly wink before going to talk to his father – *human*. An opportunistic salesman looking to take advantage of his father's distracted mind and sell him snake oil and other worthless medicines for the journey ahead – *animal*.

He still played that game from time to time. Watching people and how they treated each other. But the game always seemed to produce the same results. Animal after animal after animal.

The humans were all long gone. All animals now.

He sighed, straightened his stiff legs as he stood up and began to slowly cross Hanbury Street.

CHAPTER 32

8th September 1888, Whitechapel, London

Annie thought she heard the light tapping of shoe soles across the street.

'Hello?' She got up off the low wall. 'Hello? Someone there?'

Then it was gone. She chided herself for being so silly and jumpy. If it was anything, it was a fox. Those animals practically owned the streets once humankind had gone to bed. She slowly sat down again on the wall, praying for the last few hours of dark to hurry up and end. The faint peel of a bell chimed the hour: it was four in the morning. Another hour and the first workers would be getting up, making the street a safer place for her once more. And half an hour after that, the sky would be a pallid grey, and even here in Whitechapel, one or two foolhardy birds would have some desultory tune they wanted to sing.

Annie was feeling hopeful about today. Just a few more hours and then she was going to make her way west, towards the City and Fleet Street. And who knows? Perhaps she was going to be enjoying a hearty breakfast of sausages and bacon, with money in her bag for the story and the picture.

She heard the soft brushing of movement – cloth swishing against cloth.

Right behind her.

She'd just started to turn around when she felt a hand roughly mash her lips against her teeth, her nose pinched firmly, someone pulling her back off the low wall. She landed on her back in a small yard, looking up at a very dark sky. She tried screaming into the palm, hoping in the stillness of the night that the other two girls might still just about hear her cry. But the best she could muster was a muffled whimper.

'Best to be quiet now, Annie Chapman.' A gentle whisper from above. 'I don't wish to use the knife, but I shall if I need to.'

She felt something sharp probing her left ear and recoiled from it. 'Be still now. That's the tip of my blade in your ear. One little push and it'll be through your eardrum as if it were a pie crust and into your brain in no time.'

She stilled herself immediately.

'I'm going to remove my hand and you and I are going to talk. If you're a good, helpful girl, Annie, you're going to walk away with some money in your pocket. If you're not . . .' There really was no need to finish that.

She nodded.

Babbitt lifted his hand off her lips. 'Annie, dear Annie. Things are not so good for you, are they? You should be tucked up in a bed at this hour of the morning.'

'G-got no money.'

'Hmmm, I suspected that. No business for you this evening?'

Her mouth opened; she wanted to say something.

'Go on, what is it?'

'Are y-you . . . are you . . . ?'

'Am I the one who killed Bill? Polly?'

No point lying to her. She'd guess. More importantly, he needed to earn a little of her trust right now; he needed to give her a toe-hold of hope. Sense the possibility that co-operation with him was a way out for her.

'I won't lie to you, Annie. Yes, regretfully that was me. They weren't as helpful as I'm hoping you're going to be.'

'You . . . you want that l-locket b-back?'

He shrugged and smiled, not that she could see his lips in the gloom, but she could hear it in his voice. 'Oh, I have that already. Lovely little piece, isn't it? I had a goldsmith look at it. Very nice piece. No, it's not that I'm after, Annie.'

'The p-picture . . . the picture inside! I got it! I got it right on me!'

She seemed so very keen to talk. The blade tickling her ear lobe was helping, of course.

'In me bag!' she gasped. 'R-right 'ere in m-me bag!'

He looked down at the threadbare floral printed bag on the muddy ground beside her in the small yard. He reached for it and tipped it out beside her head. 'My dear, I presume these are all your worldly possessions?'

She nodded.

'Not really very much to show for a lifetime on this earth, is it?' he asked as his fingers picked through the meagre offering of personal effects scattered beside her.

'I 'ad me own 'ome once,' she replied.

Babbitt smiled at her distractedly. 'Really?' The poor woman was showing some spirit, some shrewdness, talking to him like that. Trying to build a relationship with him in the few moments she had left.

Clever girl.

'I 'ad an 'usband, an' me b-babies, an 'ome, n-nice things an' all,' she continued.

'But somewhere it all went wrong, did it, Annie? Hmmm?'

'Me daughter d-died an' . . . an' me an' 'im split . . . an'—'

'And you took to drink, and then, finally, whoring, to pay for the drink?'

'Y-yes.'

He sighed. 'It's a horrible world, isn't it, Annie?' he replied as his fingers found a folded envelope. It rustled as he probed hopefully inside. 'Ahhhh . . . now *this* feels promising.'

'I . . . I kept it s-safe.' She swallowed anxiously. 'The m-man in the picture . . . I think it's—'

'Someone very important?'

She nodded quickly.

'Of course it is. That's why they've paid for someone like me to come and find it. Can't have "the great and the good" looking as fallible and immoral as the rest of us lowly peasants now, can we?' From inside his dark coat he pulled out a small candle and set it carefully on the ground. 'That's supposedly what sets *them* apart from us lot; the *riff-raff*. Why they have the nice things, the privileges. Because they're meant to be a cut above common folk.'

'They . . . th-they're no b-better than . . . than us . . .' she uttered quickly. Almost challenging him.

Oh, such a plucky, clever girl, trying to join a common cause with me. So often his victims tended to stare dumbstruck at him, waiting silently for their deaths like dumb animals. But this one, this Annie, had a spark of courage to her.

'Indeed,' he said, reaching into his pockets for his box of matches. 'The rich, the great and the good: they're no better than us at all.'

Over the years, working for one paymaster or another, he'd seen the degrading abuses the rich and the powerful indulged in, the disgusting carnal perversions they wallowed in, and yet there you would find them on any given Sunday morning, in their finest, on their knees in church, pillars of the community, patrons of charities. The great and the good, hands clasped piously and eyes closed, savouring the choicest moments of the night before, or ruminating on self-serving plans, transactions to improve their standing, their wealth, their influence. No different in any meaningful way to the petty arguments, the brawls, the acts of spiteful cruelty, the self-ishness in any given public house or dockside bar on any night of the week.

'You're *all* the same, to be truthful,' he uttered, pulling a match out of the box and striking it. Annie recoiled at the momentary glare, twisted her head a little to see what he was doing.

'Why . . . why y-you lightin' a c-candle?'

He ignored her question. 'I once listened to a holy man preach; a pastor, as it happens. When I first went to New York.' Babbitt settled down cross-legged beside her. He pulled the blade away from her ear. She seemed suitably cowed for him not to need to hold it there as he talked. 'Only heard him preach the once, but he said something quite remarkable. And what he said made perfect sense of this rotting world. Shall I tell you what he said?'

Annie jerked her head silently.

'He said that all the souls that God had ever planned for this world had already been born.' He looked at her and his eyes narrowed. 'That's one hell of a thing to say. Isn't that an incredible idea? That every new baby born is inhabited by a returned soul; one that has lived on this earth before. But returned here to live yet again because he or she was not moral enough, decent enough, to proceed on to the hereafter. It made sense to me, what he said. I never forgot that sermon.' He shook his head and then looked down at Annie. 'Do you see? That explains why this modern world of ours, Annie, is so wrong. Why people can do the things they do to each other so . . . so readily.'

He gazed at the candle flame flickering in its own pool of melting wax.

'I can't tell you how hard I've looked to find a truly good person. A *selfless* person. Someone who might just be a genuinely new soul.' He sighed. 'But there are none, not anymore. We're all spoiled, you see? We're all doomed to die and return, die and return, to a world that is becoming more and more like a vision of Hell itself. And I just . . .' He shook his head, 'I just can't believe this is what was meant to be. You want to know what else I think?'

Her head nodded quickly.

'I think something has gone wrong with the *machinery* of the afterlife, of purgatory. It has broken. It's like a sewage pipe, blocked and backing up.'

He looked down at her and began tapping the tip of the blade into the palm of his hand. 'This should be a deserted world by now, entirely empty. Not a single living human soul upon it. Every spirit that was ever meant to have lived and been tested on our earth should, by now, have found its way to where it needed to go. Heaven or Hell.'

'You're going to k-kill m-me, aren't you?' Annie's face finally crumpled and folded with fear. Tears rolled out of the side of her eyes and down into her hair, her ears. 'P-please . . . I'm a good girl, I am . . .'

Babbitt raised a finger to his lips to hush her. 'This is no life for you, Annie. You can see that, can't you? Whoring for a handful of small coins? Coins you spend on a little gin to numb your senses?'

'P-please . . . I never done any wrong to any—'

He pursed his lips. 'Shhhhh. Just a little sting.' He leant over her with the knife.

'Please! Don't 'urt me! You got that picture! You got what you come for—'

He clamped his palm again over her lips. 'I'm not hurting you, Annie. I'm *releasing* you.'

The tip of the blade slid quickly into the soft skin beneath her left ear, up to the hilt. And with the flick of his wrist and a hard tug upwards, it emerged out the front of her throat.

'Shhh . . . be still,' he cooed softly, lifting her chin up firmly to open the wound. 'It'll be over very soon, my dear, and you'll be free.'

He watched her hands scrabble and snatch ineffectually at his, her legs scissoring, her heels drumming and scraping against the ground.

'Just a little longer.'

He watched by the weak, guttering light of the candle as her eyes darted first one way and then the other, until they finally rolled upwards, the pupils almost invisible.

She's done.

He licked his forefinger and thumb, preparing to pinch out the flame, when a thought occurred to him. He reached down to pick up the small photograph. His clients wanted this picture back in their hands – proof the job had been successfully completed. All the awkward loose ends tied up neatly and nicely. But an unprofessional curiosity was teasing him. No . . . he didn't *need* to know which rich banker's son, which lord of the realm, or member of parliament, had foolishly had an affair with a tart and produced an illegitimate child. Not being particularly familiar with the faces of Great Britain's privileged elite, he imagined the portrait was not going to mean a great deal to him. But still . . .

He held it close to the naked flame. The young woman he noticed first. So beautiful. Such delicate and refined features. But the man standing beside her, there was more than a gentleman's lust in his eyes; it seemed like genuine infatuation.

Then his mind managed to place the young man's face in context. The distinctive bridge of his nose, the eyes, the moustache, waxed at its tips. And in a single beat of his heart, he understood why so much money was being paid. More than that, he realised he was in as much danger as that reckless ape Bill Tolly had been.

He swore softly.

CHAPTER 33

30th September 1888, Holland Park, London

Argyll savoured the warmth of her back with the tip of his finger, ran it gently down the long slender 'S' of her spine as she lay on her side. Dawn wasn't far off. By the faint grey light seeping in through the gap in the drapes of her room, he could see the coral pink rim of her ear, at sea amidst the waves and troughs of auburn hair. He watched her narrow shoulder rise and fall and listened to the soft rustling sound of her breathing, and felt the strangest thing.

He felt complete.

Last night they had made love. Mary taking the lead, showing him the things she liked, showing him how moments could be made to last hours. And finally, exhausted, contented, they both fell asleep, Mary wrapped in his thick, muscular arms.

Argyll's sleep, for once, had been entirely untroubled. No dreams or nightmares, no zoetrope flickering images of mutilation and murder. No Indians. No shaman. No shrill, hectoring voice. Just a deep, restful sleep.

The slither of grey light through the drapes had awoken him; that and the rattle of the wheels of a milk cart going past. And now he had the pleasure of watching Mary sleeping. He eased himself up on one elbow and looked down at her face. He noticed that the slight furrow of concern, that always seemed to exist in its own narrow space between her brows, was gone, her face now at rest. And her top lip, delicately curved like Cupid's bow, pushed by the pillow a little to one side to make her mouth look like it was pursed thoughtfully. A fretful decision to be made: *which yard of muslin do you think, darling? The teal . . . or the cerise?*

Beautiful. Innocent. Wise beyond her years and so very strong-willed. He imagined young Mary could be anything she put her mind to. And yet here she lay, having given herself, her heart, to him. It was such an odd, lovely feeling. Even with his past life still a mystery – and who knows, perhaps it always would be – right now, for the first time, he felt entirely complete. He realised everything he wanted, everything he needed, was in this one bedroom, embodied in this sleeping, porcelain angel beside him.

'Mary?' he whispered. She stirred and murmured, her brows flickering, her eyes dancing beneath her lids, chasing rainbows across barley fields. He had something he wanted to say out loud. To hear it. To make it real, make it something that existed *outside* of his muddled head, instead of inside. Something this precious, this wonderful, he wanted kept as far away as possible from the horrors that flitted across his mind. Not a thought. He wanted it to be something heard. Something real.

'I love you,' he whispered quietly, testing those words on her now, while she slept. The words made him tremble. He wanted to try it again. Softly. 'I love you.'

It was the purest sound. Those three words said without any hidden agenda. Honest. Argyll heard the tap of a solitary tear on the pillow beneath him. He wondered when the last time he'd cried was. If ever. He touched a craggy cheek and felt the damp. And felt more human than he ever had since waking from his troubled coma.

Once more. Still the gentlest murmur. 'I love you, Mary.' Too much of a coward to say it to her awake in case she laughed at how childlike it sounded coming out of his mouth. But perhaps over breakfast this morning. Perhaps he would reach out across their little breakfast table, hold her hands and say it.

Love, is it?

Argyll frowned irritably at the intrusion of the voice. He leant back on the pillow until his eyes were gazing up at webs of hairline cracks in the old paint on the ceiling. That voice . . . He fancied he could make its face out of the faint dry lines of peeling paint above. Yes. There. Two eyes, a pig's snout for a mouth beneath them, and above, the vague suggestion of the horns of some tormenting demon. Very apt.

Love, is it?

Yes, he replied. I love her.

You pitiful fool. Love doesn't have a place here. There is no love here.

The voice was louder in his mind than last time, as if it had found somewhere to sit and be comfortable, that was closer to him than before.

Those who can love, those capable of love, have long since gone away. All that remains is a world populated by these pitiful ghosts. Wraiths that prey on each other, cannibalise each other. There isn't love here, fool! There isn't a single act of love here. There isn't a single act of kindness here. You know that, don't you? You remember, don't you?

Mary . . . she's kind.

He hated its laugh.

Kind, is she?

Yes. All that she'd done for him these last few weeks, the last month. Caring for someone she loved and who had no memory left of the love he must have once had for her. That was kindness, wasn't it? That was love.

She is like all the others. Selfish, scheming for what she can get.

Damn you! Leave me, will you?

No.

Why will you not?

He thought he saw the eyes shift, the pig's snout snap shut. The horns twitch. *She's playing you for the fool you are . . . 'John'.*

Go away!

She's a clever one, too. Very clever. Look around you.

He wished there was something to distract him, more noises from outside in the street. He wished the clock downstairs in the hallway could tick a little louder to drown out this horrible dry rasping in his mind. It sounded childlike and spiteful.

Look around you, you empty-headed fool. This room, this house – this isn't a home. This isn't your *home!*

Yes, it is.

It's not a home; it's a cage. And she's made it for you, trapped you like a wild animal.

No.

Look! LOOK!

He didn't need to, because he had a suspicion that what this poisonous little imp was telling him might have a grain of truth to it. Small things he'd already noticed: dust sheets hastily bundled into a cupboard; a child's playroom right at the top of the house; dark patches on the walls where paintings must have hung until very recently.

Mary told him they been living here for what? A year? But

wouldn't there be more of themselves stamped on this home? More of *him*, possessions, artefacts of the old John Argyll? Instead, this home – comfortable, secure and cosy as it was – felt strangely like a stage set, like the sort of diorama one would see within a glass display case for some stuffed species of ferocious wild animal. A museum exhibit.

Do you see?

He ignored the voice. It didn't need encouraging to come and find somewhere closer to sit.

Do you remember? I think you do.

Remember what?

The devil makes work only for idle hands to do.

He stared at the creature's small squinty eyes in the ceiling, hating its squat ugliness, its snout, its stubby horns. And hairline cracks that looked like a little pair of legs belonging to a terrier dog. He stared at it and hated that such an ugly thing was here in Mary's room, looking down at them, watching her sleep.

Please, go away! Please, I want you to leave me alone!

You need me.

NO! His balled fist knuckled his temple – as if trying to dig the malignant creature from his mind. NO. I don't need you. I need Mary. I love her. I LOVE her!

Even if this home was an illusion, even if there was some part of what Mary had been telling him that didn't quite add up, make sense, some small half-truth or petty lie – he didn't care. This . . . this . . . one man, one woman, curled in a bed together and a slant of morning light resting across them, the stillness of this moment; he wished it could last for eternity. If it was an illusion, if it was a lie, little more than a museum diorama made specifically for him, then he could happily live in it forever, in this glass cage, just as long as he had Mary to share it with him.

A museum exhibit of two.

There was no answer from the pig. He waited. Listened to the receding clop of a horse's hooves, Mary's gentle breathing, the twitter of sparrows in a tree outside.

Nothing else.

Argyll smiled. It was silenced. He could hope that perhaps it was gone, even.

CHAPTER 34

9th September 1888, The Grantham Hotel, The Strand, London

It hung suspended in an empty jam jar full of cloudy water; one of Annie Chapman's kidneys. The other left on the ground in that small yard on Hanbury Street. Babbitt left it on the ground beside her head with the rest of the contents of her lower abdominal cavity; strings of offal draping back over her left shoulder to the gaping wound from her pelvis, all the way up to her sternum.

The newspapers had given her murder a lot more attention than the other two. If the accounts being reported were to be believed, her body had been discovered less than half an hour after Babbitt had finished his work there. The column writers and editors in Fleet Street were making as much as possible out of every grisly little detail they'd gotten their hands on. But Scotland Yard, despite their ineptitude and the eagerness of their officers to sell titbits to probing Fleet Street hacks waving their fat wallets, had managed to hold back one or two important details.

Babbitt smiled. All of a sudden, with this particular murder, the police were being *very* careful with the information they were parcelling out to the public. Which could only mean one thing: they – his clients – were receiving his 'message' loud and clear. That he could frame them, that he could pull them right out into the open with this, if he so chose.

Annie, poor Annie, had been left as his clear warning to them, her remains staged to frame their three symbolic penalties.

. . . And if the oath of silence I make before my brothers I break, let it be that my throat be cut across, that my left breast be torn open and my heart and vitals taken from thence and thrown over my left shoulder . . .

It had been anathema to him, counter-intuitive to be so horribly theatrical, to attract attention like this to his work. So very unprofessional. But they needed to hear his warning message immediately. He needed them to be fully aware that he had an inkling what their intentions might be. If they had no qualms about disposing of that cheap shiv man Tolly, then despite the fact that Babbitt had offered them assurances of his confidentiality, despite the fact that he was certain his clients in New York had vouched for him, these silly gentlemen may decide that once the contract was done, they might deal with him the same way.

Poor Annie's ritualistic mutilations – her tongue cut out and placed on her chest, his candle very deliberately left behind – was a clear message to his employers that he could, and quite happily would, break his personal credo of confidentiality if they were entertaining notions of double-crossing him.

The paper he was reading this morning in his room, *The Examiner,* was making the murder a front page feature for the third day in a row now. Still there was no mention of the candle left behind at the scene, nor a detailed account of the mutilations. But in various editorials, the Masons were now being euphemistically hinted at. Enough details of the ritualistic *modus operandi* must have leaked out from the policemen working the murders for them to dare suggest a Masonic connection.

He smiled. *There's your warning, gentlemen.*

Back to work.

He finished writing his account of this particular contract on the hotel's letter-headed stationery and tucked it into a manila envelope. It was all in there, every detail he'd learned from Tolly and those two tarts. In his two sides of meticulously neat handwriting, there was mention of the foolish man in the photograph. The cause of all this crimson.

The very heart of the matter.

Prince Albert Victor Christian Edward; 'Eddy' to his friends, 'Bertie' to his mother, Queen Victoria.

There was enough on those two pieces of foolscap to ignite a powder keg. Babbitt chuckled at the thought of it, like a naughty schoolboy preparing a classroom prank. The future King of England, Eddy, guilty not only of falling in love with and screwing a common girl – a French one at that, quite possibly even a Catholic – but far, far worse than that. As a result of the ill-conceived affair, he'd produced an illegitimate child. And the silent establishment –

the Masons, or perhaps some even more secret sub-set within the Masons – had carefully set about tidying up the mess left behind by the stupid prince. Their complicity was stamped all over the murders.

What mischief this note could cause.

Every day the papers were filled with stories written for the working man. Stories phrased in clever ways to anger tired men at lunchtime with the dirt of labour on their hands. Stories of the rich and privileged, stories of unspeakable extravagances, selfishness, foolishness. And Eddy, future King of England, an all too regular character in this enraging pantomime. Babbitt could only imagine what sort of revolutionary fire he could ignite by applying a single candle's flame to that kind of a tinderbox.

He dropped the small photograph into the envelope, rough and bent around the edges with flecks of the photographic emulsion peeling from too much handling, but still very clearly that stupid young prince clutching adoringly at a common-born woman. He tucked the envelope under the jam jar and, for a moment, watched the half of Annie's kidney bob in its cloudy solution.

All the evidence was there, right there on the room's writing table.

Now, there were other matters to attend to.

He already had passage booked aboard a cargo ship leaving Liverpool in approximately two months' time. Not knowing the precise details of this contract before he'd set sail from New York, he had allowed himself three months for the job to be done before returning home. His business had been wrapped up far quicker than he thought it would be, and now caution dictated he would be better finding himself a ship home soon.

But the matter was not finished yet, was it? His clients still owed him the second half of his fee and without that, the income earned from this job wasn't going to do a great deal more than cover the costs he'd incurred coming to England and his hotel suite booked for three months' use.

There was also the principle. A fee was still owed.

He stroked the bristles of his sideburns, deep in thought, watching strands of organic sediment seesaw down through the jar's murky water, past the kidney that was already beginning to wrinkle and pucker.

The rooms were already paid for, the ship was already booked. He had a couple of months ahead of him now. A couple of months which he could use to lie low, perhaps even explore London a little more. He knew the Victoria Docks quite well now and the Royal Albert Docks; Millwall, too. A warren of warehouses, backstreet water inlets and canals a man could lose himself in. A couple of months to take his time, relax, read, meditate.

All he needed to do now was arrange a time and place to collect what he was still owed, and be sure to make it very clear when they met that he had in his possession, sitting on his hotel room's writing table, enough evidence to . . . well, to cause these gentlemen some serious problems. Just in case, that is, they were entertaining the notion of jumping him before he could leave with his fee.

He picked up his ink pen and pulled out another sheet of the hotel's writing paper from the drawer and began to carefully word an advert that would appear in the *Illustrated London News* in a couple of days, if he managed to drop it downstairs in the concierge's pigeon-hole before lunch time.

CHAPTER 35

11th September 1888, Blackfriars, London

Warrington acknowledged to himself that he was trembling because he was nervous; not as he'd earlier tried to tell himself that it was because it was a surprisingly cool night for September.

'Nervous' was perhaps not the right word to use. 'Scared witless' did it more justice. He felt too exposed standing out here, even if it was the quieter end of West India Quay. He looked up at the tall brick warehouses behind him. Gaslight lit a pair of windows from within; square amber eyes that regarded him suspiciously from on high. No doubt shipping clerks working late on manifests and ledgers, ready for an early start for the dockworkers tomorrow morning.

By the wan light of the moon, playing hide and seek behind racing clouds, he checked the hour on his timepiece. It was twenty minutes past midnight.

He's late.

According to Rawlinson, the Candle Man was *never* late. Wholly reliable in every important way, that's what their American colleagues had informed them. But not reliable tonight, so it seemed.

He's playing games with us.

The murder of the tart called Chapman at the beginning of the week was his handiwork. That much was for sure. He'd made it quite clear with the ridiculously theatrical gesture: the trademark candle of his left beside her body. What was the fool thinking about, doing that? And the way he'd mutilated her? Yes, of course, they'd instructed him to make it look like the work of some deranged fool; some insane person to which no notion of motive or logic could be applied. But to mutilate her in the specific way he had . . . to leave her so *symbolically arranged*? They'd had the devil of a time over the last week keeping as much of the details as they could out of the newspapers. Even with the tacit assistance of both Scotland Yard's and the Met's chief inspectors, one of the policemen who'd first attended the scene of the crime must have spoken out of turn. Revealed enough details – none of them officially confirmed, of course – to allow the scribblers on Fleet Street to start coming up with dangerously suggestive theories about Freemasons.

He's warning us.

He knows. He suspects, at least.

That's what Warrington was beginning to suspect. The Candle Man had somehow managed to figure out that they had no intention of letting him go on his merry way back to America. The man must have figured out the stakes were too high. Which could only mean one thing.

He's seen the photograph. He knows it's Prince Albert. And if so, then he'd probably understand how desperately important it was for this indiscretion to be completely guaranteed. There were socialist rumblings in the capital; all over Europe, in fact. Next year was the centenary of the French Revolution. Socialist and working men's groups were planning a Europe-wide organisation, a congress of workers' delegates, to meet to mark the occasion. Even now, editorials were talking up the notion that something similar to the French Revolution might be sparked here in England. The Candle Man was clearly no fool. He had understood how the stability, the very future of this country – the British Empire, even – hung on how tidily Eddy's little mess was cleared up.

God help us if that's the truth.

Warrington glanced out into the dark. His five men were out there, hidden in the corners of the warehouse. Out of sight but able to see him standing in a pool of moonlight in the middle of the wide, empty floor. Faint spears of pallid light angled down through the grimy skylight in the roof, through panels missing their glass. He could hear the soft cooing of pigeons in the iron spars directly above him and the patter of dripping water somewhere inside the abandoned and empty building, echoing between the ground and the low roof.

He'd had quite enough of this game-playing. 'Hello?!'

His voice rang through the warehouse, stirring the flutter of wings from above and causing a dusting of fluffy feathers to fall down into the beams of moonlight. He hated that too-obvious tremble in his voice. He tried again, this time doing his best to infuse his voice with a tone of irritable impatience.

'Hello? Are you there, or not?'

'*Oh . . . I'm here.*' The voice was no more than a finely judged whisper. There was no need to shout in this place; every little noise seemed to carry. '*I've been here for a while.*'

Warrington's heart skipped. How long? Long enough to watch them arrive? To hear him give instructions to the others to find hiding places? *Shit*.

He heard the soft tap and scrape of footsteps approaching him. Slow and deliberate. Not a man in a hurry to do the deal. Not a man unsettled or nervous. Perhaps the suppositions were all his? Perhaps the Candle Man had no idea at all that Warrington intended him not to leave this place alive.

Just remain calm, George. Make sure the job's done. Warrington adjusted his waistcoat, cleared his throat. 'Come on out, then, where I can see you.'

Presently his eyes picked out a tall, dark shape standing cautiously just outside of the undulating pool of moonlight.

'A bit of a melodramatic place you've chosen for us to meet,' said Warrington.

'*It suits our business, George.*' He took a step closer into the edge of pallid light. Beneath the brim of a billycock, his face remained a dark, formless shadow.

'It's, uh . . . it's rather funny you picked that name for me by chance.' Warrington smiled. 'That *is* my first name. A lucky guess?'

'*As I said . . . you look like a George.*'

Warrington's perfunctory laugh sounded giddy and childish. He hated it. 'So . . . I have the other half of your fee. Do you have . . . ?'

'*Yes, I have the locket Tolly found.*'

'And the . . . uh . . .' He didn't want to attract too much attention to what was inside. 'And the contents of the locket?' he continued, his voice as casual as he could manage.

He heard a soft, breathy laugh. '*Oh, yes . . . I have that too.*'

'Good. And Tolly involved no one else?'

'*Correct.*'

Warrington bent down and picked up the small parcel at his feet. 'Then, on behalf of my colleagues, I'd like to thank you.' He held out the parcel to the Candle Man. A gloved hand stretched out through the moon beams and took it from him. Even though this man was going to be dead inside of five minutes Warrington decided that the parcel should contain real money, just in case he chose to inspect it there and then. In fact, that might be a useful distraction. As he counted his money, Warrington could touch his hat – that was the signal.

'Do you not wish to count it?'

No answer. He heard the jingle of a bag buckle, the slap of a leather flap and the parcel rustle as it was tucked away somewhere.

Warrington quickly touched the peak of his top hat. The sign for his men to close in. 'We're very pleased with how this turned out. But . . . you have caused us some difficulties with the last one. Why did you—?'

'Make it look Masonic?'

'Indeed.'

A long pause. Warrington listened intently for the approaching footfalls of his men. They were no light-footed assassins. Two of them, Smith and Warren, were detective inspectors from Scotland Yard. The other three were all veterans from that nasty little war in Afghanistan: Hain, Orman and Robson. Mercenaries now. Those three had seen enough barbarity in those far-off mountains to cope with a little shiv-work for the Lodge. Most importantly, all five of them were Masons. Junior brothers, yes, but still bound by the code of silence.

'I suspect you have made plans for me, hmm?'

Warrington did his best to look utterly bemused. 'I . . . I'm sorry?'

'A foolish prince?' The Candle Man took another step towards him and Warrington found himself nervously taking a half-step back.

'I really . . . I don't know—'

'Yes . . . but you see I do know. I know now.'

'Know what?'

'I wasn't sure. That's why I had to come. But now I know for certain.'

'For Christ's sake, what the devil are you talking about?!'

'That you, George, have plans to cross me.'

Warrington saw the blur of something large and pale flicker through the slither of moonlight, then bounce heavily and skitter across the floor, leaving an ink-black smear behind it. It took a moment for him to understand what he was looking at: the balding pate and the dark beard, a protruding tongue, thick like a cricket ball, and two eyes, glazed and strangely wistful. Detective Inspector Orville Warren.

Warrington's voice was a child's scream. 'NOW!!! KILL HIM NOW!!!'

Babbitt suspected that there were probably more of them out there. This balding, bearded one he'd almost tripped over. Too good an opportunity not to take advantage of. A hand over the hapless man's mouth and a quick slice; the patter of gushing blood had sounded like nothing more than a dripping tap.

He'd hoped to have some more time to talk to George. He'd hoped the head resting on the floor between them, a silent witness to their softly spoken discussions, might just have focused George's jittery mind a little. Caused him to wave his clumsy bloodhounds back into their corners and listen for a moment. But instead, his woman-like shriek had triggered the others. He could feel their thundering feet vibrate on the rotten planks of the wooden floor, racing towards them.

No time to talk, then.

Time to run.

He darted out of the pool of moonlight, away from the sound of rasping breath; heavyset men, from the noises they were making, and no knowing for sure how many of them exactly. He ran far more lightly than them, making much less noise. Behind him, George was barking useless orders for his men to spread out and find him, stupidly covering up the receding patter of his footsteps.

He was heading for the rear of the warehouse, the delivery entrance, double doors that rolled aside on rusty castors. The delivery entrance opened onto a small courtyard, the courtyard's gates opened onto a backstreet, the backstreet split into a three-way junction, any one way as good as the others for escape. He'd discovered this place, an abandoned print works, several days ago, and made sure to walk through the warehouse and know its layout thoroughly.

Heading for the delivery doors in the pitch black, he collided with something that grunted on impact. The next moment, he was sprawled on the wooden floor, tangled up in someone else's fleshy arms and legs.

'Fuck!' he heard a man growl. 'Over 'ere! Fucker's over 'ere!'

He felt fat fingers scrabbling at his face, finding and grabbing the lapel of his coat. He could feel the man's body tense and lurch with exertion as something swung though the air, aimed at his head. It knocked his hat off.

Babbitt's response was instinctive, silent and deadly, although the lumbering oaf on top of him wasn't going to appreciate that for at least another half a minute. For now he'd think it was a limp-wristed punch at his belly. But it wasn't; it was nine inches of slender blade embedded to the hilt, and the odd upward tugging sensation this man felt directly after was the serrated edge being yanked savagely upwards, slicing into his liver and opening his stomach, so that any attempt to get up would result in his feet tangling, and most likely tripping, in the loops of intestine that spilled out.

'Shit, 'old fuckin' still!' grunted the man, still seemingly unaware that the front of him was now open.

Babbitt was getting ready to stick him again with his knife when he felt the man's body tense and lurch again.

This time, Babbitt felt the world explode.

A shower of brilliant white sparks suddenly erupted in front, no, behind his eyes; his ears full of a shrill ringing that completely blocked out the noises of everything else. He felt the scrape of rough splinters across his left cheek and realised he was sliding across the floor.

His feet seemed to be the only part of him that could function, while the rest of him flopped rag-doll-like.

Run, fool! Run!

His feet got him off the floor as he cradled his spinning head. His legs carried him in dizzy zigzags towards a softly glowing slither of moonlight: the gap between the open delivery doors. He slammed against them, producing a rattle of chains and counterweights, rusty wheels and loose planks. Enough to broadcast to everyone inside the building exactly where he was. He heard none of that, though. His ears were still playing a deafening white noise.

He was staggering across the courtyard now, the light of the moon almost blinding like daylight by comparison to the darkness of the print works. His shoulder crashed heavily against the loose railing gate and spilled him out into the backstreet. He tripped and rolled across uneven paving slabs. Up again, his feet, his legs, undeniably the only part of him doing anything useful. And he wobbled uncertainly, his eyes now no longer showing fireworks, instead offering him a spinning kaleidoscope facsimile of the backstreet.

He picked a direction and ran; more like a drunkard's staggering waltz than a run.

His mind was still reeling from the blow, but now it was closing down. The blow had done damage to his head. A hammer, perhaps a crowbar, that's what that man had used. Losing the capacity to think straight, to do anything, he was vaguely aware that his hands were now empty, that he'd dropped his beloved knife at some point, somewhere. He was vaguely aware that the side of his head and his face were wet, streaming; that his mouth tasted of copper coins. Finally, as if it was the very next moment, although it couldn't possibly be, he was foggily aware of being slumped in the gutter of a much wider street that now glowed faint amber from a street lamp, instead of the ink-blue of moonlight. And the last thing his closing-down, dying mind managed to be aware of was a pair of small feminine hands tugging and probing the folds of his coat.

PART II

CHAPTER 36

30th September 1888 (9.00 am),
Great Queen Street, Central London

'It has been what? Two weeks?'

'Nearly three, actually, Oscar.'

Warrington looked at the other four men of 'The Steering Committee' in the room with him, the same room as last time, the log fire crackling as if it had never been out.

'Three weeks then,' continued Crosbourne. The man had the faintest hint of a European accent. Like their queen, a thin trace of Germanic heredity ran through his veins and his vowels. 'He is probably dead. You said, did you not, George, that the man's head was smashed in with an . . . an ice pick?'

'A claw hammer. It was a claw hammer.'

Warrington recalled the poor man, Detective Inspector Smith, on his knees and holding his guts in, making his shaky report. Telling him he'd landed a mortal blow on the man's head; that he'd actually had to jerk the thing out of his skull to try for another swipe.

'A claw hammer, then. It strikes me that this "Candlestick" chap,' said Oscar, with wry amusement at the theatricality of the man's professional name, 'most probably died of his wounds that night.'

'Candle Man,' corrected Warrington.

Henry Rawlinson nodded slowly, thoughtfully. 'That's the most likely thing.'

'Would someone not have found his body? Reported it to the police?'

Rawlinson set his teacup down in its saucer. 'There are a dozen bodies found every morning in London. Most of them remain unidentified, don't they, George?'

Warrington nodded.

'There, then,' said Oscar. 'He could have died during the night, he might have died of his injury the next day, or the day after. The point is, gentlemen, if he lived, surely we would have heard from him by now?'

That's what had been keeping Warrington awake at night these last few weeks, jumping in bed at the sound of every creaking timber in his grand townhouse, the rustling of foxes in his walled garden, the thought of a midnight visit from the Candle Man.

'The point is, we risk attracting attention from the Lodge if we keep using their footmen as you have been, George, to try and locate this . . . this *ghost*.'

The three men who'd survived their brush with him – Robson, Hain and Orman – were reliable Masons. Their confidentiality was assured. But they were just that: Masons, not members of this particular committee.

'Need I remind you, Oscar,' said Warrington, 'that there is evidence out there still of the prince's affair?'

The stupid prince, thinking with his stupid dick.

Like a child grabbing for a brightly coloured toy in a toyshop, he acted without conscience or any sense of responsibility. If Warrington had his way, he would have arranged for Prince 'Eddy' Albert to have been done away with, along with the woman and the baby. For now, the idiot was being kept busy with one royal engagement after another, as far from London as they could arrange.

'What is it?' asked Rawlinson with a shrug. 'Just a mere trinket, and a photograph of a man. There is no one alive now who understands the significance of the picture, yes?'

'It's a photograph of Prince Albert with an unknown woman and child! That alone is—'

'A man who merely looks a little like Albert, that is all. How many young men mimic his appearance now?' Oscar laughed. 'Every young gentleman in London apes the way the prince fashions himself.'

Rawlinson stroked his chin thoughtfully, gazing at the flames guttering noisily as they fed on the sap spitting from the end of a log. He looked up at the others.

'He had the second half of his fee on him, yes?'

Warrington nodded.

'What if someone found all that money on him?' said Rawlinson. 'On his body?'

The men looked at each other, not sure where that suggestion took them.

'Oscar,' Rawlinson continued, 'I have to say I agree with George: I am exceedingly uncomfortable with the thought that this picture might still be at large. Whether our hired man is dead or not.' He sipped his tea. 'I presume there must be rooms he took in London somewhere. If he is dead, one might presume the locket and the picture would still be sitting there?'

'Did he not have this picture on him when you met, George?' asked one of the others – Geoffrey Mumford – fiddling with the cufflinks on his evening jacket. He was impatient to leave their meeting; he had an opera to go to.

Warrington shook his head. 'I don't believe so. He knew what we were planning to do with him.'

Yes . . . he knew, all right.

'So if your men had not been quite so hasty, I presume he was on the point of giving you instructions on where exactly to retrieve them?'

Warrington stifled a grimace. Not really his men's fault. It had been his fault. His nerves rattled at the sight of poor Warren's head rocking on its side to and fro on the wooden floor between them. Not that it mattered now whose fault it was. The Candle Man clearly had a suspicion of what plans they'd had for him. Coming across Warren hiding in the dark, his suspicions would have been confirmed.

'I think the sensible course of action is to carry on with what you have been doing, George. Softly, softly, of course. There's already enough chattering going on in the ruddy newspapers. This ridiculously theatrical name they're using – what is it?'

'Jack the Ripper,' replied Oscar.

'How many hotels and lodging houses are there in London?' asked Geoffrey. 'Surely you'll not locate his rooms that way?'

'We have been making enquiries discreetly. I think he will have wanted discretion, privacy. Which is why we have restricted our attention to the more exclusive, expensive hotels.'

'The man was a savage killer for hire. I would have imagined he would have chosen something more anonymous, low-key.' said Mumford. 'Perhaps some cheap rooms above a public—'

'No.' Warrington shook his head. 'He is . . . he was . . . he came across to me as educated. And he certainly had enough money to ensure comfort, convenience and all the privacy he required. You know how it is, gentlemen: coins pressed into the palm of a foot-man, a doorman, a concierge.'

The others nodded. Warrington suspected at one time or another, everyone in this room had indulged a peccadillo of some sort in a velvet furnished room somewhere.

'You've not had any results yet?' asked Rawlinson.

'Not yet.'

'And your enquiries are discreet, you say, George?'

Warrington nodded. 'I'm certain we'll find where he was staying soon enough. At the very least, if he *is* dead, there will come a point where money becomes overdue on a room . . .'

Rawlinson smiled. 'Very good, George. Yes, of course.' He settled back in his armchair. 'All right, then. Shall we meet again? Let's say next Tuesday at the same time? Meanwhile, I will explain to the Lodge elders that I need those three chaps of yours, George, a while longer for club business.'

The others stirred, Geoffrey eager to get his waiting carriage and already making for the room's door.

'Gentlemen.' Rawlinson nodded a farewell at them all, but he looked pointedly at Warrington. 'Quiet chat, George?'

Warrington nodded. They waited for the others to leave before Rawlinson spoke. 'George, that was something of a horrendous experience for you, I know. But . . .' He sighed, taking the time to choose his words. 'But such grisly circumstances can sometimes play on your mind. Give a man nightmares.'

Warrington nodded. *Oh, I'm having those all right.* Pretty much every night for the last few weeks he'd awoken sweating, a scream dying on his lips, and his wife sitting bolt upright in bed and staring at him, dumbfounded.

'It can affect your judgement.' Rawlinson sighed again. 'I've seen men's bodies split and broken on a battlefield. I've seen the very worst we can do to each other. I know how horrible it can be. And yes, I also have nightmares. But listen . . . what you saw, what happened at that rendezvous, was jolly bad luck. That's all. Plans go awry; that's the nature of them.' He smiled.

Warrington looked at him. 'He beheaded one man and gutted another like a fish. And he managed to escape us even after his skull was smashed in.'

'Don't mythologise him, George. He had the element of surprise and he caught your men off guard. I think we're all to blame for under-estimating him. He found out we were protecting the interests of the future King of England and he understood we couldn't let him go. So he came to that meeting prepared. But he's almost certainly a dead man now. An unidentified cadaver in a morgue or rotting in an unmarked pauper's grave.' He rested a hand on Warrington's shoulder. 'Don't let this "Candle Man" become a demon in your mind, all right? He was just a normal man, just a hired man.'

Warrington nodded. 'Yes, yes of course.'

'We'll convene next Tuesday, unless your chaps come across something in the interim.'

Warrington bid farewell and stepped out of the stuffy warmth of the club's room.

Just a normal man.

Just a normal man should have died that night. A normal man would have turned up the next morning as a stiff corpse, or floating in the Thames. A normal man wouldn't have just vanished off the face of the earth like he had. Vanished like some sort of ghostly spirit.

CHAPTER 37

1st October 1888 (9.00 am), Holland Park, London

Argyll felt too unsettled, too excited, for the breakfast Mary had laid out for them. His stomach churned and fluttered in a way that made the idea of devouring a thick slice of buttered toast and a boiled egg unthinkable. They sat in an insufferably awkward silence either side of the small breakfast table, both glancing out through the lace curtains at the passing morning traffic on the avenue, commenting occasionally on banal minutiae with a forced, distracted interest.

The enormous and unmentioned fact that hung in the space between them, filled at the moment with nothing but the sound of the tinkling of a teaspoon in a china tea pot, was that they had made love together last night in the secure anonymity of darkness. Not once, but again and again. And now it was broad daylight once more and with it came, unfortunately, the polite, vaguely formal manner they'd both adopted for each other. Not a proper couple just yet.

'Tea?' asked Mary, lifting the tea pot, a pinkie extended from her hand just like a proper lady.

'Hmmm? Oh, yes, please.' He reached for his cup and lifted it towards the proffered pot, just as she leant forward and poured. A piping hot brown stream splashed onto the table and down onto his white cotton shirt.

'Ouch!' he yelled as it scalded his belly.

Mary stopped pouring, her jaw hanging open, aghast. 'Oh, good lord! John, I'm so sorry!'

He tugged the steaming brown stain away from his skin. 'God, that's hot!'

She came around the table and fussed. 'I'm so sorry! Are you all right?'

Argyll nodded. He shrugged off her concern. 'I'm quite fine. A little broiled, but otherwise, you know, I'm quite all right.'

'Oh, but your shirt! Look, I've gone and ruined it!'

He shook his head. 'Not to worry, Mary, I . . .'

'But you have so few shirts, John, and clumsy oaf me, I ruin this one, your nicest one!' She bit her lip, angry with herself for being so inept. 'I shall get it bleached and laundered. There's a launderette round the corner. If I'm quick, perhaps the stain won't settle in.'

'I'll go and change into another one,' he said, pushing his chair back.

'Yes,' she said. 'Quick as you can.'

She watched him double-time out of the morning room, still with an awkward pins-and-needles limp, and clump up the stairs. She decided she was going to buy him some more clothes whilst she was out, before he started asking why his wardrobe was so sparse. Not for the first time, she wondered why he didn't seem to query these things.

Perhaps in his past life he wasn't the kind of man who kept wardrobes full of fine clothes. Maybe he'd been the kind of man who had two shirts for the working week, one for the weekend and the best one for church on Sunday. That would seem to suit his personality. She couldn't imagine John, with his lean and weathered face, had been the kind of man who pursued the whims of fashion vigorously.

She stepped quickly out into the hallway, pulled the key out from beneath the clock on the table and unlocked the door to the cellar. Now that John's leg was working much better – although still a comedian's slapstick limp – she'd pulled the key from the row of hooks in the pantry and taken to locking the door. She didn't want him exploring down there.

She opened the door and hesitated a moment. She could hear the boards of the floor above creaking as John shuffled around his bedroom. Typical of this awkward limbo between being lovers and strangers, if she'd been standing upstairs in that room, he would undoubtedly have insisted she look away as he changed. And she would have done so. How silly.

She bustled quickly down the stairs to the cellar, leaving it open for a little more daylight. John would be a while yet, and anyway, she'd hear him clopping heavily down the stairs. He still took the steps cautiously, not fully trusting his 'woken up' leg yet. She crossed the floor, lifted the lid of the travel chest and dug into the satchel, pulling out a five pound note. Enough for the launderette, a few more suits and shirts for John, and the sundries she needed to get whilst out shopping today.

She crossed the floor, climbed the steps again, closed and locked the door with one hand, as she tucked the money into her purse with the other. She turned to head back up the hall to the front room when she saw John standing stock still at the bottom of the stairs, watching her.

'Oh, gawd!' she gasped, flapping her hand in front of her face. 'You gave me a fright.'

He stared back at her, his face clouded for a moment with confusion. He cocked his head. 'Why did you go down there?'

'Oh, no reason, really. I was . . . I thought I heard a . . .' Her voice trailed to nothing. 'Now, did you bring your dirty shirt down?' she asked, casually sliding the cellar door key back beneath the clock's brass stand and then reaching out to adjust the collar of his clean shirt for him.

He held it out.

'Good.'

She took it and stepped into the front room, grabbing her coat. 'I'll not be too long. I'll drop your shirt in at the launderette and then go and get something for our dinner, and collect the shirt on the way back.' She stepped past him into the hall and looked at a bundle of paper protruding from their letter box. 'The newspaper's been delivered. There,' she said, pulling it out and handing it to him. 'You enjoy a read, my dear. I'll be back before lunchtime. Perhaps we can take a walk this afternoon, if it's nice?'

Argyll nodded distractedly, as if his thoughts were a thousand miles away.

She reached up on tiptoes to kiss his rough cheek. He didn't stoop. 'You all right, John?'

His eyes focused back on her; the familiar friendly set of his face returned. 'Yes . . . I'm fine.'

'I said I'll be back by lunchtime.'

He smiled. 'All right, Mary.'

She turned, opened the front door and stepped outside. 'Best go and finish your breakfast, love,' she said. 'Before it gets cold.'

He nodded obediently, waved at her as she closed the front door.

See? What did I tell you? She's playing with you. Playing you for a fool.

Argyll stared at the ticking clock, filling the quiet hallway with its regular heartbeat.

Tac . . . tac . . . tac . . . tac . . .

Well? The little demon with its ugly snout was hopping excitedly in his mind, from one stunted leg to the other.

You saw what she put underneath, didn't you?

CHAPTER 38

1st October 1888 (11.00 am),
The Grantham Hotel, The Strand, London

L iz stopped on the pavement opposite the hotel. 'That's the one.'
'You sure?'

'S'what the locksmith said: The Grantham Hotel on the Strand.'

'It looks too posh an' fancy,' uttered Cath unhappily. 'They won't
let the likes of us in.'

'What's the worst that can 'appen?' She shrugged. 'They tell us to
bugger off, right?'

Cath shook her head nervously. 'I ain't ever been in a place this
fancy before, though.'

Liz ignored her, stepping across the wide thoroughfare of the
Strand, picking her way between carriages and trams and pancakes
of flattened horse manure. On the pavement and up the steps,
Liz turned her nose up at the doorman, who eyed them both suspiciously for a moment before begrudgingly opening one of the
double doors.

Inside, the hushed quiet of the foyer echoed with the jangling ring
of one of the new Bell telephones. Cath marvelled at the sight of one
of the desk staff talking into the mouthpiece and listening to some
response on the ear piece. Liz nudged her gently as she produced the
room key from the folds of her best skirt.

Liz had been in posh hotels before. In younger days, when she'd
been a much prettier prize. Nights in hotel rooms with three or four
'gentlemen', dishevelled in their expensive dinner suits, happy to fill
her up with free alcohol until she all but passed out and they could
do what they wished. She walked away with near on ten times the
money for an evening's work then as she could get now, plying her

trade on the street. She looked for the stairs and found them, then gave Cath a gentle tug on the arm. Liz was beginning to wonder why she'd brought her along, gawping like she was at the man on the telephone, then the plush marble floor, then the chandeliers, then the rich dark wood panelling. She was becoming a bloody liability.

'Excuse me?'

The voice came from behind the desk. Liz turned to see a man in a burgundy tunic, vaguely military, with twin rows of silver buttons up the front. 'Ladies? Can I help you?'

Brass it out, Liz. It always works.

Liz nodded and strode towards him impatiently. 'I've come to visit a friend,' she said, as crisp and complete as she could. 'She's in room two-hundred and seven, I do believe.'

She?

The concierge leant forward on the reception desk, taking both women in with one foot-to-head glance. 'Uh-huh. Business?'

'None of yours, as it happens,' Liz replied curtly.

Fair game. The concierge smiled wryly. *Well played, love.*

'Go on, then. I don't want any hustling for trade with the other guests, though, you understand?'

'Thank you.'

'Mind you take the service stairway up, as well. I don't want you using the main one.'

Liz was tempted to sputter outrage at him. Something along the lines of a 'who-do-you-think-you-are', but she could see he had known exactly what they were the moment they'd stepped into the lobby. They were lucky he was letting them through.

'Thanks.' She smiled. 'We shan't be long.'

The concierge watched them go, amused at the tall tart's attempt at sounding respectable. Not even a half-bad attempt, to be fair, but the faded clothes – too many frills, too much lace hemming, ill-fitting where they should be tight – gave them away. That and the gaps in their teeth; almost, but not quite, hidden by the terse-lipped way she'd spoken. And that faintly mottled skin: sure sign of the bottle.

He watched to make sure they took the service stairway. Then, out of curiosity, he decided to be sure his suspicions were right. It most definitely had to be a single gentleman staying in room 207 and not a lady. He ducked down behind the desk and fingered through the row of room ledgers to find the one for 207. Finally, he found it and pulled the leather-bound book up onto the reception desk.

He looked for the date checked in. Almost nine weeks ago now. He recognised the handwriting of his colleague, Nigel, who must have been on duty when he'd checked the guest in: one Mr Babbitt.

In Nigel's tiny, almost feminine, loops of handwriting were further details. It was a three-month booking for the room; on its own, not a particularly odd thing. There were quite often bookings of that duration. But with this one, Mr Babbitt seemed to have given some very specific instructions on his privacy as he'd checked in: that he wished for no room service; that he would ring for a chambermaid to collect his bedding when it was convenient for him; and at no other time was he to be disturbed.

On the ledger, there were a number of entries for breakfast and evening meals taken in the hotel's dining room, but none for several weeks now.

He wondered why Nigel had not mentioned this guest's particulars to him. It was pretty damned important that a duty concierge was aware of the specific instructions of a guest. But the answer was obvious. Nigel, the selfish bastard, was keeping Mr Babbitt to himself. No doubt the man was a very generous tipper. Clearly, Mr Babbitt had asked his colleague for a few little extras, and paid handsomely for them not to be a problem.

'You sneaky rascal,' he muttered under his breath. There were going to be words come the hand-over at the end of today. He was going to expect a share of Nigel's tips for letting those tarts through; that's the least he could do. Not only that but . . .

His mind stopped dead in its tracks.

He remembered . . . what was it? Yes. A busy lunchtime. A lot of guests coming in, a lot leaving with lists of instructions for him to be very clear on, things for him to deal with, cabs to hail, recommendations on places to eat, theatres and museums to visit. And yes, amid all that, there'd been that bloke; a copper or something. How long ago? About a month?

He remembered a quietly spoken man with a beard. Asked him the most pointedly stupid questions. Have you had any oddly-behaving guests? Any gentlemen behaving in a suspicious nature? Coming and going at late hours of the night? In haste? In an odd or unusual mental condition?

He would have laughed at some of those questions if the chap hadn't appeared to be a copper. The toffs who visited The Grantham were *all* bloody unusual; mad as a box of frogs, the lot of them.

But this one ledger for room 207: nothing, not a single thing for weeks. As if their guest had died or, far worse, done a runner without settling his bill. He had scribbled the policeman's name down somewhere on a scrap of paper, more to get rid of the fool than any inclination to actually make a note of all his guests' eccentric behaviours to report back to him. Good god, he'd be on the Bell telephone all the time.

He found the torn corner of foolscap tucked into the duty book. The dialling number he'd scribbled down was not the Met's switchboard. He knew that number. It was on a list behind the desk in case of 'Special Contingencies'. No, it looked like a private number. Perhaps another hotel or a private club. Odd.

You must ask to speak to 'George Warrington'.

He vaguely recalled the copper had said there'd be a tidy reward if his call turned out to be helpful in advancing their investigation. His blood ran cold at the thought that this guest, Mr Babbitt, might be a conman. Some bastard masquerading as a well-to-do businessman, racking up an enormous hotel bill and skipping off without paying. There'd be merry hell to pay for that.

He took the scrap of paper along to the end of the desk and started to dial the number, muttering to himself something about it serving Nigel right if this was going to get him in trouble with the police or the manager.

Should've bloody well shared Mr Babbitt with me, Nigel, shouldn't you?

CHAPTER 39

1st October 1888 (11.00 am),
The Grantham Hotel, The Strand, London

The room appeared to be unoccupied. Liz stepped inside cautiously. 'Anyone in 'ere?'

There was an unpleasant odour in the room. Not overpowering, but faint, like something put away to be eaten later but then forgotten about. Liz led the way in; Cath behind her, her eyes darting anxiously up and down the quiet, carpeted hallway outside.

'Come in an' close the door!' hissed Liz. Cath did as she was told and the heavy oak door clicked shut behind them. 'What if . . . what if someone's in 'ere, waitin' to jump us?' she whispered.

'No one's 'ere, silly.'

Liz looked around room 207. It was left tidy. Part of her had expected to find something macabre or sinister in here. Mary's story had worried her; to share rooms with a man she knew absolutely nothing about, especially now that it seemed there was a madman roaming the East End of London with a taste for carving up prostitutes like mutton. They were calling the murderer 'Jack the Ripper'.

'Ripper' . . . That seems about right.

Looking around the room, her concern eased a little. She saw a travel case open under the window, suits hanging from hangers in the wardrobe, socks and undergarments folded in drawers, and two pairs of clean, polished shoes lined up in a tidy row on the floor.

In the water closet, decorated with rich dark green and black ceramic tiles, was one of those modern, fancy Twyford flush-down toilets. A bowl beneath a large oval mirror and a water jug beside it. She saw a porcelain-handled shaving brush, a cut-throat razor, a well-used bar of soap, a comb. The possessions of a well-to-do and quite normal man.

She felt a rush of relief for Mary and, if truth be told, a small tug of jealousy. She always suspected Mary Kelly was somehow going to end up landing on her feet and getting out of the mire of Whitechapel. She had that air about her. An enduring optimism that had kept her from succumbing to the downward pull of gin or absinthe or opium. A relentless striving for something better. Liz always felt that Mary would one day attract good fortune her way. Perhaps even achieve something good or great.

'Hoy! Liz!'

'What?'

'What's this?'

Liz stepped out of the water closet and joined Cath, peering closely at a jam jar sitting on the writing desk by the window.

'I dunno. A pickled egg or summin'?'

'Whatever it is, it's bleedin' well gone off, it 'as. Stinks proper.'

Liz picked it up and peered closely at the murky brown liquid inside. She shook it gently, watching layers of putrid sediment twist around each other and something hidden inside bump gently against the glass. 'Ughhh! Disgusting!'

Cath picked up an envelope the jar had been sitting on. She turned it over and lifted the flap. 'It's open. Shall we look?'

'Give it to me,' said Liz, putting the jam jar back down on the table. She pulled out a couple of sheets of writing paper with *The Grantham Hotel, Strand* printed along the top. It was densely packed with lines of carefully neat handwriting. Both sides of each sheet of foolscap.

'Come on then, Liz: what's it say?'

Liz absently touched her lips with a finger to hush her. She took the pages, sat down on the end of the bed and began to read.

CHAPTER 40

1st October 1888 (11.00 am), Holland Park, London

Argyll stared at it. The worn brown leather bag and the bundles of notes inside. The bag made some sense to him. He recognised it. He could produce half a dozen memories that in some way featured this satchel: him pulling things out of it, putting things into it.

Suddenly he's a young man. He's in the middle of some battle. The air's thick with the smell of cordite. He's kneeling in the middle of a field of thickets and weeds and the twisted and mangled bodies of men wearing grey, butternut brown and dark blue uniforms. The hands of the dying, clawing at his boots, desperate for water. He's drinking water from a flask. So thirsty. It's all the smoke, drifting across the battlefield. He's drinking water and hearing a dozen of the nearest dying men screaming at him for just one sip of his water. But he calmly screws the cap back on and puts the flask back in his bag.

Another disembodied memory.

He's older now. From the satchel, he's pulling out a long, thin-bladed knife in a dimly-lit room. Is it a loft? No, not a loft . . . a cellar, not unlike this one. And there's a man tied to a wooden chair in the middle of it. A man in very fine clothes indeed. He looks like he was attending a ball or perhaps the theatre tonight. But now he's struggling and squirming and screaming and crying. The leather seat of the chair is wet between his thighs and he's saying 'I didn't mean to do it! Tell them! Tell them I'll never do it again . . . I swear!'

And another, although this one feels more recent.

A woman in a dark street, gurgling blood onto rain-wet paving stones. He's reaching into this same bag and he pulls out a small candle and he's talking to her. Telling her some nonsense about how there's no kindness left in this soulless world.

Argyll touched the leather satchel. A familiar rasp of coarse leather on the tips of his fingers, like old friends reacquainted; the bag, he was sure, was a distinct part of who he was. He sensed that; knew that for a certainty. But the money . . . The money inside this bag made no sense to him whatsoever.

It's your money. Do you see?

Argyll shook his head. No it wasn't. He didn't want it to be his money. 'No, no . . .'

It's yours. You earned it!

No, please, no. He didn't want it to be his because if it was his money then it meant . . . it meant . . .

Yes. It means she stole it from you.

'No . . . she didn't; she wouldn't!'

She's been caring for a mindless fool because of all his money.

'Dammit! Will you shut up!' he snarled out loud. 'We were . . .' His voice quickly trailed to nothing. He was going to say that before the injury, they'd been together, man and wife in all but name. But then in all the quiet moments of reflection he'd had in this home of theirs, he'd begun to ponder the many small things that had begun to not make sense to him. Why so little of either of them seemed to exist in this home. So few possessions. No childhood mementos, no keepsakes, no family photographic portraits; nothing that marked the passing of their time living together as lovers, or their lives before then.

He was beginning to wonder how much of Mary's account of their shared life before his injury was entirely reliable. Genuine, even.

Or maybe it's ALL a pack of lies. Hmmm?

Argyll felt the bottom of his small, womb-like world begin to fall away beneath his feet. He slumped down and sat on the travel chest, feeling light-headed. Sick.

An opportunist. That's what she is. A woman who found a man with an empty head and a bag full of money.

He struggled for a moment to find a response to counter that. She could have taken his money and left him at any time. Instead, Mary had stayed, spent this money – *his* money, if the stunted pig tormenting him was to be believed – on caring for him, feeding him.

Use your brain, 'John'. If you have this money, perhaps elsewhere you have much more?

'Damn you! She's here because . . . because we *love* each other!'

A snorting laugh filled his head. *She wants more than a satchel of money. She imagines you're a businessman or a plantation owner over there, somewhere in America; that it's all waiting for her. That's what she wants.*

A deep whine came out of Argyll's throat. He hated the voice. If he could have dug it out from his mind with the tip of a blunt knife, he would have.

You're her meal ticket.

'Shut up!'

You're her pet.

'Please!' He buried his face in his hands.

She even named you . . . just like you name a puppy dog. She named you!

Argyll drew down his hands and looked up. In the darkest corner of the cellar, he thought he could see his demon standing there. A twinkle in two narrow eyes, a wet pig's snout twitching with excitement, so eager to tell him a story.

'John . . . Argyll,' he whispered. 'That's my name. That's who I am.'

No. That pitiless snigger again. *She came up with a name for you. I wonder: is it the name of a real lover she once had? Or a childhood friend? Or an acquaintance? Or even someone she once hated? Or is it a name made up at random? A shop sign? A letterhead?*

'I'm John Argyll, goddammit!!'

No. You're me.

Argyll felt a solitary tear roll down his cheek. 'I hate you.'

How can you hate what you are? Hmmm?

CHAPTER 41

1st October 1888 (11.15 am),
The Grantham Hotel, The Strand, London

'Liz? What is it?'

Cath could see her friend's face had blanched. 'What's it say?'

Liz looked up from the pages of foolscap she was holding. 'Oh, god 'elp us!'

'What's it say?' Cath repeated.

Liz put the pages down beside her, got up off the end of the bed and stepped towards the writing desk, with a look of growing dread on her face.

'Liz, tell me! What's the letter say? What's the matter?'

'I need to see . . .' she said, reaching for the jam jar.

'You need to see what?' Cath frowned, confused. 'Why d'ya need to look in there, Liz?'

'It says . . . he took a . . . took a lady's kidney!'

'Whatcha talkin' 'bout?'

'The letter!' she replied, jabbing a finger at the pages of writing paper on the end of the bed. 'That letter! It's a bloody confession!'

'A confession? To what?'

'Them murders! The ones they're sayin's been done by the mad man.'

Cath's eyes widened. 'You don't mean the one what got wrote in to the paper the other—?'

'Yes! Him! Jack the Ripper!'

Liz looked down at the metal lid of the jam jar. She pointed at the pages lying on the bed. 'He said in that letter that he took a kidney from the last one. The one on Hanbury Street. He took it for proof he's who he says he is.'

Cath's hand raced to her mouth. 'And . . . and it's in there?'

'We need to see, don't we?' Liz grasped the lid in one hand and the glass jar in the other, then gave it a gentle twist. It popped softly and hissed with the release of fetid air. Liz gagged and recoiled at the sudden rush of the smell. The jar slipped from her hand, bounced and rolled on the desk, spilling its pottage of brown broth across the varnished dark wood surface.

A small bean-shaped nub of wrinkled, dark flesh the size of a walnut rolled out of the jar.

'Oh, fuck,' whispered Liz. She threw up on the floor.

Warrington arrived outside the hotel to see his two men standing there: Hain and Orman. Both wheezing and doubled over from the exhaustion of sprinting from the Lodge over on Great Queen Street. He waved them to follow him inside into The Grantham's lobby. He was also far too out of breath and unable to gasp anything intelligible just yet. He led both men across to the reception desk, doing his best to recover his composure.

'You're the concierge . . . Mr Davis, isn't it?' he said to the man behind the desk.

'That's me, sir. I'm the one who telephoned earlier. You're George Warrington?'

Warrington nodded. 'You said two women?' He wheezed. 'Are they still up there?'

The concierge nodded. 'Not come down yet, sir. I presume they're still up in two-hundred and seven: Mr Babbitt's room.'

Mr Babbitt? The odd name strangely seemed to fit the man he'd spoken to briefly two months ago.

'You said the room's not actually been entered in nearly eight weeks?'

The concierge nodded. 'Like I said, he'd left strict instructions that no one, not even the chambermaids, were to go in without prior arrangement.'

Warrington turned to look at Hain and Orman. Both men ready to receive instructions.

My god, this could be our man.

'Could you describe the gentleman in that room?'

'No, see, I wasn't on the desk when the gentleman checked in. My colleague, Nigel, was. But I do remember now, he did mention that day an odd, tall American chap. That might just be who he—'

'American?'

'Yes, sir.'

Warrington balled his fist. *That's him. It's got to be him.*

'Well, like I said to you earlier,' continued the concierge, 'we've not heard a whistle from that gentleman in quite some time—'

Warrington raised a gloved hand to silence him. 'How many keys does a guest get given when they check in? Just the one?'

'Just the one, sir.'

'And those two tarts had the key?'

He nodded.

Then he's not in his room, is he? A burning chill of realisation prickled across his scalp and made the short hairs on the nape of his neck stand up. *He's not dead. He's sent those two women on an errand to collect his things. Which means he's outside somewhere. Perhaps even watching this very hotel right now.*

'Shouldn't we go on up, sir?' asked Hain.

Orman was nodding at his colleague's suggestion. 'If there's evidence up there, sir, they could be disturbing it.'

'No.' Both men turned to look at Warrington as if he was insane. 'No,' he repeated. The locket could be up there. The portrait of the prince. Those things might well be, and he'd make it his first order of business to be the only person to go into the room and search it thoroughly. But right now, a much higher priority was on his mind. Warrington suddenly realised he was trembling at the prospect of once more coming face to face with the Candle Man. The man exuded a terrifyingly believable aura of invincibility. And god, hadn't he been fast? He'd exited that warehouse and left them looking like foolish amateurs; one of them beheaded, one gutted and the rest of them looking like a cluster of superstitious old women who thought they'd glimpsed Ol' Nick in the eyes of a black cat.

He's just a man, remember. Don't mythologise him.

If he was somewhere outside on the Strand, watching this hotel from afar, then at the first sight of Warrington and his men, he would just melt away. But these tarts, they'd have something he wanted, presumably; something he'd paid them to retrieve.

'We need to wait for those women to come back down,' he said quietly. 'Then we're going to follow them. Understand?'

Both nodded.

He turned to the concierge. 'You can point out these women to us?'

'Yes, sir. Couple of tarts. You won't miss 'em.'

Warrington looked around the lobby. On the far side of the marble floor were some high-backed leather armchairs gathered near a fireplace and a table stacked with old newspapers. 'We shall be over there. You'll give me the nod in any case, when they go out the door; is that clear?'

'Yes. Uh, sir? There was some mention of a reward . . . ?'

'Yes.' Warrington flicked the question away like a fly. 'Yes, of course. We'll arrange the details of that later.' He nodded at Hain and Orman to go and pick an armchair each. 'Oh, and no one, I mean *no one,* is to enter that room until I return; is that absolutely clear?'

He nodded.

'Good man.'

CHAPTER 42

1st October 1888 (11.30 am),
The Grantham Hotel, The Strand, London

'She's in bloody rooms with 'im!' Liz snapped. 'She's actually *living* with 'im, Cath!'

Even sleeping with him? She doing that, too?

Cath was standing out in the hallway, unwilling to spend another second in room 207, along with the human organ perched on the end of the desk. 'No way! I ain't goin' to 'er bloody 'ouse!'

Liz stepped out and joined her. 'We 'ave to warn 'er!'

'The police! We should go to the police! That's what we oughta do!'

They should. They really should. But Liz wondered how long it would take to convince them they weren't hoaxers; two gin-breathing slappers looking to have a laugh at the police's expense and perhaps even hoping to make the next day's newspapers. Liz left the room's door wide open behind her as she walked swiftly down the hallway towards the stairs, the key still grasped, forgotten for the moment, in one hand.

Cath caught up with her. 'So? Police, right? We goin' to see the police?'

Their boots clattered down the main marble stairs. '*You* go find some police, Cath. I'm goin' to find Mary.'

They were down in the lobby. She noted it was busier now than it had been half an hour ago. They swept past the doorman, out onto the broad alabaster steps that led down to the Strand, busy and noisy with the clatter and hails of mid-morning traffic.

'Liz! You shouldn't go! What if 'e's there! 'E's dangerous!'

'He ain't got a clue who 'e is, right?' replied Liz. 'His mind's completely gone. That's what Mary told me. Gone! Just like a big baby.'

Cath grasped her arm. The sight of the decomposing organ had spooked her completely. Liz could feel the trembling in the tight grasp of her hand. 'He's lying! Maybe he's lying to 'er?'

'I got to warn 'er, Cath!'

'Yer crazy!'

'Listen, I ain't bloody well goin' in; I'm just knockin', is all. Just gonna get Mary to step outside with me to talk, all right?'

'Well, I ain't going with yer! No fuckin' way!'

'Fine. Yer go do whatcha said – go find a police station. Tell 'em exactly all what we found.'

'Everythin' . . . Yeah, I will. I will.'

'All right, then.' Liz nodded. She looked down the Strand. She had enough money for a tram at least part of the way. She could bilk a free ride on a busy one if need be. One could often get a crafty couple of stops before the conductor got round to dealing with you.

She clasped her friend by the shoulders. 'I'll see yer back at Marge's later, right?'

Cath nodded quickly. 'Oh, gawd, be ever so careful, Liz!' Her voice scratched and rattled, like a cat in a box.

'I will.'

'It's that Jack the Ripper, Liz.'

'I know that . . . I know.'

Warrington watched them through the glass of the lobby doors. The two women were talking animatedly. A disagreement of some sort? They both looked over-excited. No, not excited; they looked terrified.

Then the taller of the two – a woman Warrington imagined ten years ago must have been quite a beauty, a sight to turn heads – seemed to be giving the shorter one instructions.

Damn.

That meant they were probably going in different directions. The taller one grasped the other woman's hands and squeezed them: a 'see-you-later'. Then she turned away and headed up the Strand.

Warrington muttered a curse and then turned to his two men. He pointed at Hain. 'You follow the taller one. Don't lose her, do you understand?'

The man nodded, put on his bowler hat and bustled out the lobby doors. Warrington watched him skip swiftly down the steps past the other woman who was still standing at the bottom on the busy pavement. She looked undecided.

'What about her?' said Orman.

Warrington ignored him. He was watching her. *Come on, come on . . . What are you thinking, woman?*

She was looking up and down the busy street, looking for something.

Looking for the Candle Man, perhaps?

Her manic searching suddenly stopped; her eyes had found something on the far side of the street. Warrington tried to follow her gaze, to see what she'd picked out, but a double-decker tram clattered slowly past, blocking his view.

She stepped off the pavement, down onto the busy road, glancing right and left and then towards the far side, waiting for a gap in the traffic.

'Sir? Mr Warrington?'

'Yes, come on, we need to follow her!'

They pushed their way out through the double doors and caught sight of the woman as she hefted her heavy skirts above her ankles and darted perilously across the wide road, causing cart and cab drivers to rein in their horses and swerve and hurl streams of colourful invective at her back.

Warrington and Orman followed in her wake, trying desperately not to lose sight of her burgundy frock coat and her grubby cream-coloured bonnet.

On the far side, back up on pavement once more, it was far busier with foot traffic. His glance flipped one way then the other, looking for her bonnet amidst a sea of bobbing heads; every other one, it seemed, was yet another off-white cloth bonnet.

'Over there!' gasped Orman. He stuck out a thick butcher's finger and pointed the way. Warrington followed his finger. He couldn't see her but Orman was a good five inches taller than him; he could see above the bobbing pedestrians' heads. And he saw the dark dome of a constable's helmet.

'She's talking to that constable over there, sir.'

PC Docherty sighed. 'Sorry, love. Why don't you just calm down an' try sayin' that all over again, eh?'

The woman looked to him like one of the usual Whitechapel dregs: breath like a bleedin' brewery and teeth like a drawer full of broken china.

'Me an' Liz found 'im!' she gabbled, her hand flapping at the front entrance of The Grantham Hotel across the Strand. 'Over there! The murderer!'

'Murderer, love? Which murderer's that, then?'

She nodded, florid jowls flapping with a life of their own. 'The killer what's been doin' over the women!'

Docherty rolled his eyes irritably. *Jesus, not another bloody one.* He'd wager a pound to a penny the next thing coming out of her flapping lips would be something about Jack the Ripper. All week, since some idiot had decided to write a letter and post it into the Central News Agency, staking a claim to those two recent murders and then signing off with that provocative name, their front desk sergeant had been plagued with silly fools like this one. Excitable morons claiming their neighbour, their cousin, their father, their son, their boss, their colleague, was the Whitechapel murderer. The *Ripper*!

'He's bin stayin' in that 'otel, 'e 'as. That killer, Jack the—'

'All right, love. Come on, now, that's enough.'

She snatched at his cuff with grubby hands. 'Please! Come an' see!'

'Better let go, miss . . . I mean it! Right now or I'll take you down the station.' He'd spent a good half an hour this morning ironing the creases into his tunic; he wasn't going to let some old slapper, with fingernails dirty with god-knows-what, make a mess of his uniform.

'Please! There's 'uman bits up there! BLOODY 'UMAN BITS!' She was almost screaming now. Heads of people walking past them were beginning to turn. Several had even stopped to see how this amusing little scene was going to develop. She now had the kernel of an audience. PC Docherty realised he had better bring the matter to a close. The longer he let her yap, the more out of control she was going to get.

'Right! I think that's enough nonsense from you, love!' He twisted her paw off his crumpled cuff and was about to armlock and arrest her for causing a disturbance when a couple of gentlemen pushed their way through.

'Ah! There you are!' said one of them. Posh gentleman in a smart morning suit.

'Err . . . You know this woman, sir?'

The gentleman shrugged. 'Don't actually know her . . . she just . . . she . . .'

The other man – taller, broad-shouldered – stepped in. 'This rascal just attempted to lift this gentleman's wallet.' He fished out the late Inspector Smith's warrant card and flourished it for Docherty to see briefly.

'Oh, I see . . .'

'I'll take her off your hands, lad.' He winked at him. 'And she can make as much noise as she bleedin' well wants back at the station. Right?'

PC Docherty nodded. 'Right, sir.' He let her arm go and passed her to the inspector.

'Come on, you!' he said. 'Let's get you all sobered up in a cell, shall we?'

Docherty watched them turn away with her and shook his head. The silly old bitch was trying her garbled nonsense about Jack the Ripper on the inspector now.

He shrugged. *Good luck to him.*

He sniffed the cuff of his tunic and wrinkled his nose, realising he was going to need to wash it again tonight.

CHAPTER 43

1st October 1888 (11.35 am), The Strand, London

*D*amn, *the woman can march!*
Hain was struggling to keep up with her without breaking into a jog. Thirty feet in front of him, her head and neck visible above the pavement traffic, she was weaving with a sense of urgency.

His eyes on her – he wasn't going to lose her easily, being as tall as she was – he allowed his mind to ponder. He wondered what she'd found upstairs in that hotel room.

Something grisly, no doubt.

This man they were after – he'd heard Warrington refer to him once as the 'Candlestick Man', or something like that – was a real *frightener*, and no doubt about that. Hain had seen enough blood and savagery in his twenty-two years in the army. Particularly the tribal habits of those Pashtun barbarians in Afghanistan. And even more back here in London working for various members of the Lodge in a variety of capacities. He'd seen what those godless scrotums in the shittiest rookeries of Whitechapel and Spitalfields could do to each other. Beat each other to a pulp over the contents of a purse, the favour of some dirty poxed-up slapper, or simply because they figured they'd been disrespected in some way.

As if any of them scrotes actually deserve a shred of respect.

But this man, this Candlestick Man, was something else alto-gether. Fuckin' evil. That's what it takes to carve a man's head off, like he did. To do what he did to those tarts. Not the everyday brutish, selfish evil he saw in the East End. This was *bible* evil. *Old Testament* evil. This was bloody sulphurous down in the very depths of Hell evil.

Hain remembered a painting he once saw. Last summer, he

decided to do a bit of the ol' 'High Art' with his wife and two daughters. Bit of culture and learning for 'em. Took them down for a family day out to the National Gallery off Trafalgar Square. And that's where he saw that huge horrible painting. He forgot its title but he remembered the artist's name.

Hieronymus Bosch.

Hell. That's what he figured they were looking at: a depiction of Hell. An army of skeletal imps, chimeras and monsters, carving up the innocent like so many joints of beef. Hacking at them, impaling them, dismembering them. The painting had stayed with him, disturbed him. Had, in fact, given both his little girls nightmares. They really shouldn't have lingered so long in front of it.

Ever since that night in the old abandoned warehouse, Hain had imagined this Candlestick Man to be a bit like one of those skeletal imps, those gargoyles. A mischievous demon who had somehow managed to find a winding tunnel from the depths below and emerged in the darkest part of London, to play. Since then he, Orman and Robson had discussed that night in the warehouse with hushed voices; met several times to discuss it over a pint in the quiet corner of a pub. The three of them agreed the man was most probably quite dead. But then Robson had half-jokingly wondered whether he was even a man.

His mind was thrown back into the present. The tall woman had stopped walking. She was looking back this way.

Looking at me? He wondered if she'd somehow figured out she was being followed.

Hain quickly dropped the pace of his urgent stride to a casual stroll. A slope-shouldered man behind him cursed as he almost collided with him.

What the hell is she looking at?

Hain resisted the urge to turn and follow the direction of her gaze. That would surely give him away. Instead, he decided to improvise a reason for his sudden halt and, feigning irritation, he dropped down onto one knee and started fumbling with his shoelaces. Through milling pedestrians he could still see her, a couple of dozen yards in front, craning her neck, looking back down the Strand.

Come on, what you looking for, love?

Then he realised, as he heard the jangle of a bell, the clatter of approaching hoofs. The shadow of a double-decker tram spilled over her as it slowed to a halt beside a stop. He lost sight of her for just a second; a plump lady, arm in arm with her spindle-thin husband, blocked his line of sight. Cursing, Hain quickly stood up, just in time to see the tall woman squeezing herself onto the back of the tram. A bell jangled again and the tram began to move off.

'Bloody hell!' he growled, pushing his way forward through people who scowled at him and remarked at his rudeness. But he was too slow. The tram was already too far ahead for him to try and attempt to catch it up on foot.

He looked around desperately for a hansom. But this being the Strand, every damned cab he could see in either direction already had passengers aboard.

'Argh, shit n' fuckin' bollocks!'

Liz shouldered her way inside the tram, but not so far inside she'd struggle to do a runner if the conductor clocked her for a fare. She hung on to a handrail. Like everyone else shoe-horned on, she was oblivious to the people bumping against her, lost in her own world of thoughts.

What am I doing? Cath's right. This is crazy!

She had told Cath only part of it. It was all there in that letter, that confession. All there and almost too much for her to untangle and make sense of with one quick read. The man who'd been living in room 207 – what name had he signed at the bottom? Babber? No, Babbitt, that was it – he was some sort of hired murderer. And he confessed he was the one who'd done the Hanbury Street and Bucks Row murders: Nichols and Chapman.

The organ in the jar was a part of the Chapman woman. His proof that he was not just another hoaxer having fun with the police. But then the confession got complicated. She wondered whether she'd misread the letter or misinterpreted what had been put down on those pages. The man – Babbitt – was confessing he'd been hired by a group of gentlemen who belonged to the Freemasons.

Liz, like most people, had heard of the Masons but knew very little about them. Posh gents who met in clubs, sometimes donated money to workhouses, some would say. Others? That they danced naked around virgins and conducted all sorts of dark magic in their mysterious halls.

But this group of gentlemen seemed to have a particular responsibility, a particular purpose. When she'd opened the envelope, she had given the scuffed photograph scant attention. Glanced at it and no more. A man, a woman and a baby. But, having read further . . .

Prince Albert? Really?

She tried to recall the grey image. The man with his head held up and a cocky twist to his lips beneath the meagre twirl of a thin moustache. He certainly looked like he could be royalty. There was an inbred swagger in that pose. But in truth, the only royal face she'd know anywhere was Queen Victoria's. From the few paper illustrations she'd seen of him over the years, she thought young Prince 'Eddy' had looked wholly unremarkable. It could've been him in that photograph picture. On the other hand, it could've been any fashionable young fop.

But then someone proper knowledgeable would be able to tell, wouldn't they?

A new thought sent a shiver of comprehension down her back, as if a fellow passenger had gently lifted the collar of her coat away from her neck and lightly blown inside it.

The Queen's son fucking a whore? Producing a bastard with her? It didn't take a lot of brainwork to figure out there'd be merry hell to pay if that kind of story ever made it into the news stands. The sort of merry hell that would put mobs on the streets.

Liz listened to men do their talking over an ale. While there was an affection for 'dear ol' Victoria' – that came as a caveat before ever discussing the royals – there was little love for the rest of them 'Bavarian scroungers'. Least of all the privileged and pampered Eddy, who seemed to be making it his life's mission to thumb his nose at every hard-working man with coal dust, nicks-n-cuts and calluses on his hands. Liz had even heard men muttering scary words like 'revolution' into the froth of their beer.

Mr Babbitt had been hired to kill all those who knew about Eddy's carelessness. And now, so this Babbitt appeared to be claiming, these same Mason gentlemen working hard to safeguard Eddy's reputation wanted to be absolutely certain that their hired killer, their 'Ripper', was going to be entirely silent on the matter.

Oh, god 'elp me. And now I know . . .

She felt her legs waver beneath her. For a moment, it was nothing but the swaying press of fellow passengers that was holding her on her feet. Her friend Cath knew none of this, only the few sentences she'd blurted out loud in the room; that Mary was sharing rooms with the killer of those two women – Jack the Ripper.

And Mary clearly hadn't the first clue about any of this.

Instinct told her to ring the tram's bell and jump off, to head the other way. To walk away from this right now. Not just this Ripper to fear. God help her, it was powerful men, too. She should get off, walk away. Get out of London. Disappear into some faraway country retreat and never speak to another soul as long as she lived. But then she wondered what it would do to her if she was to read in tomorrow's paper of a young woman by the name of Mary Kelly found in some yard with her throat sliced back to her spine and her innards pulled out and scattered about the place. And all she'd needed to do to save her was knock on the door and scream to Mary to get out now!

Just knockin' for 'er, that's all I'm doing. Ain't goin' inside, that's for sure.

CHAPTER 44

1st October 1888 (11.40 am), Bayswater, London

Now, here's the thing, Mary . . . it's going to happen, sooner or later. She realised there was going to come a moment when she said something to John that was a complete contradiction to some earlier lie she'd told him. She imagined he would be polite about it, ponder on it awhile, before calmly asking her to resolve the contradiction. Oh yes, he would be awfully polite about it, not angry, but that was not the point. The point was, too much of that and he would finally figure out that she had been telling him lies and her game would be up. The trust he offered her without question would be gone.

She watched a little boy chasing pigeons around the bandstand in the small park. Fat hands and chubby pink legs tormenting the pigeons eager and impatient to touch down and peck at bread crumbs someone had thrown on the ground.

She wondered if John had actually been curious enough to try the cellar door. No . . . he wouldn't, though. That was the thing; she was getting used to his little ways. He never seemed to be particularly curious; happy to take the face value of everything she told him. She'd explained it was just dusty bags of coke down there. Dirty, dark and plenty of nasty creepy crawlies. If he really wanted to go take a look, she'd take him down and show him. All the same, she wished she'd pocketed the key instead of sliding it back under the clock's stand like she had. Almost certain he hadn't seen her doing that. Almost certain.

She bit her lip.

Should have taken the key.

It was playing on her mind now.

Maybe if he did find the key, he'd unlock the door, open it, and stare down at the steps leading into the blackness. But that's all he'd do. Like a child, he hated the dark. Whether that was a fear remembered from before or whether it was all part of the damage to his mind, there was no way to know. But she was almost certain he wouldn't venture down there on his own. Still . . .

Should have taken the key.

Her thoughts drifted onto the other key; a far more important one. The one she hoped was going to tell her – for good or bad – more about who he is.

Who he was, Mary, she corrected herself. *Who he was.*

Liz said she'd come by some time in the next couple of days with any news she had. Mary was half-hoping that Liz would not turn up. That she'd just taken the money and tossed away the key, laughing at Mary's gullibility behind her back. At least there'd be no bad news. No definite end to her little fairytale.

'I'm sorry, Mary, love. It's like this: his family was up there in that room. Wife an' kids an' all. They asked me 'ow I got 'old of this key. I'm sorry, Mary . . . I 'ad to tell 'em straight; they got coppers out on the beat lookin' for 'im. They been puttin' missin' person notices in all the papers. Game's up, girl; best you let 'im go. I told 'em you been treatin' him well, carin' for him like a nurse. But they're goin' to be comin' to get 'im any time now. Might be best if you make a quick exit, love.'

That's how it was going to end, wasn't it? Maybe the smart thing to do would be to go back home right now, go straight down into the cellar, grab that bag of money, and leave sharpish, just like she should have done at the very beginning.

Oh, god . . . but the thought of doing that to him. He'd be standing there looking at her, vexed, with puppy dog eyes that asked what he'd done to upset her, wanting to know when she would be back.

'I can't do that,' she muttered.

But maintaining this fiction: it wasn't going to last forever. At some point, he was going to catch her out, or some memory would surface that completely, unambiguously, contradicted all that she'd told him. And running off with his money? Leaving him all alone? She couldn't bring herself to do that either.

That leaves telling him the truth. The thought of doing that terrified her. However, it would be far better she sat him down and told him all she knew, than him one day soon catching her out. At least then, with her being honest with him like that, he might still trust her in some small way. There might still be a thread of trust left; just enough for them to start over with. To start from scratch and perhaps, perhaps, find their way back to where they'd been last night.

Always was going to be this way anyway, wasn't it? Having to tell him.

She got up off the park bench, her arm looped through the handle of her wicker shopping basket. Things to do: a shirt to pick up from the launderette, some groceries to get.

Tonight. Tonight, over a nice supper, she decided she was going to tell him everything and hope that when she was done, he still wanted her. Then perhaps there was still a chance of that fairytale ending.

CHAPTER 45

1st October 1888 (1.00 pm), Whitechapel, London

Warrington curled his lip in disgust at the squalor of the lodging house. Its dark entrance hallway and stairwell reeked of stale piss, and more. He turned to look at Orman, who met his gaze with a likewise wrinkled nose.

'Me room's up along 'ere,' said the tart. They had her name now: Catherine Eddowes. She fumbled in a tatty bag and finally her keys, which jangled in her shaking hands. She jammed it in the lock and opened the door to her room.

The noise she was making caused someone to stir inside a room further up the dimly lit hallway. A door was wrenched open and a small woman in a shawl stepped out into the hall. She was followed by the faintest odour of cooking opium.

'That you, Mary! Where the pissin' 'ell's my money?!'

'It's me, Marge; it's Cath!'

'Fuck!' She spat the word out like it was a fly flown into her mouth. 'So where's yer fuckin' mate? This ain't a fuckin' charity shop. She owes me—'

'Marge,' Cath cautioned. 'We got visitors.'

The woman scowled down at the dark end of the hall, just inside the closed front door. 'You workin' *already*?' She sounded impressed.

'No, it's the police.'

Marge's challenging stance and tone vanished in an instant. 'Oh, good morning, genty-men!' she smiled, a mouth of gums and black teeth. 'Can I 'elp you two loves with anythin'?'

'It's good *afternoon* now,' said Warrington dryly. 'And no. We're here to talk with Catherine.'

Marge shook her head and tutted. 'Oh, yer bloody silly cow! Whatcha fuckin' gone an' done now?'

'It's about that Jack the—'

Warrington cut her off. 'It's actually none of your business, *love*.' Warrington gestured at her door, leaking the faintest twist of pipe smoke into the hallway. 'Why don't you go back inside before I send my inspector in there to turn over your rooms?'

Her head disappeared and the door slammed shut behind her. Warrington hesitated a moment, wondering whether the woman might now be a potential problem to clear up later. Just the two words she'd heard: 'Jack the—'. But quite possibly two words too many.

Later.

'In you go,' he said to Cath.

She shuffled across darkness and a moment later scratched a match and lit a paraffin lamp in the corner of the room. Orman entered behind him and closed the door on a suffocatingly small space. A bed, a wardrobe, a tiny corner table with one wooden stool beside it, and barely room to walk between them.

'Why don't you sit down, Catherine?' Warrington gestured at the end of her bed.

She did so.

'Now . . . I'm going to need your full co-operation if we're going to help your friend. Do you understand?'

She nodded, eager as a jackdaw.

'Now, you were saying earlier, the tall woman you were with this morning—'

'Liz Stride.'

'You said she's gone to warn your friend about the chap she's sharing rooms with? Is that right?'

'Yes.'

'And the address of these rooms you say you don't—'

'It's somewhere in 'olland Park is all I know. Liz got the proper address off of 'er.'

He nodded thoughtfully. 'I see.'

He hoped Hain was still following the woman. If so, then they were going to have an address. But that wasn't going to do them a lot of good if this Stride's impromptu visit spooked the gentleman in question. He wished he'd had Hain follow this one and he and Orman were with the other, then he could take charge of the situation over there. But this was what it was; he'd have to rely on his man. Hain wasn't stupid. He'd know to identify the address, then take the initiative and quickly pull the woman to one side before she could knock on the door and alert the occupants.

The other matter was the hotel room back at The Grantham. He desperately wanted to go back there and take a look for himself, to be sure this *was* the suite the Candle Man had been using.

So very slippery of him to be this patient. To actually be able to do that. To not panic and try and make a run for home. For the week following that night at the warehouse, Rawlinson had pulled some favours in from amongst their Lodge members. They had pairs of eyes on the ports and the ship booking agents – just in case their unfortunate dead colleague, Smith, had been mistaken and the blow he'd landed with his pickaxe had just been a glancing blow and not fatal.

'Orman?'

'Sir?'

He ought not to have used his man's name in front of her. Except, of course, that wasn't going to matter. This ugly bitch was already dead; she just didn't realise it yet. 'Go and get hold of our other chap, Robson. I want him guarding that room. And then I want you outside The Grantham in case Hain returns there with the other woman.'

'Liz tol' me she was goin' to bring Mary back 'ere,' Cath cut in. 'To this place.'

Warrington smiled politely at her. 'Which is why you and I shall be staying put here in this charming room of yours this afternoon.'

Orman nodded. 'Right you are, sir.' He turned to go.

'And if Hain does turn up at the hotel with an address, call Henry at the club immediately and let him know what's happened this morning. We may need some extra pairs of hands on this.'

'Yes, sir.'

'Good man.'

Orman closed the door behind him, leaving the two of them alone with the creaking of floorboards coming from the room above and the skittering sound of rats behind the plasterboard walls.

'I don't suppose you have a kettle?'

She shrugged and offered him an apologetic smile. 'I got nothin' much in 'ere, sir.' Then her shoulders lifted. 'Oh, but I do got some tack biscuits an' a bit of cheese!'

'Splendid. Shall we . . . ?'

CHAPTER 46

1st October 1888 (1.00 pm), Holland Park, London

Five steps up off Holland Park Avenue, flanked on either side by a knee-high wall, barely a lip of stone to prevent the unwary dropping down the stairwell either side that led to basement rooms and coal cellars. Five steps leading up to a dark blue front door.

Liz checked the scribbled writing on her scrap of paper. Number 67.

To the left of the front door was a bay window: tall, wide windows filled with patterned lace that looked like they once held a rose hue. A hint of movement from behind there. She saw some of the material swinging gently, as if something inside had moved swiftly, causing a draft.

She took the five steps up slowly, a part of her arguing on each step for her to turn and run as far and as fast as she could. She felt like Little Red Riding Hood approaching her grandmother's house. But unlike Red Riding Hood, actually knowing what lies behind the door. The difference was, though, that she wasn't alone in the middle of some forest. There was that.

At the top step, she turned to look over her shoulder. Holland Park Avenue was busy with both wheel and hoof traffic and pedestrians on either side. As long as she stayed on the top step in full view of all these passing strangers, she was going to be safe, she assured herself. Safe.

A steadying deep breath to calm her jangling nerves. She cleared her throat, lifted the knocker on the front door and rapped several times.

Her mind rehearsed what she was going to say to Mary. She needed her friend to step outside, she needed her to feel at ease enough to do that so they could move further away from the door, to talk without being overheard. He could be in there, behind the door, standing in the hallway, trying to earwig what they were saying. She needed Mary to step over the threshold and be standing outside.

Oh, Jesus.

She was so nervous, she wanted to pee.

'*Hullo, Mary. Nice place, love! Yer fancy takin' a bit if a walk?*' she practised with a muted whisper. '*I got one or two things me an' you need to talk to about, love.*'

She heard the rattle of a door chain and quickly put on a friendly smile as the door creaked inwards.

'Hullo, Mary—' she started.

A man stared out of the gloom of the hallway at her. 'Yes?'

Her mouth flapped uselessly as the words she'd had lined up and ready to use completely abandoned her. A sudden spasm of fear released a trickle of urine down one thigh.

Jack the Ripper.

His craggy, gaunt face gradually loosened into a smile. Eyes, dark beneath the hood of his thick brow, seemed to glint with moisture. 'A friend of Mary's, are you?'

'I . . . uh . . . yes. I'm a friend. C-can I speak to her, p-please?'

'Oh, I'm afraid that won't be possible,' he said slowly, the smile never leaving his lips, showing a tidy row of small white teeth.

All the better for eating you with, my dear.

'Why n-not? Why c-can't I s-speak with her?' Liz tried to steady her voice. Fear, *mortal terror*, was giving her away.

The man, Babbitt – she remembered his signed name – cocked his head curiously. 'Are you all right? Hmmm? You look . . . unwell.'

'Where is she?'

'Mary? Oh, I told you, didn't I? It's not possible. She's out right now.'

He's lying. Her mind filled with a vision of her restrained in this house somewhere. Whimpering through a gagged mouth at the sound of her friend's voice at the front door.

'Mary!' she called out. 'MARY!! You in there?!'

The cordial expression vanished from his face. 'I told you she's not here!' His polite smile became a snarl. For a fleeting second, she thought she saw the amber glint of Hell's fires in his dark eyes; thought she heard the deep growl of a big bad wolf underscoring his voice.

I'm safe outside. I'm safe outside. Mary's inside. Help her!

'Mary! It's Liz! Come out here! Do you hear me? Get out—'

She felt a gust of air against her cheek and instinctively clenched her eyes shut. Her lips mashed hard against her teeth. She felt herself being lifted off her feet, and a moment later the painfully hard smack of wooden floorboards against her side that left her dazed and winded. She heard the door slam with the sudden realisation that she was now on the inside of it. *Inside.* Her bladder emptied in the darkness. All she could hear was the sound of his laboured breathing, the ticking of a clock and the muted clatter of cartwheels outside; the world passing by, oblivious to what had just happened in the blink of an eye.

Argyll stared at the woman at his feet. She was stunned by the impact with the hall's floor. In shock, still. He'd just wanted her to stop shouting for Mary like that . . . but . . . his arms seemed to flex with a mind of their own and now here the pair of them were in this calm and quiet space. He realised the poor woman was terrified. He wanted to apologise.

No. She needs to be afraid. Don't you know why?

Argyll didn't.

She lifted herself and squatted against the base of the wall, trembling. 'Please . . . please . . . don't 'urt me . . .'

Argyll hunkered down beside her. He felt some of the fear himself, wondering what she was seeing as she looked at him. Wondering why she looked like the Devil himself was hovering just in front of her face. He reached out a calming hand towards her. He wanted to tell her that it was all right, that he didn't mean to hurt her. He wanted to explain that what just happened came as a surprise to him too.

Above all else, he just wanted to make her a cup of tea and say sorry.

She recoiled from his hand, whimpering as tears rolled down her cheeks and mixed with blood on her lips. 'Please . . . Mr . . .' she babbled through snot. 'Please . . . Mr B-Babbitt, d-don't d-do me up l-like the others. P-please . . . I . . . I . . .'

His hand froze in the space between them. Somewhere he heard the shuffling of pig's trotters, excited and playful, the snort of the animal and that awful, scraping voice . . .

Babbitt?

Argyll knew the name. *Goddammit.* He knew that name from somewhere.

Yes, of course we know that name. Do you see yet?

He frowned. His mind seemed to be stirring, doors opening all along the dusty, dark hallways of his memory, spilling daylight across them. A dozen different noises and voices stirring to life, like a ward of comatose patients emerging into wakefulness together, eyes once stuck fast with sleep now cracking open.

Mr Babbitt. That's who we are.

But I'm John. John Argyll.

You are Mr Babbitt. Remember? Chop, chop. Work, work. Busy, busy.

Argyll suddenly remembered so much more; not just disjointed moments, dreams and images from someone else's life. The doors in his mind creaked wide open in unison. All of a sudden, he knew his childhood was a privileged one, lived in a household full of maids and cleaners. He remembered a severe-looking bearded man whom he knew was his father, even if the finer details, like his father's name, were still yet to come to him. No . . . there it was: Gordon. His father – Gordon – a businessman. A businessman who saw opportunities in abundance on the far side of the continent . . . in a place called Oregon.

He remembered a period of worry, upset, disquiet. Their home being sold, packing cases in every room, saying farewell to favourite toys. He remembered an older brother, Lawrence, who was closer to their father than him. And a much older sister; not a girl but a young woman. Olivia. Almost like a mother to him. A mother to replace the one he never knew. He remembered a long journey across a wilderness of wide open skies and infinite landscapes of rolling hills covered in wild grass, living and sleeping in the wooden trap of their long wagon. Mornings of waking up beneath a canopy of linen stretched over bows of willow. Evenings spent around camp fires with Olivia and Lawrence and his father and other families who had joined together to comprise their train of wagons.

So close to Olivia. He felt an aching in his heart; a deep wound poked and prodded to open and weep once more. He had always been closest to her. Olivia: memories of a young woman's face, which always seemed to be just a few moments away from laughing brightly at something or other. A tanned and freckled face surrounded by a cloud of auburn hair. And lips that parted wide, constantly amused at all the silly things he said to her, bemused at his fanciful notions and endless questions.

But also growing a little closer to his normally distant father during 'the crossing'. A man whom had always appeared to be far too busy for his young son, now around the campfire in the evenings, able to tell him stories and listen to his questions. A father who finally actually noticed his youngest child and could see he had something special about him. A keen mind. A talent for planning. Far-sightedness, even.

And then the day it all came to a sudden end. The day of screaming.

He shook his head. Too many memories; too much of his life coming at him at once. And his childhood name . . . he knew what it was now. It certainly wasn't 'Mr Babbitt'.

Nor is it 'John Argyll', the dry pig-voice chuckled. *She named you like a child names a pet.*

'NO!!!!!' he screamed. His shrill voice filled the small hallway. Liz flinched and whimpered on the floor. 'MY NAME IS JOHN!!'

He saw the young boy he once was as another person. Another person, yet so alike, with so much in common. Another boy uncertain and lost in an alien world, a wilderness. Another boy cared for by, utterly reliant on, the love of a young woman.

'GO!!' he screamed again, smacking the wall with his fist. 'GO AWAY!!!!!'

Liz stared up at him, wide-eyed, the whimpering fear clogging her throat silenced for the moment. The heels of her boots scrabbled for purchase on the wooden floor.

'Me?' she whispered. 'Y-you l-lettin' me go?'

He stood up, turned away and took several strides up the hall; her snivelling voice was one too many. He could hardly hear himself think. He needed the woman on the floor to shut up.

Time to grow up. Stop being a child.

'LEAVE ME ALONE!' he screamed again, tears thickening his voice. 'Please . . .' His voice softer, pleading, desperate. His broad shoulders shaking. 'Please . . .'

Behind him, quietly daring to pull herself to her feet, trying not to make any noise that might distract him from his fugue, Liz reached for the door handle. She grasped it and grimaced at the daylight flooding into the gloomy space, the noise of Holland Park Avenue seeping in through the partially opened door. She opened it wider. She glanced back at him as he slumped against a wall, his back to her, his fists balled and flexing, his head shaking. She quickly slipped over the threshold. She fled down the steps into the street, across the pavement and onto the road, across the paths of tradesmen's carts, running heavy-heeled until she found herself gasping and grasping the iron railings of a tall, elegant townhouse on the far side.

She turned to look over her shoulder, certain Babbitt must have recovered his wits and was now weaving through traffic to get to her. But all she saw on the far side at number 67 was the front door still open, revealing the darkness inside. In the gloom beyond, she thought she could just make out the slumped form of the man.

CHAPTER 47

1st October 1888, Holland Park, London

She loves you, does she? Hmmm?

He nodded.

She is not your sister, Olivia. Your sister died a long, long time ago. You remember how she died now?

Yes, he did. He didn't need to replay that memory to know. It was all back in his head now. He wished it wasn't.

Oh . . . but Mary reminds you of Olivia, does she? A snort of derisive laughter. *You are pitiful. You are weak. You are as naïve as a baby.* The voice managed to find a timbre of tenderness. *You have to be stronger than this. You have to be as you were.*

I don't want to be like I was. I don't want to do it anymore.

The work needs doing. All the tormented ones, the bad ones, returning and poisoning everything. God gave you this work because only you can set them free.

No. Not anymore.

Think! Think how much evil you have sent away. Corrupt souls, dirty souls, evil souls, greedy souls. How many of them is it now? Do you remember?

He could count them, although he didn't need to. The number was already tallied; scored marks cut into a wooden post in his mind. Ninety-three.

Indeed. Ninety-three souls that will never return; never again extort, steal, lie, murder, cheat.

He'd killed ninety-three people. Mostly men, but a handful of women. And with every last one, he'd made sure to study them closely, look into their eyes as they died. With most of them, it had been a rotten, putrid coil of smoke that had wafted up from the extinguished candle. But with a few, just a few, there had been the faintest odour of redemption in the thin twist of rising smoke.

Yes . . . so few.

I don't want to do this anymore.

Don't want? Don't want?! The voice mimicked the whining mewl of a petulant child. *Who says you get to choose?*

I know that . . . I know that I can choose.

No! You were CHOSEN. When they let you go . . . Oh, yes, they understood what you were.

They, those Indians, the shaman. He remembered . . .

The sky above is so blue. The sun hot on my face. I'm trembling uncontrollably, hands lashed behind me around one of the poles they use to stretch and cure buffalo hides. They're all dead now: Father, Olivia, Lawrence, the other families. A morning and an afternoon of slaughter right there before me. The whole tribe partaking in the ritual. The women of the tribe, it seems, are the best schooled in extracting the maximum pain, as they insert smouldering and sharpened sticks through clenched eyelids. Pushing and pushing them through ruined eyes until the wood snaps and splinters.

I've dirtied myself many times over. I've screamed and cried and fainted, over and over.

And now it's so quiet. They've left me to the very last. An old man approaches, holding a smouldering strip of human hide in one shaking hand. The old man settles cross-legged in front of me, eyes studying me intently. The rest of the tribe are sitting down quietly, watching their elder.

I open my mouth to beg but can produce only a croak.

The old man shuffles closer on his rump. His nose, narrow, almost beak-like, inches from my face. I can hear air whistling into his nostrils. He's smelling me. Surely the only smell here is my own shit, drying on the parched grass between my feet.

The old man's eyes narrow, as if he's discovered something that intrigues him. He holds the smouldering strip of hide up between us, chanting softly under his breath. It burns like a candle wick, an ash grey tip in the afternoon sunlight; but if it was dark, it would be a glowing ember.

I want to die. Please, something quick so I can join the others, wherever they are. It's over for them now and I envy them that.

The old man reaches a thumb and forefinger to his mouth, licks them and then pinches the end of the strip of hide. I hear the slightest sizzle of spit as the ember is extinguished. He watches a twist of smoke drift, spin and vanish. The old man seems to read something in that. He nods slowly then reaches a hand out and pats my head gently, ruffling my hair with what seems like . . . affection.

I don't die that day. The tribe adopt me. Only for a year. A hunting season passes, a winter passes; not enough time for me to learn much of their language. But I learn that a dog is called a chinpadda, *the sun is* hatat. *That's about all.*

Eventually, one morning, the tribe encounters another train of wagons. I'm frightened I'll witness another day like that one from nearly a year ago. But instead the old man approaches me, grasps my arm and walks me forward across the swaying grass towards the wagons. There are white men with guns raised warily. For a moment, I'm afraid both me and the old man are going to die in a hail of musket balls. But they see I'm a white boy and they refrain from firing.

The old man kneels beside me. There is no love between us. No bond. I can't feel anything for this man who killed my family. But over the year, an understanding between us has developed. These people communicate not with writing, but with pictures. And I understand what the old man has shown me.

Father Sky sees only an imbalance in the white faces. Their world has become bad. This is why they flood in such great numbers across land that is not theirs. The old man presses a strip of hide into my hand. I look down and see it, painted, decorated, with what look like simple representations of faces. He says something and gently places his hand between my shoulders and pushes me forward towards the waiting wagons.

In all my years since, I've never understood what the old man actually said. But I am almost certain I now understand what he was telling me.

You were tested. Now test others.

A ticking clock echoes in a hallway thirty years later.

You don't get to choose. You were chosen.

For a long while, the pig-voice fell silent. Argyll was dimly aware of the sounds coming through the open front door, the braying cough of a horse as it clopped by. He stood up, walked up the hallway towards the front door and gently pushed it to. It closed with a heavy thud that left him in a gloom lit only by the second-hand light coming through the open doorway to the morning room.

On the breakfast table in there stood his pot of tea, his boiled egg, his toast, all long since gone cold.

That hateful, rasping cackle filled his head once more, and for a fleeting moment the voice, thin and reedy, reminded him of the old Indian shaman. But, of course, the words were now English.

I have an idea.

CHAPTER 48

1st October 1888 (3.00 pm), Whitechapel, London

It took her most of the afternoon to make her way back across London. Every jostled, harried minute of it wondering what she should do for the best. Stop the nearest copper? Walk into a police station and tell all? And who the hell was going to believe a squalid-looking creature as her, smelling as she did of her own drying urine and old tobacco?

A sobering thought silenced the panicked babbling in her head.

Prince Eddy. They need this to remain secret.

They. Gentlemen in secret clubs. The authorities.

And that chilling thought came with another, hot on its heels. *They will want me and Cath dead.*

It was gone four in the afternoon when her weary heels clacked onto the cobbles of Millers Court. It was quiet as usual. This time in the afternoon, the evening meals were already being prepared, wood burners stoked, paraffin hobs fired up, children called in off the street to help with the peeling, scraping and chopping, and the men, most of them still two or three hours away from the end of their working day.

She passed by a couple of young boys, hunkered over the bodies of several dozen rats which they had laid out like a platoon of soldiers on the pavement, bickering over how many each of them had caught. She knew their dirt-smudged faces, both annoying little brats with shaved heads like bullets and pink jug ears begging to be grabbed and roughly twisted. They were brothers. Lived next door to Marge's lodging house.

'Oi, love!' said the older one. ''Ow much?' He stood up and started air-humping like a dog on heat.

'Piss off!' she hissed as she hustled up the three steps and pushed the unlocked front door inwards.

Dirty little bastards.

The hallway was never lit. 'I ain't gettin' rent off the 'allway, am I?' was what Marge said. 'Waste of bloody gas.' Liz had only rented a room here for a few months. Long enough to know she'd rather lodge elsewhere. But Cath still kept her room because it was relatively cheap.

She closed the front door behind her and stepped across the creaking boards to tap lightly on what used to be Mary's old door.

'Mary? Love? You in there?'

She tried the handle. The door was locked. She knocked again. A hope had been growing in her as she'd hurried from one tram to another that maybe the girl had come across to their neck of the woods to see if she'd found out anything about that key. Perhaps she was in Cath's room, talking to her?

She walked past another door on her left. She could faintly hear bumping going on and the bellows' wheeze of a man grunting like a farmyard animal. A new girl must have moved in. A new girl getting some early trade in.

The next door was Cath's. She rapped her knuckles lightly. 'Cath? You in?'

She heard the muted scrape of shoes. Several quick steps and the door clicked and opened ajar. In the faint pall of light coming from the small bedroom window, she saw the outline of her friend's head and shoulders.

'Liz?' Cath hissed.

'Yeah.'

'Thank, gawd. I was gettin' so worried!'

Liz pushed the door inwards. 'Cath! He *is* that killer! The crazy bastard nearly—' Her eyes registered the man sitting on a stool beside the window. She stopped. Eyes wide.

'Don't fret! He's some sort of copper,' said Cath quickly. 'It's all right. We're safe 'ere!'

'Is this your friend?' said the man. His eyes narrowed, peering into the dark. 'Is this Mary Kelly?' He looked nothing like a copper to Liz. Expensive clothes, polished shoes, neatly-trimmed moustache and sideburns. Not like any plain clothes copper she'd ever seen.

'No, it's me mate, Liz.'

He stood up, smiled, beckoned her in. 'Relax, my dear, you're quite safe. My name's George. Catherine, here, has been telling me quite a remarkable story! That you may have, shall I say, *stumbled* upon the man who's responsible for the Hanbury Street and Bucks Row killings? The chap the papers are calling "Jack the Ripper"?'

Cath nodded eagerly. 'I told 'em about the body parts in 'is jam jar!' *Parts.* Typical of Cath, in her excitement, exaggerating the story by one degree. 'An' that letter 'e wrote! That letter confessin' to all of it!'

Liz would rather she hadn't gushed everything out like that. She didn't know the half of what was in that letter. Better perhaps that she didn't.

'So, you were also in this man's room at The Grantham Hotel?' asked the well-dressed gentleman. George. If that was his real name.

She nodded. 'I was . . . yes.'

'And do you also believe, like Catherine, that the room has been occupied by the murderer? This so called "Ripper" chap?'

Liz realised Cath had already told them too much for her to offer a guarded response. 'He has and no mistake.'

'And you know where he is right now?'

She nodded quickly. 'I . . . I just come from where 'e's staying. 'E nearly . . .' She hesitated, but realised she'd given this man too much already to start being coy with the truth. ''E nearly killed me!'

'Good god!' gasped the man. 'Tell me what happened! Please!'

'I knocked, wanting to speak to Mary. 'E answered the door and . . .' Liz realised her voice was catching with emotion: delayed shock. She was going to cry if she didn't draw a breath and slow herself down. ''E . . . pulled me inside . . . but I managed to escape.'

'And your friend, Mary   was she in there?'

Liz shook her head. 'I shouted for 'er . . . but she never replied.'

'Oh gawd!' cried Cath. 'The poor love's already dead!'

Warrington nodded thoughtfully. 'I'm afraid that's a possibility we may have to consider.'

'You got to send someone over there! Now!' said Liz. 'She might not be—'

'Calm down,' said Warrington. 'My men and I were watching the hotel. And you,' he said, tipping a nod at Liz, 'were followed by one of my chaps. He has that address and I'm expecting he will have already called it in. Some of our boys will be on their way over right now.' He offered her a sympathetic smile. 'We can hope your friend is all right. There's still hope.'

Liz frowned. She was remembering something. 'I got the feelin' she was out, though,' she said. 'When I knocked, I think 'e was expecting 'er, or summin'.'

'Then perhaps our men may get there first,' said Warrington. 'Before she returns. Perhaps, as you said,' he nodded at Cath, 'perhaps she's on her way here to see you?'

Liz looked at him, feeling a little less troubled with the idea of confiding what she knew with the man. He didn't seem like a dark-hooded conspirator. He seemed as genuinely concerned as them. In any case, that letter was just sitting up there in room 207; they were going to find it and read it sooner rather than later.

'There's something said in that letter, in the hotel room.'

'Oh?'

''E . . . 'e said . . .' Liz frowned, thinking how best to relay the things she'd hastily read. 'He said summin' about the royal prince. That 'e's been . . .' It sounded utterly unlikely now, like the utterings of a drunk or an idiot. 'That the prince got some tart pregnant. That there was a baby and—'

Cath turned to look at her, her eyes wide, almost perfect circles. 'What?!'

The gentleman raised his hand. 'I think we should just deal with apprehending this man first, then we can investigate the contents of this hotel room of his in due course.' He pursed his lips. 'Your friend, Mary, may still be perfectly all right. And if she is, we would very much like to speak with her.' Again, a comforting smile that assured Liz the worst of this awful business was over; that she and Cath had done the right thing offloading what they knew onto him. That it was all in the capable hands of the police now. Liz felt the weight come off her shoulders and a sense of exhaustion kick in.

'Yes,' said Liz. 'I hope so.'

'We'll know soon enough about this man's motives.' He sighed. 'But, you know, alcohol, opiates, those sorts of vices, can make an already troubled mind believe quite insane things.'

Liz nodded. Yes, having some more time to dwell on it, thinking about it, that rambling letter had sounded quite ridiculous.

'We shall have this troubled man in irons soon enough,' said Warrington, 'and an end to this Ripper nonsense.'

CHAPTER 49

1st October 1888 (3.00 pm), Holland Park, London

He heard the front door click open.

'John?' Mary's voice; quiet, apologetic. The door clunked shut. 'I'm sorry I've been so long . . . The man in the laundrette lost your bloomin' shirt!' She sounded out of breath, like she'd been hurrying home.

Footsteps down the hallway.

'John? You in there?' she called into the morning room.

Footsteps again, past the ticking clock on the hall table then, all of a sudden, her footsteps ceased. He heard her breath catch. She had spotted the cellar door was open.

Footsteps again down the hallway, towards him.

'John?' This time her voice was much quieter, less assured. 'John?'

Her head craned round into the small kitchen. He looked up from the large notes of money spread across the round wooden table in front of him. He'd been counting them. Four thousand, three hundred and seventy-five pounds.

A lot of money.

Beneath the table, one fist gently squeezed the handle of a bread knife. He'd been holding it, absently caressing the worn wooden handle for what seemed like hours. He couldn't remember actually picking it up, couldn't remember deciding the thing ought to be out of the drawer and in his hands. It had somehow just ended up there in his lap. He wasn't entirely sure why.

'Oh, god,' she whispered at the sight of the leather bag on the table and the money spread out beside it.

Remember what I told you? said the pig-voice. *She will lie to you about all this. Just you see if she doesn't.*

Argyll said nothing. His lips clamped shut. His face immobile, hiding a raging battlefield of emotions. A discordant chorus of voices in his head, all screaming different things:

Run, Mary! Save yourself!

Why, Mary, why the lies?

You duplicitous bitch!

I love you.

I HATE YOU!

And like a conductor calling an orchestra to order, the rasping voice of that stump-legged pig hushed them all.

She'll tell a dirty lie and then you'll see she's like all the other soiled wretches. Greedy, deceitful, selfish, spiteful.

Mary hesitated in the doorway of the kitchen. She glanced over her shoulder, back down the hallway. A quick glance that looked as if she was measuring her chances of an escape.

Yes, oh yes. Even better; she'll run for it. Go on, Mary . . . Why not run? See how far you can get. His leg is much better now. Just you see, girl.

Argyll's lips trembled. He desperately wanted to warn her that the very next thing she might decide to say, to do, could very well be the end of her. He wasn't sure if the pig in his mind was himself. He wasn't even sure if this body was his anymore, whether he – 'John Argyll' – was no more than an imposter, a trespasser, no more than a passing tenant. The pig-voice, the person Argyll once was, now returned to take control of things.

Mary stared at him, then down at all that money spread across the table.

The rasping voice giggled with barely-contained excitement. *She wants that money! She's going to tell you it's hers. Any second now . . . Come on, dear, come on, let's have that lie. Say it.*

She took a step into the small kitchen. Lowered the bundle of folded shirts she had in her hands – his freshly laundered one and several new ones – onto the table, her shopping basket down onto the floor.

'I . . . I bought some pork for our tea,' she murmured hollowly.

Look at her! Oh, she's so very clever! Look at her! Do you see her thinking? Scheming? Hmmm?

Slowly, she pulled a chair out from beneath the table. Its legs scraped noisily across the stone floor. His fist clenched tightly around the knife's handle. A part of him didn't want to hear her talk; didn't want her to say anything. A part of him that was fading away fast . . . dying. John Argyll.

'Mary, please don't . . .'

Shut up! Let the bitch talk! I want you to listen to her fucking lie!

She raised a finger to hush him. A tear rolled down her cheek and her lips curled and quivered. 'I . . .'

Here it is! Here it comes!

'Mary . . . please . . . don't say any—'

Shut up! Let her do it! Let her . . . let her . . . LET HER!!!!

'John, I . . .' Her voice quavered.

The pig grasped the knife more tightly, as if to be sure he was holding it, not that *imposter*, Argyll. Under the table, the tip of the blade trembled, almost as if it had an eager hunger of its own.

'I . . . I've not been honest with you,' she said eventually. 'This house? You and me? It's all been me lying to you!' Her shoulders shook as she began to sob uncontrollably. 'It's yours . . . this money. It's your money. I . . . I don't know why I thought this would ever . . .' Her voice was lost as she dropped her face, mottled pink with shame, into her hands. The rest of her faltering words were an incomprehensible babble that spilled into her lap.

Quietly, Argyll loosened his tight grip on the blade. Then he tucked it away into a deep inside pocket of his coat. The pig was silent. It had nothing to say. It snorted with disgust, and he sensed it retiring to a dark corner of his mind.

She isn't like all the others.

'Mary,' Argyll said softly. 'I know. I remember everything now. *Everything*. I remember you and I were . . .' He looked down at the table, as if the words he needed were nestling there amongst the five pound notes. 'We weren't anything. Strangers. We hadn't met. I know that now.'

She looked up from her hands, eyes red-rimmed, her breath hitching. 'It started out . . . I just wanted your money. But . . .'

He nodded. He reached out for her small balled fist; shaking white knuckles and flexing tendons. 'I understand. What happened between you and me, it wasn't in your plan. But it happened nonetheless.' A winsome smile spread across his lips. 'Never trust a plan; they always go awry.'

She nodded silently.

'It's . . . *love* . . . isn't it?' He dared to say that word.

She looked at him and nodded again, her face crumpled. 'Yes, yes it is!'

'Well then . . . all the rest of it.' He shrugged. 'It's another life. Someone else's. And I don't want that life anymore.' He looked around the kitchen. 'I want *this*. This home that you invented. Even though it all started out as pretence.' He sighed. 'Even though this has just been pretend, I still want it. I want *this*. Us.'

His pig was silent, furious, chastened. Argyll thought he could hear its shifting movements coming from the dusty attic of his mind. Scraping, snorting angrily. No longer the master of ceremonies now; merely a disgruntled imp, a dark urge. An itch, banished to the rafters.

Mary looked up from her hands, red-eyed, cheeks blotchy and pink. Beautiful even in shame. 'I'm so sorry, I'm so sorry.'

Argyll stepped around the table and knelt beside her. He held her oval chin in one hand, dimpled and creased and quivering as her breath caught.

'Mary, I need you.'

The kitchen filled with the bark of a chair leg on the stone floor. More than that: a sob, a half-cry, a whimper of relief from her. She wrapped her arms around him. 'Oh, John, I'm sorry. I'm sorry. I'm sorry.' Her muttered words soaked into his shoulder.

'Listen, Mary,' said Argyll. 'You and me, we've got to leave this place.'

She wasn't listening. Her tears dampened his neck, her hands tugged and pulled at his shoulders as if she wanted to climb inside him, hide within the warmth and safety of Mr Argyll. He pulled her firmly away from him, his expression stern.

'Listen to me! We have to leave right now.'

She was hearing it, but not understanding it. 'Leave?'

'Yes. Get your things. Whatever's important to you. One bag. And fill it quickly!'

She sniffed, dabbed at her eyes. 'Why?' She looked at him. For the first time she noticed that he had his coat on. 'Where . . . where are we going?'

He cupped her small jaw again in his hand; the very same hand that only moments ago had been ready to thrust the end of a bread knife deep into her neck. 'Do you trust me?'

She nodded shakily.

'Good.' He lifted her arms off him and began gathering up the money. 'We have to leave this place as soon as possible. We're in danger.'

CHAPTER 50

1st October 1888 (3.15 pm), Holland Park, London

Sir Henry Rawlinson's carriage turned off Clarendon Road onto Holland Park Avenue. He felt a burning indigestion in the pit of his stomach. He hated haste. He hated being in a hurry. It upset him. Especially directly after eating so heavily.

If there was one lesson in life that he'd learned thoroughly, it was that great haste preceded many an error. A hurried plan was little more than deferred chaos. Nothing worth anything in this world was ever conceived or constructed in haste. And if it was, then it wasn't long before it started to unravel.

'Nearly there, sir.'

Rawlinson nodded at Robson sitting opposite him, rocking from side to side as the carriage barrelled along the street, faster than city ordinance allowed. A common hansom rattling along at this sort of pace would probably have been waved down by a copper by now, but Rawlinson's carriage – black lacquered and impractically long – was a caution to any young man in uniform not to waste the time of the Very Important Person inside with some finger-wagging.

Robson's boxer's hands absently played with the cylinder of his revolver. It clicked as chamber after chamber circled past the tip of the hammer. Good man, Robson, according to George Warrington. Glacially calm in a crisis. Apparently he'd seen a fair bit of action before leaving Her Majesty's service. Ostensibly, he was just a doorman for their little club. More than that, of course; he was their Lodge's sergeant at arms. He acknowledged even the higher members with a grumpy, grudging parade-ground demeanour that they all found rather amusing and vaguely charming.

Rawlinson was satisfied that the broad-shouldered man – with a chest and stomach like a cider barrel, still managing to maintain army fitness despite his middling years – was going to be enough, with his revolver, to deal with the Candle Man. This hired killer was, after all, just a ruddy man.

Robson shifted in his seat to look out the carriage window, scanning the numbers on the doors along the avenue.

'Sixty-seven, wasn't it, sir?'

Rawlinson nodded.

'We just passed fifty-nine. We're getting close. Perhaps best if we stop a little downwind?'

'Yes, quite right, Robson. Don't want to spook the game.' He leant forward, pulled aside a hatch and tapped the driver's back through it. 'Just here is fine, Colin, if you please!' he called out.

'Right y'are, sir,' the driver bellowed back, before reigning in the horses and clucking at them to settle down. The carriage came to a halt and Robson reached for the door handle.

'Robson?'

'Sir?'

'If he's inside, don't waste a single second. Do you understand? You fire your gun the instant you set eyes on him.'

Robson looked uncertain. 'It's quite busy right now, sir. Lot of people are going to hear a gun shot—'

'That's not your concern.' He offered the man a reassuring nod. 'Nothing we can't tidy up later on.'

'Right you are.' Robson nodded. 'Shoot first it is then, sir.'

'And you be sure to shoot for a *kill*. We have absolutely no need at all to talk to this gentleman. Do you understand?'

Robson pushed the carriage door open and stepped smartly out into the road, the revolver tucked discreetly into his coat. Rawlinson followed him out and together they stepped up onto the busy pavement, their eyes picking out the dark front door of 67, thirty yards ahead.

They made their way towards the property, stepping aside for a pair of young nannies pushing prams side by side and lost in their conversation, then weaving around a coal delivery man as he hefted a sack of coal past them and down a metal stairway into a basement entrance. A child's toy fell from one of the prams and Robson instinctively reached down, scooped it up and handed it to one of the young ladies with a tip of his hat.

Rawlinson tutted. Now wasn't the time for a theatrical display of good manners. He jabbed his man in the back with his walking cane.

'Come along, Robson,' he hissed as they stepped aside for a couple striding past; a tall, lean, middle-aged gentleman, laughing merrily at something the frizzy-haired young lady on his arm had just said. They strode past, oblivious, full of joy, her pretty oval face the very picture of youthful exuberance and excitement.

Lovers. Henry winked at them as he stepped aside. Long time since *he'd* had such a delightful creature as that on his old arm. The man smiled back at him.

Finally they were looking up six steps to the front door of number 67. Rawlinson nodded at Robson and they quickly climbed the steps. At the top, Robson reached out for the door knocker.

'Whoever answers, we push our way in, Robson.' Rawlinson glanced at the busy street behind him. It was busier than he'd have liked. 'Better we do what needs to be done inside, behind a closed door.'

'Right you are, sir.'

As Robson reached to knock, he noticed the door was slightly ajar. 'It's already open, sir.'

Rawlinson gave him the nod to go in. 'Be careful.'

Robson pulled the gun out of his pocket, shielding it from any curious passers-by with his back. He pushed the door open.

Argyll flagged a hansom on the opposite side of the street. The driver touched the peak of his cap and pulled over on the far side as he waited for them to cross the busy traffic and join him. Climbing aboard the open fronted cart, Argyll gave the driver instructions to take them to Euston station.

The carriage began to clatter down Holland Park Avenue and Argyll turned in his seat to watch those two men they'd just passed by, now taking the steps up to their front door.

A Mason and his foot soldier. He'd noted the older man's cravat pin. A square and compass.

He managed to contain a gasp of relief. Good god, a moment or two more fussing around inside and they would have been caught in the house.

'John? John?'

He realised Mary had been saying something to him. 'I'm sorry?'

'Why are we in such a hurry? You said something about being in danger? Please tell me . . . Where are we going? What's going on?'

He looked out at the driver sitting on the jockey board in front of them, the bouncing flanks of the horse, the rhythmic rise and dip of its head.

'Not here, not right now, Mary,' he uttered quietly.

'John . . . this is all . . . Why are we in danger? I'm frightened.'

'We're safe for the moment.' He held her hand. 'I'm taking care of *you* now.'

She shook her head, a buzzing beehive of questions. 'You said your memories have all come back? You said that back in the house.'

He nodded. 'I know who I am now. And I'm going to tell you all about me. Soon. We're going to find somewhere else to stay. Then I promise I'll tell you everything.'

Everything?

No. Just as much as she needed to know, but not all. She would run from him if she knew all the things his hands had done. Run for her life. There was much of it now he'd be happy to leave behind as well, to forget about. He was running *from* his life.

Today was going to be a new beginning. A goodbye to everything that came before.

'I'll tell you everything,' he said again. 'I promise.'

She nodded, prepared to accept that for the moment, watching the street widen as they entered Notting Hill. The traders were beginning to close their stalls as the late afternoon traffic was on the wane.

'It's awful!' she said suddenly. 'I only know you as John. It's the first name I could think of,' she said guiltily. She shook her head. 'It's so strange. You *are* John to me, but what's your real name? Can you remember it?'

He nodded.

'Tell me! What is it?'

He had a name, but not one anyone had used in years. He had pseudonyms aplenty; 'Babbitt' just one of many. Names he'd invented, names and identities he'd stolen from dead men's wallets. All part of the craft, the art of being what he'd been: an executioner for hire, an extinguisher of human rubbish. But his name, his *real* name, was all that he had left of 'before'. And the last person who'd ever spoken that name out loud had been Olivia. Not even spoken; it had been screamed.

Another time. Another life. He closed his eyes and closed a door on all of that.

'Mary . . .' He chewed his lip in thought. 'I really don't want to be who I was. Could you and I agree that I'm John Argyll?'

She frowned, mock-serious. 'Oh, come on. I want to know all about you.' She squeezed his hand. 'I love you. That's all I—'

'Please?' His smile was a plea. 'You know, I rather like this name. I've grown used to it.'

She studied his face for a moment, her eyes narrowed as a faint smile twisted the corner of her lips. 'John, you're even more of a puzzle to me now than you were.'

He shrugged an apology.

'Will you at least tell me where we're off to and why the rush?'

'I was . . . in London on important business.'

'What business?'

'Business,' he said firmly. 'Best I leave it at that. But there are men who, let me just say, don't want me to conclude my business.'

'John? Please, you're scaring me!'

'Not now. I can't explain it all now.' He smiled, reached for her hand. 'You and I, we're going to travel. See some places. And then when we find somewhere we like, we'll start again. A new life.'

She nodded.

'So, where would you like to go?'

Her eyes widened. 'Anywhere?'

'Anywhere.'

'Oh . . . I . . .' She shook her head. 'I suppose we could get a train down to Southend-on-Sea?'

He sighed and waggled his hand as if the idea sounded boring. 'I was thinking somewhere further afield.'

She gasped and her jaw hung. 'You don't mean *Brighton*?!'

Argyll stroked his chin. 'I was thinking more along the lines of . . . America?'

She sputtered and laughed. 'Oh, go on with you!'

'I'm quite serious.'

Her lips clamped shut and there wasn't another word from her all the way to the station.

Robson came down the stairs. 'All empty, sir. It looks like he's done a runner.'

Rawlinson mouthed a curse. This matter could've been wrapped up here and now. He could have laughed out loud at his wise old musings of ten minutes ago.

Not bloody hasty enough this time, ol' son.

'He wasn't living alone, sir. There's lady's things upstairs in one of the rooms. Must have left in a hurry; not much taken and it's quite a mess.'

Rawlinson turned his back on Robson and wandered down the hallway, deep in thought. So this morning they'd learned their man was actually very much alive and well. And now on the run. That made him even more dangerous. If he felt he had nowhere to turn, he might just do something very foolish. Something very public.

He wandered into the kitchen at the back of the house, still considering their options. Perhaps a much larger settlement. Five or ten times the original fee. A grand gesture of contrition on their part for mistakenly assuming he was no better than a common shiv-man. The New York Lodge had said he was a complete professional. Utterly reliable. Utterly confidential.

'Dammit,' he spat under his breath. Their little committee had been too eager to have this matter tightly parcelled up.

Robson entered the room behind him, giving the kitchen a quick and cursory second glance. He opened a door that led onto a small pantry: just empty shelves.

'Feels like a household closed down for the summer,' said Robson. 'Do you think, sir?'

Rawlinson nodded. Yes, it had that feeling. The vague smell of mothballs and dust about it.

'Hang on.' Robson strode across the kitchen and reached for something on a shelf. An envelope. 'It's a letter, sir. Says on the envelope, "For George".'

'Let me see, please?'

Robson passed it across the table to him. The envelope wasn't glued down. He lifted the flap open and impatiently pulled out the letter inside.

George,

It appears you and your colleagues acted precipitously in this matter. The act of betrayal was frankly impolite, extremely amateur and entirely unnecessary. I made no attempt to raise my fee on discovering exactly whose dirty peccadilloes you and your colleagues were attempting to cover up, did I? And yet I can only presume you thought I would attempt some sort of a blackmail at a later date.

Well, now things have gotten out of hand.

Perhaps it is time to conclude this matter. Despite your

unforgivable behaviour, I have no plans at this stage to get even with you. I do, however, wish to return to my own affairs in one piece, if possible, without having to maintain a watchful eye for those heavy-handed clods you employ.

I will, in due course, make contact in the already established way and perhaps we can settle this matter face to face.

Until then, George, you and your colleagues can wait.

Candle Man

CHAPTER 51

1st October 1888 (7.00 pm), Whitechapel, London

Warrington was getting twitchy with impatience. The afternoon had passed into early evening stuck in this small, squalid room with these two women. He had a feeling he'd extracted every last nugget of useful information out of the pair of them without even having to lift a finger, no less. They both seemed utterly relieved to unburden themselves of their story. Quite convinced they were talking to some senior, non-uniformed representative of Scotland Yard. The taller one, Liz, had been a little more wary than the other one, who kept mentioning things that Liz could only then ruefully, reluctantly acknowledge.

Such was how he learned all about their mutual friend – Mary Kelly.

He marvelled at this young girl's ingenuity. She'd come across their man in rather poor shape, then discovered he had money. Moreover, discovered he had no memories whatsoever of how he came to be where she'd discovered him. 'Amnesia', Warrington believed the official medical term was. And this Mary had convinced him that the pair of them were sweethearts.

Absolutely ingenious.

Not for the first time this afternoon, he was learning how clever and conniving the gutter class could be. So easy to write them off as little more than freshly scrubbed and shaved primates in clothes, as he'd been hitherto inclined to do. They might sound sub-normal with their swallowed half-words and incomprehensibly garbled sentences, but this girl, Kelly, sounded every bit as divisive and sharp-witted as some of the more duplicitous barristers he crossed paths with from time to time.

Clever girl. Pity, though . . . Pity.

All of them heard the front door's handle rattling as it was turned then a moment later the door clicking open, followed by the scrape and fall of footsteps outside in the hallway. They heard that appalling creature Marge emerging from her rooms like a spider down one thread of her web, enquiring who was there. Warrington heard Robson's voice as he bluntly shooed her away.

A rap on the door. On opening it, Warrington was surprised to see Sir Henry Rawlinson standing outside in the dark hallway.

'Good grief, Henry! I didn't expect you to come down here!'

The old man removed his top hat. 'George. What an eventful afternoon, eh?'

Robson stepped in behind him, his bowler hat respectfully grasped in both hands.

'We missed him, George. The chap bolted before we could get there. He's not alone, either. We think he has a lady friend with him.'

'Yes, these two,' Warrington gestured at Liz and Cath, '*ladies* . . . know of her. She's an associate of theirs. A woman called Mary Kelly.'

Rawlinson raised a snow-white feathered brow. 'A hostage to fortune, is she?'

'Perhaps.' Warrington explained quickly what the women had told him.

Rawlinson produced the letter. 'The rascal left this behind. He must have guessed we were coming for him.'

Warrington read the note quickly. 'I think I know exactly where he'll be going.'

'Where?'

'Euston station. He's leaving the country. He'll try for a train up to Liverpool tonight. I'm certain of it. If we're quick, we could catch up with him at the station.'

Rawlinson considered that in silence.

'Henry?'

'Perhaps it might be better if we *don't* try to catch him.'

Warrington looked around the room; too many damned ears listening for them to talk openly. He went to the door, pulled it open and stepped into the dark hallway. 'Henry? A word, sir?'

Rawlinson followed him and the pair of them walked down the hall, pulled the front door open and stepped outside. The sun was just above the slate roof opposite and the narrow street was a little busier, with men returning home from work. They looked too conspicuous: a pair of very well-to-do gentlemen standing on the doorstep of a dilapidated lodging house, talking in whispers . . . But needs must.

'Henry, we have to at least *try* and follow him. We can't let him completely disappear like he did last time!'

The old man pursed his lips for a moment. 'All right, George. All right. But would you be able to properly identify him in a crowd?'

Warrington had met him twice now and on both occasions he had been unable to see his face; quite deliberate, of course. He had an idea of the man's approximate build – tall and lean – and an impression of the man's agility. But that was all.

'I could take one of those two women.' He tipped his head at the door behind them. 'They know Kelly. I could take the taller woman with me to the station. If she can point out Kelly, then we'd have him.'

'Hmm. That's true.'

'And if I take Robson and Hain with me, if they get on a train, we'll get on it too. Once they've gone to ground and we know where they're staying, I'll put in a call.'

Rawlinson nodded. 'All right, but listen, George. We really can't afford a big scene at the station, you understand?' He lowered his voice. 'We do not have infinite resources to play around with. There are only so many favours I can pull in from our colleagues on the force. Just follow him, that's all.'

'Of course.'

'You can take my hansom. It's waiting at the end of Dorset Street.'

Warrington turned to go back inside, then stopped. 'The other woman, Cath; what are we doing with her?'

Rawlinson's long sigh carried a note of regret. 'This Whitechapel murderer the newspapers seem to be wholly in love with . . . I have a feeling he may just strike again tonight.'

'Both of them?'

He turned his nose up, as if the decision had its own odour. 'Once she manages to point out her friend, send her back here in a cab. You're probably best promising her a reward. I'll have one of our chaps take care of things.'

'What about the room at The Grantham Hotel?'

'We stopped by there. Hain took care of those things. That confession and the piece of . . . organ are ashes now.'

'In that case, we could have a go at killing him! We could produce evidence that frames him as the murderer. We could easily—'

'George, no. We're having to react to events far too quickly. There'll be a dreadful mistake in there somewhere that will hang us!' He stroked the tip of his long nose. 'Two more missing tarts in Whitechapel is one thing, but a man shot dead right in the middle of Euston station is quite another.'

Warrington drew a breath. The old man was right.

'Follow him until he goes to ground, then we'll discuss what needs to happen next.'

'Right.'

Rawlinson gestured with his hand. 'Go on then, George; you'd better get a move on to Euston station.'

CHAPTER 52

1st October 1888 (6.30 pm), Euston Station, London

Euston was busier than Mary imagined it would be; the main hall before the departure and arrival platforms was thick with porters and passengers, knots of people waiting for arrivals or saying farewells.

Argyll led Mary by the hand through the bustling crowd, the main hall echoing with the sounds of trains readying for departure or rolling in to clunk gently against the buffer-stops and bellow geysers of steam to announce their arrival.

Mary had only ever been on a train once before and that was several years ago: her journey to London, away from the stultifying valleys of Carmarthenshire. She'd felt like this then, trembling uncontrollably with excitement at the prospect of stepping over the threshold into a new world, a brand new life. But this time, for this far bigger journey, she had John Argyll holding her hand.

Liverpool. Liverpool! And after that, as soon as he could organise things, a ship to America!

She wished she could contain the foolish gape on her face. She imagined she must look very much like some sort of village idiot being led by the hand along the concourse.

Argyll found space on a wooden bench. 'Take a seat, Mary. I shall go and get us some tickets.'

She nodded obediently, sat down and watched him go. He was a whole head taller than most of the bustling crowd. She eventually lost sight of him, only to spot him a moment later scooting athletically up the sweeping marble staircase at the end of the hall, taking three steps at a time and causing a couple of elderly women to shake their heads disapprovingly and a porter to bark out something in his wake. He walked along the gallery and into the booking office.

She was excited, yes, but also nervous. John was suddenly so very different. Almost another person to the one she'd clumsily poured tea over at breakfast this morning. He still looked the same, he still spoke the same; that soft, exotic accent that hinted at exciting frontiers of untamed wilderness. He still treated her with a gentle formality, treated her like a lady. And yet one thing was gone from him – that childlike vulnerability, the wide-eyed man lost at sea, holding onto her like a life vest.

He didn't *need* her anymore. *He* was the carer now, the grown-up, and she the child. Which made her wonder how long it would be before he tired of her. How long this part of the fairytale would last. Yesterday, he would have been entirely lost without her. Today, she was just a young working-class woman – *oh, be honest, a common tart* – who somehow had managed to catch the eye of this wholly mysterious man. How long before he let go of that needful devotion to her, now he seemed so different, so in control. So awake.

She chastised herself. *Don't think that way! He loves you . . . He does!*

Then, not forgotten, there was the matter of that word 'danger'. John had used that word just the once and had not offered another word of explanation as to why. Mary was no fool; there must be people who were after John, for whatever reason. There was a reason why they'd left in such a dreadful hurry. Just like there was a reason why he had all that money on him. Just like there was a reason why she'd found him weeks ago, his skull stove in, and covered in so much blood.

She wasn't stupid. This much she could guess at: whomever he was running from had done that to him, tried to kill him once before. And when she'd *claimed* him like lost property from St Bartholomew's hospital, perhaps she'd unwittingly saved him, whisked him away from his pursuers. But now, whoever they were, they had somehow managed to find him again.

That could only mean she was in some sort of danger too.

She looked around at the swirling waltz of people: gentlemen in bowlers and billycock hats, hurrying to catch trains home; flustered women in bustles and feathers; and bewildered children holding hands so tightly in fear of becoming lost and separated in the crowd. So many bustling, busy people; surely nothing was going to happen to her or John? Not here, not in front of all these people?

Ten minutes passed before she caught sight of him returning, pressing through and offering his polite pardon-me's as he made his way across the concourse.

'The next available train to Liverpool is at nine o'clock.' He turned to look at the large clock face overlooking the concourse. 'We have a couple of hours.'

There was a space beside her on the bench; she beckoned him to sit down with her. With a quick glance around the milling faces, he did.

'John,' she said quietly, 'what's happening? What's this all about? Leavin' the house like that, so sudden?'

Argyll's jaw set, his eyes narrowed. 'Please. I can't explain right now.'

'You said there was danger . . .' A thought suddenly occurred to her. 'Is it the police?' she asked. 'Is that who we're runnin' from: the police?'

He glanced at her with dark, deep-set eyes that, for a moment, probed her, tried to read her face. 'No, it's not the police.'

'Them ones who attacked you, John . . . Do you remember? Is it them?'

He nodded.

'For your money? Was that it?'

'No . . . It wasn't for the money.'

'Then what? Please . . . Tell me what this is all about!'

'It's a matter that's behind me. Done. All done, and it's something I wish not to return to.' He reached out for her hand and squeezed it affectionately; his arm he put around her narrow shoulders and pulled her gently towards him until his lips were tickled by the curls of hair beside her ear.

A whisper. 'The less you know . . . the better.'

He was going to say 'the less you know about my past', but it would have invited more questions from her right now. Questions he wouldn't want to answer even if they were completely alone in this station. Even if they were the last two people in this world. His mind was a quiet place for the moment, not troubled with the vicious snarl of that voice he truly hated. His mind was settled on a purpose; silenced by a very simple goal. Just to escape those foolish men, escape his past, escape a duty that he no longer wanted to be his.

If this world was really so bad, so irredeemable, populated only by the souls God Himself couldn't stomach to let through, then where did this young lady sitting beside him fit in to all of that?

Let someone else snuff out damned candles if that's what needs to be done.

He kissed the pink rim of her ear and whispered, 'I'm John Argyll now.'

She closed her eyes and turned her cheek towards his hand, savouring his touch.

You, Mary Kelly, saved me from becoming who I was.

CHAPTER 53

1st October 1888 (8.30 pm), Euston Station, London

The hansom dropped them outside the archway at the front of Euston Station on Drummond Street, thick with other carriages and cabs picking up and dropping off. Warrington glanced at his timepiece: it was just gone half-past-eight. Hain told them along the way that the London and North Western Rail usually had a final train of the day leaving at nine in the evening for Liverpool.

This Candle Man – Mr Babbitt was his alias, presumably – might well have managed to catch the early afternoon train if he'd been very lucky, but it was unlikely. Equally, though, he might not even be heading for Liverpool. There were suppositions ladled on top of suppositions to think they might actually find him here. There were other ports of departure.

He grasped the tall tart's arm and raced her across a pavement littered with an archipelago of suitcases and travel trunks. 'Come along! Let's see if we can find your friend Mary.'

Passing through the huge Doric archway of the entrance and the congested vestibule beyond, they were in the Great Hall: three stories of cavernous interior lined with classical Roman columns that stretched all the way up to the coffered ceiling sixty feet above them. At one end was a theatrically grand stairway that led up to a gallery one storey up, which ran all the way around the hall. Hain and Robson followed closely behind them.

All four of them scanned the busy hall.

'We'll not see much from down here, sir,' said Robson. He nodded up at the gallery. Warrington followed his gaze.

'Good idea. I'll take her up there with me and you two stay

down here on the floor. If she spots them, she can point them out to you.'

'What if they're already on the train, sir?' He gestured towards the departure platform stretching out beneath the station's long skylight roof, laced with arches of wrought iron. Candelabras of large electric light bulbs descended to bathe the platform with a warm, steady glow. An engine huffed impatiently, billowing a column of steam. It was still twenty-five minutes until the train for Liverpool was due to leave.

'They don't open the platform until fifteen minutes before,' said Hain. Warrington had a feeling the man was right. There was only one departure platform and the luggage porters needed the platform space to unload and load luggage. If Babbitt and the girl were planning on getting that train, then they were surely in here, in the Great Hall, somewhere.

'Watch for me closely,' said Warrington. 'If we see him, I don't want to have to be waving my arms around like a lunatic to attract your attention.' Then he turned and led the way towards the stairs to the gallery, Liz staying close by his side, her eyes anxiously darting from face to face in the crowd.

At the top of the second flight of white marble steps, they turned to rest on the gallery's mahogany elbow rail and look down on the Great Hall's floor. Warrington promptly looped his arm through hers and took a step closer so that their hips bumped gently together.

'Hoy! What you think you're doin'?' said Liz.

'We should try not to look too conspicuous, don't you think? Sweethearts embarking on a holiday together; that's what we shall pretend to be.' He wasn't sure anyone walking past them on the gallery would be convinced that they were lovers or betrothed, but from afar, from the floor below, huddled close together like a couple gazing down would be better than them appearing like two watchful prison officers suspiciously scanning an exercise yard.

'Just look for her, will you?' Warrington ordered.

Liz turned to study the milling knots of people against the geometric designs on the marble floor. A confusing kaleidoscope of pattern and movement, a thousand pale ovals of flesh beneath bonnets and hats, smiling, talking, laughing, scowling . . . and just one of them, in amongst them somewhere, was Mary. She didn't even have any idea what Mary might be wearing today; her clothes were all new, not the familiar old gone-to-rags she used to wear.

Come on, love . . . Where are you?

Argyll looked at the large clock on the wall at the end of the main hall. 'Not long. The porter said we'll be able to board in just five minutes.'

Mary nodded absently, holding onto his arm and watching the goings-on around her.

They were standing in the middle of the floor now. Instinctively he felt more comfortable here, where the press of people was the greatest, than seated on one of the benches around the side.

For the first time since abandoning the womb-like sanctuary of that house on Holland Park Avenue, he had a few moments to evaluate his situation. He thought he'd been too hasty and skittish, dragging the poor girl away like this with nothing to call her own but whatever she'd managed to cram into the small bag she was holding. But seeing those two men taking the steps up to their home, as they'd passed on the avenue, he realised then that his instinct to flee had been right.

See? You need me. The unwelcome snort, the rasping voice of Mr Babbitt, the scrape of his restless trotters.

Argyll clenched his teeth, silently bidding the creature to go back into his corner and shut up. The truth was though, he needed the intuition, he needed the finely-honed instinct of his old self: Mr Babbitt and a hundred other aliases. John Argyll needed them, for the moment. Needed them until he was safe aboard a ship bound for New York. Perhaps then, when the shore of Great Britain was no more than a pencil line on the grey Atlantic horizon, perhaps then that snorting voice could be forcefully retired, banished forever, and he could be properly reborn as Mr John Argyll.

A pleasant dream. He squeezed Mary's arm against his side and she squeezed back in silent complicity. *Mr Argyll and Miss Kelly take on the New World.*

Not just a rebirth but perhaps the start of a wonderful adventure for the pair of them. With a bag full of money and the quick-witted street-smarts Mary clearly had, there was a world of opportunity awaiting them. The far side of the continent, the new state of California, train lines linking the east to the west, émigrés from the world over flooding to this promised land . . . A couple like Mr Argyll and Miss Kelly, with a bag of money, could make their fortunes.

He smiled.

Liz shook her head. 'It's too difficult. People are all movin' about.'

'Just keep your eyes peeled,' said Warrington. 'Her life depends on you.' He looked at her. 'You don't want her ending up like those other poor women, do you?'

Liz's mind filled with the recollection of their gruesome find this morning; that rotting organ in a jam jar, spilling its foul contents across the writing desk. She shook her head. Not poor young Mary.

'I don't know what she's wearin' . . .'

'But she's a good friend, isn't she? You know her face? If you see her down there, you'll recognise her, whatever she has on. Just keep looking.'

Warrington caught sight of his two men standing at the side of the hall, looking intently up at him; looking too damned obviously at him.

Bloody clods. Can they not be more subtle?!

He was about to mutter something under his breath about the clumpy practical boots men who used to be in the army were in the habit of wearing; how ex-army men had an all too obvious way they stood, arms behind their backs, legs planted sturdily apart. They stood out like a pair of sore thumbs. But then he felt Liz's arm tense against his own.

'There!' she whispered, pointing into the crowd.

'Don't fucking point, you silly bitch!' he hissed back.

She dropped her hand back to the railing. 'Sorry.'

Warrington looked at where she had pointed. And despite having no idea at all what Mary Kelly looked like, he was certain the small-framed girl, with frizzy strawberry-blonde hair tied up in a bun, was her. Looping her arm was a tall, slender man with dark features and deep-set eyes that seemed lost beneath thick brows.

His stomach lurched, making him feel momentarily queasy.

My god, that's him.

The hair on the back of Argyll's neck prickled. He knew, he simply *knew*, that the woman up on the gallery had just pointed them out. A second quick glance and he recognised her as the woman who had come to speak to Mary earlier today. And the man standing next to her was . . .

George!

A snort and a dry cackle from inside. *Yes, the silly fool who tried to betray us.*

He watched George trying to nod, to point towards them subtly. Which meant he was trying to point them out to someone else; someone down here on the floor of the Great Hall with them.

Argyll turned casually, as if to catch a glance of the hall's large clock. He spotted two men across the way, standing beside one of the columns, their heads both tilted up towards the gallery; as conspicuous as a pair of ink spots on a freshly laundered bed sheet.

You need me still, the pig rasped. *You still need me, 'John'.*

The two men by the column with their plain clothes, their stiff posture, screamed 'police' at him. They were looking his way, heads bobbing from side to side to get a better look through the milling crowd.

Be relaxed. The pig was right; the only card he could play right now was to make it appear that he was utterly oblivious to their presence. To give them a false sense of security. He'd let them think they had the drop on him. He casually wrapped an arm around Mary and pulled her close to him. He nuzzled her hair affectionately.

Very well done, John. But you have to move. You have to move now!

'I need to leave you for a moment,' he said. 'Stay here.'

She looked up at him, concern written on her face. 'What's the matter?'

'The gentlemen's cloakroom.' He smiled. 'I shan't be long.'

'Oh.' She smiled back. 'Right.'

Argyll weaved his way through the crowd. It was beginning to thicken before the chained entrance to the departure platform, passengers eager to board. Ahead of him, between two columns, were double doors of dark wood and a brass plaque indicating the cloakroom. Above it hung flower baskets that spilled over with bright purple and white pansies.

Hain watched him go. 'I'll follow 'im. You keep an eye on the tart.'

'Right-o,' said Robson.

Hain squeezed through the crowd, cursing as he tripped over a low travel trunk some fool had decided to deposit amid the press of bodies. He rubbed his barked shin as he desperately tried to re-acquire visual contact with the man. It wasn't too hard. This Babbitt fellow was tall enough not to lose easily. There he was now, approaching the public lavvies.

So he just needs a piss, is all? He smiled. *Human after all, then.*

Hain glanced up at the gallery and saw Warrington looking down at him, overseeing proceedings. What was that? The man nodded? He wasn't sure. Yes, there it was: another very affirmative nod. He wasn't sure what that meant. Follow him? Wait for him outside? Take him?

He nodded back, not entirely sure now what instruction he was confirming. His hand discreetly fumbled into his jacket pocket for the reassuring grip of his gun.

Argyll walked over to the public conveniences and nodded politely at the cloakroom attendant standing just outside the double doors. The attendant pushed the doors open for him and Argyll stepped inside. Frosted windows and several bulbs in ornate wire-frame cages provided a steady but dim light. The Great Hall's marbled floor had given way to black and white chequered tiles. Along the left wall was a row of porcelain urinals. Opposite was a row of spotless hand bowls, each with its own oval mirror above it, rimmed with highly-polished brass.

At the far end of the cloakroom, a row of a dozen private water closets, each with a deliberately thick oak door to mute the noises and spare the blushes of an occupier. The cloakroom was busy with four other gentlemen. He heard a muted whistle coming from out in the Great Hall and the others all suddenly hurried to finish their business. The departure platform must have just opened. He could hear a wave of voices raised in unison: 'Ahhh's and 'about-bleedin-time's, and a sound like tumbling shingle on a wave-swept beach as several hundred pairs of feet began shuffling impatiently forward through the unchained barrier and onto the platform.

Argyll found himself alone but knew that it wasn't going to be for very long. He crossed the tiled floor, picked one of the private water closets and turned the brass handle. The heavy door clicked open and he stepped inside, pulling it to almost fully behind him.

Oh, yes . . . One of them's coming. Be patient.

He was right. There, through the crack in the door, he could see one of those two men, most probably civilian-clothed policemen.

You must be so very careful, John . . . He will have a gun.

The man quickly determined that Argyll was in one of the private booths and he stepped slowly forward, the soles of his shoes lightly tapping the tiles. The man hesitated a couple of yards from Argyll's door, clearly, by the anxious way he was tugging on his lip, undecided as to what to do next. To check the booths? Or not?

A small nod of his head – a decision made – and he stepped forward and tried the door of the booth to the right. Argyll heard the handle rattle and through the wall, a disgruntled complaint.

'Ahhh . . . I do apologise, sir!'

Argyll saw an old man in a top hat step past him, glaring, crimson-faced at the intrusion on his privacy. Too embarrassed or too infuriated, he didn't bother to stop and wash his hands.

Alone again. The man rapped his knuckles on another door. 'Anyone in there?' Then a moment later, a little further away, another rap of the knuckles. 'Anyone in there?'

Argyll's hand fumbled absently into the pocket inside his coat as he listened to the tap and scrape of the man's feet and the rap of his knuckles again on another door, this time closer.

Yes. That's quite right, the voice chimed approvingly. *Be ready.* Argyll looked down at his hand and realised he was holding the very same knife that he'd been clasping beneath the kitchen table earlier this afternoon. A knife for cutting bread.

All of a sudden, through the hairline crack of the door, he noticed the cloakroom was now blotted out by the dark outline of a shifting form. Argyll pulled back quickly to avoid getting bumped by the door as the brass handle dipped. With a sharp tug on the handle, Argyll wrenched the door inwards.

The man, taken by surprise, his hand yanked by the handle, staggered off-balance and took a corrective step forwards into the cubicle. Enough. Argyll's free hand grabbed a fistful of his jacket collar and pulled him head-first into the cubicle.

The man's head cracked heavily against the rim of the toilet basin and blood smeared and spattered against the white porcelain as he collapsed on his back in the narrow space between the bowl and the booth's tiled wall. Blood was streaming from a cut in his hairline, down his forehead and into his clenched shut eyes as he fumbled, blindly, with his gun, cocking it, ready to fire.

Don't let him use it!

Argyll prised the gun out of his hand before he could squeeze the trigger and quickly tucked it into his side pocket. He then held the tip of his knife in front of the policeman's face.

The man wiped blood out of his eyes, smearing a streak across his cheeks. He finally dared to open his eyes wide at the sight of the knife, the tip of it almost tickling the end of his nose.

'Jesus!'

'Why?'

The man looked nonplussed, his gaze comically cross-eyed at the blade.

'Why are you people so damned persistently stupid!' hissed Argyll, surprised at the sudden surge of anger. 'I've assured your people, quite clearly I believe, that I have no damned interest in gossiping about your affairs!'

The man shook his head, his jowls quivering. 'I . . . I'm just . . . P-please! Don't kill me!'

Questions. Questions . . . Go on! You should ask him. Make the most of him!

Argyll nodded. He squatted down in front of the man. 'How many of you? How many here at the station?'

Blood was trickling down from his hairline, soaking his brows and trickling into his eyes again. He clenched them shut. 'Just . . . just three of us . . . and that tart!'

That was all Argyll had managed to spot, but there might just be more of them.

'Tell me the truth or I'll take your left eye out!'

Yesssss! That's the spirit, 'John'.

'Honest! Just us! It's just us!'

'That's not many.'

The policeman, his eyes still clenched shut, sneered humourlessly. 'Well . . . you fu-fuckin' well already c-carved up two of us. What do you fu-fuckin' expect?'

I like him. He's funny. Pity.

'You people don't learn, though.' Argyll prodded his cheek with the tip of his blade. 'Do you?'

'I . . . I just work f-for 'em, right? Do . . . do what the L-Lodge asks of me.'

Far away, he heard the muted sound of a whistle blowing again. There was a train to catch. And Mary was out there on her own. He had to hurry up.

'I want you to go and tell them others—'

No, 'John'. No! There is no 'go and tell'. You finish him!

Argyll shook his head. 'It's . . . I . . . don't need to—'

Finish him!

The policeman cracked open one eye, blinking the blood out of it. 'Wh-what?'

FINISH HIM!

Argyll gripped the knife hard; he wanted to hurl it far away, but he couldn't. That little bastard inside his head was stamping around like an angry boar in a china shop.

KILL HIM!!!

Argyll winced at the screaming, shrill voice. 'I'm . . . sorry . . .' he finally muttered.

'What?' The man's eyes shot wide open. 'No, please!' He struggled and kicked on the floor, suddenly realising what 'sorry' meant for him.

Argyll punched the blade of his knife into the man's chest, up to the hilt. A relatively quick kill, as it skewered the left ventricle of his heart, sending the organ into a shuddering paroxysm. Less messy, too. There were no jets of blood to dot Argyll's shirt; the trauma was all on the inside of the man. A dark bloom of crimson spread across his pinstriped shirt and his wide, blood-caked eyes rolled slowly to one side as his feet kicked and scraped the tiled floor pointlessly. Then he was still.

'I'm sorry,' whispered Argyll again.

Warrington cursed under his breath. No, he hadn't wanted that idiot Hain to follow the man into the cloakrooms; he'd just wanted him to keep a discreet watch on the doorway. The last thing he could afford to have happen was for the slippery bastard to catch wind that they were watching him. All he had was two men, just two. If Babbitt took flight, they'd lose him for sure.

If he didn't have to keep an eye on this tart, there'd be three of them. He glanced sideways at her. The woman was plainly here because she wanted to help; as far as she was concerned, they were the police. He decided he could take a risk and let her go.

He pulled a leather wallet out of his morning coat. 'Here,' he said, digging some coins out. 'Thank you for assisting us and pointing them out. This could get very nasty. Probably best you get yourself safely back home. You can take a cab.'

She took the money off him quickly.

'A cab, all right? Not a bloody bottle of cheap gin.'

She nodded. 'What about Mary?'

'She's going to be fine. We're not going to let this man disappear with her. I'll make quite sure of that.'

Liz turned to go and then stopped. 'And what about the reward?'

Warrington flicked an impatient smile at her. 'Yes, yes, of course. We have your address. I'll make sure one of our boys comes by your lodgings later. Best remain there tonight. Now, go on. Off you trot.'

CHAPTER 54

1st October 1888 (8.50 pm), Euston Station, London

Mary was beginning to get a bit concerned. The departure platform had opened and the congregation of passengers and porters peppered with islands of baggage in the middle of the Great Hall had begun to migrate towards the gate. An officious-looking LNWR clerk, with a walrus-like face full of grey whiskers, was carefully examining every ticket and ushering the passengers through.

Where is he?

She glanced at the big clock; it showed eight minutes to nine. No need to panic just yet; there was still enough time before the train was due to depart, but she wondered if there were going to be enough seats aboard the train for everyone. And if they were the last ones through the gate, might there be none left for them?

She stood anxiously on tiptoes and cursed under her breath as three gentlemen in top hats blocked her view of the cloakroom doors.

Robson shook his head. *The poor young girl looks frantic.*

Hopping around out there from one foot to the other. She looked like a rabbit in a wheat field, perched up on its hind legs, ready to scarper at the first sight of a farmer's dog. She looked so young; barely more than a child.

What the hell is she doing going on the run with this man, anyway?

Robson had a niece her age, or thereabouts. Rebecca. Between him and his brother still serving in the army, they were managing to pay for her to stay at a small finishing school. It was costing them a king's ransom, but with no children of his own, Robson was happy that money he might otherwise have thrown away on a card table was buying his niece a much better chance in life than this poor lost child stuck out there in the middle of the Great Hall.

He vaguely recalled a nursery rhyme, or was it a story? About a butterfly attracted to a candle flame. A butterfly who flew too close and burnt to death. Quite a horrible story, really. He was about to ponder on the grim, unforgiving morality of tales that lurked beneath the surface of many a bedtime story when he felt the lightest tickling at the back of his neck. He reached to scratch it.

'I'd suggest you remain perfectly still,' a voice whispered in his ear.

Robson turned his head and the tickling became, very quickly, a sharp jabbing pain.

'Be still! Yes, that's the tip of a knife you're feeling,' the deep voice murmured next to his ear. 'I think you're one of the chaps who've already witnessed what I can do with a knife. Hmmm?'

He nodded. 'Yeah, I was . . . I was there at the warehouse.' He glanced quickly up to the gallery, hoping Warrington was looking this way and had already spotted that he was in trouble. 'You got the jump on us pretty well,' he added.

Warrington wasn't watching; he was saying something to that tart he'd brought along.

A hand lightly grasped the crook of his arm and guided Robson a step backwards into the walkway behind the columns. The glow of light from the ornate chandeliers high above was wasted here in the shadows beneath the gallery floor.

'Now, if you'll just come along with me . . .'

Robson stood rigid. The knife dug into his skin. His mouth was suddenly as dry as parchment. 'G-go easy there, ch-chap . . . I . . . I . . .'

'Ahhh. In here will do perfectly.' He heard the click of a door opening behind him, felt a gentle insistent tug on the crook of his arm and that jabbing, tickling, of the knife at the base of his skull. He obediently shuffled backwards into a dark room and the door closed in front of him, pitching them into complete blackness. Robson was vaguely aware that he'd begun to piss himself.

A single bulb in a wire cage snapped on. He saw shelves stacked with soaps and cloakroom hand towels, large metal mop buckets on the floor, mops and brushes lined up against one wall. The room reeked of polish and turpentine.

'I do apologise. I'm going to have to be very quick with you. I have a train to catch.'

'Please, mate . . . Th-there's no . . . n-need . . .'

Robson felt a hand probe the pockets of his coat, locate the heavy lump of his gun and then remove it. The tickle of the blade at the base of his neck stopped.

'Yes, you can turn round now, if you want.'

He turned his head to look at the man. His first proper, close look at him. Beneath the glare of the bulb, his eyes were lost in the pooling darkness below a prominent brow. The angular geometry of his face left spills of shadow running vertically from the recessed orbits of his eyes, down gaunt cheeks to a thin-lipped mouth.

'L-look . . . there's really no . . . n-need to—'

'Oh, I don't intend to *kill* you. Just *incapacitate* you. Now, why don't you sit down?'

The man pulled a wooden chair from the corner of the small storeroom and placed it on the floor beside Robson. 'Sit.'

Robson did as he was told, his eyes still on the knife but feeling a surge of relief. Until, that is, he thought he saw a smear of blood on its tip.

'Whose blood is that?'

'Your colleague's.' The man pouted a lip with mock sympathy. 'Oh, he's quite dead.'

'J-Jesus Christ!'

The man rummaged along one of the shelves with his spare hand. 'You see any rope here? Some twine, perhaps?'

Robson twisted in his seat at the mention of rope, a little more hopeful that he was going to get out of this room alive. 'There!' He pointed. 'There! See? S-second shelf d-down!'

'Ahh! Thank you.'

Argyll unravelled a couple of yards from the ball of green twine and cut it with his knife. He turned round and looked down at the thick-set man sitting on the chair; it creaked and rattled under his weight as he trembled uncontrollably.

'Have you noticed how rude people are to each other? Hmmm?'

The man stared up at him, bewildered. 'I . . . I . . . no . . .'

Oh yes, of course . . . the voice rasped. He's the polite one, if I recall correctly.

'It's the small gestures, I think,' said Argyll absently.

Small things . . . yes. You recall? In the busy street? This one bent down, picked up a child's toy, gave it to the chattering woman with the pram. Such a small thing. A kindness. Hmmm. You can let him live, if you must.

A whistle blew outside, muted by the storeroom's thick door. Argyll's attention focused back on Robson. 'No, I'm not going to kill you. But I do need you *not* to follow me.' He dangled the twine in front of him.

Robson eagerly presented his hands to be tied.

'Not necessary.' Argyll stepped forward quickly and punched the knife deep into the man's thigh, leaving the handle protruding like a flagstaff.

Robson screamed. 'FUCK!!!' Looking down boggle-eyed at the wooden handle, he reached to pull it out.

'No. You should leave it there,' said Argyll. He stooped down and quickly wound the twine around the top of the man's thigh. He reached for a slating peg on the storage shelf beside him and inserted it into the loop of the twine. He twisted it several times, cinching it tight. Robson gritted his teeth with the pain.

Argyll grabbed one of the man's shaking hands and placed it on the peg. 'Like that, all right? You'll need to hold it as tight as you can, for as long as you can, if you wish to live.'

'FUCK!!' Robson grunted again. 'FUCK!!' His forehead was dotted with beads of sweat.

'And I really wouldn't suggest that you try getting up. You'll open the wound and bleed out. If you stay right there, you'll be just fine.'

Argyll turned back to the door and switched off the electric light. 'I'll send someone along in due course.' He stepped outside and closed the door gently behind him.

CHAPTER 55

1st October 1888 (8.56 pm), Euston Station, London

Now Robson was damn well gone as well. Warrington couldn't see any sign of the man. He'd been distracted, talking to the tart for less than a minute, and in that time Robson seemed to have vanished into thin air! He could still see the girl though, still standing in the middle of the Great Hall next to her bag on the floor, looking anxiously around her at the last of the passengers funnelling through past the ticket clerk.

The floor was almost empty now. Most of those who intended to get the nine o'clock train for Liverpool were now already on the train or on the departure platform saying their goodbyes.

Warrington wondered whether Robson had followed Hain into the cloakroom. Perhaps, whilst he'd been busy dealing with the tart, Robson had made his way across to help. Perhaps Hain had actually taken the initiative and made a move and taken the man by surprise, with his trousers down, quite literally.

In which case, excellent! To hell with Rawlinson's instructions not to approach the Candle Man. If Hain had actually managed to drop the bastard right there in the public toilets, then Warrington was going to make sure the reckless, disobedient, son-of-a-whore Hain got a damned bonus for using his initiative.

He let go of the railings and began to hurriedly make his way down the stairs from the gallery when his eyes caught a quick scooting movement across the floor below. Mary Kelly was being hustled by a tall dark figure towards the departure platform.

Warrington stopped dead in his tracks.

It's Babbitt. Where the hell are . . . ? There was no damned sign of those other two fools. Hain he'd seen disappear into the public conveniences and Robson had just disappeared.

He watched Babbitt and the Kelly girl approach the ticket clerk, the man waving his ticket at the clerk frantically. Warrington glanced up at the clock; it was three minutes to nine.

Dammit!

Something must have happened in the toilets. Something must have gone wrong for Hain and now that slippery American bastard knew he'd been followed here to the station. All of a sudden, he wasn't quite so sure Hain was going to get his bonus. He wasn't quite so sure the poor bastard was going to be doing anything anymore. He cursed under his breath. Perhaps the same fate had befallen Robson as well.

How the hell did he manage to . . . ?

Warrington carried on down the steps until he reached the polished granite floor of the Great Hall. His eyes locked firmly onto the backs of the girl and Babbitt, proceeding more calmly now down the departure platform.

It's just me now.

A guard blew his whistle and the engine at the far end of the platform impatiently huffed a column of billowing steam that rose up towards the underside of the wrought iron roof and then rolled along it, scattering pigeons that had been roosting on the spars.

'Where were you?!' cried Mary. 'I was getting so worried about you!'

'There was a god-awful long queue in the cloakroom,' he replied. 'Quite the wait.'

She held his hand, which felt clammy and warm. Concerned, she touched the back of her hand against his cheek. 'You're hot, John. And you're shaking. What's the matter?'

'I'm fine. Come along.' He smiled. 'We don't want to miss our train.'

Further up the platform, he could see several guards walking through the wraiths of steam that billowed out from beneath the carriages, down the side of the train, closing the doors left open and politely cajoling embracing sweethearts to conclude their goodbyes.

He looked through the compartment windows they passed as they made their way up the platform, seeking a compartment that was empty, or at least if not that, then not full. 'Here . . . this one looks good for us.' He pulled the door open and offered Mary a hand as she stepped up into the carriage.

'A quick thing I have to do,' he said.

'John?'

'I'll be back in just a moment.' He handed her his satchel and, leaving the door open, he double-timed back down the platform towards the clerk. It was then that he saw a gentleman remonstrating with the ticket clerk.

George.

'I'm sorry, sir, if you 'aven't got a ticket, you can't come through!'

Warrington bared his teeth in frustration. 'Goddammit, man, this is . . . this is police business! I need to get on that train right now!'

The clerk shrugged. 'Well, if it's police business, sir, then I'm going to have to ask you to identify yourself properly.'

Warrington cursed and then tried to push past the man.

'Sir!' The clerk grabbed hold of his arm firmly. A surprisingly strong grip for such an old man. 'I'm sorry, sir, you can't go through!'

'Is this man troubling you?'

Warrington turned away from the walrus-whiskered clerk to see Babbitt standing a few feet away. He stopped struggling with the clerk immediately.

'George!' said Babbitt, as if greeting a long-lost cousin. 'How are you, old chap?'

Warrington stared at him dumbfounded; a perfectly still moment between both men that seemed to last an eternity.

'Sir,' the clerk replied to Babbitt, 'I can deal well enough with this customer, thank you very much! You'll need to board the train now. It's due to leave.'

Argyll acknowledged him with the faintest nod, but his eyes remained on Warrington. 'George, I'll be leaving soon. Going home. I suggest you tell your friends that our business together is finished now.' He smiled. 'It's perfectly safe with me.'

'The girl . . .' Warrington glanced quickly at the clerk. 'Let go of me, damn you!' The clerk loosened the firm hold on his arm. He'd really much rather this conversation wasn't being held like this: conspicuous and overheard. There were several other guards walking down the platform to see what was going on. 'The girl?' he said to Babbitt. 'How much have you told her?'

Babbitt said nothing.

'She knows . . . doesn't she? She knows what you are? What you've done?'

'She's not your concern,' Babbitt replied coolly.

'Gentlemen, if you *please*!' said the clerk.

'She's a damned liability now you've involved her,' hissed Warrington. 'You know we can't leave it at that!'

The clerk had had enough. He turned to Babbitt. 'Sir! If you want to take this train, you need to board it *now*! And you, sir.' He turned to Warrington. 'Would you mind buggering off? This gent needs to leave. Now!'

'We might have let you go, but not . . .' Warrington shook his head. He wanted to say 'but not with some young slapper who might drink a little too much one night and tell a tale'. He didn't need to, though. The Candle Man narrowed his eyes with a tacit understanding and the slightest nod. He took a step backwards away from the clerk and Warrington.

'I'll be in touch, George. Make sure you read the papers.' He turned quickly and headed for the train, pulling open the last door of the rear-most carriage, to the clerk's obvious relief.

'We'll find you, you know!' shouted Warrington. 'We'll have men watching the ships!'

Babbitt stopped. Looked back at Warrington. 'Who said anything about ships?' he called back. 'Oh, George, by the way –' he pointed toward the Great Hall – 'caretaker's storeroom . . . chap of yours might appreciate some help.' He stepped up into the carriage and pulled the door closed with a slam that echoed along the platform.

Several guards' whistles blew and finally a green flag was raised. With the distant scream of steam from the locomotive at the front, the train suddenly lurched forward, the trucks and wheels beneath each coach chattering one after the other as the slack was taken up and the final carriage began to move away slowly.

Warrington saw Babbitt again, his head appearing out of the door's window; eyes that he could have sworn glinted a sulphurous red within the dark orbits beneath his brow. The bastard even managed a cheerful wave for him.

PART III

CHAPTER 56

7th November 1888, Liverpool

Mary watched the stevedores and lumpers working industriously along the Waterloo Dock quayside. To the left of the quay, a row of sail and steam ships of all sizes were lined up, smoke stacks puffing dirty columns up into the thick grey sky. A jam of handcarts and wagons filled the quay, laden with rain-dampened wooden packing crates and canvas sacks of produce coming in from all corners of the world. To the right of the quay, a continuous wall of storage warehouses, their yawning fronts open wide, both disgorging and swallowing up a steady convoy of top-heavy carts and weary-looking lumpers. A parade of relentless activity as far as the eye could see that put the paltry scale of the London docks to shame.

Through the tea shop window, she could hear steam whistles, the clank of heavy chains working, swinging crane arms, and the colourful language of master stevedores bellowing profanities that would make a priest's toes curl, as they cajoled their men to put their 'bloody backs' into it.

Watching it all, she felt a touch of excitement roll down her spine. It felt like that thing John did in bed: a gentle finger rolling down the bumps of her vertebrae, one after the other, like a harpist stroking the catgut chords on his instrument.

She would have loved to have taken rooms nearer the Prince's Landing Stage. Close enough to see the Cunard, Pacific and White Star passenger ships coming and going, the broad thoroughfare filled with people of all classes, from all corners of the world, embarking or disembarking together. To see all the wonderful clothes of the first-class passengers; the plumes of ostrich feathers and the fine layers of lace, the wonderfully precise cut of felt on the men's suits. But John had convinced her it would be better picking a smaller, less obvious hotel. Quite sensible, really.

'Another slice of your usual cake, ma'am?' asked the waitress.

Mary shook her head. 'I'm fine, thank you.'

'Yes, ma'am.'

The pink-faced girl all but seemed to curtsey as she backed up a step and returned to stand dutifully behind the tea shop's counter. Mary had been into this place enough times now over the past few weeks that they'd spoken together a little. The waitress was just a year younger than Mary and yet she treated her with complete class-based deference.

That was me a few weeks ago, Mary mused.

No, perhaps she was flattering herself. It wasn't. In the stratified bands of social class that existed in the East End, being a 'seam-stress' – a codified way of admitting she *occasionally* took men for money – meant she would have been dipping her head deferentially even to a shop girl.

Now though . . . now she got a 'ma'am'. And not said with a sarcastic tone or the sceptical cocking of an eyebrow, either. Up here in Liverpool, it seemed she actually really could pass as a lady. The occasional slipped vowel and omitted consonant – and to be fair she was getting so much better at not doing those things – were nuances that were so easily lost and less noticeable compared to the regional differences in the sound of their vowels. Indeed, simply not having a broad northern accent seemed to mark her out as somebody to offer that little extra gesture of courtesy to.

John sometimes chastised her gently for worrying so much about her airs and graces. His attitude was so typically American: that a person is judged on what it is they have to say, not on what sounds their words make. On the other side of that ocean, she was going to find a very different world, he kept telling her; not like this stultify-ing one where every child was doomed to follow the profession of their parents; where waitresses, footmen, market porters, coal men, were simply born several sizes too small to fit their uniforms of servitude.

Anyway, he'd told her many times over that it was her *soul* that so bewitched him. Her soul, her spirit, her zest. Not whether she could say 'how' instead of ''ow', or 'butter' instead of 'bu'er'. Mary smiled as she sipped her tea and watched the dock workers through the window.

So American. So refreshingly not *English.*

Thinking about it, Mary was rather glad they weren't booking to go on one of those posh White Star or Cunard liners. Partly because those same elegantly-dressed lady passengers she longed to see more closely were most likely to be the sort of pursed-lipped stuck-up cows who would spot what she was in an instant and derive a fortnight's worth of sport out of trying to trip a social gaff out of her common mouth. But also, not to forget, the money they would save taking passage on a freight ship.

John said their ship was due in soon. There would be several days' turnaround as the ship was emptied of sacks of tea, coffee, sugar, and loaded up with a consignment of engineering tools due to be delivered and offloaded in New York. And, of course, enough room aboard for a small number of passengers paying a fraction of the fare that they would aboard a liner like the SS Celtic, as long as they didn't mind eating alongside the ship's crew.

Just another few days now, according to him. He was expecting their ship any day. If she didn't trust him – *completely* trust him as she had in the four weeks since they left London – she might have begun to wonder whether there really *was* a ship booked for America. But the question never even crossed her mind. She knew her very own Mr Argyll wouldn't be untruthful with her. She knew he couldn't be deceitful, even if he tried. Even harmless white lies tripped him up. The other day, for example, he'd bought her a beautiful little cameo carved exquisitely into pink shell and had intended to give it to her over dinner, but had been so worked up and impatient about the surprise that he'd caved in during the afternoon and given it to her over tea. John was as honest a man as she could hope for. Far more honest than she deserved, given the duplicitous genesis of their love. If he said 'soon', then it was to be soon and she had no reason at all in the world to doubt that.

Soon would be good, though. Whilst sipping tea and pretending to be a lady was a pleasant enough fiction, she couldn't wait for their new life together to begin in earnest.

The other day, John had entranced her with the possibilities that their bag of money could offer them. He had built a dream in his mind already: a hardware merchants in a place called Fort Casey, Colorado. He told her the recently constructed railways were bring-ing hordes of people from the east, travelling not all the way to the west now but stopping along the way to take advantage of the cheap prairie land on offer to turn into farms. People who had sold everything and were looking to start anew. A hardware store right beside the railway station. It would be one of the first places a new farmer would want to visit.

But they'd be travel-weary. Mary suddenly had a marvellous idea that she could add to his. What about a lodging house? A small hotel, small enough for the pair of them to run? Just a few bedrooms and perhaps a tearoom like this one? John could run the store and she the hotel. Mary pressed her lips together, trying hard to give her tired mouth a rest from smiling.

It sounded wonderful.

He should be back soon. John said he had some business to attend to with the shipping merchant this morning. She couldn't wait for him to return so she could tell him about the idea.

'That's fifty-one words in your message, sir,' said the clerk. In his head he totalled the sum that was due for payment. 'That'll be two and a farthing, please, sir.'

'And this will make tomorrow's issue?'

'If I wire it through to London now, sir, yes, it should be in for tomorrow. They don't roll the printing presses until three in the afternoon normally.'

'Fine.' Argyll fumbled in his pocket for some coins, paid the clerk and then stepped out of the telegram office and onto the street. The air was damp with rain as fine as spray; 'drizzle' they called it over here. He turned the collar of his Mackintosh up beneath the broad brim of his slouch hat and began to make his way south towards the docks.

You know there's no other way.

Absently, he thumbed the rubber stopper of the small glass bottle of chloral hydrate in his pocket. The pharmacist had tried to sell him half a dozen other miracle cures for insomnia, but Argyll had used the stuff before as a sedative; given in the right dose, it worked quickly, without any unsettling side-effects.

You're doing the right thing, the pig whispered approvingly.

'Be quiet,' he muttered under his breath.

Argyll tried to avoid listening to that scratchy, hectoring voice. It was right, yes, he could see that now; this was the way he had to do things. But he didn't need to hear this wretched, deformed freak telling him that.

'Freak?' You should show me a little more gratitude. Hmmm? I saw them first. Not you.

George and his fellows must have decided to take this business to the police, because he was certain he'd spotted them several times up here in Liverpool, at the Prince's Landing Stage. Pairs of them watching discreetly, so they thought, as passengers boarded the liners. In pairs. So unmistakably coppers. Argyll was also quite certain every passenger liner booking agent was being carefully watched. The moment that he and Mary attempted to buy tickets, the moment they attempted to climb the steps for a ship to America, they were taking an enormous gamble.

You know it makes sense . . .

Argyll balled his fist and would happily have smacked his temple to shut the fucking thing up; would happily have shoved the long tip of a stiletto blade deep into his temple if he could be sure it would skewer that little bastard in there.

. . . to give them what they want.

And the little pig-voice being right just made it worse. It was the only way, wasn't it? If George and his colleagues had roped in the police, as it appeared they had, then he was well and truly cornered.

She's just a dirty tart. Dirty. How many stinking old men do you think she's had? How many shit-covered fingernails grabbing and poking inside her for the price of a bed or a meal? How many of them, before she found foolish you? How many—

'Shut up!' he barked.

He turned onto a busier street, avoiding a puddle that spread across the pavement. Mary was in her favourite tea shop just up ahead. No doubt right by the window, her favourite table in there, watching the dockers load and unload the ships. He hated the voice being anywhere near her. He hated the thought it could even be in the same room as her.

'I'm doing what you said!' he snapped beneath the dripping brim of his hat. 'Now go away! Please. Just give me tonight *alone* with her. Please!'

His aching head was quiet for a few steps. Babbitt-the-pig's scraping hoof and his self-satisfied snort was all the answer Argyll got for a while. Then, as he passed the curtained window and saw her small oval face light up at seeing him through the rain-spattered window, it rasped once again.

I'll go . . . for now.

CHAPTER 57

8th November 1888, Great Queen Street, Central London

'Good god, this is a damned relief!' said Rawlinson. 'I thought he'd slipped through our fingers!'

Warrington nodded slowly. 'Indeed.'

He was tired. Bone-weary tired, with the constant gnawing stress of this damnable situation. The number of restful nights in the last month that had begun and ended with a kiss from his wife he could count on the fingers of one hand. The rest had been nights of tossing and turning and imagining scenarios in which this slippery bastard and the girl he had with him were far, far away. Far enough away to feel quite happy sharing their fascinating tale entitled '*A Prince, His Whore, Her Bastard and the Ripper of London*' with some New York newspaper.

What easy headlines a story like that was going to make.

His sleepless nights were mixed with those worries and the very unwelcome flashing zoetrope images of dark crimson spattering across cotton white. Of eyes round with shock, surprise, a complete lack of comprehension in them.

Good grief, he'd even tried to calmly explain to the taller one, Liz, why it was that they both had to die. Warrington wondered what he'd hoped to gain by rationalising it to the whore; as if she was going to calmly listen to what he had to say, nod agreeably that it was perhaps the most sensible course of action for queen and country, and present her bare throat for his man to slit?

Orman had done his best with both of them to make it appear to be the work of the Candle Man. The first one, Liz Stride, he managed to do little more than nearly sever her head. He would have done more with her body but they'd been disturbed, nearly spotted by a man on his way to work in the early hours. The other one, an hour later, they'd been better prepared for. Orman, bless the man's strong stomach, had needed no help from him. What he'd left of Catherine Eddowes more accurately resembled the earlier victims. A regrettable business. And now the London press were excitedly screaming that 'The Leather Apron' – or his more headline-friendly moniker, 'Jack the Ripper' – had claimed two more victims . . . in one night, no less!

'Tomorrow it is, then,' said Rawlinson to the others gathered in the reading room. He turned to Warrington. 'George, you'll meet him again, if you're feeling up to it?'

He nodded. It wasn't really a question, was it? This was his responsibility. His task. His mess.

The newspaper rustled as Rawlinson carefully inspected the column of personal messages once again. 'By the way he's worded this, it certainly does seem that he's prepared to settle this matter the way we'd prefer it to be settled.'

'Quite so,' said Warrington. 'It appears we have him trapped.'

'I'm surprised,' said Oscar. 'There are a lot of ships a man could catch up there in Liverpool. Surely he could find at least *one* to escape on?'

'Yes, of course,' said Warrington. 'But we have quite a few policemen up there.'

They'd pulled in a lot of favours for this. Debts that their little 'Steering Committee' would end up in hock to for many years to come. Pairs of boots from the Lancashire constabulary all over the docks; plain-clothes boots, but probably obvious enough that they might as well have been wearing uniforms. But that was the point. They wanted the Candle Man to know the docksides were being watched.

'He must probably think that every ship and agent is being watched.' Rawlinson fumbled with a ginger biscuit that he had little appetite for. 'He's cautious. Boarding a ship represents too much of a danger, I fancy. That's why he's agreed to meet us.'

'And do we try and kill him again?' asked Geoffrey. 'Even if he is prepared to hand us the girl?'

Warrington looked to Rawlinson. That would be his decision.

Rawlinson ran a tongue over dry lips, picking up several biscuit crumbs. 'I'm afraid this horrible mess is too important for us to have this man wandering around, knowing all he knows. I accept he is a . . . *professional*,' he said, with a hint of distaste for the word. 'I accept our colleagues in New York are more than happy to vouch for his indefinite discretion, but . . .' He sighed. 'These wretched newspapers making so damned much of this story, turning what could easily have been – should have been – a few unfortunate, unlinked murders.' He glanced pointedly at Warrington. 'That really was stupid, George, making it look like the same man's work.'

Warrington nodded, looked down at his feet. The pair of them had already had this conversation in private.

'Point is,' continued Rawlinson, 'now we have the press believing their theatrically-named villain has killed *four* women now. That's exactly what those awful bloody parasites want. It's selling their papers for them.' Rawlinson sat back in his armchair. 'The whole thing has become quite ridiculous. We need a satisfactory conclusion to this quickly, now, before this preposterous "Ripper" character takes a firm hold of the public's imagination.'

'Making those last two look the same, Henry,' said Geoffrey. 'I thought that was quite clever of George. We can attribute them *all* to this Candle chap. Alive or dead, if we put a butcher's knife in his hand and it happens that a leather apron is found upon his person, the people will have no doubt that their "Ripper" has been caught, and this business will soon be forgotten about.'

Oscar shook his head. 'George, you should have briefed this man differently. These deaths should have been made to look more varied. The newspapers report a dozen or more murders every day. Unconnected murders would have passed without notice.'

'Hindsight's a very useful thing, Oscar,' said Geoffrey.

'We are where we are,' said Rawlinson with a sigh. 'There's little to be gained raking over this, gentlemen.'

'The Candle Man,' said Warrington. 'He *will* be this Jack the Ripper. The police will find him with enough evidence framing him.' He looked at all of them. 'Other than the prince's indiscretion, there is no possible way to link the four women. They were all cheap tarts who happened to be plying their trade at the wrong time, in the wrong place. The metropolitan police and Scotland Yard will have a credible culprit. They will be the heroes of the hour, and law and order will be seen to have prevailed.'

'Five,' said Geoffrey.

Warrington cocked his head. 'What?'

'Five tarts. The Kelly girl . . . ?'

He nodded. 'Yes, of course.'

'And this Kelly lived in the same boarding house as one of the others?' asked Oscar.

'Yes, one of them. But these women change rooms all the time. They miss a rent, they lose their bed, they find another. It is not implausible that two of these whores might have shared the same lodging house at one time or another. We can use or dismiss these casual associations to whatever end we want.'

The room was quiet. Through the wood-panelled walls, they heard the faint sound of several raised jovial voices coming from the Chelmsford Room. In the club's main lounge, an energetic game of poker was in progress. Warrington was sure the Lodge's sergeant-at-arms would whisper quietly for the gentlemen in question to pipe down.

'This chap will have to die. And this time, George, do please be sure he doesn't slip through your fingers. And with regret, this Kelly girl, too. Do be *very* sure we have her whereabouts before you dispose of the man.'

Warrington nodded. 'Of course.'

'But – and listen closely, George – his body will *not* be presented as this "Ripper" character.'

Warrington's head jerked. 'Why ever not?'

'If the police have a body, if anybody recognises his face – that concierge, for example, at The Grantham – then we're leaving too many lines of enquiry open. I want you to kill him, George, and dispose of the body. That is all. He's going to vanish and that will be all.'

'But without the corpse, Henry, this Ripper story will just continue. You know what these awful bloody newspapers are like. The next tart who happens to die in a bloody manner will be the Ripper's next victim; and so on and so on. We give them a body and this ridiculous story will die.'

'If we give the public a body, we give this Jack the Ripper a face. And how long before some enterprising writer or journalist decides there's money to be made in investigating and writing this Ripper's life story?'

The others nodded at that.

'I would like this matter concluded as simply, as cleanly and as invisibly as possible. By the time you have finished meeting him tomorrow, I want the body of one last Ripper victim and this Candle Man back in London, in a sack . . . at the bottom of the bloody Thames.'

CHAPTER 58

8th November 1888, Liverpool

The small balcony outside their hotel window looked out upon the Mersey. Even at night, the docks all the way along the busy waterway were still alive with industry. Orange gas lamps and burning pyres in metal bins dotted the quayside, their amber glow reflected on rain-slick brick and concrete.

The sky had cleared a space in the clouds for the moment, allowing the moon a chance to decorate the warehouse rooftops with its sparkling quicksilver reflection. A two-tone glistening industrial landscape of cool moon blues dotted with pinpricks of orange. Quite beautiful.

'They never stop, do they?' said Mary. Even up here on the third floor of the hotel, she could hear the occasional clatter and grind of cranes working and the echoing voices of men barking orders at each other.

'Never,' whispered Argyll into her hair.

She shifted within the comforting cradle of his firm arms, tilted her head backwards to look up at him. The moon picked out the firm, slender line of his nose, the line of his jaw, the diagonal twitch of a muscle across his lean cheek and poet's eyes that glinted deep within pools of shadow. So very, very handsome.

I love this man. She was aware she said it aloud far too often. It cheapened the words and she worried it made her seem too needy. How strange a pair they were. Just over a month ago, it was she caring for him. She was the adult, the mentor, the one to be wholly responsible for the other. And now it was utterly reversed; now she was being taken care of. Almost like a child once again: carefree, unburdened with worries, able just to sit and play with fantasies whilst someone else worried about the mundane matters of tickets and payments and precisely which dock they needed to present themselves at, and when, and to whom, and so on.

John's 'soon' had all of a sudden become 'tomorrow'.

This evening they were staring out one last time from their hotel balcony at the rooftops and cranes, chimney pots and masts. This evening was a celebration. A bottle of nice red wine with a posh-sounding name. Mary had tried wines before, but always the cheapest, and found the taste quite revolting. But this wine was lovely. She sipped again from her china teacup, a two-piece set he'd bought her last week after she'd fallen in love with them in a shop window. Despite eating not so long ago, it had quickly gone to her head. She wanted to giggle with pleasure, giggle with excitement.

'Tomorrow our adventure begins,' she whispered.

'Mmmmm.' She felt his chest vibrate deeply.

'I never even dreamed of America when I was young. The best dream I ever had was of escaping to London; can you believe that?' She shook her head at how limited her imagination was, how parochial her dreams had been. It all seemed so far away now, the soot-black and hopeless warrens of Whitechapel. The ever-present smell of decaying rubbish, the sharp tang of burning coke, the meaty odour of a labourer's sweat and the stale stew of alcohol on their breath. A dark hell of hopeless, rotting souls, grey-skinned mole men and women living, so it seemed, in an eternal twilight of gas-lamp nights and fog-choked days. And so much further away, the always wet, brooding valleys of Wales, embracing suffocatingly small villages of narrow streets paved with slate.

'Tell me something more,' she said. He knew the sort of things she liked to hear about. He'd told her pillow stories of all the wonderful things that they were going to see and do together in that big, wild country.

'You'll see that new statue they built in the middle of the bay,' his deep voice softly rumbled. A soothing vibration. 'That's the first thing we shall see: Laboulaye's lady, Liberty, golden bronze and holding her candle, towering above our ship. We'll sail into New York harbour and you'll see the Brooklyn Bridge ahead of you. And as many ships coming in and going out as we've seen here.'

'Tell me about the wilderness, the frontier.' She loved how he described it. The scale of it.

'There's so much sky, Mary. Horizons that seem to stretch to infinity. Out on the prairies, you can stand in the middle of a hundred square miles and not see a single tree. Just the sweeping hummocks of spurs and hills covered in grass, and nothing but the soft whisper of it all stirring . . .'

She closed her eyes and tried to imagine it. A world of deep blue sky and a rich, swaying carpet of olive green. And air so clean. And no sounds of factory whistles, nor the sharp brittle snarling of bad-tempered men returning home after work, nor the muted whimper of tears through a bedroom wall, the clunk of boots wearily undone and carelessly dropped on a bare wooden floor above. Nor the muted murmurs that suddenly, without warning, became a man's bark and the sound of a fist making contact. A million miserable noises from a million desperate people living cheek by jowl in a man-made hell.

As he talked of the crystal white peaks of the Sierra Nevada mountains, the Platte River's endless, looping energy, the haunting salt flats of Utah, he felt Mary's weight in his arms and against his chest grow heavier. And finally, when he stopped talking, he could hear her breath, deep and even.

She's asleep now.

He bent down and scooped her legs up with his right arm and stepped back off the balcony, back inside to their hotel room. Carefully, still wary he might wake her, he laid her on the bed.

You know exactly what to do.

Argyll nodded.

So do it, then.

He looked down at her, fast asleep, a half-smile on her face. 'She won't feel a thing.'

That's right.

'She won't feel a thing,' he said to himself again.

Best to get on with it. Hmmm?

Argyll wasn't sure how long the chloral hydrate powder would last. He'd stirred two spoonfuls into her first cup of wine and another two into her second, which was only half-finished. The pharmacist had assured him that just one teaspoon of the powder stirred into a cup of tea was enough to guarantee a good and long night's sleep. By the look of her, she was thoroughly sedated.

Get the knife and get started. Remember, 'John' . . . you have a train for London to catch.

He looked at the room's clock. It was five minutes past seven. His train down to Euston was due to leave at eight o'clock. Time enough to do what was needed and make his way to the station. Time enough if, like the pig was saying, he got started now.

Argyll stepped away from the bed and reached for what he needed on the small round table beside the balcony door.

He realised his face was damp with tears as he stood over her. He knelt down beside her and stroked her pale cheek. 'I'm sorry . . . so very sorry,' he whispered into her ear.

And then he began his work.

CHAPTER 59

9th November 1888 (12.00 pm), Blackfriars, London

Warrington was completely bemused by the man's choice of meeting place. The very same place: the disused printer's warehouse. If the fool had the intention of evading them a second time, then he was feeling particularly optimistic. This time around, all the exits were known about and covered with men.

This time he had his two remaining Lodge men – Orman and Robson, the latter still limping noticeably from his last encounter with the Candle Man – and also two dozen constables and a chief inspector, a member of their Lodge, commanding them. They were posted outside the building. They were going to see nothing of what went on inside and were under orders to prevent anyone leaving until told otherwise.

What was perhaps more odd about this meeting was the time he'd chosen for it: midday. Although one would describe it as gloomy in here beneath the roof of metal spars, there were enough holes and gaps in the moss-clouded glass tiles above that it was certainly not a darkness that this slippery bastard could take any advantage of. Pallid lances of light from the overcast November sky outside stabbed the gravel and concrete floor. It was a still and quiet place, save for the soft burble of pigeons in the rafters.

This time, we'll see and hear him coming.

He checked his timepiece; it was a couple of minutes to midday, according to the small gold arms on its enamel face. Warrington stroked the handle of the revolver in his coat pocket. *He* was going to do it. He was going to be the one to pull the trigger.

It was his choice. He needed to do this. He needed to see the man dead.

The nights were becoming something of a problem. The sleeplessness. He realised it had very much been a mistake. Not the actual killing of those two tarts. No, obviously they had both needed to be hushed. But it was how it had happened. It was unprofessional, it was foolish, it was reckless, and he'd been angry, enraged, that Babbitt had slipped out of his fingers like that. Rawlinson was right: both women could easily have been throttled and dumped in some coal shed, or just bundled over a low brick wall into the Thames. But he . . . well, Warrington had no idea what he'd been thinking. 'Shred them like the Ripper's work,' he'd told Orman. And good god, the man had done just that. Warrington had nearly vomited as he and Orman had emerged from that narrow passage to Mitre Square, covered in the second woman's blood.

It had been dark enough that most of what he'd done to her had been little more than a wet glint here and there. But it was the sounds he'd not been spared. Her dying noises. It was the sense of bath-like warmth from the dots of blood on his cheeks. The glimpse of the catastrophic wound, the pulled out loops and coils of her still-tepid offal, draped across her chest and shoulder. Just like the Candle Man had done with the last woman. Warrington wanted to mimic that, to ensure Babbitt was seen as guilty for the deaths of those two. That's what his thinking had been. And doing what they were doing – if only for the few quick minutes he'd been down that passageway – he felt like he had *become* him. Because – Warrington was absolutely certain of this – he couldn't have ordered such horrendous butchery to be done while he was himself. Not as George Warrington, a good Christian family man with many charity projects and good public deeds to his name.

No. For a minute or two, he suspected some dark force must have entered him; whatever evil it was inside this chap had somehow found its way inside him.

That's why he needed this. That's why he wanted to pull the trigger. He was going to kneel over Babbitt's dying body and look into his eyes so that he could know for sure that whatever had got inside him, and fleetingly turned him into a monster, was back inside Babbitt and dying with him.

They say that the last image caught on a dying man's retina is an open window to his soul. Maybe, just maybe, in Babbitt's eyes, he'd catch the faint glow of dying red embers, and that whiff of sulphur and evil inside the man.

Then, perhaps, his nightmares would stop.

A voice called out. It was Robson. 'Someone enterin' the delivery yard!'

No point trying to fool the Candle Man that he was alone. They'd tried that last time, with night on their side, and it hadn't fooled him. Hadn't turned out too well for either Warren or Smith.

'All right!' he called back, his voice echoing interminably across the empty building. It finally faded enough that he could hear the pigeons again, the tap of dripping water . . . and yes, faintly, the slow, deliberate *crunch* of boot heels across loose gravel, then a steady *clack* onto concrete floor.

Framed in a doorway, he saw the man's tall figure silhouetted.

'You're exactly on time by my watch!' Warrington nervously called out.

The Candle Man slowly crossed the vacant floor of the warehouse until finally, a few yards short of Warrington, he stopped. 'Only an amateur would turn up late, George.'

'I . . . I should warn you that . . . I'm not alone.'

Babbitt chuckled. 'Really?'

Warrington needed to get this done. Get this over with. First order of business was that girl who'd run off to Liverpool with him.

'Where's Mary Kelly? You understand there's no way we can conclude this business between us until we know where she is.'

He nodded. 'Of course.'

'I don't know how much she knows, how much you've told her about all this; it really doesn't matter. She represents too much of a risk to—'

'I shan't lie to you, George. She knows *everything* about me. Who I am, what I do.' He cocked his head slightly. '*What* I am.' He shrugged. 'I can quite understand why you want her dead. She is such a *chatty* little soul.'

What I am? Those words struck home. Warrington realised that, for a while now, he hadn't actually been thinking of this man as a *him* or a *he*. The Candle Man had become an *it*. A phenomenon, a principle. Almost a force of bloody nature.

He remembered Rawlinson's reassuring words. *Don't mythologise him.*

Easier said than done when you weren't looking into these sunken, glinting eyes.

'So then . . .' Warrington steadied his voice as a finger caressed the smooth, warm metal in his coat pocket. 'Where can we find her?'

Warrington watched as the Candle Man fumbled for something

beneath the fold of his coat and, for a desperate moment, thought he was struggling clumsily to pull out a gun of his own. Instead he saw a flicker of movement and heard the slap of something heavy on the floor between them.

Please not another head. He didn't think he could cope with that again, particularly the head of some young woman. He flinched involuntarily before he realised he was staring down at a worn leather satchel.

'Why don't you take a look inside?'

Warrington looked down at it. The bulge inside the bag was too small. He felt a small tickle of relief.

The Candle Man smiled; his straight thin lips were little more than the puckered edges of a wound. 'Go on, George, why don't you take a look?'

Warrington found himself obediently stooping down and carefully, with one finger, flicking the flap of the satchel back. The leather, worn rough inside the flap, was wet and dark. Avoiding the wet, which was almost certainly blood, he lifted the mouth of the bag open and peered inside . . .

Jesus.

CHAPTER 60

9th November 1888 (8.00 am), Whitechapel, London

It was quiet this morning. Argyll had paid the cabby at the top of Whitechapel Road, ten minutes' walk away from the address he had. The cab driver seemed quite bemused as to why a gentleman would want to be dropped in a place as grim as Whitechapel at six in the morning. The morning had yet to wake itself up, the sky still a half-dark, low, heavy and grey, and promising another day of spirit-sapping drizzle.

He'd passed dozens of men bundled up and huddled against the spit in the air as they shuffled through the half-light to work. Argyll made to appear likewise: just another worker in a thick coat striding towards a place he'd rather not be.

As he turned off Dorset Street and entered Millers Court, he picked out the house numbers, finally locating the one he was after. He took the three steps up off the narrow pavement and saw it was a door that had a corroding lock. He tried it, and yes, as Mary had told him, it wasn't locked. The door swung gently inwards, creaking and wobbling flimsily. A front door thick with rot and held together only by layers of paint and rusting metal brackets nailed on the inside.

The hallway was oppressively dark, but by the wan light of the grey dawn, he could make out the doors on his left. The second . . .

Mary's old room.

For a moment, he felt his heart pull painfully.

She lived in there . . . once upon a time. He shook his head and banished that. Now he needed a clear mind and an unclouded conscience.

The second door on the right was the one he was after. He stepped quietly over to the side of the passage, avoiding the middle, where old floorboards tended to bow and creak. Standing in front of the door, he saw the fading name scrawled untidily on a scrap of paper and tacked to the door.

He pulled out a knife and eased the tip of the blade into the gap between door and frame. It found the bevelled tongue of the lock and with a practised flip of his wrist, he teased it open with a soft *clack*.

Inside the small room, he found Marge fast asleep on her bed, snoring as she lay on her back. He knelt down beside her, inspecting her by the light seeping in through a gap in the closed linen drapes. He guessed she was in her early thirties, which was perhaps a touch too old, but she was short and slight, her hair a similar dirty strawberry-blonde.

'You'll do,' he said softly.

She stirred, her eyes blinking. Full of sleep one moment, wide awake the next.

'Shhhh.' His hand clamped over her mouth. He pressed the tip of the blade into the puffy flesh below her eye. She whimpered.

'You and I need to take a quick stroll. And not a sound from you, please, is that understood?'

She didn't nod, for fear of the blade jabbing her eye, but her grunt beneath his hand was clearly an affirmative.

'If you're a good girl and answer some questions for me, I have a very nice parcel of opium in my pocket for you.'

He led her out into the hall, across to Mary's old door. He jimmied the locked door like he had Marge's, only this time the tongue refused to yield. Argyll cursed softly.

'I got a master key,' said Marge. She pulled a key chain out from the folds of her nightgown. Several keys jangled as she picked out the right one. She pushed it into the lock, pulling the door towards her as she turned the key. 'Stiff bloody lock,' she explained.

It clicked.

She looked at him. 'This about Kelly?'

Argyll put up a finger to hush her. She had too loud a voice. He nodded.

They stepped inside the room and he gently closed the door after them.

'What's the silly cow gone an' done now?'

Argyll motioned for her to sit down on the bed. The room looked spare. It looked like a place that had simply been forgotten. 'Sorry about the knife,' he said, tucking it away. 'I just needed you to be very quiet.' He looked around the room. 'This room – have you rented it out since she left?'

She shook her head. 'Can't find tenants wanting to stay round here these days, what with 'em murders goin' on.' Marge eyed him suspiciously. 'Who are yer? You ain't no copper.'

Argyll forced a guilty shrug. 'No, indeed I'm not.'

He pulled the room's one wooden chair up beside the narrow bed and sat down, facing her. 'I'm working for a gentleman client.'

'Gentleman, eh?' Marge frowned. 'I 'eard the girls sayin' summin' 'bout 'er shackin' up with a rich gent an' all. She really go an' do that?'

Argyll raised his finger. Her voice was getting too loud. He nodded.

Marge cursed and shook her head. 'Lucky little bitch,' she whispered.

'You didn't like her?'

'Not really. She thought she was better 'an us; better than me an' the other girls. Told me once she wanted better.' Marge shrugged. 'I told 'er "who the 'ell do yer think yer are? You're a tart, like us. Once yer done it a first time, that makes yer a tart for always." She done it with gents for money, but she kept sayin' she wasn't no whore.'

Argyll nodded sympathetically. 'Didn't know her place, eh?'

Marge nodded. 'Ain't got time for a stuck-up bitch like that—' She stopped herself. 'Hoy! 'Ang on!' She grinned knowingly. 'Are yer . . .' Her eyes narrowed. 'Are yer the gent she's gone an' shacked up with?'

Argyll pursed his lips and offered her a small, confessional nod. 'Yes . . . yes, I am.'

Her eyes widened. She giggled excitedly. 'Well, aren't yer a daft bugger then! What? She done a runner on yer? Eh? Nicked yer wallet an' done a runner?'

Her voice was getting loud again. He could hear someone stirring in the room above. Heavy workman's boots scraping on a bare floor. He needed to finish his business here.

'I could've told yer for nuffin' she's no good. If you'd asked me I could of told yer all about the little selfish cunt. She always thought she was better an' us.'

Argyll offered her a knowing nod. 'Yes, she can come across like that.'

'Yeah. I slapped that smug look off 'er mug coupla times. Bitch was askin' for it.'

Argyll leant forward until his face was close to hers. Looking intently into her fidgeting eyes for a long while. Finally, Marge, uncomfortable, shrugged. 'So? You said yer got summin' nice for me in yer pocket?'

'Just one more question, Marge. Then you can have it.'

'All right.'

'If you could escape this . . .' he said, gesturing at the room, 'would you?'

'What d'ya mean?' She frowned at the oddness of his question.

He shrugged. 'This place . . . London . . . this life you've chosen.'

She pouted a lip. 'I do all right 'ere, I 's'pose.' She cocked an eyebrow, leant a little further forward, offering him a glimpse down the front of her loosely buttoned nightgown. 'Why? Yer gonna whisk *me* away instead, love?'

He smiled genuinely and not unkindly. 'I'm sorry . . . no.'

'Aww, well.' A finger reached out and teasingly stroked his knee. 'Now, what 'bout me treat? I been a good, 'elpful girl for yer, 'aven't I?'

'Close your eyes.'

She laughed a little nervously. 'I ain't doin' that. What you up to?'

'Trust me.'

'Look, I ain't gonna fuck yer for nuffin', if that's whatcha after?'

He shook his head. 'I just want this to be easy for you.'

He reached into the leather bag slung over his shoulder and pulled out a small white candle. Then a box of matches. He struck one and carefully lit the candle.

'Very romantic.' She smiled. Intrigued. 'Whatcha up to, love?'

Argyll hesitated with his hand in his pocket, resting on the knife's handle.

It has to be done, said Babbitt. *You want Mary to live, don't you?*

Argyll nodded.

Then let me do what needs to be done. Look away, if you must.

He smiled sadly at Marge as he pulled out the knife. A long, thin fishmonger's filleting knife, almost like the one he used to have and lost. Perfect for the job. 'I think it's time for you to rest, Marge.'

She shuffled back across the bed, backing away from him.

'You're tired. I can see that in you. Tired of the struggle every day.'

'P-please, mister . . . I don't know . . .'

He cocked his head, curious. 'Why is it? Why do you girls all seem to struggle so much?'

At the mention of 'girls', Marge whimpered. 'Oh god . . . oh g-god 'elp me . . .'

'This,' he said, gesturing at the room they were sitting in, 'this isn't a life, Marge. It's an eternal prison sentence. It's purgatory.'

'God! Y-you're that . . . R-Rip . . . Rip . . .' Her mouth trembled so much, she struggled to say the word.

'The Ripper?' He looked down at his hands. 'Mr Leather Apron?' He hunched his shoulders. 'I'm a way out, Marge, that's all. A way out for you.' Her eyes were focused on the glinting metal in his hand.

He rested a hand gently on her knee. 'You know, it's best if you don't look at it. Just close your eyes.'

She edged back across the far side of the bed, a slippered foot feeling over the edge for the floor.

'It's an easy way to go, I promise you.' He reached out and grasped her hand before she could pull it away from him. Gently, he stroked the back of it with his thumb. 'A moment, just for a moment, it stings. No worse than a splinter in your foot, hmmm? Then it's just like falling asleep. I promise.'

She was crying. 'I . . . don't w-wanna die—'

'Marge.' He shook his head sympathetically. 'You're already dead, my dear. All of you . . . you're lost souls, ghosts. Don't you feel that? Don't you wake up sometimes and wonder why every day seems like the last?' He shuffled across the bed to sit beside her. Springs creaked beneath them. From another room somewhere in the house, a faint muffled male voice shouted cruelly.

The hand holding his knife slid along the back of her narrow shoulders; instinctively, she tried to pull away from him. He held her tight, feeling the frizz of her hair tickle his cheek.

'Do you remember the last time you woke up and thought about leaving all of this behind? Leaving London?'

He could feel her trembling, shuddering uncontrollably. But her head managed a small nod.

'Perhaps you were much younger the last time you dreamed of better?' He rubbed his cheek against her hair, ignoring the rank odour of lacquer, the smell of stale tobacco. 'There was an energy to that idea, wasn't there? A spark? As if the idea itself felt like it was alive?' Her head was bowed. He could feel a steady rhythm of warm tears tapping the back of his hand as it rested in her lap, gently caressing her own hand. 'And then the idea died. It just vanished, didn't it? Went away and never came back?'

She nodded as she whimpered.

'That was the day you really died, Marge; not this morning. Every day since that you've woken up wanting nothing more than to stew your head with alcohol and opium; every night that you let one dirty bastard after another enter you and leave their mess running down your legs; every grey dawn you've watched creep across your ceiling – all those days, my dear, were the very same one.'

He pushed the tip of the blade into the soft skin beneath her ear, quickly but not roughly, sliding it in as easily as a well-greased door bolt. With a firm flick of his wrist, he pulled it forward and the blade opened her throat. She lurched in his arms, her legs scissoring on the bed.

'Shhhh. That was the sting; now the rest is easy. Relax.'

He let go of her hand and grasped her shoulders as they flexed and heaved. He pushed her back until she was lying on the bed. 'There . . . that's it. Just falling asleep now, just falling asleep.'

Her eyes rolled to look at him, her mouth trying to gurgle something.

'Shhh . . . Best to lie still. Don't fight it, my dear.'

A hand flailed and flapped up at him, and finally found his hand, the one that had been caressing hers. It grasped his tightly, like life-long friends embracing. He squeezed back.

'When you wake up, Marge, I promise you, it's all going to be so different.'

Her red-rimmed eyes seemed to find something to focus on, something beyond the low, cracked, damp-stained ceiling. Something beyond the lodging house itself, beyond the low pall of smog over the dark necropolis.

'That's it,' he whispered. 'Off you go.'

He sensed her leave. And when her last breath had finished bubbling through the ragged gash beneath her chin, he reached across and pinched the burning wick with his fingers until smoke coiled above it, danced momentarily and then vanished.

He heard heavy footsteps scuff along the hallway just outside, the clatter of the front door slamming shut a moment later. Someone on their way to work.

The bed frame creaked again as he stood up to inspect her body splayed across the thin mattress. There was a butcher's work to be done. He was going to leave her like the others, to be sure they understood it was his handiwork; but more than that, to be sure he could convince them he'd done what they wanted. There was a face to ruin – and a totem to extract.

CHAPTER 61

9th November 1888 (12.00 pm), Blackfriars, London

Argyll watched Warrington staring down at the wet organ nestling at the bottom of the satchel; he could see revulsion stretch across his curling mouth before he managed to wrest control of his face once more.

'This is . . . this is Mary Kelly's?'

'Yes.'

He looked down at it again. 'It looks . . . fresh . . . Did you kill her this morning?'

'I brought her back down with me. You'll find her in her old room in Millers Court.'

'Orman!' Warrington called out.

'Sir?' a voice replied from a dark corner of the warehouse.

'Kelly's body is to be found at her lodging room. Go and check on that.'

'Aye.'

He looked again at the organ. 'She's dead?' A stupid question, and apparently Warrington realised that as soon as he'd asked. 'We didn't say for you to *kill* her. That was unnecessary. We just wanted to talk to her. Find out how much she knows.'

'Just talk to her? Like those two other tarts?'

Warrington flinched at their mention.

'I presume they must have overheard you mention Prince Albert? How careless of you.'

'They knew that anyway, from the confessional you decided to leave in your hotel room. They were dead the moment they clapped eyes on that.' Warrington tried a smile that ended up looking like a wince. 'So their blood is on *your* hands, actually.'

'I have no problem with having blood on my hands, George. It's what I do.' He sighed softly. 'But I suspect you have troubled nights, hmmm? I read some details in the newspapers. How the second one was gutted like a fish. A difficult thing to do first time round. It leaves troublesome images in your mind, right?'

Warrington couldn't stop himself nodding. 'It wasn't pleasant, no.'

He offered Warrington an encouraging smile. 'Well, if it's any consolation, George, it gets easier, this kind of business. Particularly when you begin to realise that in most cases, you're doing them a favour, doing the rest of the world a favour. Once you understand that, it becomes easy, actually . . . almost *satisfying*.'

Warrington's eyes narrowed. 'What we did *had* to be done. That foolish—' He stopped himself and chose words from a more tactful palette. 'The prince made a mistake that could have cost this nation everything. *Everything*. Anarchy, riots, a complete collapse of order, many more deaths. I – *we* – did what was needed and no more. It certainly wasn't for sport.'

'*I* . . . *we*?' Argyll's lips spread apart in a sneer. 'You sound so unsure, George. Or perhaps that's how you're dealing with the blood on your fingers – sharing it out with your colleagues? "We" killed them, not "I"?'

'It really is none of your business, Mr Babbitt.'

Argyll noticed Warrington flexing a hand buried deep in a coat pocket. He could guess what was there.

'Babbitt, I presume, is an alias. Not your real name?'

Argyll shrugged. 'One of a long line of aliases, if you really want to know. But, truth be told, this name has grown on me a touch.' He smiled. 'I rather like this one.'

'Perhaps you'd tell me your *real* name? Just your first name? You know mine, after all.'

Argyll pursed his lips with deliberation. 'Hmmm, do you know, George, I honestly can't recall it anymore. I've used so many names over the years. Been so many different people.'

Warrington huffed humourlessly. 'One of those women said you'd lost your memory, after the last time we met?'

'After you attempted to double-cross me, you mean?'

Warrington ignored that. 'Is it true? Did you forget who you were?'

'Yes, it's true. I was, I suppose you could say, *lost* for a while. But it all came back to me eventually.'

They stared at each other in silence, long enough for them both to realise there was little more to be said.

Warrington eased the gun out of his pocket. 'You know, we really can't let you go, Mr Babbitt. With this particular job, there was always too much at stake for us to actually let our hired man just walk away from the job.'

'I suspected as much.'

Warrington shook his head, confused. 'Then why the hell did you arrange this meeting?'

'To finish our business, of course, George. To give you the Kelly girl. I am a hopeless completist.' He laughed softly. 'I do so hate leaving things unfinished.'

'You could have tried to escape us. Why not? Why didn't you try to?'

He took a deep breath, but gave no answer.

'You could have tried another port. We could only manage to muster a few dozen men to watch the ships.' Warrington seemed eager for an answer. 'We even thought you might already have gone, you know? You could so easily have escaped! You're a puzzle to me, Mr Babbitt. Why the hell are you here? I mean . . . really?'

Warrington was studying him intently, as if trying to read the answer in the expression written on his face.

'Perhaps, George, it's not *you* I wanted to escape.'

Argyll's head was suddenly filled with the sound of restlessness; the scraping and scratching of sharp-edged hooves. The hiss of an enraged voice as brittle and unpleasant as a fingernail dragged down a blackboard. It wanted control of him again. It wanted escape. In his own coat pocket, his fingers flexed around the handle of his knife. A knife that could be drawn out and slashed across the throat of this bumbling, nervous gentleman in less time than it would take him to raise his aim, cock the hammer and squeeze the trigger.

DO IT!!

Argyll winced at the piercing volume in his mind. He wished he had the strength of will to dig a blade deep into his own head and scoop the vicious bastard out. To see it squirming on the floor, to actually see it *outside* his head, like some kind of aborted, horned foetus, curling, gurgling. To be able to crush its misshapen head beneath his booted heel and see its poison splatter across the floor in visceral comma marks of gore.

It – Babbitt, the pig – raged inside his head, stamping and snorting like an enraged bull, now fully awake to the treachery

Argyll had been quietly intending. It snarled orders, orders that his fingers instinctively seemed to want to obey, tightening their grasp on the knife handle.

Warrington, the fool, was still watching him intently, his gun still angled carelessly at the floor. He was unaware that Argyll was wrestling with the pig; a bare-chested wrestling match on the sawdust pit in his mind. Argyll heard Warrington say something, all but drowned out by the shrill raging coming from inside. The man's voice was far away now, and still bleating that silly, irrelevant question . . .

'Come on, Babbitt. I'm curious – why? What exactly were you hoping to achieve by coming here?'

Argyll felt his control slipping, losing his turf war with Babbitt, with the Candle Man. His body was fast finding its allegiance to a much stronger, smarter, worldly-wise voice, and a far more compelling imperative to survive. Argyll rallied what was left of himself; a part of himself that was unspoiled, almost a separate person. A person who'd lived only a life of a dozen weeks. *John Argyll.* A person born to the world the day Mary walked into that hospital ward and gave him a name. Such a short life as John Argyll.

But a wonderful life.

Babbitt-the-pig roared at him to stop his childlike mewling, to grab hold of his knife and finish the idiot standing in front of him. Argyll's struggle was waning. The best he could manage was to whimper a muted warning to Warrington.

'Kill me . . . now!'

Kill me. Those were the two words that Warrington thought he heard the Candle Man gasp. Looking back on it in later years to come, as he did almost every night he closed his eyes to try and sleep, he found himself wondering whether he'd glimpsed tears on the man's cheeks or whether that was an embellishment of the memory. Good god, it had actually almost sounded like a plea. Hadn't it?

Kill me – would you?

He was never going to know for sure.

Immediately following that mucous-thick rasp of a voice, the Candle Man lunged forward with a knife produced seemingly out of thin air. Warrington's gun erupted in his hand as his finger tensed with surprise. The shot *pinged* off the floor with a spark and a spurt of grit and dust erupted from a divot that was dug in the concrete.

A strong hand was suddenly wrapped around the wrist of his gun hand. The moment telescoped in time, feeling not like a half or a quarter second, but like a minute counted patiently. His eyes followed the blurred glint of a long serrated blade whipping up from waist height with a murderous arc of intent towards his throat.

That eternal minute ended quite suddenly with the boom of another gun fired from somewhere inside the warehouse. Warrington lost his balance and found himself on his back on the floor, looking up at rafters of corroded iron and lances of pale daylight spearing down through the roof, and a cascade, like snowfall, of bird fluff from the startled pigeons taking flight across the abandoned warehouse.

Regaining his senses, he sat quickly up to see Babbitt, the Candle Man, kneeling on the floor beside him. He was burping gouts of blood from his mouth and down the front of his cotton shirt.

The Candle Man's hand slapped the floor, fumbling to find his dropped knife. Warrington had dropped his own gun in the panic. Both of them now unarmed, on their knees, staring at each other in a wordless silence.

The Candle Man's fumbling hand found the blade and raised it half-heartedly. It wavered for just a second in the space between them, then a second boom, much louder, much closer, knocked the man back as if a kick had been landed under his jaw. The Candle Man flopped to the floor, beside a tuft of nettles pushing defiantly up through a crack in the old warehouse floor.

Warrington heard the uneven approaching footsteps of a limping walk and looked up at the hand proffered to him, and Orman's face beneath the brim of his billycock. 'You all right, sir?'

'I'm fine. Quite all right.'

Blood bubbled out of the ragged hole in Argyll's throat. He could feel it all slipping away – life, thoughts, sensations, all growing indistinct. The bitter, angry shriek of Babbitt receding, dying with him. Cursing his betrayal, his stupidity, and finally leaving him alone in the final few seconds, while his brain fed on the last of the blood in his head. Giving him time for one more thought, one moment of satisfaction, contentment even.

Mary Kelly. You're free. Fly away, my dear. Fly away.

CHAPTER 62

9th November 1888, (2.00 pm), Liverpool

Mary looked up the gangway, only four feet wide and busy with stevedores in heavy boots carrying oak crates of something fragile up towards a master, barking orders at the top. She had the booking slip in her hand with instructions on whom to make herself known to; her few worldly possessions were packed tightly into a new travel valise. All that was left now for her to do, for the rest of her life to properly begin, was take two dozen steps up the iron gangway and board the steamship.

She realised she was trembling like a mangy dog tied up outside a pub on a harsh winter's day. A heady mixture of anxiety and excitement. Mostly the first. Mary wasn't sure she had the gumption to do this all on her own; another country, a whole other continent. And Mary Argyll – the name John had booked her passage under – facing all the unknowns it had to offer on her own.

All she had was his promise to follow her very shortly. She had it tucked into the pocket of her coat, still in the torn-open envelope she'd found tucked beneath her pillow. Words she'd read through a dozen times before she properly understood she was taking this ship alone.

Dear Mary,

I suspect you are aware there's much about me that has come back to my mind, and yet I have kept it from you. Trust me when I say it is better that way. It feels very odd to be two people at once: the person I was, and the person I am. The person I was, I wish to have no more to do with, and it is for this reason I have to go back down to London and conclude some matters.

But this is very important, Mary. You must go ahead and board the ship I have booked. The people I am going to see are dangerous. They are after you, as much as me, because they will suspect you know all the things I have been keeping secret from you. You must *board for your own safety. DO NOT delay here in Liverpool waiting for me. I hope this is clear.*

I have left you the money. It is yours to use how you wish. I know you will spend it shrewdly. I suspect you have a far wiser head on your shoulders than most men twice your age. I want only happiness for you and opportunities that someone of your back-ground could never hope to find in England. I have little doubt you will achieve so much over there.

I have a train to catch, so this letter only says half the things I want to say. But know this: our weeks in London together, and here in Liverpool, have been a happy time for me. I have never been so happy as I have been as John Argyll. It is a good name.

I will follow you across, 'Miss Argyll'. That is a promise. If you leave details of where you are with the shipping agent on the other side, I shall find you easily enough.

Fondest affections,
John

'Hoy! You down there!'

Mary's head cleared and she glanced around, panicked for a moment that the mysterious men John referred to had finally clapped eyes on her.

'Yes! You, love!' She glanced past the broad shoulders of a bald man clomping noisily down the gangplank to retrieve another sack of potatoes for the ship's galley. At the top of the gangplank she saw a man wearing a dark forage cap and leaning on the ship's railing. 'Are you our fare?'

Mary nodded.

'Right then, you comin' aboard, or what?'

Well? Mary?

She looked along the quayside uncertainly, hoping to catch sight of John racing towards her to board the ship with her. But no . . . She was alone.

She looked up at the man in the cap. 'All right . . . I'm coming up!'

A sharp gust of cool breeze spilled off the Mersey and sent her skirts and bonnet fluttering. She grasped at her dancing hem for modesty and then finally, sucking in a deep breath and waiting to allow the surly-looking broad-shouldered man to step past her with his sack of potatoes, she followed him up the gangway.

EPILOGUE

1912, RMS Titanic

The girl, Miss Hammond, stared at him in silence.

'Good god,' she whispered after a while.

The hubbub of noise outside the reading room had changed in nature over the last hour. No longer was it the polite curiosity at an unscheduled stop; the gentlemen standing outside in their dinner jackets were now wearing life preservers, their voices raised with increasing concern as the ship's crew busied themselves with uncovering the lifeboats and working the winches.

'This is . . .' Her words were slurred from the brandy. 'This is . . . a *true* story? Prince Albert . . . ?'

The old man nodded. 'It's perhaps a lucky thing that he died so young. I shudder to think what other indiscretions might have needed to be cleaned up in his wake, if the silly fool had gone on to become king. God help us.'

Her bright eyes, although glazed by the brandy, remained wide and round with incredulity. 'But you . . . are a Mason . . . and you've now told me this story!'

He shrugged. 'A secret needs to be passed along, my dear, or it just dies. It needs . . .' He pressed his lips together thoughtfully as he hunted for the right word. 'It needs a host. Someone who can carry it for a while before choosing another to pass it on to.'

'But . . . but why?' She pressed a hand to her lips to suppress a belch. 'You and your friends, you say you *killed* those poor women to keep a secret? Now you're telling me?'

'Times have changed. We live in a new century, with different values, with new things to worry about. Not stupid princes that need to keep their flies buttoned.'

She gawped drunkenly at that.

'Countries are readying for a war.' He shrugged again. 'It's not such big beer anymore, my deathbed story. And anyway, I'm the only one of our little privileged group left alive. I'm the only one left who knows about it.' He glanced up at Reginald, the chief steward who'd wheeled her in here earlier, striding swiftly towards them, a younger steward beside him.

'And now you know, Miss Hammond.' He smiled and spoke quietly as the stewards approached. 'It's *your* secret now. *Yours* to decide what you do with.'

'All right, Miss Hammond?' said Reginald. 'We got a space for you on a lifeboat on the port side. Best get a move on, though; the boats are gettin' filled quickly.' He turned to the young steward beside him. 'Liam, lad, go make a last check on them cabins on our floor. Make sure we ain't missed anyone.'

'Aye.'

Reginald grasped the handles of her wheelchair and began to take her away.

'Wait!' She twisted in her chair towards the old man. 'Is there not space for Mr Larkin too?'

'Sorry, love, it's women and children only, I'm afraid.'

'I'm fine,' he said, raising his brandy glass. 'You go on, Miss Hammond. I have a hope, no, a feeling, that you'll enjoy quite a few more summers, hmmm?'

She returned his warm smile. 'I'll . . . look after it, you know?' Her eyes locked on his, her voice a whisper. 'The secret.'

'I'm sure you will. Now best you get going, my dear; you've a boat to catch.'

As Reginald wheeled her out of the room, he caught one last glance of her face, eyes still saucer-wide.

Alone again, Warrington topped up his brandy glass one last time and settled back into his armchair to listen to the growing cacophony of the approaching end. Not just voices raised in panic now, but the sporadic crash of crockery from tables set in the dining room next door, wine glasses and top-heavy champagne flutes toppling and smashing, and the distant pop of another rocket exploding in the night sky.

He pulled out a folded corner of newspaper and looked at it once again. The print of the photograph was smeared from being thumbed these last couple of years, the paper beginning to yellow very slightly. But the face was still determinable, and yes, it could just be the same face. The features, as he vaguely remembered them in that crowded station hall, could quite possibly be hers. Obviously she was a middle-aged woman now, but still a strikingly beautiful woman as well.

He'd lied, of course, the Candle Man did. The body they found at the boarding house in Millers Court wasn't that of Kelly. They found that out later, after the news had hit the papers, too late to want to attract attention by changing the victim's name. And too late to find the young girl. She was going to be long gone to bother watching the ships and checking in with the shipping agents again under her name Kelly, or the name they later discovered the pair of them had been using in Liverpool – Mr and Mrs Argyll.

He looked once more at the photograph cut from a newspaper: a strong woman standing tall and proud behind a lectern, flanked on one side by two gentlemen politely clapping. It was hard to be certain from just this one blurry newspaper photograph. But Warrington was very good with faces. Never forgot a face. And he was sure it was the very same woman. Sure enough to have booked his fare over and try and arrange a meeting with her.

He wasn't sure what he wanted to do. Not kill her, for sure. The woman either knew nothing, or she'd chosen not to talk. And in the end, as he'd told that charming young lady, it really didn't matter anymore. A different world, with different things to worry about. Warrington just wanted to talk to her about the Candle Man. Perhaps she knew a little more about him; perhaps she could put some of his own demons to rest. Perhaps she could strip some of the mythology away from the man. Reassure Warrington that, in the end, the chap was just a very proficient shiv-man. Nothing more than that.

Just a talk, that's all he wanted. Peace of mind for whatever time he had left.

Warrington looked down at his newspaper cutting and read the caption beneath the photograph once more. Yes, the woman had sensibly changed her name – not Mary Kelly anymore. But, by god, that was definitely her.

'In the centre, Mary Argyll, voted in yesterday for the state of Montana, America's first woman in Congress.'